Robert Barr (16 September 1849 – 21 October 1912) was a Scottish-Canadian short story writer and novelist. Robert Barr was born in Barony, Lanark, Scotland to Robert Barr and Jane Watson. In 1854, he emigrated with his parents to Upper Canada at the age of four years old. His family settled on a farm near the village of Muirkirk. Barr assisted his father with his job as a carpenter, and developed a sound work ethic. Robert Barr then worked as a steel smelter for a number of years before he was educated at Toronto Normal School in 1873 to train as a teacher. After graduating Toronto Normal School, Barr became a teacher, and eventually headmaster/principal of the Central School of Windsor, Ontario in 1874. While Barr worked as head master of the Central School of Windsor, Ontario, he began to contribute short stories—often based on personal experiences, and recorded his work. On August 1876, when he was 27, Robert Barr married Ontario-born Eva Bennett, who was 21. (Source: Wikipedia)

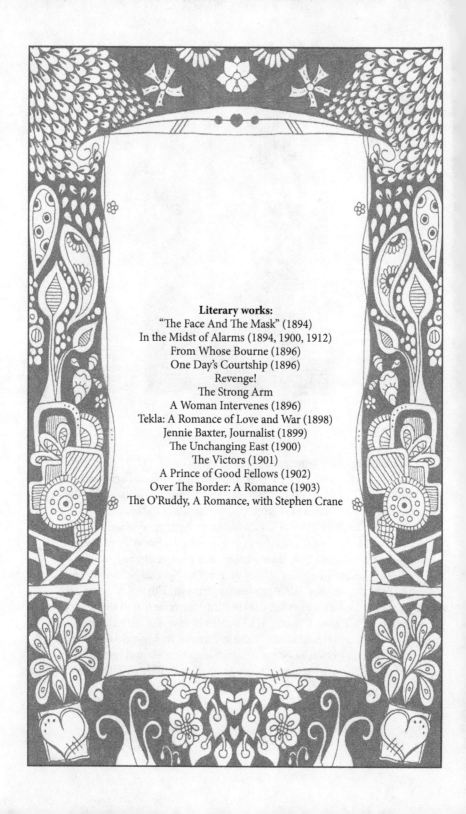

Literary works:
"The Face And The Mask" (1894)
In the Midst of Alarms (1894, 1900, 1912)
From Whose Bourne (1896)
One Day's Courtship (1896)
Revenge!
The Strong Arm
A Woman Intervenes (1896)
Tekla: A Romance of Love and War (1898)
Jennie Baxter, Journalist (1899)
The Unchanging East (1900)
The Victors (1901)
A Prince of Good Fellows (1902)
Over The Border: A Romance (1903)
The O'Ruddy, A Romance, with Stephen Crane

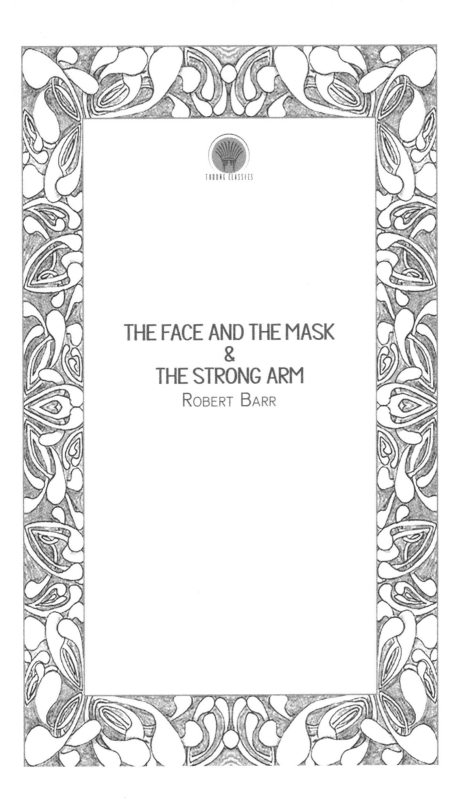

THRONE CLASSICS

THE FACE AND THE MASK
&
THE STRONG ARM

ROBERT BARR

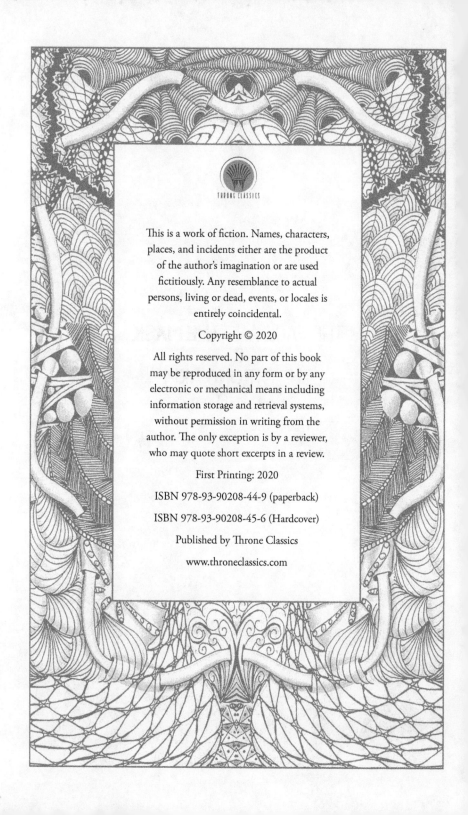

First Printing: 2020

ISBN 978-93-90208-44-9 (paperback)

ISBN 978-93-90208-45-6 (Hardcover)

Published by Throne Classics

www.throneclassics.com

Contents

THE FACE AND THE MASK
&
THE STRONG ARM

THE FACE AND THE MASK

THE WOMAN OF STONE.

Lurine, was pretty, petite, and eighteen. She had a nice situation at the Pharmacie de Siam, in the Rue St. Honoré. She had no one dependent upon her, and all the money she earned was her own. Her dress was of cheap material perhaps, but it was cut and fitted with that daintiness of perfection which seems to be the natural gift of the Parisienne, so that one never thought of the cheapness, but admired only the effect, which was charming. She was book-keeper and general assistant at the Pharmacie, and had a little room of her own across the Seine, in the Rue de Lille. She crossed the river twice every day—once in the morning when the sun was shining, and again at night when the radiant lights along the river's bank glittered like jewels in a long necklace. She had her little walk through the Gardens of the Tuileries every morning after crossing the Pont Royal, but she did not return through the gardens in the evening, for a park in the morning is a different thing to a park at night. On her return she always walked along the Rue de Tuileries until she came to the bridge. Her morning ramble through the gardens was a daily delight to her, for the Rue de Lille is narrow, and not particularly bright, so it was pleasant to walk beneath the green trees, to feel the crisp gravel under her feet, and to see the gleaming white statues in the sunlight, with the sparkle on the round fountain pond, by the side of which she sometimes sat. Her favorite statue was one of a woman that stood on a pedestal near the Rue de Rivoli. The arm was thrown over her head, and there was a smile on the marble face which was inscrutable. It fascinated the girl as she looked up to it, and seemed to be the morning greeting to her busy day's work in the city. If no one was in sight, which was often the case at eight o'clock in the morning, the girl kissed the tips of her fingers, and tossed the salute airily up to the statue, and the woman of stone always smiled back at her the strange mystical smile which seemed to indicate that it knew much more of this world and its ways than did the little Parisienne who daily gazed up at her.

Lurine was happy, as a matter of course, for was not Paris always beautiful? Did not the sun shine brightly? And was not the air always clear?

What more, then, could a young girl wish? There was one thing which was perhaps lacking, but that at last was supplied; and then there was not a happier girl in all Paris than Lurine. She almost cried it aloud to her favorite statue the next morning, for it seemed to her that the smile had broadened since she had passed it the morning before, and she felt as if the woman of stone had guessed the secret of the woman of flesh.

Lurine had noticed him for several days hovering about the Pharmacie, and looking in at her now and then; she saw it all, but pretended not to see. He was a handsome young fellow with curly hair, and hands long, slender, and white as if he were not accustomed to doing hard, manual labor. One night he followed her as far as the bridge, but she walked rapidly on, and he did not overtake her. He never entered the Pharmacie, but lingered about as if waiting for a chance to speak with her. Lurine had no one to confide in but the woman of stone, and it seemed by her smile that she understood already, and there was no need to tell her, that the inevitable young man had come. The next night he followed her quite across the bridge, and this time Lurine did not walk so quickly. Girls in her position are not supposed to have normal introductions to their lovers, and are generally dependent upon a haphazard acquaintance, although that Lurine did not know. The young man spoke to her on the bridge, raising his hat from his black head as he did so.

"Good evening!" was all he said to her.

She glanced sideways shyly at him, but did not answer, and the young man walked on beside her.

"You come this way every night," he said. "I have been watching you. Are you offended?"

"No," she answered, almost in a whisper.

"Then may I walk with you to your home?" he asked.

"You may walk with me as far as the corner of the Rue de Lille," she replied.

"Thank you!" said the young fellow, and together they walked the short distance, and there he bade her good night, after asking permission to meet her at the corner of the Rue St. Honoré, and walk home with her, the next night.

"You must not come to the shop," she said.

"I understand," he replied, nodding his head in assent to her wishes. He told her his name was Jean Duret, and by-and-by she called him Jean, and he called her Lurine. He never haunted the Pharmacie now, but waited for her at the corner, and one Sunday he took her for a little excursion on the river, which she enjoyed exceedingly. Thus time went on, and Lurine was very happy. The statue smiled its enigmatical smile, though, when the sky was overcast, there seemed to her a subtle warning in the smile. Perhaps it was because they had quarrelled the night before. Jean had seemed to her harsh and unforgiving. He had asked her if she could not bring him some things from the Pharmacie, and gave her a list of three chemicals, the names of which he had written on a paper.

"You can easily get them," he had said; "they are in every Pharmacie, and will never be missed."

"But," said the girl in horror, "that would be stealing."

The young man laughed.

"How much do they pay you there?" he asked. And when she told him, he laughed again and said,

"Why, bless you, if I got so little as that I would take something from the shelves every day and sell it."

The girl looked at him in amazement, and he, angry at her, turned upon his heel and left her. She leaned her arms upon the parapet of the bridge, and looked down into the dark water. The river always fascinated her at night, and she often paused to look at it when crossing the bridge, shuddering as she did so. She cried a little as she thought of his abrupt departure, and wondered if she had been too harsh with him. After all, it was not very much he had asked her to do, and they did pay her so little at the Pharmacie. And then perhaps her lover was poor, and needed the articles he had asked her to get. Perhaps he was ill, and had said nothing. There was a touch on her shoulder. She looked round. Jean was standing beside her, but the frown had not yet disappeared from his brow.

"Give me that paper," he said, abruptly.

She unclosed her hand, and he picked the paper from it, and was turning away.

"Stop!" she said, "I will get you what you want, but I will myself put the money in the till for what they cost."

He stood there, looking at her for a moment, and then said—"Lurine, I think you are a little fool. They owe you ever so much more than that. However, I must have the things," and he gave her back the paper with the caution—"Be sure you let no one see that, and be very certain that you get the right things." He walked with her as far as the corner of the Rue de Lille. "You are not angry with me?" he asked her before they parted.

"I would do anything for you," she whispered, and then he kissed her good night.

She got the chemicals when the proprietor was out, and tied them up neatly, as was her habit, afterwards concealing them in the little basket in which she carried her lunch. The proprietor was a sharp-eyed old lynx, who looked well after his shop and his pretty little assistant.

"Who has been getting so much chlorate of potash?" he asked, taking down the jar, and looking sharply at her.

The girl trembled.

"It is all right," she said. "Here is the money in the till."

"Of course," he said. "I did not expect you to give it away for nothing. Who bought it?"

"An old man," replied the girl, trembling still, but the proprietor did not notice that—he was counting the money, and found it right.

16

"I was wondering what he wanted with so much of it. If he comes in again look sharply at him, and be able to describe him to me. It seems suspicious." Why it seemed suspicious Lurine did not know, but she passed an anxious time until she took the basket in her hand and went to meet her lover at the corner of the Rue des Pyramides. His first question was—

"Have you brought me the things?"

"Yes," she answered. "Will you take them here, now?"

"Not here, not here," he replied hurriedly, and then asked anxiously, "Did anyone see you take them?"

"No, but the proprietor knows of the large package, for he counted the money."

"What money?" asked Jean.

"Why, the money for the things. You didn't think I was going to steal them, did you?"

The young man laughed, and drew her into a quiet corner of the Gardens of the Tuileries.

"I will not have time to go with you to the Rue de Lille to-night," he said.

"But you will come as usual to-morrow night?" she asked, anxiously.

"Certainly, certainly," he replied, as he rapidly concealed the packages in his pockets.

The next night the girl waited patiently for her lover at the corner where they were in the habit of meeting, but he did not come. She stood under the glaring light of a lamp-post so that he would recognize her at once. Many people accosted her as she stood there, but she answered none, looking straight before her with clear honest eyes, and they passed on after a moment's hesitation. At last she saw a man running rapidly down the street, and as he passed a brilliantly-lighted window she recognized Jean. He came quickly towards her.

"Here I am," she cried, running forward. She caught him by the arm, saying, "Oh, Jean, what is the matter?"

He shook her rudely, and shouted at her—"Let me go, you fool!" But she clung to him, until he raised his fist and struck her squarely in the face. Lurine staggered against the wall, and Jean ran on. A stalwart man who had spoken to Lurine a few moments before, and, not understanding her silence, stood in a doorway near watching her, sprang out when he saw the assault, and thrust his stick between the feet of the flying man, flinging him face forward on the pavement. The next instant he placed his foot upon Jean's neck holding him down as if he were a snake.

"You villain!" he cried. "Strike a woman, would you?"

Jean lay there as if stunned, and two gens d'armes came pantingly upon the scene.

"This scoundrel," said the man, "has just assaulted a woman. I saw him."

"He has done more than that," said one of the officers, grimly, as if, after all, the striking of a woman was but a trivial affair.

They secured the young man, and dragged him with them. The girl came up to them and said, falteringly—

"It is all a mistake, it was an accident. He didn't mean to do it."

"Oh, he didn't, and pray how do you know?" asked one of the officers.

"You little devil," said Jean to the girl, through his clinched teeth, "it's all your fault."

The officers hurried him off.

"I think," said one, "that we should have arrested the girl; you heard what she said."

"Yes," said the other, "but we have enough on our hands now, if the crowd find out who he is."

Lurine thought of following them, but she was so stunned by the words that her lover had said to her, rather than by the blow he had given her that she turned her steps sadly towards the Pont Royal and went to her room.

The next morning she did not go through the gardens, as usual, to her work, and when she entered the Pharmacie de Siam, the proprietor cried out, "Here she is, the vixen! Who would have thought it of her? You wretch, you stole my drugs to give to that villain!"

"I did not," said Lurine, stoutly. "I put the money in the till for them."

"Hear her! She confesses!" said the proprietor.

The two concealed officers stepped forward and arrested her where she stood as the accomplice of Jean Duret, who, the night before, had flung a bomb in the crowded Avenue de l'Opéra.

Even the prejudiced French judges soon saw that the girl was innocent of all evil intent, and was but the victim of the scoundrel who passed by the name of Jean Duret. He was sentenced for life; she was set free. He had tried to place the blame on her, like the craven he was, to shield another woman. This was what cut Lurine to the heart. She might have tried to find an excuse for his crime, but she realized that he had never cared for her, and had but used her as his tool to get possession of the chemicals he dared not buy.

In the drizzling rain she walked away from her prison, penniless, and broken in body and in spirit. She passed the little Pharmacie de Siam, not daring to enter. She walked in the rain along the Rue des Pyramides, and across the Rue de Rivoli, and into the Tuileries Gardens. She had forgotten about her stone woman, but, unconsciously her steps were directed to her. She looked up at her statue with amazement, at first not recognizing it. It was no longer the statue of a smiling woman. The head was thrown back, the eyes closed. The last mortal agony was on the face. It was a ghastly monument to Death. The girl was so perplexed by the change in her statue that for the moment she forgot the ruin of her own life. She saw that the smiling face was but a mask, held in place by the curving of the left arm over it. Life, she realized now, was made up of tragedy and comedy, and he who sees but the smiling face, sees but the half of life. The girl hurried on to the bridge, sobbing quietly to herself, and looked down at the grey river water. The passers-by paid no attention to her. Why, she wondered, had she ever thought the river cold and cruel and merciless? It is the only home of the homeless, the only lover that does not change. She turned back to the top of the flight of steps which lead down, to the water's brink. She looked toward the Tuileries Gardens, but she could not see her statue for the trees which intervened. "I, too, will be a woman of stone," she said, as she swiftly descended the steps.

THE CHEMISTRY OF ANARCHY.

It has been said in the London papers that the dissolution of the Soho Anarchist League was caused by want of funds. This is very far from being the case. An Anarchist League has no need for funds and so long as there is money enough to buy beer the League is sure of continued existence. The truth about the scattering of the Soho organization was told me by a young newspaper-man who was chairman at the last meeting.

The young man was not an anarchist, though he had to pretend to be one in the interests of his paper, and so joined the Soho League, where he made some fiery speeches that were much applauded. At last Anarchist news became a drug in the market, and the editor of the paper young Marshall Simkins belonged to, told him that he would now have to turn his attention to Parliamentary work, as he would print no more Anarchist news in the sheet.

One might think that young Simkins would have been glad to get rid of his anarchist work, as he had no love for the cause. He was glad to get rid of it, but he found some difficulty in sending in his resignation. The moment he spoke of resigning, the members became suspicious of him. He had always been rather better dressed than the others, and, besides, he drank less beer. If a man wishes to be in good standing in the League he must not be fastidious as to dress, and he must be constructed to hold at least a gallon of beer at a sitting. Simkins was merely a "quart" man, and this would have told against him all along if it had not been for the extra gunpowder he put in his speeches. On several occasions seasoned Anarchists had gathered about him and begged him to give up his designs on the Parliament buildings.

The older heads claimed that, desirable as was the obliteration of the Houses of Parliament, the time was not yet ripe for it. England, they pointed out, was the only place where Anarchists could live and talk unmolested, so, while they were quite anxious that Simkins should go and blow up Vienna, Berlin, or Paris, they were not willing for him to begin on London. Simkins was usually calmed down with much difficulty, and finally, after hissing "Cowards!" two or three times under his breath, he concluded with, "Oh, very well, then, you know better than I do—I am only a young recruit; but allow me at least to blow up Waterloo Bridge, or spring a bomb in Fleet Street just to show that we are up and doing."

But this the Anarchists would not sanction. If he wanted to blow up bridges, he could try his hand on those across the Seine. They had given their word that there would be no explosions in London so long as England afforded them an asylum.

"But look at Trafalgar Square," cried Simkins angrily; "we are not allowed to meet there."

"Who wants to meet there?" said the chairman. "It is ever so much more comfortable in these rooms, and there is no beer in Trafalgar Square." "Yes, yes," put in several others; "the time is not yet ripe for it." Thus was Simkins calmed down, and beer allowed to flow again in tranquillity, while some foreign Anarchist, who was not allowed to set foot in his native country, would get up and harangue the crowd in broken English and tell them what great things would yet be done by dynamite.

But when Simkins sent in his resignation a change came over their feelings towards him, and he saw at once that he was a marked man. The chairman, in a whisper, advised him to withdraw his resignation. So Simkins, who was a shrewd young fellow, understanding the temper of the assembly, arose and said:—

"I have no desire to resign, but you do nothing except talk, and I want to belong to an Anarchist Society that acts." He stayed away from the next meeting, and tried to drop them in that way, but a committee from the League called upon him at his lodgings, and his landlady thought that young Simkins had got into bad ways when he had such evil-looking men visiting him.

Simkins was in a dilemma, and could not make up his mind what to do. The Anarchists apparently were not to be shaken off. He applied to his editor for advice on the situation, but that good man could think of no way out of the trouble.

"You ought to have known better," he said, "than to mix up with such people."

"But how was I to get the news?" asked Simkins, with some indignation. The editor shrugged his shoulders. That was not his part of the business; and if the Anarchists chose to make things uncomfortable for the young man, he could not help it.

Simkins' fellow-lodger, a student who was studying chemistry in London, noticed that the reporter was becoming gaunt with anxiety.

"Simkins," said Sedlitz to him one morning, "you are haggard and careworn: what is the matter with you? Are you in love, or is it merely debt that is bothering you?"

"Neither," replied Simkins.

"Then cheer up," said Sedlitz. "If one or the other is not interfering with you, anything else is easily remedied."

"I am not so sure of that," rejoined Simkins; and then he sat down and told his friend just what was troubling him.

"Ah," said Sedlitz, "that accounts for it. There has been an unkempt ruffian marching up and down watching this house. They are on your track, Simkins, my boy, and when they discover that you are a reporter, and therefore necessarily a traitor, you will be nabbed some dark night."

"Well, that's encouraging," said Simkins, with his head in his hands.

"Are these Anarchists brave men, and would they risk their lives in any undertaking?" asked Sedlitz.

"Oh, I don't know. They talk enough, but I don't know what they would do. They are quite capable, though, of tripping me up in a dark lane."

"Look here," said Sedlitz, "suppose you let me try a plan. Let me give them a lecture on the Chemistry of Anarchy. It's a fascinating subject."

"What good would that do?"

"Oh, wait till you have heard the lecture. If I don't make the hair of some of them stand on end, they are braver men than I take them to be. We have a large room in Clement's Inn, where we students meet to try experiments and smoke tobacco. It is half club, and half a lecture- room. Now, I propose to get those Anarchists in there, lock the doors, and tell them something about dynamite and other explosives. You give out that I am an Anarchist from America. Tell them that the doors will be locked to prevent police interference, and that there will be a barrel of beer. You can introduce me as a man from America, where they know as much about Anarchism in ten minutes as they do here in ten years. Tell them that I have spent my life in the study of explosives. I will have to make-up a little, but you know that I am a very good amateur actor, and I don't think there will be any trouble about that. At the last you must tell them that you have an appointment and will leave me to amuse them for a couple of hours."

"But I don't see what good it is all going to do, though I am desperate," said Simkins, "and willing to try anything. I have thought some of firing a bomb off myself at an Anarchist meeting."

When the Friday night of meeting arrived the large hall in Clement's Inn was filled to the doors. Those assembled there saw a platform at one end of the apartment, and a door that led from it to a room at the back of the hall. A table was on the platform, and boxes, chemical apparatus, and other scientific-looking paraphernalia were on it. At the hour of eight young Simkins appeared before the table alone.

"Fellow Anarchists," he said, "you are well aware that I am tired of the great amount of talk we indulge in, and the little action which follows it. I have been fortunate enough to secure the co-operation of an Anarchist from America, who will tell you something of the cause there. We have had the doors locked, and those who keep the keys are now down at the entrance of the Inn, so that if a fire should occur, they can quickly come and let us out. There is no great danger of fire, however, but the interruption of the police must be guarded against very carefully. The windows, as you see, are shuttered and barred, and no ray of light can penetrate from this room outside. Until the lecture is over no one can leave the room, and by the same token no one can enter it, which is more to the purpose.

"My friend, Professor Josiah P. Slivers, has devoted his life to the Chemistry of Anarchy, which is the title of this lecture. He will tell you of some important discoveries, which are now to be made known for the first time. I regret to say that the Professor is not in a very good state of health, because the line of life which he has adopted has its drawbacks. His left eye has been blown away by a premature explosion during his experiments. His right leg is also permanently disabled. His left arm, as you will notice, is in a sling, having been injured by a little disaster in his workshop since he came to London. He is a man, as you will see, devoted body and soul to the cause, so I hope you will listen to him attentively. I regret that I am unable to remain with you to-night, having other duties to perform which are imperative. I will therefore, if you will permit me, leave by the back entrance after I have introduced the Professor to you."

At this moment the stumping of a wooden leg was heard, and those in the audience saw appear a man on crutches, with one arm in a sling and a bandage over an eye, although he beamed upon them benevolently with the other.

"Fellow Anarchists," said Simkins, "allow me to introduce to you Professor Josiah P. Slivers, of the United States."

The Professor bowed and the audience applauded. As soon as the applause began the Professor held up his unmaimed arm and said, "Gentlemen, I beg that you will not applaud."

It seems the fashion in America to address all sorts and conditions of men as "Gentlemen."

The Professor continued, "I have here some explosives so sensitive that the slightest vibration will cause them to go off, and I therefore ask you to listen in silence to what I have to say. I must particularly ask you also not to stamp on the floor."

25

Before these remarks were concluded Simkins had slipped out by the back entrance, and somehow his desertion seemed to have a depressing effect upon the company, who looked upon the broken-up Professor with eyes of wonder and apprehension.

The Professor drew towards him one of the boxes and opened the lid. He dipped his one useful hand into the box and, holding it aloft, allowed something which looked like wet sawdust to drip through his fingers. "That, gentlemen," he said, with an air of the utmost contempt, "is what is known to the world as dynamite. I have nothing at all to say against dynamite. It has, in its day, been a very powerful medium through which our opinions have been imparted to a listening world, but its day is past. It is what the lumbering stage-coach is to the locomotive, what the letter is to the telegram, what the sailing-vessel is to the steamship. It will be my pleasant duty to-night to exhibit to you an explosive so powerful and deadly that hereafter, having seen what it can accomplish, you will have nothing but derision for such simple and harmless compounds as dynamite and nitro-glycerine."

The Professor looked with kindly sympathy over his audience as he allowed the yellow mixture to percolate slowly through his fingers back into the box again. Ever and anon he took up a fresh handful and repeated the action.

The Anarchists in the audience exchanged uneasy glances one with the other.

"Yet," continued the Professor, "it will be useful for us to consider this substance for a few moments, if but for the purpose of comparison. Here," he said, diving his hand into another box and bringing up before their gaze a yellow brick, "is dynamite in a compressed form. There is enough here to wreck all this part of London, were it exploded. This simple brick would lay St. Paul's Cathedral in ruins, so, however antiquated dynamite may become, we must always look upon it with respect, just as we look upon reformers of centuries ago who perished for their opinions, even though their opinions were far behind what ours are now. I shall take the liberty of performing some experiments with this block of dynamite." Saying which the Professor, with his free arm, flung the block of dynamite far down the aisle, where it fell on the floor with a sickening thud. The audience sprang from their seats and tumbled back one over the other. A wild shriek went up into the air, but the Professor gazed placidly on the troubled mob below him with a superior smile on his face. "I beg you to seat yourselves," he said, "and for reasons which I have already explained, I trust that you will not applaud any of my remarks. You have just now portrayed one of the popular superstitions about dynamite, and you show by your actions how necessary a lecture of this sort is in order that you may comprehend thoroughly the substance with which you have to deal. That brick is perfectly harmless, because it is frozen. Dynamite in its frozen state will not explode—a fact well understood by miners and all those who have to work with it, and who, as a rule, generally prefer to blow themselves to pieces trying to thaw the substance before a fire. Will you kindly bring that brick back to me, before it thaws out in the heated atmosphere of this room?"

One of the men stepped gingerly forward and picked up the brick, holding it far from his body, as he tip-toed up to the platform, where he laid it down carefully on the desk before the Professor.

"Thank you," said the Professor, blandly.

The man drew a long breath of relief as he went back to his seat.

"That is frozen dynamite," continued the Professor, "and is, as I have said, practically harmless. Now, it will be my pleasure to perform two startling experiments with the unfrozen substance," and with that he picked up a handful of the wet sawdust and flung it on a small iron anvil that stood on the table. "You will enjoy these experiments," he said, "because it will show you with what ease dynamite may be handled. It is a popular error that concussion will cause dynamite to explode. There is enough dynamite here to blow up this hall and to send into oblivion every person in it, yet you will see whether or not concussion will explode it." The Professor seized a hammer and struck the substance on the anvil two or three sharp blows, while those in front of him scrambled wildly back over their comrades, with hair standing on end. The Professor ceased his pounding and gazed reproachfully at them;

then something on the anvil appeared to catch his eye. He bent over it and looked critically on the surface of the iron. Drawing himself up to his full height again, he said,

"I was about to reproach you for what might have appeared to any other man as evidence of fear, but I see my mistake. I came very near making a disastrous error. I have myself suffered from time to time from similar errors. I notice upon the anvil a small spot of grease; if my hammer had happened to strike that spot you would all now be writhing in your death-agonies under the ruins of this building. Nevertheless, the lesson is not without its value. That spot of grease is free nitro- glycerine that has oozed out from the dynamite. Therein rests, perhaps, the only danger in handling dynamite. As I have shown you, you can smash up dynamite on an anvil without danger, but if a hammer happened to strike a spot of free nitroglycerine it would explode in a moment. I beg to apologize to you for my momentary neglect."

A man rose up in the middle of the hall, and it was some little time before he could command voice enough to speak, for he was shaking as if from palsy. At last he said, after he had moistened his lips several times:—

"Professor, we are quite willing to take your word about the explosive. I think I speak for all my comrades here. We have no doubt at all about your learning, and would much prefer to hear from your own lips what you have to say on the subject, and not have you waste any more valuable time with experiments. I have not consulted with my comrades before speaking, but I think I voice the sense of the meeting." Cries of "You do, you do," came from all parts of the hall. The Professor once more beamed upon them benevolently.

"Your confidence in me is indeed touching," he said, "but a chemical lecture without experiments is like a body without a soul. Experiment is the soul of research. In chemistry we must take nothing for granted. I have shown you how many popular errors have arisen regarding the substance with which we are dealing. It would have been impossible for these errors to have arisen if every man had experimented for himself; and although I thank you for the mark of confidence you have bestowed upon me, I cannot bring myself

28

to deprive you of the pleasure which my experiments will afford you. There is another very common error to the effect that fire will explode dynamite. Such, gentlemen, is not the case."

The Professor struck a match on his trousers-leg and lighted the substance on the anvil. It burnt with a pale bluish flame, and the Professor gazed around triumphantly at his fellow Anarchists.

While the shuddering audience watched with intense fascination the pale blue flame the Professor suddenly stooped over and blew it out. Straightening himself once more he said, "Again I must apologize to you, for again I have forgotten the small spot of grease. If the flame had reached the spot of nitro-glycerine it would have exploded, as you all know. When a man has his thoughts concentrated on one subject he is apt to forget something else. I shall make no more experiments with dynamite. Here, John," he said to the trembling attendant, "take this box away, and move it carefully, for I see that the nitro-glycerine is oozing out. Put it as tenderly down in the next room as if it were a box of eggs."

As the box disappeared there was a simultaneous long-drawn sigh of relief from the audience.

"Now, gentlemen," said the Professor, "we come to the subject that ought to occupy the minds of all thoughtful men." He smoothed his hair complacently with the palm of his practicable hand, and smiled genially around him.

"The substance that I am about to tell you of is my own invention, and compares with dynamite as prussic acid does with new milk as a beverage." The Professor dipped his fingers in his vest pocket and drew out what looked like a box of pills. Taking one pill out he placed it upon the anvil and as he tip-toed back he smiled on it with a smile of infinite tenderness. "Before I begin on this subject I want to warn you once more that if any man as much as stamps upon the floor, or moves about except on tip-toe this substance will explode and will lay London from here to Charing Cross in one mass of indistinguishable ruins. I have spent ten years of my life in completing this invention. And these pills, worth a million a box, will cure all ills to which the flesh is heir."

"John," he said, turning to his attendant, "bring me a basin of water!" The basin of water was placed gingerly upon the table, and the Professor emptied all the pills into it, picking up also the one that was on the anvil and putting it with the others.

"Now," he said, with a deep sigh, "we can breathe easier. A man can put one of these pills in a little vial of water, place the vial in his vest-pocket, go to Trafalgar Square, take the pill from the vial, throw it in the middle of the Square, and it will shatter everything within the four-mile radius, he himself having the glorious privilege of suffering instant martyrdom for the cause. People have told me that this is a drawback to my invention, but I am inclined to differ with them. The one who uses this must make up his mind to share the fate of those around him. I claim that this is the crowning glory of my invention. It puts to instant test our interest in the great cause. John, bring in very carefully that machine with the electric-wire attachment from the next room."

The machine was placed upon the table. "This," said the Professor, holding up some invisible object between his thumb and forefinger, "is the finest cambric needle. I will take upon the point of it an invisible portion of the substance I speak of." Here he carefully picked out a pill from the basin, and as carefully placed it upon the table, where he detached an infinitesimal atom of it and held it up on the point of the needle. "This particle," he said, "is so small that it cannot be seen except with the aid of a microscope. I will now place needle and all on the machine and touch it off with electric current;" and as his hand hovered over the push-button there were cries of "Stop! stop!" but the finger descended, and instantly there was a terrific explosion. The very foundation seemed shaken, and a dense cloud of smoke rolled over the heads of the audience. As the Professor became visible through the thinning smoke, he looked around for his audience. Every man was under the benches, and groans came from all parts of the hall. "I hope," said the Professor, in anxious tones, "that no one has been hurt. I am afraid that I took up too much of the substance on the point of the needle, but it will enable you to imagine the effect of a larger quantity. Pray seat yourselves again. This is my last experiment."

As the audience again seated itself, another mutual sigh ascended to the roof. The Professor drew the chairman's chair towards him and sat down, wiping his grimy brow.

A man instantly arose and said, "I move a vote of thanks to Professor Slivers for the interesting——"

The Professor raised his hand. "One moment," he said, "I have not quite finished. I have a proposal to make to you. You see that cloud of smoke hovering over our heads? In twenty minutes that smoke will percolate down through the atmosphere. I have told you but half of the benefits of this terrific explosive. When that smoke mixes with the atmosphere of the room it becomes a deadly poison. We all can live here for the next nineteen minutes in perfect safety, then at the first breath we draw we expire instantly. It is a lovely death. There is no pain, no contortion of the countenance, but we will be found here in the morning stark and stiff in our seats. I propose, gentlemen, that we teach London the great lesson it so much needs. No cause is without its martyrs. Let us be the martyrs of the great religion of Anarchy. I have left in my room papers telling just how and why we died. At midnight these sheets will be distributed to all the newspapers of London, and to-morrow the world will ring with our heroic names. I will now put the motion. All in favor of this signify it by the usual upraising of the right hand."

The Professor's own right hand was the only one that was raised.

"Now all of a contrary opinion," said the Professor, and at once every hand in the audience went up.

"The noes have it," said the Professor, but he did not seem to feel badly about it. "Gentlemen," he continued, "I see that you have guessed my second proposal, as I imagined you would, and though there will be no newspapers in London to-morrow to chronicle the fact, yet the newspapers of the rest of the world will tell of the destruction of this wicked city. I see by your looks that you are with me in this, my second proposal, which is the most striking thing ever planned, and is that we explode the whole of these pills in the basin. To make sure of this, I have sent to an agent in Manchester the full account of how it was done, and the resolutions brought forward at this meeting, and which doubtless you will accept.

"Gentlemen, all in favor of the instant destruction of London signify it in the usual manner."

"Mr. Professor," said the man who had spoken previously, "before you put that resolution I would like to move an amendment. This is a very serious proposal, and should not be lightly undertaken. I move as an amendment, therefore, that we adjourn this meeting to our rooms at Soho, and do the exploding there. I have some little business that must be settled before this grand project is put in motion."

The Professor then said, "Gentlemen, the amendment takes precedence. It is moved that this meeting be adjourned, so that you may consider the project at your club-rooms in Soho."

"I second that amendment," said fifteen of the audience rising together to their feet.

"In the absence of the regular chairman," said the Professor, "it is my duty to put the amendment. All in favor of the amendment signify it by raising the right hand."

Every hand was raised. "The amendment, gentlemen, is carried. I shall be only too pleased to meet you to-morrow night at your club, and I will bring with me a larger quantity of my explosive. John, kindly go round and tell the man to unlock the doors."

When Simkins and Slivers called round the next night at the regular meeting-place of the Anarchists, they found no signs of a gathering, and never since the lecture has the Soho Anarchist League been known to hold a meeting. The Club has mysteriously dissolved.

THE FEAR OF IT.

The sea was done with him. He had struggled manfully for his life, but exhaustion came at last, and, realizing the futility of further fighting, he gave up the battle. The tallest wave, the king of that roaring tumultuous procession racing from the wreck to the shore, took him in its relentless grasp, held him towering for a moment against the sky, whirled his heels in the air, dashed him senseless on the sand, and, finally, rolled him over and over, a helpless bundle, high up upon the sandy beach.

Human life seems of little account when we think of the trifles that make toward the extinction or the extension of it. If the wave that bore Stanford had been a little less tall, he would have been drawn back into the sea by one that followed. If, as a helpless bundle, he had been turned over one time more or one less, his mouth would have pressed into the sand, and he would have died. As it was, he lay on his back with arms outstretched on either side, and a handful of dissolving sand in one clinched fist. Succeeding waves sometimes touched him, but he lay there unmolested by the sea with his white face turned to the sky.

Oblivion has no calendar. A moment or an eternity are the same to it. When consciousness slowly returned, he neither knew nor cared how time had fled. He was not quite sure that he was alive, but weakness rather than fear kept him from opening his eyes to find out whether the world they would look upon was the world they had last gazed at. His interest, however, was speedily stimulated by the sound of the English tongue. He was still too much dazed to wonder at it, and to remember that he was cast away on some unknown island in the Southern Seas. But the purport of the words startled him.

"Let us be thankful. He is undoubtedly dead." This was said in a tone of infinite satisfaction.

There seemed to be a murmur of pleasure at the announcement from those who were with the speaker. Stanford slowly opened his eyes, wondering what these savages were who rejoiced in the death of an inoffensive stranger cast upon their shores. He saw a group standing around him, but his attention speedily became concentrated on one face. The owner of it, he judged, was not more than nineteen years of age, and the face—at least so it seemed to Stanford at the time—was the most beautiful he had ever beheld. There was an expression of sweet gladness upon it until her eyes met his, then the joy faded from the face, and a look of dismay took its place. The girl seemed to catch her breath in fear, and tears filled her eyes.

"Oh," she cried, "he is going to live."

She covered her face with her hands, and sobbed.

Stanford closed his eyes wearily. "I am evidently insane," he said to himself. Then, losing faith in the reality of things, he lost consciousness as well, and when his senses came to him again he found himself lying on a bed in a clean but scantily furnished room. Through an open window came the roar of the sea, and the thunderous boom of the falling waves brought to his mind the experiences through which he had passed. The wreck and the struggle with the waves he knew to be real, but the episode on the beach he now believed to have been but a vision resulting from his condition.

A door opened noiselessly, and, before he knew of anyone's entrance, a placid-faced nurse stood by his bed and asked him how he was.

"I don't know. I am at least alive."

The nurse sighed, and cast down her eyes. Her lips moved, but she said nothing. Stanford looked at her curiously. A fear crept over him that he was hopelessly crippled for life, and that death was considered preferable to a maimed existence. He felt wearied, though not in pain, but he knew that sometimes the more desperate the hurt, the less the victim feels it at first.

"Are—are any of my—my bones broken, do you know?" he asked.

"No. You are bruised, but not badly hurt. You will soon recover."

"Ah!" said Stanford, with a sigh of relief. "By the way," he added, with sudden interest, "who was that girl who stood near me as I lay on the beach?"

"There were several."

"No, there was but one. I mean the girl with the beautiful eyes and a halo of hair like a glorified golden crown on her head."

"We speak not of our women in words like those," said the nurse, severely; "you mean Ruth, perhaps, whose hair is plentiful and yellow."

Stanford smiled. "Words matter little," he said.

"We must be temperate in speech," replied the nurse.

"We may be temperate without, being teetotal. Plentiful and yellow, indeed! I have had a bad dream concerning those who found me. I thought that they—but it does not matter. She at least is not a myth. Do you happen to know if any others were saved?"

"I am thankful to be able to say that every one was drowned."

Stanford started up with horror in his eyes. The demure nurse, with sympathetic tones, bade him not excite himself. He sank back on his pillow.

"Leave the room," he cried, feebly, "Leave me—leave me." He turned his face toward the wall, while the woman left as silently as she had entered.

When she was gone Stanford slid from the bed, intending to make his way to the door and fasten it. He feared that these savages, who wished him dead, would take measures to kill him when they saw he was going to recover. As he leaned against the bed, he noticed that the door had no fastening. There was a rude latch, but neither lock nor bolt. The furniture of the room was of the most meagre description, clumsily made. He staggered to the open window, and looked out. The remnants of the disastrous gale blew in upon him and gave him new life, as it had formerly threatened him with death. He saw that he was in a village of small houses, each cottage standing in its own plot of ground. It was apparently a village of one street, and over the roofs of the houses opposite he saw in the distance the white waves of the sea. What astonished him most was a church with its tapering spire at the end of the street—a wooden church such as he had seen in remote American settlements. The street was deserted, and there were no signs of life in the houses.

"I must have fallen in upon some colony of lunatics," he said to himself. "I wonder to what country these people belong—either to England or the United States, I imagine—yet in all my travels I never heard of such a community."

There was no mirror in the room, and it was impossible for him to know how he looked. His clothes were dry and powdered with salt. He arranged them as well as he could, and slipped out of the house unnoticed. When he reached the outskirts of the village he saw that the inhabitants, both men and women, were working in the fields some distance away. Coming towards the village was a girl with a water-can in either hand. She was singing as blithely as a lark until she saw Stanford, whereupon she paused both in her walk and in her song. Stanford, never a backward man, advanced, and was about to greet her when she forestalled him by saying:

"I am grieved, indeed, to see that you have recovered."

The young man's speech was frozen on his lip, and a frown settled off his brow. Seeing that he was annoyed, though why she could not guess, Ruth hastened to amend matters by adding:

"Believe me, what I say is true. I am indeed sorry."

"Sorry that I live?"

"Most heartily am I."

"It is hard to credit such a statement from one so—from you."

"Do not say so. Miriam has already charged me with being glad that you were not drowned. It would pain me deeply if you also believed as she does."

The girl looked at him with swimming eyes, and the young man knew not what to answer. Finally he said:

"There is some horrible mistake. I cannot make it out. Perhaps our words, though apparently the same, have a different meaning. Sit down,

Ruth, I want to ask you some questions."

Ruth cast a timorous glance towards the workers, and murmured something about not having much time to spare, but she placed the water-cans on the ground and sank down on the grass. Stanford throwing himself on the sward at her feet, but, seeing that she shrank back, he drew himself further from her, resting where he might gaze upon her face.

Ruth's eyes were downcast, which was necessary, for she occupied herself in pulling blade after blade of grass, sometimes weaving them together. Stanford had said he wished to question her, but he apparently forgot his intention, for he seemed wholly satisfied with merely looking at her. After the silence had lasted for some time, she lifted her eyes for one brief moment, and then asked the first question herself.

"From what land do you come?"

"From England."

"Ah! that also is an island, is it not?"

He laughed at the "also," and remembered that he had some questions to ask.

"Yes, it is an island—also. The sea dashes wrecks on all four sides of it, but there is no village on its shores so heathenish that if a man is cast upon the beach the inhabitants do not rejoice because he has escaped death."

Ruth looked at him with amazement in her eyes.

"Is there, then, no religion in England?"

"Religion? England is the most religious country on the face of the earth. There are more cathedrals, more churches, more places of worship in England than in any other State that I know of. We send missionaries to all heathenish lands. The Government, itself, supports the Church."

"I imagine, then, I mistook your meaning. I thought from what you said that the people of England feared death, and did not welcome it or rejoice when one of their number died."

"They do not fear death, and they do not rejoice when it comes. Far from it. From the peer to the beggar, everyone fights death as long as he can; the oldest cling to life as eagerly as the youngest. Not a man but will spend his last gold piece to ward off the inevitable even for an hour."

"Gold piece—what is that?"

Stanford plunged his hand into his pocket.

"Ah!" he said, "there are some coins left. Here is a gold piece."

The girl took it, and looked at it with keen interest.

"Isn't it pretty?" she said, holding the yellow coin on her pink palm, and glancing up at him.

"That is the general opinion. To accumulate coins like that, men will lie, and cheat, and steal—yes, and work. Although they will give their last sovereign to prolong their lives, yet will they risk life itself to accumulate gold. Every business in England is formed merely for the gathering together of bits of metal like that in your hand; huge companies of men are formed so that it may be piled up in greater quantities. The man who has most gold has most power, and is generally the most respected; the company which makes most money is the one people are most anxious to belong to."

Ruth listened to him with wonder and dismay in her eyes. As he talked she shuddered, and allowed the yellow coin to slip from her hand to the ground. "No wonder such a people fears death."

"Do you not fear death?"

"How can we, when we believe in heaven?"

"But would you not be sorry if someone died whom you loved?"

"How could we be so selfish? Would you be sorry if your brother, or someone you loved, became possessed of whatever you value in England—a large quantity of this gold, for instance?"

"Certainly not. But then you see—well, it isn't exactly the same thing. If one you care for dies you are separated from him, and——"

"But only for a short time, and that gives but another reason for welcoming death. It seems impossible that Christian people should fear to enter Heaven. Now I begin to understand why our forefathers left England, and why our teachers will never tell us anything about the people there. I wonder why missionaries are not sent to England to teach them the truth, and try to civilize the people?"

"That would, indeed, be coals to Newcastle. But there comes one of the workers."

"It is my father," cried the girl, rising. "I fear I have been loitering. I never did such a thing before."

The man who approached was stern of countenance.

"Ruth," he said, "the workers are athirst."

The girl, without reply, picked up her pails and departed.

"I have been receiving," said the young man, coloring slightly, "some instruction regarding your belief. I had been puzzled by several remarks I had heard, and wished to make inquiries concerning them."

"It is more fitting," said the man, coldly, "that you should receive instruction from me or from some of the elders than from one of the youngest in the community. When you are so far recovered as to be able to listen to an exposition of our views, I hope to put forth such arguments as will convince you that they are the true views. If it should so happen that my arguments are not convincing, then I must request that you will hold no communication with our younger members. They must not be contaminated by the heresies of the outside world."

Stanford looked at Ruth standing beside the village well.

"Sir," he said, "you underrate the argumentative powers of the younger members. There is a text bearing upon the subject which I need not recall to you. I am already convinced."

THE METAMORPHOSES OF JOHNSON.

I was staying for some weeks at a lovely town in the Tyrol which I shall take the liberty of naming Schwindleburg. I conceal its real title because it charges what is termed a visitors' tax, and a heavy visitors' tax, exacting the same from me through the medium of my hotel bill. The town also made me pay for the excellent band that performs morning and afternoon in the Kurpark. Many continental health resorts support themselves by placing a tax upon visitors, a practice resorted to by no English town, and so I regard the imposition as a swindle, and I refuse to advertise any place that practises it. It is true that if you stay in Schwindleburg less than a week they do not tax you, but I didn't know that, and the hotel man, being wise in his own generation, did not present his bill until a day after the week was out, so I found myself in for the visitors' tax and the music money before I was aware of it. Thus does a foolish person accumulate wisdom by foreign travel. I stayed on at this picturesque place, listening to the band every day, trying to get value for my money. I intended to keep much to myself, having work to do, and make no acquaintances, but I fell under the fascination of Johnson, thus breaking my rule. What is the use of making a rule if you can't have the pleasure of breaking it?

I think the thing that first attracted me to Johnson was his utter negligence in the matter of his personal appearance. When he stepped down from the hotel 'bus he looked like a semi-respectable tramp. He wore a blue woolen shirt, with no collar or necktie. He had a slouch hat, without the usual affectation of a Tyrolese feather in it. His full beard had evidently not been trimmed for weeks, and he had one trouser-leg turned up. He had no alpenstock, and that also was a merit. So I said to myself, "Here is a man free from the conventionalities of society. If I become acquainted with anybody it will be with him."

I found Johnson was an American from a Western city named Chicago, which I had heard of, and we "palled on." He was very fond of music, and the band in the Kurpark was a good one, so we went there together twice a day, and talked as we walked up and down the gravel paths. He had been everywhere, and knew his way about; his conversation was interesting. In about a week I had come to love Johnson, and I think he rather liked me.

One day, as we returned together to the Hotel Post, he held out his hand.

"I'm off to-morrow," he said; "off to Innsbruck. So I shall bid you good-bye. I am very glad indeed to have met you."

"Oh, I'm sorry to hear that," I replied. "But I won't say good-bye now, I'll see you to the station to-morrow."

"No, don't do that. I shall be away before you are up. We'll say good- bye here."

We did, and when I had breakfast next morning I found Johnson had left by the early train. I wandered around the park that forenoon mourning for Johnson. The place seemed lonely without him. In the afternoon I explored some of the by-paths of the park within hearing distance of the band, when suddenly, to my intense surprise, I met my departed friend.

"Hello! Johnson," I cried, "I thought you left this morning."

The man looked at me with no recognition in his face.

"I beg your pardon," he said, "my name is Baumgarten."

Looking more closely at him I at once saw I was mistaken. I had been thinking of Johnson at the time, which probably accounted for the error. Still, his likeness to Johnson was remarkable—to Johnson well groomed. He had neatly-trimmed side-whiskers and moustache, while Johnson had a full beard. His round hat was new, and he wore an irreproachable collar, and even cuffs. Besides this he sported a cane, and evidently possessed many weaknesses to which Johnson was superior. I apologized for my mistake, and was about to walk on when Baumgarten showed signs of wishing to become acquainted.

"I have just arrived," he said, "and know nothing of the place. Have you been here long?"

"About two weeks," I answered.

"Ah! then, you are a resident as it were. Are there any good ascents to be made around here?"

"I have not been informed that there are. I am not a climber myself, except by funicular railway. I am always content to take other people's figures for the heights. The only use I have for a mountain is to look at it."

Then Baumgarten launched into a very interesting account of mountain dangers he had passed through. I found him a most entertaining talker, almost as fascinating as Johnson himself. He told me he was from Hanover, but he had been educated in Great Britain, which accounted for his perfect English.

"What hotel are you at?" he asked, as the band ceased playing.

"I am staying at the Post," I answered. "And you?"

"I am at the Adler. You must come to dine with me some evening, and I will make it even by dining with you. We can thus compare table d'hôtes."

Baumgarten improved on acquaintance in spite of his foppishness in dress. I almost forgot Johnson until one day I was reminded of him one day by Baumgarten saying, "I leave to-night for Innsbruck."

"Innsbruck? Why, that's where Johnson is. You ought to meet him. He's an awfully good fellow. A little careless about his clothes, that's all."

"I should like to meet him. I know no one in Innsbruck. Do you happen to know the name of his hotel?"

"I do not. I don't even know Johnson's first name. But I'll write you a note of introduction on my card, and if you should come across him, give him my regards."

Baumgarten accepted the card with thanks, and we parted.

Next day, being warm, I sat on a bench in the shade listening to the music. Now that Baumgarten had gone, I was meditating on his strange resemblance to Johnson, and remembering things. Someone sat down beside me, but I paid no attention to him. Finally he said: "This seems to be a very good band."

I started at the sound of his voice, and looked at him too much astonished to reply.

He wore a moustache, but no whiskers, and a green Tyrolese felt hat with a feather in it. An alpenstock leaned against the bench beside him, its iron point in the gravel. He wore knickerbockers; in fact, his whole appearance was that of the conventional mountaineer-tourist. But the voice! And the expression of the eyes!

"What did you say?"

"I said the band is very good."

"Oh, yes. Quite so. It's expensive, and it ought to be good. I'm helping to pay for it. By the way, you arrived this morning, I take it?"

"I came last night."

"Oh, indeed. And you depart in a few days for Innsbruck?"

"No, I go to Salzburg when I leave here."

"And your name isn't Johnson—or—or Baumgarten, by any chance?"

"It is not."

"You come neither from Chicago nor Hanover?"

"I have never been in America, nor do I know Hanover. Anything else?"

"Nothing else. It's all right. It's none of my business, of course."

"What is none of your business?"

"Who are you."

"Oh, there's no secret about that. I am a Russian. My name is Katzoff. At least, these are the first and last syllables of my name. I never use my full name when I travel; it is too complicated."

"Thanks. And how do you account for your perfect English? Educated in England, I presume? Baumgarten was."

"No, I was not. You know we Russians are reputed to be good linguists."

"Yes, I had forgotten that. We will now return to the point from which we started. The band is excellent, and it is about to play one of four favorite selections, Mr. Katzburg."

"Katzoff is the name. As to the selection, I don't know much about music, although I am fond of popular pieces."

Katzoff and I got along very nicely, although I did not seem to like him as well as either Johnson or Baumgarten. He left for Salzburg without bidding me good-bye. Missing him one day, I called at the Angleterre, and the porter told me he had gone.

Next day I searched for him, wondering in what garb I should find him. I passed him twice as he sat on the bench, before I was sure enough to accost him. The sacrifice of his moustache had made a remarkable difference. His clean-shaven face caused him to look at least ten years younger. He wore a tall silk hat, and a long black morning coat. I found myself hardly able to withdraw my eyes from the white spats that partially covered his polished boots. He was reading an English paper, and did not observe my scrutiny. I approached him.

"Well, Johnson," I said, "this is a lay out. You're English this time, I suppose?"

The man looked up in evident surprise. Fumbling around the front of his waistcoat for a moment, he found a black silk string, which he pulled, bringing to his hand a little round disc of glass. This he stuck in one eye, grimacing slightly to keep it in place, and so regarded me apparently with some curiosity. My certainty that it was Johnson wavered for a moment, but I braved it out.

"That monocle is a triumph, Johnson. In combination with the spats it absolutely staggers me. If you had tried that on as Baumgarten I don't know that I should have recognized you. Johnson, what's your game?"

"You seem to be laboring under some delusion," he said at last. "My name is not Johnson. I am Lord Somerset Campbell, if you care to know."

"Really? Oh, well, that's all right. I'm the Duke of Argyll, so we must be relatives. Blood is thicker than water, Campbell. Confess. Whom have you murdered?"

"I knew," said his lordship, slowly, "that the largest lunatic asylum in the Tyrol is near here, but I was not aware that the patients were allowed to stroll in the Kurpark."

"That's all very well, Johnson, but——"

"Campbell, if you please."

"I don't please, as it happens. This masquerade has gone on long enough. What's your crime? Or are you on the other side of the fence? Are you practising the detective business?"

"My dear fellow, I don't know you, and I resent your impertinent curiosity. Allow me to wish you good-day."

"It won't do, Johnson, it has gone too far. You have played on my feelings, and I won't stand it. I'll go to the authorities and relate the circumstances. They are just suspicious enough to——"

"Which? The authorities or the circumstances?" asked Johnson, sitting down again.

"Both, my dear boy, both, and you know it. Now, Johnson, make a clean breast of it, I won't give you away."

Johnson sighed, and his glass dropped from his eye. He looked around cautiously. "Sit down," he said.

"Then you are Johnson!" I cried, with some exultation.

"I thought you weren't very sure," began Johnson. "However, it doesn't matter, but you should be above threatening a man. That was playing it low down."

"I see you're from Chicago. Go on."

"It's all on account of this accursed visitors' tax. That I decline to pay. I stay just under the week at a hotel, and then take a 'bus to the station, and another 'bus to another hotel. Of course my mistake was getting acquainted with you. I never suspected you were going to stay here a month."

"But why didn't you let me know? Your misdemeanor is one I thoroughly sympathize with. I wouldn't have said anything."

Johnson shook his head.

"I took a fellow into my confidence once before. He told it as a dead secret to a friend, and the friend thought it a good joke, and related it, always under oath that it should go no further. The authorities had me arrested before the week was out, and fined me heavily besides exacting the tax."

"But doesn't the 'bus fares, the changing, and all that amount to as much as the tax?"

"I suppose it does. It isn't the money I object to, it's the principle of the thing."

This interview was the last I ever had with Johnson. About a week later I read in the Visitors' List that Lord Somerset Campbell, who had been a guest of the Victoria (the swell hotel of the place), had left Schwindleburg for Innsbruck.

THE RECLAMATION OF JOE HOLLENDS.

The public-houses of Burwell Road—and there were many of them for the length of the street—were rather proud of Joe Hollends. He was a perfected specimen of the work a pub produces. He was probably the most persistent drunkard the Road possessed, and the periodical gathering in of Joe by the police was one of the stock sights of the street. Many of the inhabitants could be taken to the station by one policeman; some required two; but Joe's average was four. He had been heard to boast that on one occasion he had been accompanied to the station by seven bobbies, but that was before the force had studied Joe and got him down to his correct mathematical equivalent. Now they tripped him up, a policeman taking one kicking leg and another the other, while the remaining two attended to the upper part of his body. Thus they carried him, followed by an admiring crowd, and watched by other envious drunkards who had to content themselves with a single officer when they went on a similar spree. Sometimes Joe managed to place a kick where it would do the most good against the stomach of a policeman, and when the officer rolled over there was for a few moments a renewal of the fight, silent on the part of the men and vociferous on the part of the drunkard, who had a fine flow of abusive language. Then the procession went on again. It was perfectly useless to put Joe on the police ambulance, for it required two men to sit on him while in transit, and the barrow is not made to stand such a load.

Of course, when Joe staggered out of the pub and fell in the gutter, the ambulance did its duty, and trundled Joe to his abiding place, but the real fun occurred when Joe was gathered in during the third stage of his debauch. He passed through the oratorical stage, then the maudlin or sentimental stage, from which he emerged into the fighting stage, when he was usually ejected into the street, where he forthwith began to make Rome howl, and paint the town red. At this point the policeman's whistle sounded, and the force knew Joe was on the warpath, and that duty called them to the fray.

It was believed in the neighborhood that Joe had been a college man, and this gave him additional standing with his admirers. His eloquence was undoubted, after several glasses varying in number according to the strength of their contents, and a man who had heard the great political speakers of the day admitted that none of them could hold a candle to Joe when he got on the subject of the wrongs of the working man and the tyranny of the capitalist. It was generally understood that Joe might have been anything he liked, and that he was no man's enemy but his own. It was also hinted that he could tell the bigwigs a thing or two if he had been consulted in affairs of State.

One evening, when Joe was slowly progressing as usual, with his feet in the air, towards the station, supported by the requisite number of policemen, and declaiming to the delight of the accompanying crowd, a woman stood with her back to the brick wall, horror-stricken at the sight. She had a pale, refined face, and was dressed in black. Her self-imposed mission was among these people, but she had never seen Joe taken to the station before, and the sight, which was so amusing to the neighborhood, was shocking to her. She enquired about Joe, and heard the usual story that he was no man's enemy but his own, although they might in justice have added the police. Still, a policeman was hardly looked upon as a human being in that neighborhood. Miss Johnson reported the case to the committee of the Social League, and took counsel. Then it was that the reclamation of Joe Hollends was determined on.

Joe received Miss Johnson with subdued dignity, and a demeanor that delicately indicated a knowledge on his part of her superiority and his own degradation. He knew how a lady should be treated even if he was a drunkard, as he told his cronies afterwards. Joe was perfectly willing to be reclaimed. Heretofore in his life, no one had ever extended the hand of fellowship to him. Human sympathy was what Joe needed, and precious little he had had of it. There were more kicks than halfpence in this world for a poor man. The rich did not care what became of the poor; not they—a proposition which Miss Johnson earnestly denied.

It was one of the tenets of the committee that where possible the poor should help the poor. It was resolved to get Joe a decent suit of clothes and endeavor to find him a place where work would enable him to help himself.

Miss Johnson went around the neighborhood and collected pence for the reclamation. Most people were willing to help Joe, although it was generally felt that the Road would be less gay when he took on sober habits. In one room, however, Miss Johnson was refused the penny she pleaded for.

"We cannot spare even a penny," said the woman, whose sickly little boy clung to her skirts. "My husband is just out of work again. He has had only four weeks' work this time."

Miss Johnson looked around the room and saw why there was no money. It was quite evident where the earnings of the husband had gone.

The room was much better furnished than the average apartment of the neighborhood. There were two sets of dishes where one would have been quite sufficient. On the mantelshelf and around the walls were various unnecessary articles which cost money.

Miss Johnson noted all this but said nothing, although she resolved to report it to the committee. In union is strength and in multitude of counsel there is wisdom. Miss Johnson had great faith in the wisdom of the committee.

"How long has your husband been out of work?" she asked.

"Only a few days, but times are very bad and he is afraid he will not get another situation soon."

"What is his trade?"

"He is a carpenter and a good workman—sober and steady."

"If you give me his name I will put it down in our books. Perhaps we may be able to help him."

"John Morris is his name."

Miss Johnson wrote it down on her tablets, and when she left, the wife felt vaguely grateful for benefits to come.

The facts of the case were reported to the committee, and Miss Johnson was deputed to expostulate with Mrs. Morris upon her extravagance. John

Morris's name was put upon the books among the names of many other unemployed persons. The case of Joe Hollends then came up, and elicited much enthusiasm. A decent suit of clothing had been purchased with part of the money collected for him, and it was determined to keep the rest in trust, to be doled out to him as occasion warranted.

Two persuasive ladies undertook to find a place for him in one of the factories, if such a thing were possible.

Joe felt rather uncomfortable in his new suit of clothes, and seemed to regard the expenditure as, all in all, a waste of good money. He was also disappointed to find that the funds collected were not to be handed over to him in a lump. It was not the money he cared about, he said, but the evident lack of trust. If people had trusted him more, he might have been a better man. Trust and human sympathy were what Joe Hollends needed.

The two persuasive ladies appealed to Mr. Stillwell, the proprietor of a small factory for the making of boxes. They said that if Hollends got a chance they were sure he would reform. Stillwell replied that he had no place for anyone. He had enough to do to keep the men already in his employ. Times were dull in the box business, and he was turning away applicants every day who were good workmen and who didn't need to be reformed. However, the ladies were very persuasive, and it is not given to every man to be able to refuse the appeal of a pretty woman, not to mention two of them. Stillwell promised to give Hollends a chance, said he would consult with his foreman, and let the ladies know what could be done.

Joe Hollends did not receive the news of his luck with the enthusiasm that might have been expected. Many a man was tramping London in search of employment and finding none, therefore even the ladies who were so solicitous about Joe's welfare thought he should be thankful that work came unsought. He said he would do his best, which is, when you come to think of it, all that we have a right to expect from any man.

Some days afterwards Jack Morris applied to Mr. Stillwell for a job, but he had no sub-committee of persuasive ladies to plead for him. He would be willing to work half-time or quarter-time for that matter. He had a wife and boy dependent on him. He could show that he was a good workman and he did not drink. Thus did Morris recite his qualifications to the unwilling ears of Stillwell the box maker. As he left the place disheartened with another refusal, he was overtaken by Joe Hollends. Joe was a lover of his fellow-man, and disliked seeing anyone downhearted. He had one infallible cure for dejection. Having just been discharged, he was in high spirits, because his prediction of his own failure as a reformed character, if work were a condition of the reclamation, had just been fulfilled.

"Cheer up, old man," he cried, slapping Morris on the shoulder, "what's the matter? Come and have a drink with me. I've got the money."

"No," said Morris, who knew the professional drunkard but slightly, and did not care for further acquaintance with him, "I want work, not beer."

"Every man to his taste. Why don't you ask at the box factory? You can have my job and welcome. The foreman's just discharged me. Said I wouldn't work myself, and kept the men off theirs. Thought I talked too much about capital and labor."

"Do you think I could get your job?"

"Very likely. No harm in trying. If they don't take you on, come into the Red Lion—I'll be there—and have a drop. It'll cheer you up a bit."

Morris appealed in vain to the foreman. They had more men now in the factory than they needed, he said. So Morris went to the Red Lion, where he found Hollends ready to welcome him. They had several glasses together, and Hollends told him of the efforts of the Social League in the reclamation line, and his doubts of their ultimate success. Hollends seemed to think the ladies of the League were deeply indebted to him for furnishing them with such a good subject for reformation. That night Joe's career reached a triumphant climax, for the four policeman had to appeal to the bystanders for help in the name of the law.

Jack Morris went home unaided. He had not taken many glasses, but he knew he should have avoided drink altogether, for he had some experience of its power in his younger days. He was, therefore, in a quarrelsome mood, ready to blame everyone but himself.

He found his wife in tears, and saw Miss Johnson sitting there, evidently very miserable.

"What's all this?" asked Morris.

His wife dried her eyes, and said it was nothing. Miss Johnson had been giving her some advice, which she was thankful for. Morris glared at the visitor.

"What have you got to do with us?" he demanded rudely. His wife caught him by the arm, but he angrily tossed aside her hand. Miss Johnson arose, fearing.

"You've no business here. We want none of your advice. You get out of this." Then, impatiently to his wife, who strove to calm him, "Shut up, will you?"

Miss Johnson was afraid he would strike her as she passed him going to the door, but he merely stood there, following her exit with lowering brow.

The terrified lady told her experience to the sympathizing members of the committee. She had spoken to Mrs. Morris of her extravagance in buying so many things that were not necessary when her husband had work. She advised the saving of the money. Mrs. Morris had defended her apparent lavish expenditure by saying that there was no possibility of saving money. She bought useful things, and when her husband was out of work she could always get a large percentage of their cost from the pawnbroker. The pawnshop, she had tearfully explained to Miss Johnson, was the only bank of the poor. The idea of the pawnshop as a bank, and not as a place of disgrace, was new to Miss Johnson, but before anything further could be said the husband had come in. One of the committee, who knew more about the district than Miss Johnson, affirmed that there was something to say for the pawnbroker as the banker of the poor. The committee were unanimous in condemning the conduct of Morris, and it says much for the members that, in spite of the provocation one of them had received, they did not take the name of so undeserving a man from their list of the unemployed.

The sad relapse of Joe Hollends next occupied the attention of the League. His fine had been paid, and he had expressed himself as deeply grieved at his own frailty. If the foreman had been less harsh with him and had given him a chance, things might have been different. It was resolved to send Joe to the seaside so that he might have an opportunity of toning up his system to resist temptation. Joe enjoyed his trip to the sea. He always liked to encounter a new body of police unaccustomed to his methods. He toned up his system so successfully the first day on the sands that he spent the night in the cells.

Little by little, the portable property in the rooms of the Morrises disappeared into the pawnshop. Misfortune, as usual, did not come singly. The small boy was ill, and Morris himself seemed to be unable to resist the temptation of the Red Lion. The unhappy woman took her boy to the parish doctor, who was very busy, but he gave what attention he could to the case. He said all the boy needed was nourishing food and country air. Mrs. Morris sighed, and decided to take the little boy oftener to the park, but the way was long, and he grew weaker day by day.

At last, she succeeded in interesting her husband in the little fellow's condition. He consented to take the boy to the doctor with her.

"The doctor doesn't seem to mind what I say," she complained. "Perhaps he will pay attention to a man."

Morris was not naturally a morose person, but continued disappointment was rapidly making him so. He said nothing, but took the boy in his arms, and, followed by his wife, went to the doctor.

"This boy was here before," said the physician, which tended to show that he had paid more attention to the case than Mrs. Morris thought. "He is very much worse. You will have to take him to the country or he will die."

"How can I send him to the country?" asked Morris, sullenly. "I've been out of work for months."

"Have you friends in the country?"

"No."

"Hasn't your wife any friends in the country who would take her and the lad for a month or so?"

"No."

"Have you anything to pawn?"

"Very little."

"Then I would advise you to pawn everything you own, or sell it if you can, and take the boy on your back and tramp to the country. You will get work there probably more easily than in the city. Here are ten shillings to help you."

"I don't want your money," said Morris, in a surly tone. "I want work."

"I have no work to give you, so I offer you what I have. I haven't as much of that as I could wish. You are a fool not to take what the gods send."

Morris, without replying, gathered up his son in his arms and departed.

"Here is a bottle of tonic for him." said the doctor to Mrs. Morris.

He placed the half-sovereign on the bottle as he passed it to her. She silently thanked him with her wet eyes, hoping that a time would come when she could repay the money. The doctor had experience enough to know that they were not to be classed among his usual visitors. He was not in the habit of indiscriminately bestowing gold coins.

It was a dreary journey, and they were a long time shaking off the octopus-like tentacles of the great city, that reached further and further into he country each year, as if it lived on consuming the green fields. Morris walked ahead with the boy on his back, and his wife followed. Neither spoke, and the sick lad did not complain. As they were nearing a village, the boy's head sunk on his father's shoulder. The mother quickened her pace, and came up to them stroking the head of her sleeping son. Suddenly, she uttered a smothered cry and took the boy in her arms.

"What's the matter?" asked Morris, turning round.

She did not answer, but sat by the roadside with the boy on her lap, swaying her body to and fro over him, moaning as she did so. Morris needed no answer. He stood on the road with hardening face, and looked down on his wife and child without speaking.

The kindly villagers arranged the little funeral, and when it was over Jack Morris and his wife stood again on the road.

"Jack, dear," she pleaded, "don't go back to that horrible place. We belong to the country, and the city is so hard and cruel."

"I'm going back. You can do as you like." Then, relenting a little, he added, "I haven't brought much luck to you, my girl."

She knew her husband was a stubborn man, and set in his way, so, unprotesting, she followed him in, as she had followed out, stumbling many times, for often her eyes did not see the road. And so they returned to their empty rooms.

Jack Morris went to look for work at the Red Lion. There he met that genial comrade, Joe Hollends, who had been reformed, and who had backslid twice since Jack had foregathered with him before. It is but fair to Joe to admit that he had never been optimistic about his own reclamation, but being an obliging man, even when he was sober, he was willing to give the Social League every chance. Jack was deeply grieved at the death of his son, although he had said no word to his wife that would show it. It therefore took more liquor than usual to bring him up to the point of good comradeship that reigned at the Red Lion. When he and Joe left the tavern that night it would have taken an expert to tell which was the more inebriated. They were both in good fighting trim, and were both in the humor for a row. The police, who had reckoned on Joe alone, suddenly found a new element in the fight that not only upset their calculations but themselves as well. It was a glorious victory, and, as both fled down a side street, Morris urged Hollends to come along, for the representatives of law and order have the habit of getting reinforcements which often turn a victory into a most ignominious defeat.

"I can't," panted Hollends. "The beggars have hurt me."

"Come along. I know a place where we are safe."

Drunk as he was, Jack succeeded in finding the hole in the wall that allowed him to enter a vacant spot behind the box factory. There Hollends lay down with a groan, and there Morris sank beside him in a drunken sleep. The police were at last revenged, and finally.

When the grey daylight brought Morris to a dazed sense of where he was, he found his companion dead beside him. He had a vague fear that he would be tried for murder, but it was not so. From the moment that Hollends, in his fall, struck his head on the curb, the Providence which looks after the drunken deserted him.

But the inquest accomplished one good object. It attracted the attention of the Social League to Jack Morris, and they are now endeavoring to reclaim him.

Whether they succeed or not, he was a man that was certainly once worth saving.

THE TYPE-WRITTEN LETTER.

When a man has battled with poverty all his life, fearing it as he fought it, feeling for its skinny throat to throttle it, and yet dreading all the while the coming of the time when it would gain the mastery and throttle him—when such a man is told that he is rich, it might be imagined he would receive the announcement with hilarity. When Richard Denham realized that he was wealthy he became even more sobered than usual, and drew a long breath as if he had been running a race and had won it. The man who brought him the news had no idea he had told Denham anything novel.

He merely happened to say, "You are a rich man, Mr. Denham, and will never miss it."

Denham had never before been called a rich man, and up to that moment he had not thought of himself as wealthy. He wrote out the check asked of him, and his visitor departed gratefully, leaving the merchant with something to ponder over. He was as surprised with the suddenness of the thing as if someone had left him a legacy. Yet the money was all of his own accumulating, but his struggle had been so severe, and he had been so hopeless about it, that from mere habit he exerted all his energies long after the enemy was overcome—just as the troops at New Orleans fought a fierce battle not knowing that the war was over. He had sprung from such a hopelessly poor family. Poverty had been their inheritance from generation to generation. It was the invariable legacy that father had left to son in the Denham family. All had accepted their lot with uncomplaining resignation, until Richard resolved he would at least have a fight for it. And now the fight had been won. Denham sat in his office staring at the dingy wall-paper so long, that Rogers, the chief clerk, put his head in and said in a deferential voice:

"Anything more to-night, Mr. Denham?"

Denham started as if that question in that tone had not been asked him every night for years.

"What's that, what's that?" he cried.

Rogers was astonished, but too well trained to show it.

"Anything more to-night, Mr. Denham?"

"Ah, quite so. No, Rogers, thank you, nothing more."

"Good-night, Mr. Denham."

"Eh? Oh, yes. Good-night, Rogers, good-night."

When Mr. Denham left his office and went out into the street everything had an unusual appearance to him. He walked along, unheeding the direction. He looked at the fine residences and realized that he might have a fine residence if he wanted it. He saw handsome carriages; he too might set up an equipage. The satisfaction these thoughts produced was brief. Of what use would a fine house or an elegant carriage be to him? He knew no one to invite to the house or to ride with him in the carriage. He began to realize how utterly alone in the world he was. He had no friends, no acquaintances even. The running dog, with its nose to the ground, sees nothing of the surrounding scenery. He knew men in a business way, of course, and doubtless each of them had a home in the suburbs somewhere, but he could not take a business man by the shoulders and say to him, "Invite me to your house; I am lonely; I want to know people."

If he got such an invitation, he would not know what to do with himself. He was familiar with the counting-room and its language, but the drawing-room was an unexplored country to him, where an unknown tongue was spoken. On the road to wealth he had missed something, and it was now too late to go back for it. Only the day before, he had heard one of the clerks, who did not know he was within earshot, allude to him as "the old man." He felt as young as ever he did, but the phrase, so lightly spoken, made him catch his breath.

As he was now walking through the park, and away from the busy streets, he took off his hat and ran his fingers through his grizzled hair, looking at his hand when he had done so, as if the grey, like wet paint, might have come off. He thought of a girl he knew once, who perhaps would have married him if he had asked her, as he was tempted to do. But that had always been the mistake of the Denhams. They had all married young except himself, and so sunk deeper into the mire of poverty, pressed down by a rapidly-increasing progeny. The girl had married a baker, he remembered. Yes, that was a long time ago. The clerk was not far wrong when he called him an old man. Suddenly, another girl arose before his mental vision—a modern girl—very different indeed to the one who married the baker. She was the only woman in the world with whom he was on speaking terms, and he knew her merely because her light and nimble fingers played the business sonata of one note on his office typewriter. Miss Gale was pretty, of course— all typewriter girls are—and it was generally understood in the office that she belonged to a good family who had come down in the world. Her somewhat independent air deepened this conviction and kept the clerks at a distance. She was a sensible girl who realized that the typewriter paid better than the piano, and accordingly turned the expertness of her white fingers to the former instrument. Richard Denham sat down upon a park bench. "Why not?" he asked himself. There was no reason against it except that he felt he had not the courage. Nevertheless, he formed a desperate resolution.

Next day, business went on as usual. Letters were answered, and the time arrived when Miss Gale came in to see if he had any further commands that day. Denham hesitated. He felt vaguely that a business office was not the proper place for a proposal; yet he knew he would be at a disadvantage anywhere else. In the first place, he had no plausible excuse for calling upon the young woman at home, and, in the second place, he knew if he once got there he would be stricken dumb. It must either be at his office or nowhere.

"Sit down a moment, Miss Gale," he said at last; "I wanted to consult you about a matter—about a business matter."

Miss Gale seated herself, and automatically placed on her knee the shorthand writing-pad ready to take down his instructions. She looked up at him expectantly. Denham, in an embarrassed manner, ran his fingers through his hair.

"I am thinking," he began, "of taking a partner. The business is very prosperous now. In fact, it has been so for some time."

"Yes?" said Miss Gale interrogatively.

"Yes. I think I should have a partner. It is about that I wanted to speak to you."

"Don't you think it would be better to consult with Mr. Rogers? He knows more about business than I. But perhaps it is Mr. Rogers who is to be the partner?"

"No, it is not Rogers. Rogers is a good man. But—it is not Rogers."

"Then I think in an important matter like this Mr. Rogers, or someone who knows the business as thoroughly as he does, would be able to give you advice that would be of some value."

"I don't want advice exactly. I have made up my mind to have a partner, if the partner is willing."

Denham mopped his brow. It was going to be even more difficult than he had anticipated.

"Is it, then, a question of the capital the partner is to bring in?" asked Miss Gale, anxious to help him.

"No, no. I don't wish any capital. I have enough for both. And the business is very prosperous, Miss Gale—and—and has been."

The young woman raised her eyebrows in surprise.

"You surely don't intend to share the profits with a partner who brings no capital into the business?"

"Yes—yes, I do. You see, as I said, I have no need for more capital."

"Oh, if that is the case, I think you should consult Mr. Rogers before you commit yourself."

"But Rogers wouldn't understand."

"I'm afraid I don't understand either. It seems to me a foolish thing to do—that is, if you want my advice."

"Oh, yes, I want it. But it isn't as foolish as you think. I should have had a partner long ago. That is where I made the mistake. I've made up my mind on that."

"Then I don't see that I can be of any use—if your mind is already made up."

"Oh, yes, you can. I'm a little afraid that my offer may not be accepted."

"It is sure to be, if the man has any sense. No fear of such an offer being refused! Offers like that are not to be had every day. It will be accepted."

"Do you really think so, Miss Gale? I am glad that is your opinion. Now, what I wanted to consult you about, is the form of the offer. I would like to put it—well—delicately, you know, so that it would not be refused, nor give offence."

"I see. You want me to write a letter to him?"

"Exactly, exactly," cried Denham with some relief. He had not thought of sending a letter before. Now, he wondered why he had not thought of it. It was so evidently the best way out of a situation that was extremely disconcerting.

"Have you spoken to him about it?"

"To him? What him?"

"To your future partner, about the proposal?"

"No, no. Oh, no. That is—I have spoken to nobody but you."

"And you are determined not to speak to Mr. Rogers before you write?"

"Certainly not. It's none of Roger's business."

"Oh, very well," said Miss Gale shortly, bending over her writing-pad.

It was evident that her opinion of Denham's wisdom was steadily lowering. Suddenly, she looked up.

"How much shall I say the annual profits are? Or do you want that mentioned?"

"I—I don't think I would mention that. You see, I don't wish this arrangement to be carried out on a monetary basis—not altogether."

"On what basis then?"

"Well—I can hardly say. On a personal basis, perhaps. I rather hope that the person—that my partner—would, you know, like to be associated with me."

"On a friendly basis, do you mean?" asked Miss Gale, mercilessly.

"Certainly. Friendly, of course—and perhaps more than that."

Miss Gale looked up at him with a certain hopelessness of expression.

"Why not write a note inviting your future partner to call upon you here, or anywhere else that would be convenient, and then discuss the matter?"

Denham looked frightened.

"I thought of that, but it wouldn't do. No; it wouldn't do. I would much rather settle everything by correspondence."

"I am afraid I shall not be able to compose a letter that will suit you. There seem to be so many difficulties. It is very unusual."

"That is true, and that is why I knew no one but you could help me, Miss Gale. If it pleases you, it will please me."

Miss Gale shook her head, but, after a few moments, she said, "How will this do?"

"Dear Sir"—

"Wait a moment," cried Mr. Denham; "that seems rather a formal opening, doesn't it? How would it read if you put it 'Dear friend'?"

"If you wish it so." She crossed out the "sir" and substituted the word suggested. Then, she read the letter:

"Dear Friend,—I have for some time past been desirous of taking a partner, and would be glad if you would consider the question and consent to join me in this business. The business is, and has been for several years, very prosperous, and, as I shall require no capital from you, I think you will find my offer a very advantageous one. I will——"

"I—I don't think I would put it quite that way," said Denham, with some hesitation. "It reads as if I were offering everything, and that my partner—well, you see what I mean."

"It's the truth," said Miss Gale, defiantly.

"Better put it on the friendly basis, as you suggested a moment ago."

"I didn't suggest anything, Mr. Denham. Perhaps it would be better if you would dictate the letter exactly as you want it. I knew I could not write one that would please you."

"It does please me, but I'm thinking of my future partner. You are doing first-rate—better than I could do. But just put it on the friendly basis."

A moment later she read:

"... join me in this business. I make you this offer entirely from a friendly, and not from a financial, standpoint, hoping that you like me well enough to be associated with me."

"Anything else, Mr. Denham?"

"No. I think that covers the whole ground. It will look rather short, type-written, won't it? Perhaps you might add something to show that I shall be exceedingly disappointed if my offer is not accepted."

"No fear," said Miss Gale. "I'll add that though. 'Yours truly,' or 'Yours very truly'?"

"You might end it 'Your friend.'"

The rapid click of the typewriter was heard for a few moments in the next room, and then Miss Gale came out with the completed letter in her hand.

"Shall I have the boy copy it?" she asked.

"Oh, bless you, no!" answered Mr. Denham, with evident trepidation.

The young woman said to herself, "He doesn't want Mr. Rogers to know, and no wonder. It is a most unbusiness-like proposal."

Then she said aloud, "Shall you want me again to-day?"

"No, Miss Gale; and thank you very much."

Next morning, Miss Gale came into Mr. Denham's office with a smile on her face.

"You made a funny mistake last night, Mr. Denham," she said, as she took off her wraps.

"Did I?" he asked, in alarm.

"Yes. You sent that letter to my address. I got it this morning. I opened it, for I thought it was for me, and that perhaps you did not need me to-day. But I saw at once that you put it in the wrong envelope. Did you want me to-day?"

It was on his tongue to say, "I want you every day," but he merely held out his hand for the letter, and looked at it as if he could not account for its having gone astray.

The next day Miss Gale came late, and she looked frightened. It was evident that Denham was losing his mind. She put the letter down before him and said:

"You addressed that to me the second time, Mr. Denham."

There was a look of haggard anxiety about Denham that gave color to her suspicions. He felt that it was now or never.

"Then why don't you answer it, Miss Gale?" he said gruffly.

She backed away from him.

64

"Answer it?" she repeated faintly.

"Certainly. If I got a letter twice, I would answer it."

"What do you mean?" she cried, with her hand on the door-knob.

"Exactly what the letter says. I want you for my partner. I want to marry you, and d—n financial considerations——"

"Oh!" cried Miss Gale, in a long-drawn, quivering sigh. She was doubtless shocked at the word he had used, and fled to her typewriting room, closing the door behind her.

Richard Denham paced up and down the floor for a few moments, then rapped lightly at her door, but there was no response. He put on his hat and went out into the street. After a long and aimless walk, he found himself again at his place of business. When he went in, Rogers said to him:

"Miss Gale has left, sir."

"Has she?"

"Yes, and she has given notice. Says she is not coming back, sir."

"Very well."

He went into his own room and found a letter marked "personal" on his desk. He tore it open, and read in neatly type-written characters:

"I have resigned my place as typewriter girl, having been offered a better situation. I am offered a partnership in the house of Richard Denham. I have decided to accept the position, not so much on account of its financial attractions, as because I shall be glad, on a friendly basis, to be associated with the gentleman I have named. Why did you put me to all that worry writing that idiotic letter, when a few words would have saved ever so much bother? You evidently need a partner. My mother will be pleased to meet you any time you call. You have the address,—Your friend,

"MARGARET GALE."

"Rogers!" shouted Denham, joyfully.

"Yes, sir," answered that estimable man, putting his head into the room.

"Advertise for another typewriter girl, Rogers."

"Yes, sir," said Rogers.

THE DOOM OF LONDON.

I.—THE SELF-CONCEIT OF THE 20TH CENTURY.

I trust I am thankful my life has been spared until I have seen that most brilliant epoch of the world's history—the middle of the 20th century. It would be useless for any man to disparage the vast achievements of the past fifty years, and if I venture to call attention to the fact, now apparently forgotten, that the people of the 19th century succeeded in accomplishing many notable things, it must not be imagined that I intend thereby to discount in any measure the marvellous inventions of the present age. Men have always been somewhat prone to look with a certain condescension upon those who lived fifty or a hundred years before them. This seems to me the especial weakness of the present age; a feeling of national self-conceit, which, when it exists, should at least be kept as much in the background as possible. It will astonish many to know that such also was a failing of the people of the 19th century. They imagined themselves living in an age of progress, and while I am not foolish enough to attempt to prove that they did anything really worth recording, yet it must be admitted by any unprejudiced man of research that their inventions were at least stepping-stones to those of to-day. Although the telephone and telegraph, and all other electrical appliances, are now to be found only in our national museums, or in the private collections of those few men who take any interest in the doings of the last century, nevertheless, the study of the now obsolete science of electricity led up to the recent discovery of vibratory ether which does the work of the world so satisfactorily. The people of the 19th century were not fools, and although I am well aware that this statement will be received with scorn where it attracts any attention whatever, yet who can say that the progress of the next half-century may not be as great as that of the one now ended, and that the people of the next century may not look upon us with the same contempt which we feel toward those who lived fifty years ago?

Being an old man, I am, perhaps, a laggard who dwells in the past rather than the present; still, it seems to me that such an article as that which appeared recently in Blackwood from the talented pen of Prof. Mowberry, of Oxford University, is utterly unjustifiable. Under the title of "Did the People of London Deserve their Fate?" he endeavors to show that the simultaneous blotting out of millions of human beings was a beneficial event, the good results of which we still enjoy. According to him, Londoners were so dull-witted and stupid, so incapable of improvement, so sodden in the vice of mere money- gathering, that nothing but their total extinction would have sufficed, and that, instead of being an appalling catastrophe, the doom of London was an unmixed blessing. In spite of the unanimous approval with which this article has been received by the press, I still maintain that such writing is uncalled for, and that there is something to be said for the London of the 19th century.

WHY LONDON, WARNED, WAS UNPREPARED.

The indignation I felt in first reading the article alluded to still remains with me, and it has caused me to write these words, giving some account of what I must still regard, in spite of the sneers of the present age, as the most terrible disaster that ever overtook a portion of the human race. I shall not endeavor to place before those who read, any record of the achievements pertaining to the time in question. But I would like to say a few words about the alleged stupidity of the people of London in making no preparations for a disaster regarding which they had continual and ever-recurring warning. They have been compared with the inhabitants of Pompeii making merry at the foot of a volcano. In the first place, fogs were so common in London, especially in winter, that no particular attention was paid to them. They were merely looked upon as inconvenient annoyances, interrupting traffic and prejudicial to health, but I doubt if anyone thought it possible for a fog to become one vast smothering mattress pressed down upon a whole metropolis, extinguishing life as if the city suffered from hopeless hydrophobia. I have read that victims bitten by mad dogs were formerly put out of their sufferings in that way, although I doubt much if such things were ever actually done, notwithstanding the charges of savage barbarity now made against the people of the 19th century.

Probably, the inhabitants of Pompeii were so accustomed to the eruptions of Vesuvius that they gave no thought to the possibility of their city being destroyed by a storm of ashes and an overflow of lava. Rain frequently descended upon London, and if a rainfall continued long enough it would certainly have flooded the metropolis, but no precautions were taken against a flood from the clouds. Why, then, should the people have been expected to prepare for a catastrophe from fog, such as there had never been any experience of in the world's history? The people of London were far from being the sluggish dolts present-day writers would have us believe.

THE COINCIDENCE THAT CAME AT LAST.

As fog has now been abolished both on sea and land, and as few of the present generation have even seen one, it may not be out of place to give a few lines on the subject of fogs in general, and the London fogs in particular, which through local peculiarities differed from all others. A fog was simply watery vapor rising from the marshy surface of the land or from the sea, or condensed into a cloud from the saturated atmosphere. In my day, fogs were a great danger at sea, for people then travelled by means of steamships that sailed upon the surface of the ocean.

London at the end of the 19th century consumed vast quantities of a soft bituminous coal for the purpose of heating rooms and of preparing food. In the morning and during the day, clouds of black smoke were poured forth from thousands of chimneys. When a mass of white vapor arose in the night these clouds of smoke fell upon the fog, pressing it down, filtering slowly through it, and adding to its density. The sun would have absorbed the fog but for the layer of smoke that lay thick above the vapor and prevented the rays reaching it. Once this condition of things prevailed, nothing could clear London but a breeze of wind from any direction. London frequently had a seven days' fog, and sometimes a seven days' calm, but these two conditions never coincided until the last year of the last century. The coincidence, as everyone knows, meant death—death so wholesale that no war the earth has ever seen left such slaughter behind it. To understand the situation, one has only to imagine the fog as taking the place of the ashes at Pompeii, and the coal-smoke as being the lava that covered it. The result to the inhabitants in both cases was exactly the same.

THE AMERICAN WHO WANTED TO SELL.

I was at the time confidential clerk to the house of Fulton, Brixton & Co., a firm in Cannon Street, dealing largely in chemicals and chemical apparatus. Fulton I never knew; he died long before my time. Sir John Brixton was my chief, knighted, I believe, for services to his party, or because he was an official in the City during some royal progress through it; I have forgotten which. My small room was next to his large one, and my chief duty was to see that no one had an interview with Sir John unless he was an important man or had important business. Sir John was a difficult man to see, and a difficult man to deal with when he was seen. He had little respect for most men's feelings, and none at all for mine. If I allowed a man to enter his room who should have been dealt with by one of the minor members of the company, Sir John made no effort to conceal his opinion of me. One day, in the autumn of the last year of the century, an American was shown into my room. Nothing would do but he must have an interview with Sir John Brixton. I told him that it was impossible, as Sir John was extremely busy, but that if he explained his business to me I would lay it before Sir John at the first favorable opportunity. The American demurred at this, but finally accepted the inevitable. He was the inventor, he said, of a machine that would revolutionize life in London, and he wanted Fulton, Brixton & Co. to become agents for it. The machine, which he had in a small handbag with him, was of white metal, and it was so constructed that by turning an index it gave out greater or less volumes of oxygen gas. The gas, I understood, was stored in the interior in liquid form under great pressure, and would last, if I remember rightly, for six months without recharging. There was also a rubber tube with a mouthpiece attached to it, and the American said that if a man took a few whiffs a day, he would experience beneficial results. Now, I knew there was not the slightest use in showing the machine to Sir John, because we dealt in old-established British apparatus, and never in any of the new- fangled Yankee contraptions. Besides, Sir John had a prejudice against Americans, and I felt sure this man would exasperate him, as he was a most cadaverous specimen of the race, with high nasal tones, and a most deplorable pronunciation, much given to phrases savoring of slang; and he exhibited also a certain nervous familiarity of demeanor towards people to whom he was all but a complete stranger. It was impossible for me to allow such a man to enter the presence of Sir John Brixton, and when he returned some days later I explained to him, I hope with courtesy, that the head of the house regretted very much his inability to consider his proposal regarding the machine. The ardor of the American seemed in no way dampened by this rebuff. He said I could not have explained the possibilities of the apparatus properly to Sir John; he characterized it as a great invention, and said it meant a fortune to whoever obtained the agency for it. He hinted that other noted London houses were anxious to secure it, but for some reason not stated he preferred to deal with us. He left some printed pamphlets referring to the invention, and said he would call again.

THE AMERICAN SEES SIR JOHN.

Many a time I have since thought of that persistent American, and wondered whether he left London before the disaster, or was one of the unidentified thousands who were buried in unmarked graves. Little did Sir John think when he expelled him with some asperity from his presence, that he was turning away an offer of life, and that the heated words he used were, in reality, a sentence of death upon himself. For my own part, I regret that I lost my temper, and told the American his business methods did not commend themselves to me. Perhaps he did not feel the sting of this; indeed, I feel certain he did not, for, unknowingly, he saved my life. Be that as it may, he showed no resentment, but immediately asked me out to drink with him, an offer I was compelled to refuse. But I am getting ahead of my story. Indeed, being unaccustomed to writing, it is difficult for me to set down events in their proper sequence. The American called upon me several times after I told him our house could not deal with him. He got into the habit of dropping in upon me unannounced, which I did not at all like, but I gave no instructions regarding his intrusions, because I had no idea of the extremes to which he was evidently prepared to go. One day, as he sat near my desk reading a paper, I was temporarily called from the room. When I returned I thought he had gone, taking his machine with him, but a moment later I was shocked to hear his high nasal tones in Sir John's room alternating with the deep notes of my chief's voice, which apparently exercised no such dread upon the American as upon those who were more accustomed to them. I at once entered the room, and was about to explain to Sir John that the American was there through no connivance of mine, when my chief asked me to be silent, and, turning to his visitor, gruffly requested him to proceed with his interesting narration. The inventor needed no second invitation, but went on with his glib talk, while Sir John's frown grew deeper, and his face became redder under his fringe of white hair. When the American had finished, Sir John roughly bade him begone, and take his accursed machine with him. He said it was an insult for a person with one foot in the grave to bring a so-called health invention to a robust man who never had a day's illness, I do not know why he listened so long to the American, when he had made up his mind from the first not to deal with him, unless it was to punish me for inadvertently allowing the stranger to enter. The interview distressed me exceedingly, as I stood there helpless, knowing Sir John was becoming more and more angry with every word the foreigner uttered, but, at last, I succeeded in drawing the inventor and his work into my own room and closing the door. I sincerely hoped I would never see the American again, and my wish was gratified. He insisted on setting his machine going, and placing it on a shelf in my room. He asked me to slip it into Sir John's room some foggy day and note the effect. The man said he would call again, but he never did.

HOW THE SMOKE HELD DOWN THE FOG.

It was on a Friday that the fog came down upon us. The weather was very fine up to the middle of November that autumn. The fog did not seem to have anything unusual about it. I have seen many worse fogs than that appeared to be. As day followed day, however, the atmosphere became denser and darker, caused, I suppose, by the increasing volume of coal- smoke poured out upon it. The peculiarity about those seven days was the intense stillness of the air. We were, although we did not know it, under an air-proof canopy, and were slowly but surely exhausting the life-giving oxygen around us, and replacing it by poisonous carbonic acid gas. Scientific men have since showed that a simple mathematical calculation might have told us exactly when the last atom of oxygen would have been consumed; but it is easy to be wise after the event. The body of the greatest mathematician in England was found in the Strand. He came that morning from Cambridge. During the fog there was always a marked increase in the death rate, and on this occasion the increase was no greater than usual until the sixth day. The newspapers on the morning of the seventh were full of startling statistics, but at the time of going to press the full significance of the alarming figures was not realized. The editorials of the morning papers on the seventh day contained no warning of the calamity that was so speedily to follow their appearance. I lived then at Ealing, a Western suburb of London, and came every morning to Cannon Street by a certain train. I had up to the sixth day experienced no inconvenience from the fog, and this was largely due, I am convinced, to the unnoticed operations of the American machine.

On the fifth and sixth days Sir John did not come to the City, but he was in his office on the seventh. The door between his room and mine was closed. Shortly after ten o'clock I heard a cry in his room, followed by a heavy fall. I opened the door, and saw Sir John lying face downwards on the floor. Hastening towards him, I felt for the first time the deadly effect of the deoxygenized atmosphere, and before I reached him I fell first on one knee and then headlong. I realized that my senses were leaving me, and instinctively crawled back to my own room, where the oppression was at once lifted, and I stood again upon my feet, gasping. I closed the door of Sir John's room, thinking it filled with poisonous fumes, as, indeed, it was. I called loudly for help, but there was no answer. On opening the door to the main office I met again what I thought was the noxious vapor. Speedily as I closed the door, I was impressed by the intense silence of the usually busy office, and saw that some of the clerks were motionless on the floor, and others sat with their heads on their desks as if asleep. Even at this awful moment I did not realize that what I saw was common to all London, and not, as I imagined, a local disaster, caused by the breaking of some carboys in our cellar. (It was filled with chemicals of every kind, of whose properties I was ignorant, dealing as I did with the accountant, and not the scientific side of our business.) I opened the only window in my room, and again shouted for help. The street was silent and dark in the ominously still fog, and what now froze me with horror was meeting the same deadly, stifling atmosphere that was in the rooms. In falling I brought down the window, and shut out the poisonous air. Again I revived, and slowly the true state of things began to dawn upon me.

I was in an oasis of oxygen. I at once surmised that the machine on my shelf was responsible for the existence of this oasis in a vast desert of deadly gas. I took down the American's machine, fearful in moving it that I might stop its working. Taking the mouthpiece between my lips I again entered Sir John's room, this time without feeling any ill effects. My poor master was long beyond human help. There was evidently no one alive in the building except myself. Out in the street all was silent and dark. The gas was extinguished, but here and there in shops the incandescent lights were still weirdly burning, depending, as they did, on accumulators, and not on direct engine power. I turned automatically towards Cannon Street Station, knowing my way to it even if blindfolded, stumbling over bodies prone on the pavement, and in crossing the street I ran against a motionless 'bus, spectral in the fog, with dead horses lying in front, and their reins dangling from the nerveless hand of a dead driver. The ghostlike passengers, equally silent, sat bolt upright, or hung over the edge boards in attitudes horribly grotesque.

THE TRAIN WITH ITS TRAIL OF THE DEAD.

If a man's reasoning faculties were alert at such a time (I confess mine were dormant), he would have known there could be no trains at Cannon Street Station, for if there was not enough oxygen in the air to keep a man alive, or a gas-jet alight, there would certainly not be enough to enable an engine fire to burn, even if the engineer retained sufficient energy to attend to his task. At times instinct is better than reason, and it proved so in this case. The railway from Ealing in those days came under the City in a deep tunnel. It would appear that in this underground passage the carbonic acid gas would first find a resting-place on account of its weight; but such was not the fact. I imagine that a current through the tunnel brought from the outlying districts a supply of comparatively pure air that, for some minutes after the general disaster, maintained human life. Be this as it may, the long platforms of Cannon Street Underground Station presented a fearful spectacle. A train stood at the down platform. The electric lights burned fitfully. This platform was crowded with men, who fought each other like demons, apparently for no reason, because the train was already packed as full as it could hold. Hundreds were dead under foot, and every now and then a blast of foul air came along the tunnel, whereupon hundreds more would relax their grips, and succumb. Over their bodies the survivors fought, with continually thinning ranks. It seemed to me that most of those in the standing train were dead. Sometimes a desperate body of fighters climbed over those lying in heaps and, throwing open a carriage door, hauled out passengers already in, and took their places, gasping. Those in the train offered no resistance, and lay motionless where they were flung, or rolled helplessly under the wheels of the train. I made my way along the wall as well as I could to the engine, wondering why the train did not go. The engineer lay on the floor of his cab, and the fires were out.

Custom is a curious thing. The struggling mob, fighting wildly for places in the carriages, were so accustomed to trains arriving and departing that it apparently occurred to none of them that the engineer was human and subject to the same atmospheric conditions as themselves. I placed the mouthpiece between his purple lips, and, holding my own breath like a submerged man, succeeded in reviving him. He said that if I gave him the machine he would take out the train as far as the steam already in the boiler would carry it. I refused to do this, but stepped on the engine with him, saying it would keep life in both of us until we got out into better air. In a surly manner he agreed to this and started the train, but he did not play fair. Each time he refused to give up the machine until I was in a fainting condition with holding in my breath, and, finally, he felled me to the floor of the cab. I imagine that the machine rolled off the train as I fell and that he jumped after it. The remarkable thing is that neither of us needed the machine, for I remember that just after we started I noticed through the open iron door that the engine fire suddenly became aglow again, although at the time I was in too great a state of bewilderment and horror to understand what it meant. A western gale had sprung up—an hour too late. Even before we left Cannon Street those who still survived were comparatively safe, for one hundred and sixty-seven persons were rescued from that fearful heap of dead on the platforms, although many died within a day or two after, and others never recovered their reason. When I regained my senses after the blow dealt by the engineer, I found myself alone, and the train speeding across the Thames near Kew. I tried to stop the engine, but did not succeed. However, in experimenting, I managed to turn on the air brake, which in some degree checked the train, and lessened the impact when the crash came at Richmond terminus. I sprang off on the platform before the engine reached the terminal buffers, and saw passing me like a nightmare the ghastly trainload of the dead. Most of the doors were swinging open, and every compartment was jammed full, although, as I afterwards learned, at each curve of the permanent way, or extra lurch of the train, bodies had fallen out all along the line. The smash at Richmond made no difference to the passengers. Besides myself, only two persons were taken alive from the train, and one of these, his clothes torn from his back in the struggle was sent to an asylum, where he was never able to tell who he was; neither, as far as I know, did anyone ever claim him.

THE PREDICAMENT OF DE PLONVILLE.

This story differs from others in having an assortment of morals. Most stories have one moral; here are several. The moral usually appears at the end—in this case a few are mentioned at the beginning, so that they may be looked out for as the reading progresses. First: it is well for a man—especially a young man—to attend to his own business. Second: in planning a person's life for some little distance ahead, it will be a mistake if an allowance of ten per cent. at least, is not made for that unknown quantity—woman. Third: it is beneficial to remember that one man rarely knows everything. Other morals will doubtless present themselves, and at the end the cynically-inclined person may reflect upon the adage about the frying-pan and the fire.

Young M. de Plonville of Paris enjoyed a most enviable position. He had all the money he needed, which is quite a different thing from saying he had all the money he wanted. He was well educated, and spoke three languages, that is, he spoke his own well and the other two badly, but as a man always prides himself on what he is least able to do, De Plonville fancied himself a linguist. His courage in speaking English to Englishmen and German to Germans showed that he was, at least, a brave man. There was a great deal of good and even of talent in De Plonville. This statement is made at the beginning, because everyone who knows De Plonville will at once unhesitatingly contradict it. His acquaintances thought him one of the most objectionable young men in Paris, and naval officers, when his name was mentioned, usually gave themselves over to strong and unjustifiable language. This was all on account of De Plonville's position, which, although enviable had its drawbacks.

His rank in the navy was such that it entitled him to no consideration whatever, but, unfortunately for his own popularity, De Plonville had a method of giving force to his suggestions. His father was a very big man in the French Government. He was so big a man that he could send a censure to the commander of a squadron in the navy, and the commander dare not talk back. It takes a very big man indeed to do this, and that was the elder De Plonville's size. But then it was well known that the elder De Plonville was an easy-going man who loved comfort, and did not care to trouble himself too much about the navy in his charge, and so when there was trouble, young De Plonville got the credit of it; consequently, the love of the officers did not flow out to him.

Often young De Plonville's idiotic impetuosity gave color to these suspicions. For instance, there is the well-known Toulon incident. In a heated controversy young De Plonville had claimed that the firing of the French ironclads was something execrable, and that the whole fleet could not hold their own at the cannon with any ten of the British navy. Some time after, the naval officers learned that the Government at Paris was very much displeased with the inaccurate gun practice of the fleet, and the hope was expressed that the commander would see his way to improving it. Of course, the officers could do nothing but gnash their teeth, try to shoot better, and hope for a time to come when the Government then in power would be out, and they could find some tangible pretence for hanging young De Plonville from the yard-arm.

All this has only a remote bearing upon this story, but we now come to a matter on which the story sinks or swims. De Plonville had a secret— not such a secret as is common in Parisian life, but one entirely creditable to him. It related to an invention intended to increase the efficiency of the French army. The army being a branch of the defences of his country with which De Plonville had nothing whatever to do, his attention naturally turned towards it. He spoke of this invention, once, to a friend, a lieutenant in the army. He expected to get some practical suggestions. He never mentioned it again to anyone.

"It is based on the principle of the umbrella," he said to his friend; "in fact, it was the umbrella that suggested it to me. If it could be made very light so as not to add seriously to the impedimenta at present carried by the soldier, it seems to me it would be exceedingly useful. Instead of being circular as an umbrella is, it must be oblong with sharp ends. It would have to be arranged so as to be opened and closed quickly, with the cloth thin, but impervious to water. When the army reached a river each soldier could open this, place it in the water, enter it with some care, and then paddle himself across with the butt-end of his gun, or even with a light paddle, if the carrying of it added but little to the weight, thus saving the building of temporary bridges. It seems to me such an invention ought to be of vast use in a forced march. Then at night it might be used as a sort of tent, or in a heavy rain it would form a temporary shelter. What do you think of the idea?" His friend had listened with half-closed eyes. He blew a whiff of cigarette smoke from his nostrils and answered:

"It is wonderful, De Plonville," he said drawlingly. "Its possibilities are vast—more so than even you appear to think. It would be very useful in our Alpine corps as well."

"I am glad you think so. But why there?"

"Well, you see, if the army reached a high peak looking into a deep valley, only to be reached over an inaccessible precipice, all the army would have to do would be to spread out your superb invention and use it as a parachute. The sight of the army of France gradually floating down into the valley would be so terrifying to the nations of Europe, that I imagine no enemy would wait for a gun to be fired. De Plonville, your invention will immortalize you, and immortalize the French army."

Young De Plonville waited to hear no more, but turned on his heel and strode away.

This conversation caused young De Plonville to make two resolutions; first, to mention his scheme to no one; second, to persevere and perfect his invention, thus causing confusion to the scoffer. There were several sub-resolutions dependent on these two. He would not enter a club, he would abjure society, he would not speak to a woman—he would, in short, be a hermit until his invention stood revealed before an astonished world.

All of which goes to show that young De Plonville was not the conceited, meddlesome fop his acquaintances thought him. But in the large and small resolutions he did not deduct the ten per cent. for the unknown quantity.

Where? That was the question. De Plonville walked up and down his room, and thought it out. A large map of France was spread on the table. Paris and the environs thereof were manifestly impossible. He needed a place of seclusion. He needed a stretch of water. Where then should be the spot to which coming generations would point and say, "Here, at this place, was perfected De Plonville's celebrated parachute-tent- bateau invention."

No, not parachute. Hang the parachute! That was the scoffing lieutenant's word. De Plonville paused for a moment to revile his folly in making a confidant of any army man.

There was a sufficiency of water around the French coast, but it was too cold at that season of the year to experiment in the north and east. There was left the Mediterranean. He thought rapidly of the different delightful spots along the Riviera—Cannes, St. Raphael, Nice, Monte Carlo,—but all of these were too public and too much thronged with visitors. The name of the place came to him suddenly, and, as he stopped his march to and fro, De Plonville wondered why it had not suggested itself to him at the very first. Hyères! It seemed to have been planned in the Middle Ages for the perfecting of just such an invention. It was situated two or three miles back from the sea, the climate was perfect, there was no marine parade, the sea coast was lonely, and the bay sheltered by the islands. It was an ideal spot.

De Plonville easily secured leave of absence. Sons of fathers high up in the service of a grateful country seldom have any difficulty about a little thing like that. He purchased a ticket for that leisurely train which the French with their delicious sense of humor call the "Rapide," and in due time found himself with his various belongings standing on the station platform at Hyères.

Few of us are as brave as we think ourselves. De Plonville flinched when the supreme moment came, and perhaps that is why the Gods punished him. He had resolved to go to one of the country inns at Carqueyranne on the coast, but this was in a heroic mood when the lieutenant had laughed at his project. Now in a cooler moment he thought of the cuisine of Carqueyranne and shuddered. There are sacrifices which no man should be called upon to endure, so the naval officer hesitated, and at last directed the porter to put his luggage on the top of the Costebelle Hotel "bus." There would be society at the hotel it is true, but he could avoid it, while if he went to the rural tavern he could not avoid the cooking. Thus he smothered his conscience. Lunch at Costebelle seemed to justify his choice of an abiding-place. The surroundings of the hotel were dangerously charming to a man whose natural inclination was towards indolent enjoyment. It was a place to "Loaf and invite your soul," as Walt Whitman phrases it. Plonville, who was there incognito, for he had temporarily dropped the "De," strolled towards the sea in the afternoon, with the air of one who has nothing on his mind. No one to see him would have suspected he was the future Edison of France. When he reached the coast at the ruins of the ancient Roman naval station called Pomponiana, he smote his thigh with joy. He had forgotten that at this spot there had been erected a number of little wooden houses, each larger than a bathing-machine and smaller than a cottage, which were used in summer by the good people of Hyères, and in winter were silently vacant. The largest of these would be exactly the place for him, and he knew he would have no difficulty in renting it for a month or two. Here, he could bring down his half- finished invention; here, work at it all day unmolested; and here test its sailing qualities with no onlookers.

He walked up the road, and hailed the ancient bus which jogs along between Toulon and Hyères by way of the coast; mounted beside the driver, and speedily got information about the owner of the cottages at Pomponiana.

As he expected, he had no difficulty in arranging with the proprietor for the largest of the little cottages, but he thought he detected a slight depression on the right eyelid as that person handed him the key. Had the owner suspected his purpose? he asked himself anxiously, as he drove back from the town to Costebelle. Impossible. He felt, however, that he could not be too secret about his intentions. He had heard of inventors being forestalled just at the very moment of success.

He bade the driver wait, and placed that part of his luggage in the cab which consisted of his half-finished invention and the materials for completing it. Then he drove to the coast, and after placing the packages on the ground, paid and dismissed the man. When the cab was out of sight, he carried the things to the cottage and locked them in. His walk up the hill to the hotel rendered the excellent dinner provided doubly attractive.

Next morning he was early at work, and speedily began to realize how many necessary articles he had forgotten at Paris. He hoped he would be able to get them at Hyères, but his remembrance of the limited resources of the town made him somewhat doubtful. The small windows on each side gave him scarcely enough light, but he did not open the door, fearing the curiosity of a chance passer-by. One cannot be too careful in maturing a great invention.

Plonville had been at work for possibly an hour and a half, when he heard someone singing, and that very sweetly. She sang with the joyous freedom of one who suspected no listener. The song came nearer and nearer. Plonville standing amazed, dropped his implements, and stole to the somewhat obscure little window. He saw a vision of fresh loveliness dressed in a costume he never before beheld on a vision. She came down the bank with a light, springy step to the next cottage, took a key that hung at her belt, and threw open the door. The song was hushed, but not silenced, for a moment, and then there came from out the cottage door the half of a boat that made Plonville gasp. Like the costume, he had never before seen such a boat. It was exactly the shape in which he had designed his invention, and was of some extra light material, for the sylph-like girl in the extraordinary dress pushed it forth without even ceasing her song. Next moment, she came out herself and stood there while she adjusted her red head-gear. She drew the boat down to the water, picked out of it a light, silver-mounted paddle, stepped deftly aboard, and settled down to her place with the airy grace of a thistle-down. There was no seat in the boat, Plonville noted with astonishment. The sea was very smooth, and a few strokes of the paddle sent girl and craft out of sight along the coast. Plonville drew a deep breath of bewilderment. It was his first sight of a Thames boating costume and a canoe.

This, then, was why the man winked when he gave him the key. Plonville was in a quandary. Should he reveal himself when she returned? It did not seem to be quite the thing to allow the girl to believe she had the coast to herself when in fact she hadn't. But then there was his invention to think of. He had sworn allegiance to that. He sat down and pondered. English, evidently. He had no idea English girls were so pretty, and then that costume! It was very taking. The rich, creamy folds of the white flannel, so simple, yet so complete, lingered in his memory. Still, what was he there for? His invention certainly. The sneer of the lieutenant stung his memory. That Miss Whatever-her- name-might-be had rented the next box was nothing to him; of course not. He waved her aside and turned to his work. He had lost enough of time as it was; he would lose no more.

Although armed with this heroic resolution, his task somehow did not seem so interesting as before, and he found himself listening now and then for the siren's song. He dramatized imaginary situations, which is always bad for practical work. He saw the frail craft shattered or overturned, and beheld himself bravely buffeting the waves rescuing the fair girl in white. Then he remembered with a sigh that he was not a good swimmer. Possibly she was more at home in the waves than he was. Those English seemed on such terms of comradeship with the sea.

At last, intuition rather than hearing told him she had returned. He walked on tip-toe to the dingy window. She was pulling the light canoe up from the water. He checked his impulse to offer assistance. When the girl sprang lightly up the bank, Plonville sighed and concluded he had done enough work for the day. As he reached the road, he noticed that the white figure in the distance did not take the way to the hotel, but towards one of the neighboring Chateaux.

In the afternoon, Plonville worked long at his invention, and made progress. He walked back to his hotel with the feeling of self- satisfaction which indolent men have on those rare occasions when they are industrious. He had been uninterrupted, and his resolutions were again heroic. What had been done one afternoon might be done all afternoons. He would think no more of the vision he had seen and he would work only after lunch, thus avoiding the necessity of revealing himself, or of being a concealed watcher of her actions. Of course she came always in the morning, for the English are a methodical people, and Plonville was so learned in their ways that he knew what they did one day they were sure to do the next. An extraordinary nation, Plonville said to himself with a shrug of his shoulders, but then of course, we cannot all be French.

It is rather a pity that temptation should step in just when a man has made up his mind not to deviate from a certain straight line of conduct. There was to be a ball that night at the big hotel. Plonville had refused to have anything to do with it. He had renounced the frivolities of life. He was there for rest, quiet, and study. He was adamant. That evening the invitation was again extended to him, the truth being that there was a scarcity of young men, as is usually the case at such functions. Plonville was about to re-state his objections to frivolity when through the open door he caught a glimpse of two of the arriving guests ascending the stair. The girl had on a long opera cloak with some fluffy white material round the neck and down the front. A filmy lace arrangement rested lightly on her fair hair. It was the lady of the canoe—glorified. Plonville wavered and was lost. He rushed to his room and donned his war paint. Say what you like, evening dress improves the appearance of a man. Besides this, he had resumed the De once more, and his back was naturally straighter. De Plonville looked well.

They were speedily introduced, of course. De Plonville took care of that, and the manager of the ball was very grateful to him for coming, and for looking so nice. There was actually an air of distinction about De Plonville. She was the Hon. Margaret Stansby, he learned. Besides being unfair, it would be impossible to give their conversation. It would read like a section from Ollendorf's French-English exercises. De Plonville, as has been said, was very proud of his English, and, unfortunately, the Hon. Margaret had a sense of humor. He complimented her by saying that she talked French even better than he talked English, which, while doubtless true, was not the most tactful thing De Plonville might have said. It was difficult to listen to such a statement given in his English, and refrain from laughing. Margaret, however, scored a great victory and did not laugh. The evening passed pleasantly, she thought; delightfully, De Plonville thought.

It was hard after this to come down to the prosaic work of completing a cloth canoe-tent, but, to De Plonville's credit, he persevered. He met the young lady on several occasions, but never by the coast. The better they became acquainted the more he wished to have the privilege of rescuing her from some deadly danger; but the opportunity did not come. It seldom does, except in books, as he bitterly remarked to himself. The sea was exasperatingly calm, and Miss Margaret was mistress of her craft, as so many charming women are. He thought of buying a telescope and watching her, for she had told him that one of her own delights was looking at the evolutions of the ironclads through a telescope on the terrace in front of the Chateau.

At last, in spite of his distractions, De Plonville added the finishing touches to his notable invention, and all that remained was to put it to a practical test. He chose a day when that portion of the French navy which frequents the Rade d'Hyères was not in sight, for he did not wish to come within the field of the telescope at the Chateau terrace. He felt that he would not look his best as he paddled his new-fangled boat. Besides, it might sink with him.

There was not a sail in sight as he put forth. Even the fishing boats of Carqueyranne were in shelter. The sea was very calm, and the sun shone brightly. He had some little difficulty in getting seated, but he was elated to find that his invention answered all expectations. As he went further out he noticed a great buoy floating a long distance away. His evil genius suggested that it would be a good thing to paddle out to the buoy and back. Many men can drink champagne and show no sign, but few can drink success and remain sober. The eccentric airs assumed by noted authors prove the truth of this. De Plonville was drunk, and never suspected it. The tide, what little there is of it in the Mediterranean, helped him, and even the gentle breeze blew from the shore. He had some doubts as to the wisdom of his course before he reached the gigantic red buoy, but when he turned around and saw the appalling distance to the coast, he shuddered.

The great buoy was of iron, apparently boiler plate, and there were rings fastened to its side. It was pear-shaped with the point in the water, fastened to a chain that evidently led to an anchor. He wondered what it was for. As he looked up it was moved by some unseen current, and rolled over as if bent on the destruction of his craft. Forgetting himself, he sprang up to ward it off, and instantly one foot went through the thin waterproof that formed the bottom and sides of his boat. He found himself struggling in the water almost before he realized what had happened. Kicking his foot free from the entanglement that threatened to drag him under, he saw his invention slowly settle down through the clear, green water. He grasped one of the rings of the buoy, and hung there for a moment to catch his breath and consider his position. He rapidly came to the conclusion that it was not a pleasant one, but further than that he found it difficult to go. Attempting to swim ashore would be simply one form of suicide. The thing to do was evidently to get on top of the buoy, but he realized that if he tried to pull himself up by the rings it would simply roll him under. He was surprised to find, however, that such was not the case. He had under- estimated both its size and its weight.

He sat down on top of it and breathed heavily after his exertions, gazing for a few moments at the vast expanse of shimmering blue water. It was pretty, but discouraging. Not even a fishing-boat was in sight, and he was in a position where every prospect pleases, and only man is in a vile situation. The big iron island had an uncomfortable habit every now and then of lounging partly over to one side or the other, so that De Plonville had to scramble this way or that to keep from falling off. He vaguely surmised that his motions on these occasions lacked dignity. The hot sun began to dry the clothes on his back, and he felt his hair become crisp with salt. He recollected that swimming should be easy here, for he was on the saltest portion of the saltest open sea in the world. Then his gaze wandered over the flat lands about Les Salins where acres of ground were covered artificially with Mediterranean water so that the sun may evaporate it, and leave the coarse salt used by the fishermen of the coast. He did not yet feel hungry, but he thought with regret of the good dinner which would be spread at the hotel that evening, when, perhaps, he would not be there.

He turned himself around and scanned the distant Islands of Gold, but there was as little prospect of help from that quarter as from the mainland. Becoming more accustomed to the swayings of the big globe, he stood up. What a fool he had been to come so far, and he used French words between his teeth that sounded terse and emphatic. Still there was little use thinking of that. Here he was, and here he would stay, as a President of his country had once remarked. The irksomeness and restraint of his position began to wear on his nerves, and he cried aloud for something—anything—to happen rather than what he was enduring.

Something happened.

From between the Islands, there slowly appeared a great modern French ship of war, small in the distance. Hope lighted up the face of De Plonville. She must pass near enough to enable his signalling to be seen by the lookout. Heavens! how leisurely she moved! Then a second war vessel followed the first into view, and finally a third. The three came slowly along in stately procession. De Plonville removed his coat and waved it up and down to attract attention. So intent was he upon this that he nearly lost his footing, and, realizing that the men-of- war were still too far away, he desisted. He sat down as his excitement abated, and watched their quiet approach. Once it seemed to him they had stopped, and he leaned forward, shading his eyes with his hand, and watched them eagerly. They were just moving—that was all.

Suddenly, from the black side of the foremost battle-ship, there rolled upward a cloud of white smoke, obscuring the funnels and the rigging, thinning out into the blue sky over the top-masts. After what seemed a long interval the low, dull roar of a cannon reached him, followed by the echo from the high hills of the island, and later by the fainter re-echo from the mountains on the mainland. This depressed De Plonville, for, if the ships were out for practice, the obscuring smoke around them would make the seeing of his signalling very improbable; and then that portion of the fleet might return the way it came, leaving him in his predicament. From the second ironclad arose a similar cloud, and this time far to his left there spurted up from the sea a jet of water, waving in the air like a plume for a moment, then dropping back in a shower on the ruffled surface.

The buoy was a target!

As De Plonville realized its use, he felt that uncomfortable creeping of the scalp which we call, the hair standing on end. The third cannon sent up its cloud, and De Plonville's eyes extended at what they saw. Coming directly towards him was a cannon ball, skipping over the water like a thrown pebble. His experience in the navy—at Paris—had never taught him that such a thing was possible. He slid down flat on the buoy, till his chin rested on the iron, and awaited the shock. A hundred yards from him the ball dipped into the water and disappeared. He found that he had ineffectually tried to drive his nails into the boiler plate, until his fingers' ends were sore. He stood up and waved his arms, but the first vessel fired again, and the ball came shrieking over him so low that he intuitively ducked his head. Like a pang of physical pain, the thought darted through his brain that he had instigated a censure on the bad firing of these very boats. Doubtless they saw a man on the buoy, but as no man had any business there, the knocking of him off by a cannon ball would be good proof of accuracy of aim. The investigation which followed would be a feather in the cap of the officer in charge, whatever the verdict. De Plonville, with something like a sigh, more than suspected that his untimely death would not cast irretrievable gloom over the fleet.

Well, a man has to die but once, and there is little use in making a fuss over the inevitable. He would meet his fate calmly and as a Frenchman should, with his face to the guns. There was a tinge of regret that there would be no one to witness his heroism. It is always pleasant on such occasions to have a war correspondent, or at least a reporter, present. It is best to be as comfortable as possible under any circumstances, so De Plonville sat down on the spheroid and let his feet dangle toward the water. The great buoy for some reason floated around until it presented its side to the ships. None of the balls came so near as those first fired—perhaps because of the accumulated smoke. New features of the situation continued to present themselves to De Plonville as he sat there. The firing had been going on for some time before he reflected that if a shot punctured the buoy it would fill and sink. Perhaps their orders were to fire until the buoy disappeared. There was little comfort in this suggestion.

Firing had ceased for some minutes before he noticed the fact. A bank of thinning smoke rested on the water between the buoy and the ships. He saw the ironclads move ponderously around and steam through this bank turning broadside on again in one, two, three, order. He watched the evolution with his chin resting on his hands, not realizing that the moment for signalling had come. When the idea penetrated his somewhat dazed mind, he sprang to his feet, but his opportunity had gone. The smoke of the first gun rose in the air, there was a clang of iron on iron, and De Plonville found himself whirling in space: then sinking in the sea. Coming breathless to the surface, he saw the buoy revolving slowly, and a deep dinge in its side seemed to slide over its top and disappear into the water, showing where the shot had struck. The second boat did not fire, and he knew that they were examining the buoy with their glasses. He swam around to the other side, intending to catch a ring and have it haul him up where he could be seen. Before he reached the place the buoy was at rest again, and as he laboriously climbed on top more dead than alive, the second ship opened fire. He lay down at full length exhausted, and hoped if they were going to hit they would hit quick. Life was not worth having on these conditions. He felt the hot sun on his back, and listened dreamily to the cannon. Hope was gone, and he wondered at himself for feeling a remote rather than an active interest in his fate. He thought of himself as somebody else, and felt a vague impersonal pity. He criticised the random firing, and suspected the hit was merely a fluke. When his back was dry he rolled lazily over and lay gazing up at the cloudless sky. For greater comfort he placed his hands beneath his head. The sky faded, and a moment's unconsciousness intervened.

"This won't do," he cried, shaking himself. "If I fall asleep I shall roll off."

He sat up again, his joints stiff with his immersion, and watched the distant ironclads. He saw with languid interest a ball strike the water, take a new flight, and plunge into the sea far to the right. He thought that the vagaries of cannon-balls at sea would make an interesting study.

"Are you injured?" cried a clear voice behind him.

"Mon Dieu!" shouted the young man in a genuine fright, as he sprang to his feet.

"Oh, I beg pardon," as if a rescuer need apologize, "I thought you were M. De Plonville."

"I am De Plonville."

"Your hair is grey," she said in an awed whisper; then added, "and no wonder."

"Mademoiselle," replied the stricken young man, placing his hand on his heart, "it is needless to deny—I do not deny—that I was frightened— but—I did not think—not so much as that, I regret. It is so—so— theatrical—I am deeply sorrowful."

"Please say no more, but come quickly. Can you come down? Step exactly in the middle of the canoe. Be careful—it is easily upset—and sit down at once. That was very nicely done."

"Mademoiselle, allow me at least to row the boat."

"It is paddling, and you do not understand it. I do. Please do not speak until we are out of range. I am horribly frightened."

"You are very, very brave."

"Hs—s—sh."

Miss Stansby wielded the double-bladed paddle in a way a Red Indian might have envied. Once she uttered a little feminine shriek as a cannon ball plunged into the water behind them; but as they got further away from the buoy those on the iron-clads appeared to notice that a boat was within range, and the firing ceased.

Miss Stansby looked fixedly at the solemn young man sitting before her; then placed her paddle across the canoe, bent over it, and laughed. De Plonville saw the reaction had come. He said sympathetically:—

"Ah, Mademoiselle, do not, I beg. All danger is over, I think."

"I am not frightened, don't think it," she cried, flashing a look of defiance at him, and forgetting her admission of fear a moment before. "My father was an Admiral. I am laughing at my mistake. It is salt."

"What is?" asked her astonished passenger.

"In your hair."

He ran his fingers through his hair, and the salt rattled down to the bottom of the canoe. There was something of relief in his laugh.

De Plonville always believes the officers on board the gunboats recognized him. When it was known in Paris that he was to be married to the daughter of an English Admiral, whom rumor said he had bravely saved from imminent peril, the army lieutenant remarked that she could never have heard him speak her language—which, as we know, is not true.

A NEW EXPLOSIVE.

The French Minister of War sat in his very comfortable chair in his own private yet official room, and pondered over a letter he had received. Being Minister of War, he was naturally the most mild, the most humane, and least quarrelsome man in the Cabinet. A Minister of War receives many letters that, as a matter of course, he throws into his waste basket, but this particular communication had somehow managed to rivet his attention. When a man becomes Minister of War he learns for the first time that apparently the great majority of mankind are engaged in the manufacture or invention of rifles, gunpowders, and devices of all kinds for the destruction of the rest of the world.

That morning, the Minister of War had received a letter which announced to him that the writer of it had invented an explosive so terrible that all known destructive agencies paled before it. As a Frenchman, he made the first offer of his discovery to the French Government. It would cost the Minister nothing, he said, to make a test which would corroborate his amazing claims for the substance, and the moment that test was made, any intelligent man would recognize the fact that the country which possessed the secret of this destructive compound would at once occupy an unassailable position in a contentious world.

The writer offered personally to convince the Minister of the truth of his assertions, provided they could go to some remote spot where the results of the explosion would do no damage, and where they would be safe from espionage. The writer went on very frankly to say that if the Minister consulted with the agents of the police, they would at once see in this invitation a trap for the probable assassination of the Minister. But the inventor claimed that the Minister's own good sense should show him that his death was desired by none. He was but newly appointed, and had not yet had time to make enemies. France was at peace with all the world, and this happened before the time of the Anarchist demonstrations in Paris. It was but right, the letter went on, that the Minister should have some guarantee as to the bona fides of the inventor. He therefore gave his name and address, and said if the Minister made inquiries from the police, he would find nothing stood in their books against him. He was a student, whose attention, for years, had been given to the subject of explosives. To further show that he was entirely unselfish in this matter, he added that he had no desire to enrich himself by his discovery. He had a private income quite sufficient for his needs, and he intended to give, and not to sell, his secret to France. The only proviso he made was that his name should be linked with this terrible compound, which he maintained would secure universal peace to the world, for, after its qualities were known, no nation would dare to fight with another. The sole ambition of the inventor, said the letter in conclusion, was to place his name high in the list of celebrated French scientists. If, however, the Minister refused to treat with him he would go to other Governments until his invention was taken up, but the Government which secured it would at once occupy the leading position among nations. He entreated the Minister, therefore, for the sake of his country, to make at least one test of the compound.

It was, as I have said, before the time of the Paris explosions, and ministers were not so suspicious then as they are now. The Minister made inquiries regarding the scientist, who lived in a little suburb of Paris, and found that there was nothing against him on the books of the police. Inquiry showed that all he had said about his own private fortune was true. The Minister therefore wrote to the inventor, and named an hour at which he would receive him in his private office.

The hour and the man arrived together. The Minister had had some slight doubts regarding his sanity, but the letter had been so straightforwardly written, and the appearance of the man himself was so kindly and benevolent and intelligent that the doubts of the official vanished.

"I beg you to be seated," said the Minister. "We are entirely alone, and nothing you say will be heard by any one but myself."

"I thank you, Monsieur le Ministre," replied the inventor, "for this mark of confidence; for I am afraid the claims I made in the letter were so extraordinary that you might well have hesitated about granting me an interview."

The Minister smiled. "I understand," he said, "the enthusiasm of an inventor for his latest triumph, and I was enabled thus to take, as it were, some discount from your statements, although I doubt not that you have discovered something that may be of benefit to the War Department."

The inventor hesitated, looking seriously at the great official before him.

"From what you say," he began at last, "I am rather afraid that my letter misled you, for, fearing it would not be credited I was obliged to make my claims so mild that I erred in under-estimating rather than in over-stating them. I have the explosive here in my pocket."

"Ah!" cried the Minister, a shade of pallor coming over his countenance, as he pushed back his chair. "I thought I stated in my note that you were not to bring it."

"Forgive me for not obeying. It is perfectly harmless while in this state. This is one of the peculiarities—a beneficent peculiarity if I may so term it—of this terrible agent. It may be handled with perfect safety, and yet its effects are as inevitable as death," saying which, he took out of his pocket and held up to the light a bottle filled with a clear colorless liquid like water.

"You could pour that on the fire," he said, "with no other effect than to put out the blaze. You might place it under a steam hammer and crush the bottle to powder, yet no explosion would follow. It is as harmless as water in its present condition."

"How, then," said the Minister, "do you deal with it?"

Again the man hesitated.

"I am almost afraid to tell you," he said; "and if I could not demonstrate to your entire satisfaction that what I say is true, it would be folly for me to say what I am about to say. If I were to take this bottle and cut a notch in the cork, and walk with it neck downwards along the Boulevard des Italiens, allowing this fluid to fall drop by drop on the pavement, I could walk in that way in safety through every street in Paris. If it rained that day nothing would happen. If it rained the next or for a week nothing would happen, but the moment the sun came out and dried the moisture, the light step of a cat on any pavement over which I had passed would instantly shatter to ruins the whole of Paris."

"Impossible!" cried the Minister, an expression of horror coming into his face.

"I knew you would say that. Therefore I ask you to come with me to the country, where I can prove the truth of what I allege. While I carry this bottle around with me in this apparently careless fashion, it is corked, as you see with the utmost security. Not a drop of the fluid must be left on the outside of the cork or of the bottle. I have wiped the bottle and cork most thoroughly, and burned the cloth which I used in doing so. Fire will not cause this compound, even when dry, to explode, but the slightest touch will set it off. I have to be extremely careful in its manufacture, so that not a single drop is left unaccounted for in any place where it might evaporate."

The Minister, with his finger-tips together and his eyes on the ceiling, mused for a few moments on the amazing statement he had heard.

"If what you say is true," he began at last, "don't you think it would be more humane to destroy all traces of the experiments by which you discovered this substance, and to divulge the secret to no one? The devastation such a thing would cause, if it fell into unscrupulous hands, is too appalling even to contemplate."

"I have thought of that," said the inventor; "but some one else—the time may be far off or it may be near—is bound to make the discovery. My whole ambition, as I told you in my letter, is to have my name coupled with this discovery. I wish it to be known as the Lambelle Explosive. The secret would be safe with the French Government."

"I am not so sure of that," returned the Minister. "Some unscrupulous man may become Minister of War, and may use his knowledge to put himself in the position of Dictator. An unscrupulous man in the possession of such a secret would be invincible."

"What you say," replied the inventor, "is undoubtedly true; yet I am determined that the name of Lambelle shall go down in history coupled with the most destructive agent the world has ever known, or will know. If the Government of France will build for me a large stone structure as secure as a fortress, I will keep my secret, but will fill that building with bottles like this, and then——"

"I do not see," said the Minister, "that that would lessen the danger, if the unscrupulous man I speak of once became possessed of the keys; and, besides, the mere fact that such a secret existed would put other inventors upon the track, and some one else less benevolent than yourself would undoubtedly make the discovery. You admitted a moment ago that the chances were a future investigator would succeed in getting the right ingredients together, even without the knowledge that such an explosive existed. See what an incentive it would be to inventors all over the world, if it were known that France had in its possession such a fearful explosive! No Government has ever yet been successful in keeping the secret of either a gun or a gunpowder."

"There is, of course," said Lambelle, "much in what you say; but, equally of course, all that you say might have been said to the inventor of gunpowder, for gunpowder in its day was as wonderful as this is now."

Suddenly the Minister laughed aloud.

"I am talking seriously with you on this subject," he exclaimed, "as if I really believed in it. Of course, I may say I do nothing of the kind. I think you must have hypnotized me with those calm eyes of yours into crediting your statements for even a few moments."

"All that I say," said the inventor quietly, "can be corroborated to-morrow. Make an appointment with me in the country, and if it chances to be a calm and sunny day you will no longer doubt the evidence of your own eyes."

"Where do you wish the experiment to be made?" asked the Minister.

"It must be in some wild and desolate region, on a hill-top for preference.

There should be either trees or old buildings there that we can destroy, otherwise the full effects can hardly be estimated."

"I have a place in the country," said the Minister, "which is wild and desolate and unprofitable enough. There are some useless stone buildings, not on a hill-top, but by the edge of a quarry which has been unworked for many years. There is no habitation for several miles around. Would such a spot be suitable?"

"Perfectly so. When would it be convenient for you to go?"

"I will leave with you to-night," said the Minister, "and we can spend the day to-morrow experimenting."

"Very well," answered Lambelle, rising when the Minister had told him the hour and the railway station at which they should meet.

That evening, when the Minister drove to the railway station in time for his train, he found Lambelle waiting for him, holding, by a leash, two sorry-looking dogs.

"Do you travel with such animals as these?" asked the Minister.

"The poor brutes," said Lambelle, with regret in his voice, "are necessary for our experiments. They will be in atoms by this time to- morrow."

The dogs were put into the railway-van, and the inventor brought his portmanteau with him into the private carriage reserved for the use of the Minister.

The place, as the Minister of War had said, was desolate enough. The stone buildings near the edge of the deserted quarry were stout and strong, although partly in ruins.

"I have here with me in my portmanteau," said Lambelle, "some hundreds of metres of electric wire. I will attach one of the dogs by this clip, which we can release from a distance by pressing an electric button. The moment the dog escapes he will undoubtedly explode the compound."

The insulated wire was run along the ground to a distant elevation.

The dog was attached by the electric clip, and chained to a doorpost of one of the buildings. Lambelle then carefully uncorked his bottle, holding it at arm's length from his person. The Minister looked on with strange interest as Lambelle allowed the fluid to drip in a semicircular line around the chained dog. The inventor carefully re-corked the bottle, wiped it thoroughly with a cloth he had with him, and threw the cloth into one of the deserted houses.

They waited near, until the spots caused by the fluid on the stone pavement in front of the house had disappeared.

"By the time we reach the hill," said Lambelle, "it will be quite dry in this hot sun."

As they departed towards the elevation, the forlorn dog howled mournfully, as if in premonition of his fate.

"I think, to make sure," said the inventor, when they reached the electrical apparatus, "that we might wait for half an hour."

The Minister lit a cigarette, and smoked silently, a strange battle going on in his mind. He found himself believing in the extraordinary claims made by the inventor, and his thought dwelt on the awful possibilities of such an explosive.

"Will you press the electric lever?" asked Lambelle quietly. "Remember that you are inaugurating a new era."

The Minister pressed down the key, and then, putting his field-glass to his eye, he saw that the dog was released, but the animal sat there scratching its ear with its paw. Then, realizing that it was loose, it sniffed for a moment at the chain. Finally, it threw up its head and barked, although the distance was too great for them to hear any sound. The dog started in the direction the two men had gone, but, before it had taken three steps, the Minister was appalled to see the buildings suddenly crumble into dust, and a few moments later the thunder of the rocks falling into the deserted quarry came toward them. The whole ledge had been flung forwards into the chasm. There was no smoke, but a haze of dust hovered over the spot.

"My God!" cried the Minister. "That is awful!"

"Yes," said Lambelle quietly; "I put more of the substance on the flagging than I need to have done. A few drops would have answered quite as well, but I wanted to make sure. You were very sceptical, you know."

The Minister looked at him. "I beg of you, M. Lambelle, never to divulge this secret to the Government of France, or to any other power. Take the risk of it being discovered in the future. I implore you to reconsider your original intention. If you desire money, I will see that you get what you want from the secret funds."

Lambelle shrugged his shoulders.

"I have no desire for money," he said; "but what you have seen will show you that I shall be the most famous scientist of the century. The name of Lambelle will be known till the end of the world."

"But, my God, man!" said the Minister, "the end of the world is here the moment your secret is in the possession of another. With you or me it would be safe: but who can tell the minds of those who may follow us? You are putting the power of the Almighty into the hands of a man."

Lambelle flushed with pride as the pale-faced Minister said this.

"You speak the truth!" he cried, "it is the power of Omnipotence."

"Then," implored the Minister, "reconsider your decision."

"I have labored too long," said Lambelle, "to forego my triumph now. You are convinced at last, I see. Now then, tell me: will you, as Minister of France, secure for your country this greatest of all inventions?"

"Yes," answered the Minister; "no other power must be allowed to obtain the secret. Have you ever written down the names of the ingredients?"

"Never," answered Lambelle.

"Is it not possible for any one to have suspected what your experiments were? If a man got into your laboratory—a scientific man—could he not, from what he saw there, obtain the secret?"

"It would be impossible," said Lambelle. "I have been too anxious to keep the credit for myself, to leave any traces that might give a hint of what I was doing."

"You were wise in that," said the Minister, drawing a deep breath. "Now let us go and look at the ruins."

As they neared the spot the official's astonishment at the extraordinary destruction became greater and greater. The rock had been rent as if by an earthquake, to the distance of hundreds of yards.

"You say," said the Minister, "that the liquid is perfectly safe until evaporation takes place."

"Perfectly," answered Lambelle. "Of course one has to be careful, as I told you, in the use of it. You must not get a drop on your clothes, or leave it anywhere on the outside of the bottle to evaporate."

"Let me see the stuff."

Lambelle handed him the bottle.

"Have you any more of this in your laboratory?"

"Not a drop."

"If you wished to destroy this, how would you do it?"

"I should empty the bottle into the Seine. It would flow down to the sea, and no harm would be done."

"See if you can find any traces of the dog," said the Minister. "I will clamber down into the quarry, and look there."

"You will find nothing," said Lambelle confidently.

There was but one path by which the bottom of the quarry could be reached. The Minister descended by this until he was out of sight of the man above; then he quickly uncorked the bottle, and allowed the fluid to drip along the narrowest part of the path which faced the burning sun. He corked the bottle, wiped it carefully with his handkerchief, which he rolled into a ball, and threw into the quarry. Coming up to the surface again, he said to the mild and benevolent scientist: "I cannot find a trace of the dog."

"Nor can I," said Lambelle. "Of course when you can hardly find a sign of the building it is not to be expected that there should be any remnants of the dog."

"Suppose we get back to the hill now and have lunch," said the Minister.

"Do you wish to try another experiment?"

"I would like to try one more after we have had something to eat. What would be the effect if you poured the whole bottleful into the quarry and set it off?"

"Oh, impossible!" cried Lambelle. "It would rend this whole part of the country to pieces. In fact, I am not sure that the shock would not be felt as far as Paris. With a very few drops I can shatter the whole quarry."

"Well, we'll try that after lunch. We have another dog left."

When an hour had passed, Lambelle was anxious to try his quarry experiment.

"By-and-by," he said, "the sun will not be shining in the quarry, and then it will be too late."

"We can easily wait until to-morrow, unless you are in a hurry."

"I am in no hurry," rejoined the inventor. "I thought perhaps you might be, with so much to do."

"No," replied the official. "Nothing I shall do during my administration will be more important than this."

"I am glad to hear you say so," answered Lambelle; "and if you will give me the bottle again I will now place a few drops in the sunny part of the quarry."

The Minister handed him the bottle, apparently with some reluctance.

"I still think," he said, "that it would be much better to allow this secret to die. No one knows it at present but yourself. With you, as I have said, it will be safe, or with me; but think of the awful possibilities of a disclosure."

"Every great invention has its risks," said Lambelle firmly. "Nothing would induce me to forego the fruits of my life-work. It is too much to ask of any man."

"Very well," said the Minister. "Then let us be sure of our facts. I want to see the effects of the explosive on the quarry."

"You shall," said Lambelle, as he departed.

"I will wait for you here," said the Minister, "and smoke a cigarette."

When the inventor approached the quarry, leading the dog behind him, the Minister's hand trembled so that he was hardly able to hold the field-glass to his eye. Lambelle disappeared down the path. The next instant the ground trembled even where the Minister sat, and a haze of dust arose above the ruined quarry.

Some moments after the pallid Minister looked over the work of destruction, but no trace of humanity was there except himself.

"I could not do otherwise," he murmured, "It was too great a risk to run."

THE GREAT PEGRAM MYSTERY.

(With apologies to Dr. Conan Doyle, and our mutual and lamented friend the late Sherlock Holmes.)

I dropped in on my friend, Sherlaw Kombs, to hear what he had to say about the Pegram mystery, as it had come to be called in the newspapers. I found him playing the violin with a look of sweet peace and serenity on his face, which I never noticed on the countenances of those within hearing distance. I knew this expression of seraphic calm indicated that Kombs had been deeply annoyed about something. Such, indeed, proved to be the case, for one of the morning papers had contained an article, eulogizing the alertness and general competence of Scotland Yard. So great was Sherlaw Kombs's contempt for Scotland Yard that he never would visit Scotland during his vacations, nor would he ever admit that a Scotchman was fit for anything but export.

He generously put away his violin, for he had a sincere liking for me, and greeted me with his usual kindness.

"I have come," I began, plunging at once into the matter on my mind, "to hear what you think of the great Pegram mystery."

"I haven't heard of it," he said quietly, just as if all London were not talking of that very thing. Kombs was curiously ignorant on some subjects, and abnormally learned on others. I found, for instance, that political discussion with him was impossible, because he did not know who Salisbury and Gladstone were. This made his friendship a great boon.

"The Pegram mystery has baffled even Gregory, of Scotland Yard."

"I can well believe it," said my friend, calmly. "Perpetual motion, or squaring the circle, would baffle Gregory. He's an infant, is Gregory."

This was one of the things I always liked about Kombs. There was no professional jealousy in him, such as characterizes so many other men.

He filled his pipe, threw himself into his deep-seated arm-chair, placed his feet on the mantel, and clasped his hands behind his head.

"Tell me about it," he said simply.

"Old Barrie Kipson," I began, "was a stockbroker in the City. He lived in Pegram, and it was his custom to——"

"COME IN!" shouted Kombs, without changing his position, but with a suddenness that startled me. I had heard no knock.

"Excuse me," said my friend, laughing, "my invitation to enter was a trifle premature. I was really so interested in your recital that I spoke before I thought, which a detective should never do. The fact is, a man will be here in a moment who will tell me all about this crime, and so you will be spared further effort in that line."

"Ah, you have an appointment. In that case I will not intrude," I said, rising.

"Sit down; I have no appointment. I did not know until I spoke that he was coming."

I gazed at him in amazement. Accustomed as I was to his extraordinary talents, the man was a perpetual surprise to me. He continued to smoke quietly, but evidently enjoyed my consternation.

"I see you are surprised. It is really too simple to talk about, but, from my position opposite the mirror, I can see the reflection of objects in the street. A man stopped, looked at one of my cards, and then glanced across the street. I recognized my card, because, as you know, they are all in scarlet. If, as you say, London is talking of this mystery, it naturally follows that he will talk of it, and the chances are he wished to consult me about it. Anyone can see that, besides there is always—Come in!"

There was a rap at the door this time.

A stranger entered. Sherlaw Kombs did not change his lounging attitude.

"I wish to see Mr. Sherlaw Kombs, the detective," said the stranger, coming within the range of the smoker's vision.

"This is Mr. Kombs," I remarked at last, as my friend smoked quietly, and seemed half-asleep.

"Allow me to introduce myself," continued the stranger, fumbling for a card.

"There is no need. You are a journalist," said Kombs.

"Ah," said the stranger, somewhat taken aback, "you know me, then."

"Never saw or heard of you in my life before."

"Then how in the world——"

"Nothing simpler. You write for an evening paper. You have written an article slating the book of a friend. He will feel badly about it, and you will condole with him. He will never know who stabbed him unless I tell him."

"The devil!" cried the journalist, sinking into a chair and mopping his brow, while his face became livid.

"Yes," drawled Kombs, "it is a devil of a shame that such things are done. But what would you? as we say in France."

When the journalist had recovered his second wind he pulled himself together somewhat. "Would you object to telling me how you know these particulars about a man you say you have never seen?"

"I rarely talk about these things," said Kombs with great composure. "But as the cultivation of the habit of observation may help you in your profession, and thus in a remote degree benefit me by making your paper less deadly dull, I will tell you. Your first and second fingers are smeared with ink, which shows that you write a great deal. This smeared class embraces two sub-classes, clerks or accountants, and journalists. Clerks have to be neat in their work. The ink-smear is slight in their case. Your fingers are badly and carelessly smeared; therefore, you are a journalist. You have an evening paper in your pocket. Anyone might have any evening paper, but yours is a Special Edition, which will not be on the streets for half-an-hour yet. You must have obtained it before you left the office, and to do this you must be on the staff. A book notice is marked with a blue pencil. A journalist always despises every article in his own paper not written by himself; therefore, you wrote the article you have marked, and doubtless are about to send it to the author of the book referred to. Your paper makes a specialty of abusing all books not written by some member of its own staff. That the author is a friend of yours, I merely surmised. It is all a trivial example of ordinary observation."

"Really, Mr. Kombs, you are the most wonderful man on earth. You are the equal of Gregory, by Jove, you are."

A frown marred the brow of my friend as he placed his pipe on the sideboard and drew his self-cocking six-shooter.

"Do you mean to insult me, sir?"

"I do not—I—I assure you. You are fit to take charge of Scotland Yard to-morrow———. I am in earnest, indeed I am, sir."

"Then Heaven help you," cried Kombs, slowly raising his right arm.

I sprang between them.

"Don't shoot!" I cried. "You will spoil the carpet. Besides, Sherlaw, don't you see the man means well. He actually thinks it is a compliment!"

"Perhaps you are right," remarked the detective, flinging his revolver carelessly beside his pipe, much to the relief of the third party. Then, turning to the journalist, he said, with his customary bland courtesy—

"You wanted to see me, I think you said. What can I do for you, Mr. Wilber Scribbings?"

The journalist started.

"How do you know my name?" he gasped.

Kombs waved his hand impatiently.

"Look inside your hat if you doubt your own name?"

I then noticed for the first time that the name was plainly to be seen inside the top-hat Scribbings held upside down in his hands.

"You have heard, of course, of the Pegram mystery——".

"Tush," cried the detective; "do not, I beg of you, call it a mystery. There is no such thing. Life would become more tolerable if there ever was a mystery. Nothing is original. Everything has been done before. What about the Pegram affair?"

"The Pegram—ah—case has baffled everyone. The Evening Blade wishes you to investigate, so that it may publish the result. It will pay you well. Will you accept the commission?"

"Possibly. Tell me about the case."

"I thought everybody knew the particulars. Mr. Barrie Kipson lived at Pegram. He carried a first-class season ticket between the terminus and that station. It was his custom to leave for Pegram on the 5.30 train each evening. Some weeks ago, Mr. Kipson was brought down by the influenza. On his first visit to the City after his recovery, he drew something like £300 in notes, and left the office at his usual hour to catch the 5.30. He was never seen again alive, as far as the public have been able to learn. He was found at Brewster in a first-class compartment on the Scotch Express, which does not stop between London and Brewster. There was a bullet in his head, and his money was gone, pointing plainly to murder and robbery."

"And where is the mystery, may I ask?"

"There are several unexplainable things about the case. First, how came he on the Scotch Express, which leaves at six, and does not stop at Pegram? Second, the ticket examiners at the terminus would have turned him out if he showed his season ticket; and all the tickets sold for the Scotch Express on the 21st are accounted for. Third, how could the murderer have escaped? Fourth, the passengers in the two compartments on each side of the one where the body was found heard no scuffle and no shot fired."

"Are you sure the Scotch Express on the 21st did not stop between London and Brewster?"

"Now that you mention the fact, it did. It was stopped by signal just outside of Pegram. There was a few moments' pause, when the line was reported clear, and it went on again. This frequently happens, as there is a branch line beyond Pegram."

Mr. Sherlaw Kombs pondered for a few moments, smoking his pipe silently.

"I presume you wish the solution in time for to-morrow's paper?"

"Bless my soul, no. The editor thought if you evolved a theory in a month you would do well."

"My dear sir, I do not deal with theories, but with facts. If you can make it convenient to call here to-morrow at 8 a.m. I will give you the full particulars early enough for the first edition. There is no sense in taking up much time over so simple an affair as the Pegram case. Good afternoon, sir."

Mr. Scribbings was too much astonished to return the greeting. He left in a speechless condition, and I saw him go up the street with his hat still in his hand.

Sherlaw Kombs relapsed into his old lounging attitude, with his hands clasped behind his head. The smoke came from his lips in quick puffs at first, then at longer intervals. I saw he was coming to a conclusion, so I said nothing.

Finally he spoke in his most dreamy manner. "I do not wish to seem to be rushing things at all, Whatson, but I am going out to-night on the Scotch Express. Would you care to accompany me?"

"Bless me!" I cried, glancing at the clock, "you haven't time, it is after five now."

"Ample time, Whatson—ample," he murmured, without changing his position. "I give myself a minute and a half to change slippers and dressing gown for boots and coat, three seconds for hat, twenty-five seconds to the street, forty-two seconds waiting for a hansom, and then seven at the terminus before the express starts. I shall be glad of your company."

I was only too happy to have the privilege of going with him. It was most interesting to watch the workings of so inscrutable a mind. As we drove under the lofty iron roof of the terminus I noticed a look of annoyance pass over his face.

"We are fifteen seconds ahead of our time," he remarked, looking at the big clock. "I dislike having a miscalculation of that sort occur."

The great Scotch Express stood ready for its long journey. The detective tapped one of the guards on the shoulder.

"You have heard of the so-called Pegram mystery, I presume?"

"Certainly, sir. It happened on this very train, sir."

"Really? Is the same carriage still on the train?"

"Well, yes, sir, it is," replied the guard, lowering his voice, "but of course, sir, we have to keep very quiet about it. People wouldn't travel in it, else, sir."

"Doubtless. Do you happen to know if anybody occupies the compartment in which the body was found?"

"A lady and gentleman, sir; I put 'em in myself, sir."

"Would you further oblige me," said the detective, deftly slipping half-a-sovereign into the hand of the guard, "by going to the window and informing them in an offhand casual sort of way that the tragedy took place in that compartment?"

"Certainly, sir."

We followed the guard, and the moment he had imparted his news there was a suppressed scream in the carriage. Instantly a lady came out, followed by a florid-faced gentleman, who scowled at the guard. We entered the now empty compartment, and Kombs said: "We would like to be alone here until we reach Brewster."

"I'll see to that, sir," answered the guard, locking the door.

When the official moved away, I asked my friend what he expected to find in the carriage that would cast any light on the case.

"Nothing," was his brief reply.

"Then why do you come?"

"Merely to corroborate the conclusions I have already arrived at."

"And may I ask what those conclusions are?"

"Certainly," replied the detective, with a touch of lassitude in his voice. "I beg to call your attention, first, to the fact that this train stands between two platforms, and can be entered from either side. Any man familiar with the station for years would be aware of that fact. This shows how Mr. Kipson entered the train just before it started."

"But the door on this side is locked," I objected, trying it.

"Of course. But every season ticket-holder carries a key. This accounts for the guard not seeing him, and for the absence of a ticket. Now let me give you some information about the influenza. The patient's temperature rises several degrees above normal, and he has a fever. When the malady has run its course, the temperature falls to three- quarters of a degree below normal. These, facts are unknown to you, I imagine, because you are a doctor."

I admitted such was the case.

"Well, the consequence of this fall in temperature is that the convalescent's mind turns toward thoughts of suicide. Then is the time he should be watched by his friends. Then was the time Mr. Barrie Kipson's friends did not watch him. You remember the 21st, of course. No? It was a most depressing day. Fog all around and mud under foot. Very good. He resolves on suicide. He wishes to be unidentified, if possible but forgets his season ticket. My experience is that a man about to commit a crime always forgets something."

"But how do you account for the disappearance of the money?"

"The money has nothing to do with the matter. If he was a deep man, and knew the stupidness of Scotland Yard, he probably sent the notes to an enemy. If not, they may have been given to a friend. Nothing is more calculated to prepare the mind for self-destruction than the prospect of a night ride on the Scotch Express, and the view from the windows of the train as it passes through the northern part of London is particularly conducive to thoughts of annihilation."

"What became of the weapon?"

"That is just the point on which I wish to satisfy myself. Excuse me for a moment."

Mr. Sherlaw Kombs drew down the window on the right hand side, and examined the top of the casing minutely with a magnifying glass. Presently he heaved a sigh of relief, and drew up the sash.

"Just as I expected," he remarked, speaking more to himself than to me. "There is a slight dent on the top of the window-frame. It is of such a nature as to be made only by the trigger of a pistol falling from the nerveless hand of a suicide. He intended to throw the weapon far out of the window, but had not the strength. It might have fallen into the carriage. As a matter of fact, it bounced away from the line and lies among the grass about ten feet six inches from the outside rail. The only question that now remains is where the deed was committed, and the exact present position of the pistol reckoned in miles from London, but that, fortunately, is too simple to even need explanation."

"Great heavens, Sherlaw!" I cried. "How can you call that simple? It seems to me impossible to compute."

We were now flying over Northern London, and the great detective leaned back with every sign of ennui, closing his eyes. At last he spoke wearily:

"It is really too elementary, Whatson, but I am always willing to oblige a friend. I shall be relieved, however, when you are able to work out the A B C of detection for yourself, although I shall never object to helping you with the words of more than three syllables. Having made up his mind to commit suicide, Kipson naturally intended to do it before he reached Brewster, because tickets are again examined at that point. When the train began to stop at the signal near Pegram, he came to the false conclusion that it was stopping at Brewster. The fact that the shot was not heard is accounted for by the screech of the air- brake, added to the noise of the train. Probably the whistle was also sounding at the same moment. The train being a fast express would stop as near the signal as possible. The air-brake will stop a train in twice its own length. Call it three times in this case. Very well. At three times the length of this train from the signalpost towards London, deducting half the length of the train, as this carriage is in the middle, you will find the pistol."

"Wonderful!" I exclaimed.

"Commonplace," he murmured.

At this moment the whistle sounded shrilly, and we felt the grind of the air-brakes.

"The Pegram signal again," cried Kombs, with something almost like enthusiasm. "This is indeed luck. We will get out here, Whatson, and test the matter."

As the train stopped, we got out on the right-hand side of the line. The engine stood panting impatiently under the red light, which changed to green as I looked at it. As the train moved on with increasing speed, the detective counted the carriages, and noted down the number. It was now dark, with the thin crescent of the moon hanging in the western sky throwing a weird half-light on the shining metals. The rear lamps of the train disappeared around a curve, and the signal stood at baleful red again. The black magic of the lonesome night in that strange place impressed me, but the detective was a most practical man. He placed his back against the signal-post, and paced up the line with even strides, counting his steps. I walked along the permanent way beside him silently. At last he stopped, and took a tapeline from his pocket. He ran it out until the ten feet six inches were unrolled, scanning the figures in the wan light of the new moon. Giving me the end, he placed his knuckles on the metals, motioning me to proceed down the embankment. I stretched out the line, and then sank my hand in the damp grass to mark the spot.

"Good God!" I cried, aghast, "what is this?"

"It is the pistol," said Kombs quietly.

It was!!

Journalistic London will not soon forget the sensation that was caused by the record of the investigations of Sherlaw Kombs, as printed at length in the next day's Evening Blade. Would that my story ended here. Alas! Kombs contemptuously turned over the pistol to Scotland Yard. The meddlesome officials, actuated, as I always hold, by jealousy, found the name of the seller upon it. They investigated. The seller testified that it had never been in the possession of Mr. Kipson, as far as he knew. It was sold to a man whose description tallied with that of a criminal long watched by the police. He was arrested, and turned Queen's evidence in the hope of hanging his pal. It seemed that Mr. Kipson, who was a gloomy, taciturn man, and usually came home in a compartment by himself, thus escaping observation, had been murdered in the lane leading to his house. After robbing him, the miscreants turned their thoughts towards the disposal of the body—a subject that always occupies a first-class criminal mind before the deed is done. They agreed to place it on the line, and have it mangled by the Scotch Express, then nearly due. Before they got the body half- way up the embankment the express came along and stopped. The guard got out and walked along the other side to speak with the engineer. The thought of putting the body into an empty first-class carriage instantly occurred to the murderers. They opened the door with the deceased's key. It is supposed that the pistol dropped when they were hoisting the body in the carriage.

The Queen's evidence dodge didn't work, and Scotland Yard ignobly insulted my friend Sherlaw Kombs by sending him a pass to see the villains hanged.

DEATH COMETH SOON OR LATE.

It was Alick Robbins who named the invalid the Living Skeleton, and probably remorse for having thus given him a title so descriptively accurate, caused him to make friends with the Living Skeleton, a man who seemed to have no friends.

Robbins never forgot their first conversation. It happened in this way. It was the habit of the Living Skeleton to leave his hotel every morning promptly at ten o'clock, if the sun was shining, and to shuffle rather than walk down the gravel street to the avenue of palms. There, picking out a seat on which the sun shone, the Living Skeleton would sit down and seem to wait patiently for someone who never came. He wore a shawl around his neck and a soft cloth cap on his skull. Every bone in his face stood out against the skin, for there seemed to be no flesh, and his clothes hung as loosely upon him as they would have upon a skeleton. It required no second glance at the Living Skeleton to know that the remainder of his life was numbered by days or hours, and not by weeks or months. He didn't seem to have energy enough even to read, and so it was that Robbins sat down one day on the bench beside him, and said sympathetically:—

"I hope you are feeling better to-day."

The Skeleton turned towards him, laughed a low, noiseless, mirthless laugh for a moment, and then said, in a hollow, far-away voice that had no lungs behind it: "I am done with feeling either better or worse."

"Oh, I trust it is not so bad as that," said Robbins; "the climate is doing you good down here, is it not?"

Again the Skeleton laughed silently, and Robbins began to feel uneasy. The Skeleton's eyes were large and bright, and they fastened themselves upon Robbins in a way that increased that gentleman's uneasiness, and made him think that perhaps the Skeleton knew he had so named him.

"I have no more interest in climate," said the Skeleton. "I merely seem to live because I have been in the habit of living for some years; I presume that is it, because my lungs are entirely gone. Why I can talk or why I can breathe is a mystery to me. You are perfectly certain you can hear me?"

"Oh, I hear you quite distinctly," said Robbins.

"Well, if it wasn't that people tell me that they can hear me, I wouldn't believe I was really speaking, because, you see, I have nothing to speak with. Isn't it Shakespeare who says something about when the brains are out the man is dead? Well, I have seen some men who make me think Shakespeare was wrong in his diagnosis, but it is generally supposed that when the lungs are gone a man is dead. To tell the truth, I am dead, practically. You know the old American story about the man who walked around to save funeral expenses; well, it isn't quite that way with me, but I can appreciate how the man felt. Still I take a keen interest in life, although you might not think so. You see, I haven't much time left; I am going to die at eight o'clock on the 30th of April. Eight o'clock at night, not in the morning, just after table d'hôte."

"You are going to what!" cried Robbins in astonishment.

"I'm going to die that day. You see I have got things to such a fine point, that I can die any time I want to. I could die right here, now, if I wished. If you have any mortal interest in the matter I'll do it, and show you what I say is true. I don't mind much, you know, although I had fixed April the 30th as the limit. It wouldn't matter a bit for me to go off now, if it would be of any interest to you."

"I beg you," said Robbins, very much alarmed, "not to try any experiments on my account. I am quite willing to believe anything you say about the matter—of course you ought to know."

"Yes, I do know." answered the Living Skeleton sadly. "Of course I have had my struggle with hope and fear, but that is all past now, as you may well understand. The reason that I have fixed the date for April 30th is this: you see I have only a certain amount of money—I do not know why I should make any secret of it. I have exactly 240 francs today, over and above another

100 francs which I have set aside for another purpose. I am paying 8 francs a day at the Golden Dragon; that will keep me just thirty days, and then I intend to die."

The Skeleton laughed again, without sound, and Robbins moved uneasily on the seat.

"I don't see," he said finally, "what there is to laugh about in that condition of affairs."

"I don't suppose there is very much; but there is something else that I consider very laughable, and that I will tell you if you will keep it a secret. You see, the Golden Dragon himself—I always call our innkeeper the Golden Dragon, just as you call me, the Living Skeleton."

"Oh, I—I—beg your pardon," stammered Robbins, "I——."

"It really doesn't matter at all. You are perfectly right, and I think it a very apt term. Well, the old Golden Dragon makes a great deal of his money by robbing the dead. You didn't know that, did you? You thought it was the living who supported him, and goodness knows he robs them when he has a chance. Well, you are very much mistaken. When a man dies in the Golden Dragon, he, or his friends rather, have to pay very sweetly for it. The Dragon charges them for re-furnishing the room. Every stick of furniture is charged for, all the wall-paper, and so on. I suppose it is perfectly right to charge something, but the Dragon is not content with what is right. He knows he has finally lost a customer, and so he makes all he can out of him. The furniture so paid for, is not re-placed, and the walls are not papered again, but the Dragon doesn't abate a penny of his bill on that account. Now, I have inquired of the furnishing man, on the street back of the hotel, and he has written on his card just the cost of mattress, sheets, pillows, and all that sort of thing, and the amount comes to about 50 francs. I have put in an envelope a 50-franc note, and with it the card of the furniture man. I have written a letter to the hotel-keeper, telling him just what the things will cost that he needs, and have referred the Dragon to the card of the furniture man who has given me the figures. This envelope I have addressed to the Dragon, and he will find it when I am dead. This is the joke that old man Death and myself have put up on our host, and my only regret is that I shall not be able to enjoy a look at the Dragon's countenance as he reads my last letter to him. Another sum of money I have put away, in good hands where he won't have a chance to get it, for my funeral expenses, and then you see I am through with the world. I have nobody to leave that I need worry about, or who would either take care of me or feel sorry for me if I needed care or sympathy, which I do not. So that is why I laugh, and that is why I come down and sit upon this bench, in the sunshine, and enjoy the posthumous joke."

Robbins did not appear to see the humor of the situation quite as strongly as the Living Skeleton did. At different times after, when they met he had offered the Skeleton more money if he wanted it, so that he might prolong his life a little, but the Skeleton always refused.

A sort of friendship sprang up between Robbins and the Living Skeleton, at least, as much of a friendship as can exist between the living and the dead, for Robbins was a muscular young fellow who did not need to live at the Riviera on account of his health, but merely because he detested an English winter. Besides this, it may be added, although it really is nobody's business, that a Nice Girl and her parents lived in this particular part of the South of France.

One day Robbins took a little excursion in a carriage to Toulon. He had invited the Nice Girl to go with him, but on that particular day she could not go. There was some big charity function on hand, and one necessary part of the affair was the wheedling of money out of people's pockets, so the Nice Girl had undertaken to do part of the wheedling.

She was very good at it, and she rather prided herself upon it, but then she was a very nice girl, pretty as well, and so people found it difficult to refuse her. On the evening of the day there was to be a ball at the principal hotel of the place, also in connection with this very desirable charity. Robbins had reluctantly gone to Toulon alone, but you may depend upon it he was back in time for the ball.

"Well," he said to the Nice Girl when he met her, "what luck collecting, to-day?"

"Oh, the greatest luck," she replied enthusiastically, "and whom do you think I got the most money from?"

"I am sure I haven't the slightest idea—that old English Duke, he certainly has money enough."

"No, not from him at all; the very last person you would expect it from—your friend, the Living Skeleton."

"What!" cried Robbins, in alarm.

"Oh, I found him on the bench where he usually sits, in the avenue of the palms. I told him all about the charity and how useful it was, and how necessary, and how we all ought to give as much as we could towards it, and he smiled and smiled at me in that curious way of his. 'Yes,' he said in a whisper, 'I believe the charity should be supported by everyone; I will give you eighty francs.' Now, wasn't that very generous of him? Eighty francs, that was ten times what the Duke gave, and as he handed me the money he looked up at me and said in that awful whisper of his: 'Count this over carefully when you get home and see if you can find out what else I have given you. There is more than eighty francs there.' Then, after I got home, I——"

But here the Nice Girl paused, when she looked at the face of Robbins, to whom she was talking. That face was ghastly pale and his eyes were staring at her but not seeing her.

"Eighty francs," he was whispering to himself, and he seemed to be making a mental calculation. Then noticing the Nice Girl's amazed look at him, he said:

"Did you take the money?"

"Of course I took it," she said, "why shouldn't I?"

"Great Heavens!" gasped Robbins, and without a word he turned and fled, leaving the Nice Girl transfixed with astonishment and staring after him with a frown on her pretty brow.

"What does he mean by such conduct?" she asked herself. But Robbins disappeared from the gathering throng in the large room of the hotel, dashed down the steps, and hurried along the narrow pavements toward the "Golden Dragon." The proprietor was standing in the hallway with his hands behind him, a usual attitude with the Dragon.

"Where," gasped Robbins, "is Mr.—Mr.——" and then he remembered he didn't know the name. "Where is the Living Skeleton?"

"He has gone to his room," answered the Dragon, "he went early to-night, he wasn't feeling well, I think."

"What is the number of his room?"

"No. 40," and the proprietor rang a loud, jangling bell, whereupon one of the chambermaids appeared. "Show this gentleman to No. 40."

The girl preceded Robbins up the stairs. Once she looked over her shoulder, and said in a whisper, "Is he worse?"

"I don't know," answered Robbins, "that's what I have come to see."

At No. 40 the girl paused, and rapped lightly on the door panel. There was no response. She rapped again, this time louder. There was still no response.

"Try the door," said Robbins.

"I am afraid to," said the girl.

"Why?"

"Because he said if he were asleep the door would be locked, and if he were dead the door would be open."

"When did he say that?"

"He said it several times, sir; about a week ago the last time."

Robbins turned the handle of the door; it was not locked. A dim light was in the room, but a screen before the door hid it from sight. When he passed round the screen he saw, upon the square marble-topped arrangement at the head of the bed, a candle burning, and its light shone on the dead face of the Skeleton, which had a grim smile on its thin lips, while in its clenched hand was a letter addressed to the proprietor of the hotel.

The Living Skeleton had given more than the eighty francs to that deserving charity.

HIGH STAKES.

The snow was gently sifting down through the white glare of the electric light when Pony Rowell buttoned his overcoat around him and left the Metropolitan Hotel, which was his home. He was a young man, not more than thirty, and his face was a striking one. It was clean cut and clean shaven. It might have been the face of an actor or the face of a statesman. An actor's face has a certain mobility of expression resulting from the habit of assuming characters differing widely. Rowell's face, when you came to look at it closely, showed that it had been accustomed to repress expression rather than to show emotion of any kind. A casual look at Pony Rowell made you think his face would tell you something; a closer scrutiny showed you that it would tell you nothing. His eyes were of a piercing steely gray that seemed to read the thoughts of others, while they effectually concealed his own. Pony Rowell was known as a man who never went back on his word. He was a professional gambler.

On this particular evening he strolled up the avenue with the easy carriage of a man of infinite leisure. He hesitated for a moment at an illy-lighted passage-way in the middle of a large building on a side street, then went in and mounted a stair. He rapped lightly at a door. A slide was shoved back and a man inside peered out at him for a moment. Instantly the door was opened, for Pony's face was good for admittance at any of the gambling rooms in the city. There was still another guarded door to pass, for an honest gambling-house keeper can never tell what streak of sudden morality may strike the police, and it is well to have a few moments' time in which to conceal the paraphernalia of the business. Of course, Mellish's gambling rooms were as well known to the police as to Pony Rowell, but unless some fuss was made by the public, Mellish knew he would be free from molestation.

Mellish was a careful man, and a visitor had to be well vouched for, before he gained admission. There never was any trouble in Mellish's rooms. He was often known to advise a player to quit when he knew the young gambler could not afford to lose, and instances were cited where he had been the banker of some man in despair. Everybody liked Mellish, for his generosity was unbounded, and he told a good story well.

Inside the room that Pony Rowell had penetrated, a roulette table was at its whirling work and faro was going on in another spot. At small tables various visitors were enjoying the game of poker.

"Hello, Pony," cried Bert Ragstock, "are you going to give me my revenge to-night?"

"I'm always willing to give anyone his revenge," answered Pony imperturbably, lighting a fresh cigarette.

"All right then; come and sit down here."

"I'm not going to play just yet. I want to look on for a while."

"Nonsense. I've been waiting for you ever so long already. Sit down."

"You ought to know by this time, Bert, that when I say a thing I mean it. I won't touch a card till the clock begins to strike 12. Then I'm wid ye."

"Pshaw, Pony, you ought to be above that sort of thing. That's superstition, Rowell. You're too cool a man to mind when you touch a card. Come on."

"That's all right. At midnight, I said to myself, and at midnight it shall be or not at all."

The old gamblers in the place nodded approval of this resolution. It was all right enough for Bert Ragstock to sneer at superstition, because he was not a real gambler. He merely came to Mellish's rooms in the evening because the Stock Exchange did not keep open all night. Strange to say Ragstock was a good business man as well as a cool gambler. He bemoaned the fate that made him so rich that gambling had not the exhilarating effect on him which it would have had if he had been playing in desperation.

When the clock began to chime midnight Pony Rowell took up the pack and began to shuffle.

"Now, old man," he said, "I'm going in to win. I'm after big game to-night."

"Right you are." cried Bert, with enthusiasm. "I'll stand by you as long as the spots stay on the cards."

In the gray morning, when most of the others had left and even Mellish himself was yawning, they were still at it. The professional gambler had won a large sum of money; the largest sum he ever possessed. Yet there was no gleam of triumph in his keen eyes. Bert might have been winning for all the emotion his face showed. They were a well matched pair, and they enjoyed playing with each other.

"There," cried Pony at last, "haven't you had enough? Luck's against you. I wouldn't run my head any longer against a brick wall, if I were you."

"My dear Pony, how often have I told you there is no such thing as luck. But to tell the truth I'm tired and I'm going home. The revenge is postponed. When do I meet the enemy again?"

Pony Rowell shuffled the cards idly for a few moments without replying or raising his eyes. At last he said:

"The next time I play you, Bert, it will be for high stakes."

"Good heavens, aren't you satisfied with the stakes we played for to-night?"

"No. I want to play you for a stake that will make even your hair stand on end. Will you do it?"

"Certainly. When?"

"That I can't tell just yet. I have a big scheme on hand. I am to see a man to-day about it. All I want to know is that you promise to play."

"Pony, this is mysterious. I guess you're not afraid I will flunk out. I'm ready to meet you on any terms and for any stake."

"Enough said. I'll let you know some of the particulars as soon as I find out all I want myself. Good-night."

"Good-night to you, rather," said Bert, as Mellish helped him on with his overcoat. "You've won the pile: robbing a poor man of his hard- earned gains!"

"Oh, the poor man does not need the money as badly as I do. Besides, I'm going to give you a chance to win it all back again and more."

When Ragstock had left, Pony still sat by the table absent-mindedly shuffling the cards.

"If I were you," said Mellish, laying his hand on his shoulder, "I would put that pile in the bank and quit."

"The faro bank?" asked Pony, looking up with a smile.

"No, I'd quit the business altogether if I were you. I'm going to myself."

"Oh, we all know that. You've been going to quit for the last twenty years. Well, I'm going to quit, too, but not just yet. That's what they all say, of course, but I mean it."

In the early and crisp winter air Pony Rowell walked to the Metropolitan Hotel and to bed. At 3 that afternoon the man he had an appointment with, called to see him.

"You wanted to see me about an Insurance policy," the visitor began. An agent is always ready to talk of business. "Now, were you thinking of an endowment scheme or have you looked into our new bond system of insurance? The twenty-pay-life style of thing seems to be very popular."

"I want to ask you a few questions," said Pony. "If I were to insure my life in your company and were to commit suicide would that invalidate the policy?"

"Not after two years. After two years, in our company, the policy is incontestable."

"Two years? That won't do for me. Can't you make it one year?"

"I'll tell you what I will do," said the agent, lowering his voice, "I can ante-date the policy, so that the two years will end just when you like, say a year from now."

"Very well. If you can legally fix it so that the two years come to an end about this date next year I will insure in your company for $100,000."

The agent opened his eyes when the amount was mentioned.

"I don't want endowments or bonds, but the cheapest form of life insurance you have, and——"

"Straight life is what you want."

"Straight life it is, then, and I will pay you for the two years or say, to make it sure, for two years and a half down, when you bring me the papers."

Thus it was that with part of the money he had won, Pony Rowell insured his life for $100,000, and with another part he paid his board and lodging for a year ahead at the Metropolitan Hotel.

The remainder he kept to speculate on.

During the year that followed he steadily refused to play with Bert Ragstock, and once or twice they nearly had a quarrel about it—that is as near as Pony could come to having a row with anybody, for quarrelling was not in his line. If he had lived in a less civilized part of the community Pony might have shot, but as it was quarrels never came to anything, therefore he did not indulge in any.

"A year from the date of our last game? What nonsense it is waiting all that time. You play with others, why not with me? Think of the chances we are losing," complained Bert.

"We will have a game then that will make up for all the waiting," answered Rowell.

At last the anniversary came and when the hour struck that ushered it in Pony Rowell and Bert Ragstock sat facing each other, prepared to resume business on the old stand.

"Ah," said Bert, rubbing his hands, "it feels good to get opposite you once more. Pony, you're a crank. We might have had a hundred games like this during the past year, if there wasn't so much superstition about you."

"Not quite like this. This is to be the last game I play, win or lose. I tell you that now, so that there won't be any talk of revenge if I win."

"You don't mean it! I've heard talk like that before."

"All right. I've warned you. Now I propose that this be a game of pure luck. We get a new pack of cards, shuffle them, cut, then you pull one card and I another. Ace high. The highest takes the pot. Best two out of three. Do you agree?"

"Of course. How much is the pile to be?"

"One hundred thousand dollars."

"Oh, you're dreaming."

"Isn't it enough?"

"Thunder! You never saw $100,000."

"You will get the money if I lose."

"Say, Pony, that's coming it a little strong. One hundred thousand dollars! Heavens and earth! How many business men in this whole city would expect their bare word to be taken for $100,000?"

"I'm not a business man. I'm a gambler."

"True, true. Is the money in sight?"

"No; but you'll be paid. Your money is not in sight. I trust you. Can't you trust me?

"It isn't quite the same thing, Pony. I'll trust you for three times the money you have in sight, but when you talk about $100,000 you are talking of a lot of cash."

"If I can convince Mellish here that you will get your money, will you play?"

128

"You can convince me just as easily as you can Mellish. What's the use of dragging him in?"

"I could convince you in a minute, but you might still refuse to play. Now I'm bound to play this game and I can't take any risks. If my word and Mellish's isn't good enough for you, why, say so."

"All right," cried Bert. "If you can convince Mellish that you will pay if you lose I'll play you."

Rowell and Mellish retired into an inner room and after a few minutes reappeared again.

Mellish's face was red when he went in. He was now a trifle pale.

"I don't like this, Bert," Mellish said, "and I think this game had better stop right here."

"Then you are not convinced that I am sure of my money?"

"Yes, I am, but——"

"That's enough for me. Get out your new pack."

"You've given your word, Mellish," said Pony, seeing the keeper of the house was about to speak. "Don't say any more."

"For such a sum two out of three is too sudden. Make it five out of nine," put in Bert.

"I'm willing."

The new pack of cards was brought and the wrappings torn off.

"You shuffle first; I'll cut," said Rowell. His lips seemed parched and he moistened them now and then, which was unusual for so cool a gambler. Mellish fidgeted around with lowered brow. Bert shuffled the cards as nonchalantly as if he had merely a $5 bill on the result. When each had taken a card, Bert held an ace and Pony a king. Pony shuffled and the turn up was a spot in Pony's hand and queen in that of his opponent. Bert smiled and drops began to show on Pony's forehead in spite of his efforts at self-control.

No word was spoken by either players or onlookers. After the next deal Pony again lost. His imperturbability seemed to be leaving him. He swept the cards from the table with an oath. "Bring another pack," he said hoarsely.

Bert smiled at him across the table. He thought, of course, that they were playing for even stakes.

Mellish couldn't stand it any longer. He retired to one of the inner rooms. The first deal with the new pack turned in Pony's favor and he seemed to feel that his luck had changed, but the next deal went against him and also the one following.

"It's your shuffle," said Rowell, pushing the cards towards his opponent. Bert did not touch the cards, but smiled across at the gambler.

"What's the matter with you? Why don't you shuffle?"

"I don't have to," said Bert, quietly, "I've won five."

Rowell drew his hand across his perspiring brow and stared at the man across the table. Then he seemed to pull himself together.

"So you have," he said, "I hadn't noticed it. Excuse me. I guess I'll go now."

"Sit where you are and let us have a game for something more modest. I don't care about these splurges myself and I don't suppose you do— now."

"Thanks, no. I told you this was my last game. As to the splurge, if I had the money I would willingly try it again. So long."

When Mellish came in and saw that the game was over he asked where Pony was.

"He knew when he had enough, I guess," answered Bert. "He's gone home."

"Come in here, Bert. I want to speak with you," said Mellish.

When they were alone Mellish turned to him.

"I suppose Pony didn't tell you where the money is to come from?"

130

"No, he told you. That was enough for me."

"Well, there's no reason why you should not know now. I promised silence till the game was finished. He's insured his life for $100,000 and is going to commit suicide so that you may be paid."

"My God!" cried Bert, aghast. "Why did you let the game go on?"

"I tried to stop it, but I had given my word and you——"

"Well, don't let us stand chattering here. He's at the Metropolitan, isn't he? Then come along. Hurry into your coat."

Mellish knew the number of Rowell's room and so no time was lost in the hotel office with inquiries. He tried the door, but, as he expected, it was locked.

"Who's that?" cried a voice within.

"It's me—Mellish. I want to speak with you a moment."

"I don't want to see you."

"Bert wants to say something. It's important. Let us in."

"I won't let you in. Go away and don't make a fuss. It will do no good. You can get in ten minutes from now."

"Look here, Pony, you open that door at once, or I'll kick it in. You hear me? I want to see you a minute, and then you can do what you like," said Bert, in a voice that meant business.

After a moment's hesitation Rowell opened the door and the two stepped in. Half of the carpet had been taken up and the bare floor was covered with old newspapers. A revolver lay on the table, also writing materials and a half-finished letter. Pony was in his shirt sleeves and he did not seem pleased at the interruption.

"What do you want?" he asked shortly.

"Look here, Pony," said Bert, "I have confessed to Mellish and I've come

131

to confess to you. I want you to be easy with me and hush the thing up. I cheated. I stocked the cards."

"You're a liar," said Rowell, looking him straight in the eye.

"Don't say that again," cried Ragstock, with his fingers twitching. "There's mighty few men I would take that from."

"You stocked the cards on me? I'd like to see the man that could do it!"

"You were excited and didn't notice it."

"You're not only a liar, but you're an awkward liar. I have lost the money and I'll pay it. It would have been ready for you now, only I had a letter to write. Mellish has told you about the insurance policy and my will attached to it. Here they are. They're yours. I'm no kicker. I know when a game's played fair."

Bert took the policy and evidently intended to tear it in pieces, while Mellish, with a wink at him, edged around to get at the revolver. Ragstock's eye caught the name in big letters at the head of the policy, beautifully engraved. His eyes opened wide, then he sank into a chair and roared with laughter. Both the other men looked at him in astonishment.

"What's the matter?" asked Mellish.

"Matter? Why, this would have been a joke on Pony. It would do both of you some good to know a little about business as well as of gambling. The Hardfast Life Insurance Company went smash six months ago. It's the truth this time, Pony, even if I didn't stock the cards. Better make some inquiries in business circles before you try to collect any money from this institution. Now, Pony, order up the drinks, if anything can be had at this untimely hour. We are your guests so you are expected to be hospitable. I've had all the excitement I want for one night. We'll call it square and begin over again."

"WHERE IGNORANCE IS BLISS."

The splendid steamship Adamant, of the celebrated Cross Bow line, left New York on her February trip under favorable auspices. There had just been a storm on the ocean, so there was every chance that she would reach Liverpool before the next one was due.

Capt. Rice had a little social problem to solve at the outset, but he smoothed that out with the tact which is characteristic of him. Two Washington ladies—official ladies—were on board, and the captain, old British sea-dog that he was, always had trouble in the matter of precedence with Washington ladies. Capt. Rice never had any bother with the British aristocracy, because precedence is all set down in the bulky volume of "Burke's Peerage," which the captain kept in his cabin, and so there was no difficulty. But a republican country is supposed not to meddle with precedence. It wouldn't, either, if it weren't for the women.

So it happened that Mrs. Assistant-Attorney-to-the-Senate Brownrig came to the steward and said that, ranking all others on board, she must sit at the right hand of the captain. Afterwards Mrs. Second-Adjutant-to- the-War-Department Digby came to the same perplexed official and said she must sit at the captain's right hand because in Washington she took precedence over everyone else on board. The bewildered steward confided his woes to the captain, and the captain said he would attend to the matter. So he put Mrs. War-Department on his right hand and then walked down the deck with Mrs. Assistant-Attorney and said to her:

"I want to ask a favor, Mrs. Brownrig. Unfortunately I am a little deaf in the right ear, caused, I presume, by listening so much with that ear to the fog horn year in and year out. Now, I always place the lady whose conversation I wish most to enjoy on my left hand at table. Would you oblige me by taking that seat this voyage? I have heard of you, you see, Mrs. Brownrig, although you have never crossed with me before."

"Why, certainly, captain," replied Mrs. Brownrig; "I feel especially complimented."

"And I assure you, madam," said the polite captain, "that I would not for the world miss a single word that," etc.

And thus it was amicably arranged between the two ladies. All this has nothing whatever to do with the story. It is merely an incident given to show what a born diplomat Capt. Rice was and is to this day. I don't know any captain more popular with the ladies than he, and besides he is as good a sailor as crosses the ocean.

Day by day the good ship ploughed her way toward the east, and the passengers were unanimous in saying that they never had a pleasanter voyage for that time of the year. It was so warm on deck that many steamer chairs were out, and below it was so mild that a person might think he was journeying in the tropics. Yet they had left New York in a snow storm with the thermometer away below zero.

"Such," said young Spinner, who knew everything, "such is the influence of the Gulf Stream."

Nevertheless when Capt. Rice came down to lunch the fourth day out his face was haggard and his look furtive and anxious.

"Why, captain," cried Mrs. Assistant-Attorney, you look as if you hadn't slept a wink last night."

"I slept very well, thank you, madam." replied the captain. "I always do."

"Well, I hope your room was more comfortable than mine. It seemed to me too hot for anything. Didn't you find it so, Mrs. Digby?"

"I thought it very nice," replied the lady at the captain's right, who generally found it necessary to take an opposite view from the lady at the left.

"You see," said the captain, "we have many delicate women and children on board and it is necessary to keep up the temperature. Still, perhaps the man who attends to the steam rather overdoes it. I will speak him."

Then the captain pushed from him his untasted food and went up on the

134

bridge, casting his eye aloft at the signal waving from the masthead, silently calling for help to all the empty horizon.

"Nothing in sight, Johnson?" said the captain.

"Not a speck, sir."

The captain swept the circular line of sea and sky with his glasses, then laid them down with a sigh.

"We ought to raise something this afternoon, sir," said Johnson; "we are right in their track, sir. The Fulda ought to be somewhere about."

"We are too far north for the Fulda, I am afraid," answered the captain.

"Well, sir, we should see the Vulcan before night, sir. She's had good weather from Queenstown."

"Yes. Keep a sharp lookout, Johnson."

"Yes, sir."

The captain moodily paced the bridge with his head down.

"I ought to have turned back to New York," he said to himself.

Then he went down to his own room, avoiding the passengers as much as he could, and had the steward bring him some beef-tea. Even a captain cannot live on anxiety.

"Steamer off the port bow, sir," rang out the voice of the lookout at the prow. The man had sharp eyes, for a landsman could have seen nothing.

"Run and tell the captain," cried Johnson to the sailor at his elbow, but as the sailor turned the captain's head appeared up the stairway. He seized the glass and looked long at a single point in the horizon.

"It must be the Vulcan," he said at last.

"I think so, sir."

"Turn your wheel a few points to port and bear down on her."

Johnson gave the necessary order and the great ship veered around.

"Hello!" cried Spinner, on deck. "Here's a steamer. I found her. She's mine."

Then there was a rush to the side of the ship. "A steamer in sight!" was the cry, and all books and magazines at once lost interest. Even the placid, dignified Englishman who was so uncommunicative, rose from his chair and sent his servant for his binocular. Children were held up and told to be careful, while they tried to see the dim line of smoke so far ahead.

"Talk about lane routes at sea," cried young Spinner, the knowing. "Bosh, I say. See! we're going directly for her. Think what it might be in a fog! Lane routes! Pure luck, I call it."

"Will we signal to her, Mr. Spinner?" gently asked the young lady from Boston.

"Oh, certainly," answered young Spinner. "See there's our signal flying from the masthead now. That shows them what line we belong to."

"Dear me, how interesting," said the young lady. "You have crossed many times, I suppose, Mr. Spinner."

"Oh, I know my way about," answered the modest Spinner.

The captain kept the glasses glued to his eyes. Suddenly he almost let them drop.

"My God! Johnson," he cried.

"What is it, sir?"

"She's flying a signal of distress, too!"

The two steamers slowly approached each other and, when nearly alongside and about a mile apart, the bell of the Adamant rang to stop.

"There, you see," said young Spinner to the Boston girl, "she is flying the same flag at her masthead that we are."

"Then she belongs to the same line as this boat?"

"Oh, certainly," answered Mr. Cock-Sure Spinner.

"Oh, look! look! look!" cried the enthusiastic Indianapolis girl who was going to take music in Germany.

Everyone looked aloft and saw running up to the masthead a long line of fluttering, many-colored flags. They remained in place for a few moments and then fluttered down again, only to give place to a different string. The same thing was going on on the other steamer.

"Oh, this is too interesting for anything," said Mrs. Assistant. "I am just dying to know what it all means. I have read of it so often but never saw it before. I wonder when the captain will come down. What does it all mean?" she asked the deck steward.

"They are signalling to each other, madam."

"Oh, I know that. But what are they signalling?"

"I don't know, madam."

"Oh, see! see!" cried the Indianapolis girl, clapping her hands with delight. "The other steamer is turning round."

It was indeed so. The great ship was thrashing the water with her screw, and gradually the masts came in line and then her prow faced the east again. When this had been slowly accomplished the bell on the Adamant rang full speed ahead, and then the captain came slowly down the ladder that led from the bridge.

"Oh, captain, what does it all mean?"

"Is she going back, captain? Nothing wrong, I hope."

"What ship is it, captain?"

"She belongs to our line, doesn't she?"

"Why is she going back?"

"The ship," said the captain slowly, "is the Vulcan, of the Black Bowling

Line, that left Queenstown shortly after we left New York. She has met with an accident. Ran into some wreckage, it is thought, from the recent storm. Anyhow there is a hole in her, and whether she sees Queenstown or not will depend a great deal on what weather we have and whether her bulkheads hold out. We will stand by her till we reach Queenstown."

"Are there many on board, do you think, captain?"

"There are thirty-seven in the cabin and over 800 steerage passengers," answered the captain.

"Why don't you take them on board, out of danger, captain?"

"Ah, madam, there is no need to do that. It would delay us, and time is everything in a case like this. Besides, they will have ample warning if she is going down and they will have time to get everybody in the boats. We will stand by them, you know."

"Oh, the poor creatures," cried the sympathetic Mrs. Second-Adjutant. "Think of their awful position. May be engulfed at any moment. I suppose they are all on their knees in the cabin. How thankful they must have been to see the Adamant."

On all sides there was the profoundest sympathy for the unfortunate passengers of the Vulcan. Cheeks paled at the very thought of the catastrophe that might take place at any moment within sight of the sister ship. It was a realistic object lesson on the ever-present dangers of the sea. While those on deck looked with new interest at the steamship plunging along within a mile of them, the captain slipped away to his room. As he sat there, there was a tap at his door.

"Come in," shouted the captain.

The silent Englishman slowly entered.

"What's wrong, captain," he asked.

"Oh, the Vulcan has had a hole stove in her and I signalled——"

"Yes, I know all that, of course, but what's wrong with us?"

138

"With us?" echoed the captain blankly.

"Yes, with the Adamant? What has been amiss for the last two or three days? I'm not a talker, nor am I afraid any more than you are, but I want to know."

"Certainly," said the captain. "Please shut the door, Sir John."

Meanwhile there was a lively row on board the Vulcan. In the saloon Capt. Flint was standing at bay with his knuckles on the table.

"Now what the devil's the meaning of all this?" cried Adam K. Vincent, member of Congress.

A crowd of frightened women were standing around, many on the verge of hysterics. Children clung, with pale faces, to their mother's skirts, fearing they knew not what. Men were grouped with anxious faces, and the bluff old captain fronted them all.

"The meaning of all what, sir?"

"You know very well. What is the meaning of our turning-round?"

"It means, sir, that the Adamant has eighty-five saloon passengers and nearly 500 intermediate and steerage passengers who are in the most deadly danger. The cotton in the hold is on fire, and they have been fighting it night and day. A conflagration may break out at any moment. It means, then, sir, that the Vulcan is going to stand by the Adamant."

A wail of anguish burst from the frightened women at the awful fate that might be in store for so many human beings so near to them, and they clung closer to their children and thanked God that no such danger threatened them and those dear to them.

"And dammit, sir," cried the Congressman, "do you mean to tell us that we have to go against our will—without even being consulted—back to Queenstown?"

"I mean to tell you so, sir."

"Well, by the gods, that's an outrage, and I won't stand it, sir. I must be in New York by the 27th. I won't stand it, sir."

"I am very sorry, sir, that anybody should be delayed."

"Delayed? Hang it all, why don't you take the people on board and take 'em to New York? I protest against this. I'll bring a lawsuit against the company, sir."

"Mr. Vincent," said the captain sternly, "permit me to remind you that I am captain of this ship. Good afternoon, sir."

The Congressman departed from the saloon exceeding wroth, breathing dire threats of legal proceedings against the line and the captain personally, but most of the passengers agreed that it would be an inhuman thing to leave the Adamant alone in mid-ocean in such terrible straits.

"Why didn't they turn back, Captain Flint?" asked Mrs. General Weller.

"Because, madam, every moment is of value in such a case, and we are nearer Queenstown than New York."

And so the two steamships, side by side, worried their way toward the east, always within sight of each other by day, and with the rows of lights in each visible at night to the sympathetic souls on the other. The sweltering men poured water into the hold of the one and the pounding pumps poured water out of the hold of the other, and thus they reached Queenstown.

On board the tender that took the passengers ashore at Queenstown from both steamers two astonished women met each other.

"Why! Mrs.—General—WELLER!!! You don't mean to say you were on board that unfortunate Vulcan!"

"For the land's sake, Mrs. Assistant Brownrig! Is that really you? Will wonders never cease? Unfortunate, did you say? Mightily fortunate for you, I think. Why! weren't you just frightened to death?"

"I was, but I had no idea anyone I knew was on board."

"Well, you were on board yourself. That would have been enough to have killed me."

"On board myself? Why, what do you mean? I wasn't on board the Vulcan. Did you get any sleep at all after you knew you might go down at any moment?"

"My sakes, Jane, what are you talking about? Down at any moment? It was you that might have gone down at any moment or, worse still, have been burnt to death if the fire had got ahead. You don't mean to say you didn't know the Adamant was on fire most of the way across?"

"Mrs.—General—Weller!! There's some horrible mistake. It was the Vulcan. Everything depended on her bulkheads, the captain said. There was a hole as big as a barn door in the Vulcan. The pumps were going night and day."

Mrs. General looked at Mrs. Assistant as the light began to dawn on both of them.

"Then it wasn't the engines, but the pumps," she said.

"And it wasn't the steam, but the fire," screamed Mrs. Assistant. "Oh, dear, how that captain lied, and I thought him such a nice man, too. Oh, I shall go into hysterics, I know I shall."

"I wouldn't if I were you," said the sensible Mrs. General, who was a strong-minded woman; "besides, it is too late. We're all safe now. I think both captains were pretty sensible men. Evidently married, both of 'em."

Which was quite true.

THE DEPARTURE OF CUB MCLEAN.

Of course no one will believe me when I say that Mellish was in every respect, except one, an exemplary citizen and a good-hearted man. He was generous to a fault and he gave many a young fellow a start in life where a little money or a few encouraging words were needed. He drank, of course, but he was a connoisseur in liquors, and a connoisseur never goes in for excess. Few could tell a humorous story as well as Mellish, and he seldom dealt in chestnuts. No man can be wholly bad who never inflicts an old story on his friends, locating it on some acquaintance of his, and alleging that it occurred the day before.

If I wished to write a heart-rending article on the evils of gambling, Mellish would be the man I would go to for my facts and for the moral of the tale. He spent his life persuading people not to gamble. He never gambled himself, he said. But if no attention was paid to his advice, why then he furnished gamblers with the most secluded and luxurious gambling rooms in the city. It was supposed that Mellish stood in with the police, which was, of course, a libel. The idea of the guardians of the city standing in with a gambler or a gambling house! The statement was absurd on the face of it. If you asked any policeman in the city where Mellish's gambling rooms were, you would speedily learn that not one of them had ever even heard of the place. All this goes to show how scandalously people will talk, and if Mellish's rooms were free from raids, it was merely Mellish's good luck, that was all. Anyhow, in Mellish's rooms you could have a quiet, gentlemanly game for stakes about as high as you cared to go, and you were reasonably sure there would be no fuss and that your name would not appear in the papers next morning.

One night as Mellish cast his eye around his well-filled main room he noticed a stranger sitting at the roulette table. Mellish had a keen eye for strangers and in an unobtrusive way generally managed to find out something about them. A stranger in a gambling room brings in with him a certain sense of danger to the habitués.

"Who is that boy?" whispered Mellish to his bartender, generally known as Sotty, an ex-prize fighter and a dangerous man to handle if it came to trouble. It rarely came to trouble there, but Sotty was, in a measure, the silent symbol of physical force, backing the well-known mild morality of Mellish.

"I don't know him," answered Sotty.

"Whom did he come in with?"

"I didn't see him come in. Hadn't noticed him till now."

Mellish looked at the boy for a few minutes. He had the fresh, healthy, smooth face of a lad from the country, and he seemed strangely out of place in the heated atmosphere of that room, under the glare of the gas. Mellish sighed as he looked at him, then he turned to Sotty and said:

"Just get him away quietly and bring him to the small poker room. I want to have a few words with him."

Sotty, who had the utmost contempt for the humanitarian feelings of his boss, said nothing, but a look of disdain swept over his florid features as he went on his mission. If he had his way, he would not throw even a sprat out of the net. Many a time he had known Mellish to persuade a youngster with more money than brains to go home, giving orders at the double doors that he was not to be admitted again.

The young man rose with a look of something like consternation on his face and followed Sotty. The thing was done quietly, and all those around the tables were too much absorbed in the game to pay much attention.

"Look here, my boy," said Mellish, when they were alone, "who brought you to this place?"

"I guess," said the lad, with an expression of resentment, "I'm old enough to go where I like without being brought."

"Oh, certainly, certainly," said Mellish, diplomatically, knowing how much very young men dislike being accused of youth, "but I like to know all visitors here. You couldn't get in unless you came with someone known at the door. Who vouched for you?"

"See here, Mr. Mellish," said the youth angrily, "what are you driving at? If your doorkeepers don't know their own business why don't you speak to them about it? Are you going to have me turned out?"

"Nothing of the sort," said Mellish, soothingly, putting his hand in a fatherly manner on the young fellow's shoulder. "Don't mistake my meaning. The fact that you are here shows that you have a right to be here. We'll say no more about that. But you take my advice and quit the business here and now. I was a gambler before you were born, although I don't gamble any more. Take the advice of a man who knows. It doesn't pay."

"It seems to have paid you reasonably well."

"Oh, I don't complain. It has its ups and downs like all businesses. Still, it doesn't pay me nearly as well as perhaps you think, and you can take my word that in the long run it won't pay you at all. How much money have you got?"

"Enough to pay if I lose," said the boy impudently; then seeing the look of pain that passed over Mellish's face, he added more civilly:

"I have three or four hundred dollars."

"Well, take my advice and go home. You'll be just that much better off in the morning."

"What! Don't you play a square game here?"

"Of course we play a square game here," answered Mellish with indignation. "Do you think I am a card-sharper?"

"You seem so cock-sure I'll lose my money that I was just wondering. Now, I can afford to lose all the money I've got and not feel it. Are you going to allow me to play, or are you going to chuck me out?"

"Oh, you can play if you want to. But don't come whining to me when you lose. I've warned you."

"I'm not a whiner," said the young fellow; "I take my medicine like a man."

"Right you are," said Mellish with a sigh. He realized that this fellow, young as he looked, was probably deeper in vice than his appearance indicated and he knew the uselessness of counsel in such a case. They went into the main room together and the boy, abandoning roulette, began to play at one of the card tables for ever-increasing stakes. Mellish kept an eye on him for a time. The boy was having the luck of most beginners. He played a reckless game and won hand over fist. As one man had enough and rose from the table another eagerly took his place, but there was no break in the boy's winnings.

Pony Rowell was always late in arriving at the gambling rooms. On this occasion he entered, irreproachably dressed, and with the quiet, gentlemanly demeanor habitual with him. The professional gambler was never known to lose his temper. When displeased he became quieter, if possible, than before. The only sign of inward anger was a mark like an old scar which extended from his right temple, beginning over the eye and disappearing in his closely-cropped hair behind the ear. This line became an angry red that stood out against the general pallor of his face when things were going in a way that did not please him. He spoke in a low tone to Mellish.

"What's the excitement down at the other end of the room? Every one seems congregated there."

"Oh," answered Mellish, "it's a boy—a stranger—who is having the devil's own luck at the start. It will be the ruin of him."

"Is he playing high?"

"High? I should say so. He's perfectly reckless. He'll be brought up with a sharp turn and will borrow money from me to get out of town. I've seen a flutter like that before."

"In that case," said Pony tranquilly, "I must have a go at him. I like to tackle a youngster in the first flush of success, especially if he is plunging."

"You will soon have a chance," answered Mellish, "for even Ragstock knows when he has enough. He will get up in a moment. I know the signs."

145

With the air of a gentleman of leisure, somewhat tired of the frivolities of this world, Rowell made his way slowly to the group. As he looked over their shoulders at the boy a curious glitter came into his piercing eyes, and his lips, usually so well under control, tightened. The red mark began to come out as his face paled. It was evident that he did not intend to speak and that he was about to move away again, but the magnetism of his keen glance seemed to disturb the player, who suddenly looked up over the head of his opponent and met the stern gaze of Rowell.

The boy did three things. He placed his cards face downward on the table, put his right hand over the pile of money, and moved his chair back.

"What do you mean by that?" cried Ragstock.

The youth ignored the question, still keeping his eyes on Rowell.

"Do you squeal?" he asked.

"I squeal," said Pony, whatever the question and answer might mean. Then Rowell cried, slightly raising his voice so that all might hear:

"This man is Cub McLean, the most notorious card-sharper, thief, and murderer in the west. He couldn't play straight if he tried."

McLean laughed. "Yes," he said; "and if you want to see my trademark look at the side of Greggs' face."

Every man looked at Pony, learning for the first time that he had gone under a different name at some period of his life.

During the momentary distraction McLean swept the money off the table and put it in his pockets.

"Hold on," cried Ragstock, seemingly not quite understanding the situation. "You haven't won that yet."

Again McLean laughed.

"It would have been the same in ten minutes."

He jumped up, scattering the crowd behind him.

"Look to the doors," cried Pony. "Don't let this man out."

McLean had his back to the wall. From under his coat he whipped two revolvers which he held out, one in each hand.

"You ought to know me better than that, Greggs," he said, "do you want me to have another shot at you? I won't miss this time. Drop that."

The last command was given in a ringing voice that attracted every one's attention to Sotty. He had picked up a revolver from somewhere behind the bar and had come out with it in his hand. McLean's eye seemed to take in every motion in the room and he instantly covered the bartender with one of the pistols as he gave the command.

"Drop it," said Mellish. "There must be no shooting. You may go quietly. No one will interfere with you."

"You bet your sweet life they won't," said McLean with a laugh.

"Gentlemen," continued Mellish, "the house will stand the loss. If I allow a swindler in my rooms it is but right that I alone should suffer. Now you put up your guns and walk out."

"Good old Mellish," sneered McLean, "you ought to be running a Sunday- school."

Notwithstanding the permission to depart McLean did not relax his precautions for a moment. His shoulders scraped their way along the wall as he gradually worked towards the door. He kept Pony covered with his left hand while the polished barrel of the revolver in his right seemed to have a roving commission all over the room, to the nervous dread of many respectable persons who cowered within range. When he reached the door he said to Pony:

"I hope you'll excuse me, Greggs, but this is too good an opportunity to miss. I'm going to kill you in your tracks."

"That's about your size," said Pony putting his hands behind him and standing in his place, while those near him edged away. "I'm unarmed, so it is perfectly safe. You will insure your arrest so blaze away."

"Dodge under the table, then, and I will spare you."

Pony invited him to take up his abode in tropical futurity.

Cub laughed once more good naturedly, and lowered the muzzle of his revolver. As he shoved back his soft felt hat, Mellish, who stood nearest him, saw that the hair on his temples was grey. Lines of anxiety had come into his apparently youthful face as he had scraped his way along the wall.

"Good-night, all," he shouted back from the stairway.

OLD NUMBER EIGHTY-SIX.

John Saggart stood in a dark corner of the terminus, out of the rays of the glittering arc lamps, and watched engine Number Eighty-six. The engineer was oiling her, and the fireman, as he opened the furnace-door and shovelled in the coal, stood out like a red Rembrandt picture in the cab against the darkness beyond. As the engineer with his oil can went carefully around Number Eighty-six, John Saggart drew his sleeve across his eyes, and a gulp came up his throat. He knew every joint and bolt in that contrary old engine—the most cantankerous iron brute on the road—and yet, if rightly managed, one of the swiftest and most powerful machines the company had, notwithstanding the many improvements that had been put upon locomotives since old Eighty-six had left the foundry.

Saggart, as he stood there, thought of the seven years he had spent on the foot-board of old Eighty-six, and of the many tricks she had played him during that period. If, as the poet says, the very chains and the prisoner become friends through long association, it may be imagined how much of a man's affection goes out to a machine that he thoroughly understands and likes—a machine that is his daily companion for years, in danger and out of it. Number Eighty-six and John had been in many a close pinch together, and at this moment the man seemed to have forgotten that often the pinch was caused by the pure cussedness of Eighty-six herself, and he remembered only that she had bravely done her part several times when the situation was exceedingly serious.

The cry "All aboard" rang out and was echoed down from the high-arched roof of the great terminus, and John with a sigh turned from his contemplation of the engine, and went to take his seat in the car. It was a long train with many sleeping-cars at the end of it. The engineer had put away his oil-can, and had taken his place on the engine, standing ready to begin the long journey at the moment the signal was given.

John Saggart climbed into the smoking-carriage at the front part of the train. He found a place in one of the forward seats, and sank down into it with a vague feeling of uneasiness at being inside the coach instead of on the engine. He gazed out of the window and saw the glittering electric lights slide slowly behind, then, more quickly, the red, green, and white lights of the signal lamps, and finally there flickered swiftly past the brilliant constellation of city windows, showing that the town had not yet gone to bed. At last the flying train plunged into the country, and Saggart pressed his face against the cold glass of the window, unable to shake off his feeling of responsibility, although he knew there was another man at the throttle.

He was aroused from his reverie by a touch on the shoulder, and a curt request, "Tickets, please."

He pulled out of his pocket a pass, and turned to hand it to the conductor who stood there with a glittering, plated, and crystal lantern on his arm.

"Hello, John, is this you?" cried the conductor, as soon as he saw the face. "Hang it, man, you didn't need a pass in travelling with me."

"They gave it to me to take me home," said Saggart, a touch of sadness in his voice, "and I may as well use it as not. I don't want to get you into trouble."

"Oh, I'd risk the trouble," said the conductor, placing the lantern on the floor and taking his seat beside the engineer. "I heard about your worry to-day. It's too bad. If a man had got drunk at his post, as you and I have known 'em to do, it wouldn't have seemed so hard; but at its worst your case was only an error of judgment, and then nothing really happened. Old Eighty-six seems to have the habit of pulling herself through. I suppose you and she have been in worse fixes than that, with not a word said about it."

"Oh, yes," said John, "we've been in many a tight place together, but we won't be any more. It's rough, as you say. I've been fifteen years with the company, and seven on old Eighty-six, and at first it comes mighty hard. But I suppose I'll get used to it."

"Look here, John," said the conductor, lowering his voice to a confidential tone, "the president of the road is with us to-night; his private car is the last but one on the train. How would it do to speak to him? If you are afraid to tackle him, I'll put in a word for you in a minute, and tell him your side of the story."

John Saggart shook his head.

"It wouldn't do," he said; "he wouldn't overrule what one of his subordinates had done, unless there was serious injustice in the case. It's the new manager, you know. There's always trouble with a new manager. He sweeps clean. And I suppose that he thinks by 'bouncing' one of the oldest engineers on the road, he will scare the rest."

"Well, I don't think much of him between ourselves," said the conductor. "What do you think he has done to-night? He's put a new man on Eighty-six. A man from one of the branch lines who doesn't know the road. I doubt if he's ever been over the main line before. Now, it's an anxious enough time for me anyhow with a heavy train to take through, with the thermometer at zero, and the rails like glass, and I like to have a man in front that I can depend on."

"It's bad enough not to know the road," said John gloomily, "but it's worse not to know old Eighty-six. She's a brute if she takes a notion."

"I don't suppose there is another engine that could draw this train and keep her time," said the conductor.

"No! She'll do her work all right if you'll only humor her," admitted Saggart, who could not conceal his love for the engine even while he blamed her.

"Well," said the conductor, rising and picking up his lantern, "the man in front may be all right, but I would feel safer if you were further ahead than the smoker. I'm sorry I can't offer you a berth to-night, John, but we're full clear through to the rear lights. There isn't even a vacant upper on the train."

"Oh, it doesn't matter," said Saggart. "I couldn't sleep, anyhow. I'd rather sit here and look out of the window."

"Well, so long," said the conductor. "I'll drop in and see you as the night passes on."

Saggart lit his pipe and gazed out into darkness. He knew every inch of the road—all the up grades and the down grades and the levels. He knew it even better in the murkiest night than in the clearest day. Now and then the black bulk of a barn or a clump of trees showed for one moment against the sky, and Saggart would say to himself, "Now he should shut off an inch of steam," or, "Now he should throw her wide open." The train made few stops, but he saw that they were losing time. Eighty-six was sulking, very likely. Thinking of the engine turned his mind to his own fate. No man was of very much use in the world, after all, for the moment he steps down another is ready to stand in his place. The wise men in the city who had listened to his defence knew so well that an engine was merely a combination of iron and steel and brass, and that a given number of pounds of steam would get it over a given number of miles in a given number of hours, and they had smiled incredulously when he told them that an engine had her tantrums, and informed them that sometimes she had to be coddled up like any other female. Even when a man did his best there were occasions when nothing he could do would mollify her, and then there was sure to be trouble, although, he added, in his desire to be fair, she was always sorry for it afterward. Which remark, to his confusion, had turned the smile into a laugh.

He wondered what Eighty-six thought of the new man. Not much, evidently, for she was losing time, which she had no business to do on that section of the road. Still it might be the fault of the new man not knowing when to push her for all she was worth and when to ease up. All these things go to the making of time. But it was more than probable that old Eighty-six, like Gilpin's horse, was wondering more and more what thing upon her back had got. "He'll have trouble," muttered John to himself, "when she finds out."

The conductor came in again and sat down beside the engineer. He said nothing, but sat there sorting his tickets, while Saggart gazed out of the window. Suddenly the engineer sprang to his feet with his eyes wide open. The train was swaying from side to side and going at great speed.

The conductor looked up with a smile.

"Old Eighty-six," he said, "is evidently going to make up for lost time."

152

"She should be slowing down for crossing the G. & M. line," replied the engineer. "Good heavens!" he cried a moment after, "we've gone across the G. & M. track on the keen jump."

The conductor sprang to his feet. He knew the seriousness of such a thing. Even the fastest expresses must stop dead before crossing on the level the line of another railway. It is the law.

"Doesn't that fool in front know enough to stop at a crossing?"

"It isn't that," said Saggart. "He knows all right. Even the train boys know that. Old Eighty-six has taken the bit between her teeth. He can't stop her. Where do you pass No. 6 to-night?"

"At Pointsville."

"That's only six miles ahead," said the engineer; "and in five minutes at this rate we will be running on her time and on her rails. She's always late, and won't be on the side track. I must get to Eighty-six."

Saggart quickly made his way through the baggage-coach, climbed on the express car, and jumped on the coal of the tender. He cast his eye up the track and saw glimmering in the distance, like a faint wavering star, the headlight of No. 6. Looking down into the cab he realized the situation in a glance. The engineer, with fear in his face and beads of perspiration on his brow, was throwing his whole weight on the lever, the fireman helping him. Saggart leaped down to the floor of the cab.

"Stand aside," he shouted; and there was such a ring of confident command in his voice that both men instantly obeyed.

Saggart grasped the lever, and instead of trying to shut off steam flung it wide open. Number Eighty-six gave a quiver and a jump forward. "You old fiend!" muttered John between his teeth. Then he pushed the lever home, and it slid into place as if there had never been any impediment. The steam was shut off, but the lights of Pointsville flashed past them with the empty side-track on the left, and they were now flying along the single line of rails with the headlight of No. 6 growing brighter and brighter in front of them.

"Reverse her, reverse her!" cried the other engineer, with fear in his voice.

"Reverse nothing," said Saggart. "She'll slide ten miles if you do. Jump, if you're afraid."

The man from the branch line promptly jumped.

"Save yourself," said Saggart to the stoker; "there's bound to be a smash."

"I'll stick by you, Mr. Saggart," said the fireman, who knew him. But his hand trembled.

The air-brake was grinding the long train and sending a shiver of fear through every timber, but the rails were slippery with frost, and the speed of the train seemed as great as ever. At the right moment Saggart reversed the engine, and the sparks flew up from her great drivers like catharine wheels.

"Brace yourself," cried Saggart. "No. 6 is backing up, thank God!"

Next instant the crash came. Two headlights and two cow-catchers went to flinders, and the two trains stood there with horns locked, but no great damage done, except a shaking up for a lot of panic-stricken passengers.

The burly engineer of No. 6 jumped down and came forward, his mouth full of oaths.

"What the h—l do you mean by running in on our time like this? Hello, is that you, Saggart? I thought there was a new man on to-night. I didn't expect this from you."

"It's all right, Billy. It wasn't the new man's fault. He's back in the ditch with a broken leg, I should say, from the way he jumped. Old Eighty-six is to blame. She got on the rampage. Took advantage of the greenhorn."

The conductor came running up.

"How is it?" he cried.

"It's all right. Number Eighty-six got her nose broke, and served her right, that's all. Tell the passengers there's no danger, and get 'em on board. We're going to back up to Pointsville. Better send the brakesmen to pick up the other engineer. The ground's hard tonight, and he may be hurt."

"I'm going back to talk to the president," said the conductor emphatically. "He's in a condition of mind to listen to reason, judging from the glimpse I got of his face at the door of his car a moment ago. Either he re-instates you or I go gathering tickets on a street-car. This kind of thing is too exciting for my nerves."

The conductor's interview with the president of the road was apparently satisfactory, for old Number Eighty-six is trying to lead a better life under the guidance of John Saggart.

PLAYING WITH MARKED CARDS.

"I'm bothered about that young fellow," said Mellish early one morning, to the professional gambler, Pony Rowell.

"Why?"

"He comes here night after night, and he loses more than he can afford, I imagine. He has no income, so far as I can find out, except what he gets as salary, and it takes a mighty sight bigger salary than his to stand the strain he's putting on it."

"What is his business?"

"He is cashier in the Ninth National Bank. I don't know how much he gets, but it can't be enough to permit this sort of thing to go on."

Pony Rowell shrugged his shoulders.

"I don't think I would let it trouble me, if I were you, Mellish."

"Nevertheless it does. I have advised him to quit, but it is no use. If I tell the doorkeeper not to let him in here, he will merely go somewhere else where they are not so particular."

"I must confess I don't quite understand you, Mellish, long as I have known you. In your place, now, I would either give up keeping a gambling saloon or I would give up the moral reformation line of business. I wouldn't try to ride two horses of such different tempers at the same time."

"I've never tried to reform you, Pony," said Mellish, with reproach in his voice.

"No; I will give you credit for that much sense."

"It's all right with old stagers like you and me, Pony, but with a boy just beginning life, it is different. Now it struck me that you might be able to help me in this."

"Yes, I thought that was what you were leading up to," said Rowell, thrusting his hands deep in his trousers' pockets. "I'm no missionary, remember. What did you want me to do?"

"I wanted you to give him a sharp lesson. Couldn't you mark a pack of cards and get him to play high? Then, when you have taken all his ready money and landed him in debt to you so that he can't move, give him back his cash if he promises not to gamble again."

Rowell looked across at the subject of their conversation. "I don't think I would flatter him so much as to even stock the cards on him. I'll clean him out if you like. But it won't do any good, Mellish. Look at his eyes. The insanity of gambling is in them. I used to think if I had $100,000, I would quit. I'm old enough now to know that I wouldn't. I'd gamble if I had a million."

"I stopped after I was your age."

"Oh, yes, Mellish, you are the virtuous exception that proves the rule. You quit gambling the way the old woman kept tavern," and Rowell cast a glance over the busy room.

Mellish smiled somewhat grimly, then he sighed. "I wish I was out of it," he said. "But, anyhow, you think over what I've been talking about, and if you can see your way to giving him a sharp lesson I wish you would."

"All right I will, but merely to ease your tender conscience, Mellish. It's no use, I tell you. When the snake has bitten, the victim is doomed. Gambling isn't a simple thing like the opium habit."

Reggie Forme, the bank cashier, rose at last from the roulette table. He was flushed with success, for there was a considerable addition to the sum he had in his pockets when he sat down. He flattered himself that the result was due to the system he had elaborately studied out.

Nothing lures a man to destruction quicker than a system that can be mathematically demonstrated. It gives an air of business to gambling which is soothing to the conscience of a person brought up on statistics. The system generally works beautifully at first; then a cog slips and you are mangled in the machinery before you know where you are. As young Forme left the table he felt a hand on his shoulder, and looking around, met the impassive gaze of Pony Rowell.

"You're young at the business, I see," remarked the professional quietly.

"Why do you think that?" asked the youngster, coloring, for one likes to be taken for a veteran, especially when one is an amateur.

"Because you fool away your time at roulette. That is a game for boys and women. Have you nerve enough to play a real game?"

"What do you call a real game?"

"A game with cards in a private room for something bigger than half-dollar points."

"How big?"

"Depends on what capital you have. How much capital can you command?"

The cashier hesitated for a moment and his eyes fell from the steady light of Rowell's, which seemed to have an uncomfortable habit of looking into one's inmost soul.

"I can bring $1,000 here on Saturday night."

"All right. That will do as a starter. Is it an appointment then?"

"Yes, if you like. What time?"

"I generally get here pretty late, but I can make an exception in your case. What do you say to 10 o'clock?"

"That will suit me."

"Very well, then. Don't fool away any of your money or nerve until I come. You will need all you have of both."

The professional gambler and the amateur began their series of games a few minutes after ten in a little private room. The young man became more and more excited as the play went on. As for Pony, he was cool under any circumstances. Before an hour had passed the $1,000 was transferred from the possession of Forme into the pockets of the professional, and by midnight the younger man was another $1,000 in Rowell's debt.

"It isn't my practice," said Rowell slowly, "to play with a man unless he has the money in sight. I've made an exception in your case, as luck was against you, but I think this has gone far enough. You may bring me the $1,000 you owe any day next week. No particular hurry, you know."

The young fellow appeared to be dazed. He drew his hand across his brow and then said mechanically, as if he had just heard his opponent's remark:

"No hurry? All right. Next week. Certainly. I guess I'll go home now."

Forme went out, leaving Rowell idly shuffling the cards at the small table. The moment the young man had disappeared all Rowell's indolence vanished. He sprang up and put on his overcoat, then slipped out by the rear exit into the alley. He had made up his mind what Forme would do. Mentally he tracked him from the gambling rooms to the river and he even went so far as to believe he would take certain streets on his way thither. A gambler is nothing if not superstitious and so Rowell was not in the least surprised when he saw the young man emerge from the dark stairway, hesitate for a moment between the two directions open to him, and finally choose the one that the gambler expected him to take. The cold streets were deserted and so Rowell had more difficulty in following his late victim unperceived than he would have had earlier in the evening. Several times the older man thought the pursued had become aware of the pursuit, for Forme stopped and looked around him; once coming back and taking another street as if trying to double on the man who was following him.

Rowell began to realize the difficulty of the task he had set for himself, and as he had never had any faith in it anyhow, he began to feel uncomfortable and to curse the tender heart of Mellish. If the youngster got the idea into his head that he was followed he might succeed in giving his pursuer the slip, and then Rowell would find himself with the fool's death on his conscience, and what was to him infinitely worse, with a thousand dollars in his pocket that had been unfairly won. This thought made him curse Mellish afresh. It had been entirely against his own will that he had played with marked cards, but Mellish had insisted that they should take no chances, and the veteran knew too well the uncertainties of playing a fair game where a great object lesson was to be taught. It would make them look like two fools, Mellish had said, if Forme won the money. In answer to this Rowell had remarked that they were two fools anyhow, but he had finally succumbed to Mellish as the whole scheme was Mellish's. As Rowell thought bitterly of these things his attention was diverted from the very matter he had in hand. Few men can pursue a course of thought and a fellow-creature at the same time. He suddenly realized that young Forme had escaped him. Rowell stood alone in the dimly-lighted silent street and poured unuttered maledictions on his own stupidity. Suddenly a voice rang out from a dark doorway.

"What the devil are you following me for?"

"Oh, you're there, are you?" said Pony calmly.

"I'm here. Now what do you want of me? Aren't you satisfied with what you have done to-night?"

"Naturally not, or I wouldn't be fool-chasing at such an hour as this."

"Then you admit you have been following me?"

"I never denied it."

"What do you want of me? Do I belong to myself or do you think I belong to you, because I owe you some money?"

"I do not know, I am sure, to whom you belong," said Rowell with his slow drawl. "I suspect, however, that the city police, who seem to be scarce at this hour, have the first claim upon you. What do I want of you? I want to ask you a question. Where did you get the money you played with to-night?"

"It's none of your business."

"I presume not. But as there are no witnesses to this interesting conversation I will venture an opinion that you robbed the bank."

The young man took a step forward, but Pony stood his ground, using the interval to light another cigarette.

"I will also venture an opinion, Mr. Rowell, and say that the money came as honestly into my pocket as it did into yours."

"That wouldn't be saying much for it. I have the advantage of you, however, because the nine points are in my favor. I have possession."

"What are you following me for? To give me up?"

"You admit the robbery, then."

"I admit nothing."

"It won't be used against you. As I told you, there are no witnesses. It will pay you to be frank. Where did you get the money?"

"Where many another man gets it. Out of the bank."

"I thought so. Now, Forme, you are not such a fool as you look—or act. You know where all that sort of thing leads to. You haven't any chance. All the rules of the game are against you. You have no more show than you had against me to-night. Why not chuck it, before it is too late?"

"It is easy for you to talk like that when you have my money in your pocket."

"But that simply is another rule of the game. The money of a thief is bound to go into someone else's pocket. Whoever enjoys the cash ultimately, he never does. Now if you had the money in your pocket what would you do?"

"I would go back to Mellish's and have another try."

"I believe you," said Rowell with, for the first time, some cordiality in his voice. He recognized a kindred spirit in this young man. "Nevertheless it would be a foolish thing to do. You have two chances before you. You can become a sport as I am and spend your life in gambling rooms. Or you can become what is called a respectable business man. But you can't be both. In a very short time you will not have the choice. You will be found out and then you can only be what I am— probably not as successful as I have been. If you add bank robbery to your other accomplishments then you will go to prison or, what is perhaps worse, to Canada. Which career are you going to choose?"

"Come down to plain facts. What do you mean by all this talk? If I say I'll quit gambling do you mean that you will return to me the thousand dollars and call the other thousand square?"

"If you give me your word of honor that you will quit."

"And if I don't, what then?"

"Then on Monday I will hand over this money to the bank and advise them to look into your accounts."

"And suppose my accounts prove to be all right, what then?"

Rowell shrugged his shoulders. "In that remote possibility I will give the thousand dollars to you and play you another game for it."

"I see. Which means that you cheated to-night."

"If you like to put it that way."

"And what if I denounced you as a self-confessed cheat?"

"It wouldn't matter to me. I wouldn't take the trouble to deny it. Nobody would believe you."

"You're a cool hand, Pony, I admire your cheek. Still, you've got some silly elements in you."

"Oh, you mean my trying to reform you? Don't make any mistake about that. It is Mellish's idea, not mine. I don't believe in you for a moment."

The young man laughed. He reflected for a few seconds, then said: "I'll take your offer. You give me back the money and I will promise never to gamble again in any shape or form."

"You will return the cash to the bank, if you took it from there?"

"Certainly. I will put it back the first thing on Monday morning."

"Then here is your pile," said Rowell, handing him the roll of bills.

Forme took it eagerly and, standing where the light struck down upon him, counted the bills, while Rowell looked on silently with a cynical smile on his lips.

"Thank you," said the young man, "you're a good fellow, Rowell."

"I'm obliged for your good opinion. I hope you found the money correct?"

"Quite right," said Forme, flushing a little. "I hope you did not mind my counting it. Merely a business habit, you know."

"Well, stick to business habits, Mr. Forme. Good night."

Rowell walked briskly back to Mellish's. Forme walked toward the railway station and found that there was a train for Chicago at 4 in the morning. He had one clear day and part of another before he was missed, and as it turned out all trace of him was lost in the big city. The bank found about $6,000 missing. Two years after, news came that Forme had been shot dead in a gambling hall in Southern Texas.

"We are two first-class fools," said Rowell to Mellish, "and I for one don't feel proud of the episode, so we'll say nothing more about it. The gambling mania was in his blood. Gambling is not a vice; it is a disease, latent in all of us."

THE BRUISER'S COURTSHIP.

While the Northern Bruiser sat in the chair in his corner and was being fanned he resolved to finish the fight at the next round. The superior skill of his opponent was telling upon him, and although the Bruiser was a young man of immense strength, yet, up to that time, the alertness and dexterity of the Yorkshire Chicken had baffled him, and prevented him from landing one of his tremendous shoulder thrusts. But even though skill had checkmated strength up to this point, the Chicken had not entirely succeeded in defending himself, and was in a condition described by the yelling crowd as "groggy."

When time was called the Bruiser was speedily on his feet. His face did not present the repulsive appearance so visible on the countenance of his opponent, but the Bruiser had experience enough to know that the body blows received in this fight had had their effect on his wind and staying powers; and that although the Chicken presented an appalling appearance with his swollen lips and cheeks, and his eyes nearly closed, yet he was in better trim for continuing the battle than the Bruiser.

The Chicken came up to the mark less promptly than his big antagonist, but whether it was from weakness or lack of sight, he seemed uncertain in his movements, and the hearts of his backers sank as they saw him stagger rather than walk to his place.

Before the Chicken, as it were, fully waked up to the situation, the Bruiser lunged forward and planted a blow on his temple that would have broken the guard of a man who was in better condition than the Chicken. The Yorkshireman fell like a log, and lay where he fell. Then the Bruiser got a lesson which terrified him. A sickly ashen hue came over the purple face of the man on the ground. The Bruiser had expected some defence, and the terrible blow had been even more powerful than he intended. A shivering whisper went round the crowd, "He is killed," and instantly the silenced mob quietly scattered. It was every man for himself before the authorities took a hand in the game.

The Bruiser stood there swaying from side to side, his gaze fixed upon the prostrate man. He saw himself indicted and hanged for murder, and he swore that if the Chicken recovered he would never again enter the ring. This was a phase of prize-fighting that he had never before had experience of. On different occasions he had, it is true, knocked out his various opponents, and once or twice he had been knocked out himself; but the Chicken had fought so pluckily up to the last round that the Bruiser had put forth more of his tremendous strength than he had bargained for, and now the man's life hung on a thread.

The unconscious pugilist was carried to an adjoining room. Two physicians were in attendance upon him, and at first the reports were most gloomy, but towards daylight the Bruiser learned with relief that the chances were in favor of his opponent.

The Bruiser had been urged to fly, but he was a man of strong common sense, and he thoroughly understood the futility of flight. His face and his form were too well known all around the country. It would have been impossible for him to escape, even if he had tried to do so.

When the Yorkshire Chicken recovered, the Bruiser's friends laughed at his resolve to quit the ring, but they could not shake it. The money he had won in his last fight, together with what he had accumulated before— for he was a frugal man—was enough to keep him for the rest of his days, and he resolved to return to the Border town where he was born, and where doubtless his fame had preceded him.

He buckled his guineas in a belt around him, and with a stout stick in his hand he left London for the North. He was a strong and healthy young man, and had not given way to dissipation, as so many prizefighters had done before, and will again. He had a horror of a cramped and confined, seat in a stage coach. He loved the free air of the heights and the quiet stillness of the valleys.

It was in the days of highwaymen, and travelling by coach was not considered any too safe. The Bruiser was afraid of no man that lived, if he met him in the open with a stick in his hand, or with nature's weapons, but he feared the muzzle of a pistol held at his head in the dark by a man with a mask over his face. So he buckled his belt around him with all his worldly gear in gold, took his own almost forgotten name, Abel Trenchon, set his back to the sun and his face to the north wind, and journeyed on foot along the king's highway. He stopped at night in the wayside inns, taking up his quarters before the sun had set, and leaving them when it was broad daylight in the morning. He disputed his reckonings like a man who must needs count the pennies, and no one suspected the sturdy wayfarer of carrying a fortune around his body.

As his face turned toward the North his thought went to the Border town where he had spent his childhood. His father and mother were dead, and he doubted now if anyone there remembered him, or would have a welcome for him. Nevertheless no other spot on earth was so dear to him, and it had always been his intention, when he settled down and took a wife, to retire to the quiet little town.

The weather, at least, gave him a surly welcome. On the last day's tramp the wind howled and the rain beat in gusts against him, but he was a man who cared little for the tempest, and he bent his body to the blast, trudging sturdily on. It was evening when he began to recognize familiar objects by the wayside, and he was surprised to see how little change there had been in all the years he was away. He stopped at an inn for supper, and, having refreshed himself, resolved to break the rule he had made for himself throughout the journey. He would push on through the night, and sleep in his native village.

The storm became more pitiless as he proceeded, and he found himself sympathizing with those poor creatures who were compelled to be out in it, but he never gave a thought to himself.

It was nearly midnight when he saw the square church tower standing blackly out against the dark sky; and when he began to descend the valley, on the other side of which the town stood, a thrill of fear came over him, as he remembered what he had so long forgotten—that the valley was haunted, and was a particularly dangerous place about the hour of midnight. To divert his thoughts he then began to wonder who the woman was he would marry. She was doubtless now sleeping calmly in the village on the hill, quite unconscious of the approach of her lover and her husband. He could not conceal from himself the fact that he would be reckoned a good match when his wealth was known, for, excepting the Squire, he would probably be the richest man in the place. However, he resolved to be silent about his riches, so that the girl he married would little dream of the good fortune that awaited her. He laughed aloud as he thought of the pleasure he would have in telling his wife of her luck, but the laugh died on his lips as he saw, or thought he saw, something moving stealthily along the hedge.

He was now in the depth of the valley in a most lonesome and eerie spot. The huge trees on each side formed an arch over the roadway and partially sheltered it from the rain.

He stood in his tracks, grasped his stick with firmer hold, and shouted valiantly, "Who goes there?"

There was no answer, but in the silence which followed he thought he heard a woman's sob.

"Come out into the road," he cried, "or I shall fire."

His own fear of pistols was so great that he expected everyone else to be terrorized by the threat of using them; and yet he had never possessed nor carried a pistol in his life.

"Please—please don't fire," cried a trembling voice, from out the darkness. "I will do as you tell me." And so saying the figure moved out upon the road.

Trenchon peered at her through the darkness, but whether she was old or young he could not tell. Her voice seemed to indicate that she was young.

"Why, lass," said Trenchon, kindly, "what dost thou here at such an hour and in such a night?"

"Alas!" she cried, weeping; "my father turned me out, as he has often done before, but to-night is a bitter night, and I had nowhere to go, so I came here to be sheltered from the rain. He will be asleep ere long, and he sleeps soundly. I may perhaps steal in by a window, although sometimes he fastens them down."

"God's truth!" cried Trenchon, angrily. "Who is thy brute of a father?"

The girl hesitated, and then spoke as if to excuse him, but again Trenchon demanded his name.

"He is the blacksmith of the village, and Cameron is his name."

"I remember him," said Trenchon. "Is thy mother, then, dead?"

"Yes," answered the girl, weeping afresh. "She has been dead these five years."

"I knew her when I was a boy," said Trenchon. "Thy father also, and many a grudge I owe him, although I had forgotten about them. Still, I doubt not but as a boy I was as much in fault as he, although he was harsh to all of us, and now it seems he is harsh to thee. My name is Trenchon. I doubt if any in the village now remember me, although, perhaps, they may have heard of me from London," he said, with some pride, and a hope that the girl would confirm his thoughts. But she shook her head.

"I have never heard thy name," she said.

Trenchon sighed. This, then, was fame!

"Ah, well!" he cried, "that matters not; they shall hear more of me later. I will go with thee to thy father's house and demand for thee admittance and decent usage."

But the girl shrank back. "Oh, no, no!" she cried; "that will never do. My father is a hard man to cross. There are none in the village who dare contend with him."

"That is as it may be," said Trenchon, with easy confidence. "I, for one, fear him not. Come, lass, with me, and see if I cannot, after all these years, pick out thy father's dwelling. Come, I say, thou must not longer tarry here; the rain is coming on afresh, and these trees, thick as they are, form scant protection. It is outrageous that thou should wander in this storm, while

168

thy brutal father lies in shelter. Nay, do not fear harm for either thee or me; and as for him, he shall not suffer if thou but wish it so." And, drawing the girl's hand through his arm, he took her reluctantly with him, and without direction from her soon stood before the blacksmith's house.

"You see," he said, triumphantly, "I knew the place, and yet I have not seen the town for years."

Trenchon rapped soundly on the oaken door with his heavy stick, and the blows re-echoed through the silent house. The girl shrank timidly behind him, and would have fled, but that he held her firmly by the wrist.

"Nay, nay," he said: "believe me there is naught to fear. I will see that thou art not ill-used."

As he spoke the window above was thrown up, and a string of fearful oaths greeted the two, whereat the girl once more tried to release her imprisoned wrist, but Trenchon held it lightly, though with a grip like steel.

The stout old man thrust his head through the open window.

"God's blight on thee!" he cried, "thou pair of fools who wish to wed so much that ye venture out in such a night as this. Well, have your way, and let me have my rest. In the name of the law of Scotland I pronounce ye man and wife. There, that will bind two fools together as strongly as if the Archbishop spoke the words. Place thou the money on the steps. I warrant none will venture to touch it when it belongs to me." And with that he closed the window.

"Is he raving mad or drunk?" cried Trenchon.

The girl gave a wailing cry. "Alas! alas!" she said; "he is neither. He is so used to marrying folk who come from England across the Border that he thinks not it his daughter who came with thee, but two who wished to wed. They come at all hours of the night and day, and he has married us. I am thy wife."

The astonished man dropped her wrist, and she put her hands before her eyes and wept.

"Married!" cried Trenchon. "We two married!"

He looked with interest at the girl, but in the darkness could see nothing of her. The unheeded rain pelted on them both.

"Hast thou"—he hesitated—"hast thou some other lover, since you weep?"

The girl shook her head. "No one," she said, "comes near us. They fear my father."

"Then, if this be true, why dost thou weep? I am not considered so bad a fellow."

"I weep not for myself, but for thee, who through the kindness of thy heart hast been led into this trap. Believe me, it was not my intention."

"Judging from thy voice, my girl, and if thou favorest thy mother, as I think, whom I remember well, this is a trap that I shall make little effort to get my foot out of. But thou art dripping, and I stand chattering here. Once more I will arouse my father-in-law."

So saying, he stoutly rapped again with his stick upon the door.

Once more the window was pushed up, and again the angry head appeared.

"Get you gone!" cried the maddened blacksmith, but before he could say anything further Trenchon cried out:

"It is thy daughter here who waits. Open the door, thou limb of hell, or I will burst it in and cast thee out as thou hast done thy daughter."

The blacksmith, who had never in his life been spoken to in tones or words like these, was so amazed that he could neither speak nor act, but one stout kick against the door so shook the fabric that he speedily saw another such would break into his domicile; so, leaving the window open that his curses might the better reach them, the blacksmith came down and threw the barrier from the door, flinging it open and standing on the threshold so as to bar all ingress.

170

"Out of the way," cried Trenchon, roughly placing his hand on the other's breast with apparent lightness, but with a push that sent him staggering into the room.

The young man pulled the girl in after him and closed the door.

"Thou knowest the way," he whispered. "Strike thou a light."

The trembling girl lit a candle, and as it shone upon her face Trenchon gave a deep sigh of happiness and relief. No girl in the village could be more fair.

The blacksmith stood, his fingers clenched with rage; but he looked with hesitation and respect upon the burly form of the prizefighter. Yet the old man did not flinch.

"Throw aside thy stick," he cried, "or wait until I can get me another."

Trenchon flung his stick into the corner.

"Oh! oh!" cried the girl, clasping her hands. "You must not fight." But she appealed to her husband and not to her father, which caused a glow of satisfaction to rise from the heart of the young man.

"Get thee out of this house," cried her father, fiercely, turning upon her.

"Talk not thus to my wife," said Trenchon, advancing upon him.

"Thy wife?" cried the blacksmith, in amaze.

"My wife," repeated the young man with emphasis. "They tell me, blacksmith, that thou art strong. That thou art brutal I know, but thy strength I doubt. Come to me and test it."

The old man sprang upon him, and the Bruiser caught him by the elbows and held him helpless as a child. He pressed him up against the wall, pushed his wrists together, and clasped them both in his one gigantic hand. Then, placing the other on the blacksmith's shoulder, he put his weight upon him, and the blacksmith, cursing but helpless, sank upon his knees.

"Now, thou hardened sinner," cried the Bruiser, bending over him. "Beg from thy daughter on thy knees for a night's shelter in this house. Beg, or I will thrust thy craven face against the floor."

The girl clung to her newly-found husband, and entreated him not to hurt her father.

"I shall not hurt him if he do but speak. If he has naught but curses on his lips, why then those lips must kiss the flags that are beneath him. Speak out, blacksmith: what hast thou to say?"

"I beg for shelter," said the conquered man.

Instantly the Bruiser released him.

"Get thee to bed," he said, and the old man slunk away.

"Wife," said Abel Trenchon, opening his arms, "I have come all the way from London for thee. I knew not then what drew me north, but now I know that One wiser than me led my steps hither. As far as erring man may promise I do promise thee that thou shalt ne'er regret being cast out this night into the storm."

THE RAID ON MELLISH.

Some newspapers differ from others. One peculiarity about the Argus was the frequency with which it changed its men. Managing editors came who were going to revolutionize the world and incidentally the Argus, but they were in the habit of disappearing to give place to others who also disappeared. Newspaper men in that part of the country never considered themselves full-fledged unless they had had a turn at managing the Argus. If you asked who was at the head of the Argus the answer would very likely be: "Well, So-and-so was managing it this morning. I don't know who is running it this afternoon."

Perhaps the most weird period in the history of the Argus was when the owners imported a crank from Pittsburg and put him in as local editor, over the heads of the city staff. His name was McCrasky, christened Angus or Archie, I forget which, at this period of time. In fact, his Christian name was always a moot point; some of the reporters saying it was Angus and others Archie, no one having the courage to ask him. Anyhow, he signed himself A. McCrasky. He was a good man, which was rather an oddity on the staff, and puzzled the reporters not a little. Most of his predecessors had differed much from each other, but they were all alike in one thing, and that was profanity. They expressed disapproval in language that made the hardened printers' towel in the composing room shrink.

McCrasky's great point was that the local pages of the paper should have a strong moral influence on the community. He knocked the sporting editor speechless by telling him that they would have no more reports of prize-fights. Poor Murren went back to the local room, sat down at his table and buried his head in his hands. Every man on a local staff naturally thinks the paper is published mainly to give his department a show, and Murren considered a fight to a finish as being of more real importance to the world than a presidential election. The rest of the boys tried to cheer him up. "A fine state of things," said Murren bitterly. "Think of the scrap next week between the California Duffer and Pigeon Billy and no report of it in the Argus!

Imagine the walk- over for the other papers. What in thunder does he think people want to read?"

But there was another surprise in store for the boys. McCrasky assembled them all in his room and held forth to them. He suddenly sprung a question on the criminal reporter—so suddenly that Thompson, taken unawares, almost spoke the truth.

"Do you know of any gambling houses in this city?"

Thompson caught his breath and glanced quickly at Murren.

"No," he said at last. "I don't, but perhaps the religious editor does. Better ask him."

The religious editor smiled and removed his corn-cob pipe.

"There aren't any," he said. "Didn't you know it was against the law to keep a gambling house in this state? Yes, sir!" Then he put his corn- cob pipe back in its place.

McCrasky was pleased to see that his young men knew so little of the wickedness of a great city; nevertheless he was there to give them some information, so he said quietly:

"Certainly it is against the law; but many things that are against the law flourish in a city like this. Now I want you to find out before the week is past how many gambling houses there are and where they are located. When you are sure of your facts we will organize a raid and the news will very likely be exclusive, for it will be late at night and the other papers may not hear of it."

"Suppose," said the religious editor, with a twinkle in his eye, as he again removed his corn-cob, "that—assuming such places to exist—you found some representatives of the other papers there? They are a bad lot, the fellows on the other papers."

"If they are there," said the local editor, "they will go to prison."

"They won't mind that, if they can write something about it," said Murren gloomily. In his opinion the Argus was going to the dogs.

"Now, Thompson," said McCrasky, "you as criminal reporter must know a lot of men who can give you particulars for a first-rate article on the evils of gambling. Get it ready for Saturday's paper—a column and a half, with scare heads. We must work up public opinion."

When the boys got back into the local room again, Murren sat with his head in his hands, while Thompson leaned back in his chair and laughed.

"Work up public opinion," he said. "Mac had better work up his own knowledge of the city streets, and not put Bolder avenue in the East End, as he did this morning."

The religious editor was helping himself to tobacco from Murren's drawer. "Are you going to put Mellish on his guard?" he asked Thompson.

"I don't just know what I'm going to do," said Thompson; "are you?"

"I'll think about it," replied the R. E. "Beastly poor tobacco, this of yours, Murren. Why don't you buy cut plug?"

"You're not compelled to smoke it," said the sporting editor, without raising his head.

"I am when mine is out, and the other fellows keep their drawers locked."

Thompson dropped in on Mellish, the keeper of the swell gambling rooms, to consult with him on the article for Saturday's paper. Mellish took a great interest in it, and thought it would do good. He willingly gave Thompson several instances where the vice had led to ruin of promising young men.

"All men gamble in some way or another," said Mellish meditatively. "Some take it one way and some another. It is inherent in human nature, like original sin. The beginning of every business is a gamble. If I had $30,000 I would rather run my chance of doubling it at these tables here than I would, for instance, by starting a new newspaper or putting it on wheat or in railway stocks. Take a land boom, for instance, such as there was in California or at Winnipeg—the difference between putting your money in a thing like that or going in for legitimate gambling is that, in the one case, you are sure to lose your cash, while in the other you have a chance of winning some. I hold that all kinds of gambling are bad, unless a man can easily afford to lose what he stakes. The trouble is that gambling affects some people like liquor. I knew a man once who——" but you can read the whole article if you turn up the back numbers of the Argus.

Thompson told Mellish about McCrasky. Mellish was much interested, and said he would like to meet the local editor. He thought the papers should take more interest in the suppression of gambling dens than they did, and for his part he said he would like to see them all stopped, his own included. "Of course," he added, "I could shut up my shop, but it would simply mean that someone else would open another, and I don't think any man ever ran such a place fairer than I do."

McCrasky called on the chief of police, and introduced himself as the local editor of the Argus.

"Oh," said the chief, "has Gorman gone, then?"

"I don't know about Gorman," said McCrasky; "the man I succeeded was Finnigan. I believe he is in Cincinnati now."

When the chief learned the purport of the local editor's visit he became very official and somewhat taciturn. He presumed that there were gambling houses in the city. If there were, they were very quiet and no complaints ever reached his ears. There were many things, he said, that it was impossible to suppress, and the result of attempted suppression was to drive the evil deeper down. He seemed to be in favor rather of regulating, than of attempting the impossible; still, if McCrasky brought him undoubted evidence that a gambling house was in operation, he would consider it his duty to make a raid on it. He advised McCrasky to go very cautiously about it, as the gamblers had doubtless many friends who would give a tip and so frustrate a raid, perhaps letting somebody in for damages. McCrasky said he would be careful.

Chance played into the hands of McCrasky and "blew in" on him a man who little recked what he was doing when he entered the local editor's room. Gus Hammerly, sport and man-about-town, dropped into the Argus office late one night to bring news of an "event" to the sporting editor. He knew his way about in the office, and, finding Murren was not in, he left the item on his table. Then he wandered into the local editor's room. The newspaper boys all liked Hammerly, and many a good item they got from him. They never gave him away, and he saw that they never got left, as the vernacular is.

"Good-evening. You're the new local editor, I take it. I've just left a little item for Murren, I suppose he's not in from the wrestle yet. My name's Hammerly. All the boys know me and I've known in my time fourteen of your predecessors, so I may as well know you. You're from Pittsburg, I hear."

"Yes. Sit down, Mr. Hammerly. Do you know Pittsburg at all?"

"Oh, yes. Borden, who keeps the gambling den on X street, is an old friend of mine. Do you happen to know how old Borden's getting along?"

"Yes, his place was raided and closed up by the police."

"That's just the old man's luck. Same thing in Kansas City."

"By the way, Mr. Hammerly, do you know of any gambling houses in this city?"

"Why, bless you, haven't the boys taken you round yet? Well, now, that's inhospitable. Mellish's is the best place in town. I'm going up there now. If you come along with me I'll give you the knock-down at the door and you'll have no trouble after that."

"I'll go with you," said McCrasky, reaching for his hat, and so the innocent Hammerly led the lamb into the lion's den.

McCrasky, unaccustomed to the sight, was somewhat bewildered with the rapidity of the play. There was a sort of semicircular table, around the outside rim of which were sitting as many men as could be comfortably placed there. A man at the inside of the table handled the cards. He flicked out one to each player, face downward, with an expertness and speed that dazzled McCrasky. Next he dealt out one to each player face upward and people put sums of money on the table beside their cards, after looking at them. There was another deal and so on, but the stranger found it impossible to understand or follow the game. He saw money being raked in and paid out rapidly and over the whole affair was a solemn decorum that he had not been prepared for. He had expected fierce oaths and the drawing of revolvers.

"Here, Mellish," said the innocent Hammerly, "let me introduce you to the new local editor of the Argus. I didn't catch your name," he said in a whisper.

"My name's McCrasky."

"Mr. McCrasky; Mr. Mellish. Mellish is proprietor here and you'll find him a first-rate fellow."

"I am pleased to meet you," said Mellish quietly; "any friend of Hammerly's is welcome. Make yourself at home."

Edging away from the two, Mellish said in a quick whisper to Sotty, the bartender: "Go and tell the doorkeeper to warn Thompson, or any of the rest of the Argus boys, that their boss is in here."

At 12 o'clock that night the local editor sat in his room. "Is that you, Thompson?" he shouted, as he heard a step.

"Yes, sir;" answered Thompson, coming into the presence.

"Shut the door, Thompson. Now I have a big thing on for to-night, but it must be done quietly. I've unearthed a gambling den in full blast. It will be raided to-night at 2 o'clock. I want you to be on the ground with Murren; will you need anybody else?"

"Depends on how much you wish to make of it."

"I want to make it the feature of to-morrow's paper. I think we three can manage, but bring some of the rest if you like. The place is run by a man named Mellish. Now, if you boys kept your eyes open you would know more of what is going on in your own city than you do."

"We haven't all had the advantage of metropolitan training," said Thompson humbly.

"I will go there with the police. You and Murren had better be on the ground, but don't go too soon, and don't make yourselves conspicuous or they might take alarm. Here is the address. You had better take it down."

"Oh, I'll find the place all——" Then Thompson thought a moment and pulled himself together. "Thanks," he said, carefully noting down the street and number.

The detachment of police drew up in front of the place a few minutes before 2 o'clock. The streets were deserted, and so silent were the blue coats that the footsteps of a belated wayfarer sounded sharply in the night air from the stone pavement of a distant avenue.

"Are you sure," said McCrasky to the man in charge of the police, "that there is not a private entrance somewhere?"

"Certainly there is," was the impatient reply: "Sergeant McCollum and four men are stationed in the alley behind. We know our business, sir."

McCrasky thought this was a snub, and he was right. He looked around in the darkness for his reporters. He found them standing together in a doorway on the opposite side of the street.

"Been here long?" he whispered.

Murren was gloomy and did not answer. The religious editor removed his corn-cob and said briefly; "About ten minutes, sir." Thompson was gazing with interest at the dark building across the way.

"You've seen nobody come out?"

"Nobody. On the contrary, about half a dozen have gone up that stairway."

"Is that the place, sir?" asked Thompson with the lamb-like innocence of the criminal reporter.

"Yes, upstairs there."

"What did I tell you?" said the religious editor. "Thompson insisted it was next door."

"Come along," said McCrasky, "the police are moving at last."

A big bell in the neighborhood solemnly struck two slow strokes, and all over the city the hour sounded in various degrees of tone and speed. A whistle rang out and was distantly answered. The police moved quickly and quietly up the stairway.

"Have you tickets, gentlemen," asked the man at the door politely; "this is a private assembly."

"The police," said the sergeant shortly, "stand aside."

If the police were astonished at the sight which met their gaze, their faces did not show it. But McCrasky had not such control over his features and he looked dumbfounded. The room was the same, undoubtedly, but there was not the vestige of a card to be seen. There were no tables, and even the bar had disappeared. The chairs were nicely arranged and most of them were occupied. At the further end of the room Pony Rowell stood on a platform or on a box or some elevation, and his pale, earnest face was lighted up with the enthusiasm of the public speaker. He was saying: "On the purity of the ballot, gentlemen, depends the very life of the republic. That every man should be permitted, without interference or intimidation, to cast his vote, and that every vote so cast should be honestly counted is, I take it, the desire of all who now listen to my words." (Great applause, during which Pony took a sip from a glass that may have contained water.)

The police had come in so quietly that no one, apparently, had noticed their entrance, except that good man Mellish, who hurried forward to welcome the intruders.

"Will you take a seat?" he asked. "We are having a little political talk from Mr. Rowell, sergeant."

"Rather an unusual hour, Mr. Mellish," said the sergeant grimly.

"It is a little late," admitted Mellish, as if the idea had not occurred to him before.

The police who had come in by the back entrance appeared at the other end of the room and it was evident that Rowell's oration had come to an untimely end. Pony looked grieved and hurt, but said nothing.

"We will have to search the premises, Mr. Mellish," said the sergeant.

Mellish gave them every assistance, but nothing was found.

As the four men walked back together to the Argus office, McCrasky was very indignant.

"We will expose the police to-morrow," he said. "They evidently gave Mellish the tip."

"I don't think so," said Thompson. "We will say nothing about it."

"You forget yourself, Mr. Thompson. It rests with me to say what shall go on the local page. Not with you."

"I don't forget myself," answered Thompson sadly; "I've just remembered myself. The Directors of the Argus appointed me local editor yesterday. Didn't they tell you about it? That's just like them. They forgot to mention the fact to Corbin that he had been superseded and the manager went off fishing after appointing Jonsey local editor, so that for a week we had two local editors, each one countermanding the orders of the other. It was an awful week. You remember it, Murren?" Murren's groan seemed to indicate that his recollection of the exciting time was not a pleasant memory.

"In case of doubt," murmured the religious editor, this time without removing his corn-cob, "obey the orders of the new man where the Argus is concerned. Thompson, old man, I'm wid you. When did the blow fall?"

"Yesterday afternoon," said Thompson, almost with a sob; "I'll be dismissed within a month, so I am rather sorry. I liked working on the Argus—as a reporter. I never looked for such ill luck as promotion. But we all have our troubles, haven't we, Mac?"

McCrasky did not answer. He is now connected with some paper in Texas.

STRIKING BACK.

George Streeter was in Paris, because he hoped and expected to meet Alfred Davison there. He knew that Davison was going to be in Paris for at least a fortnight, and he had a particular reason for wishing to come across him in the streets of that city rather than in the streets of London.

Streeter was a young author who had published several books, and who was getting along as well as could be expected, until suddenly he met a check. The check was only a check as far as his own self-esteem was concerned; for it did not in the least retard the sale of his latest book, but rather appeared to increase it. The check was unexpected, for where he had looked for a caress, he received a blow. The blow was so well placed, and so vigorous, that at first it stunned him. Then he became unreasonably angry. He resolved to strike back.

The review of his book in the Argus was vigorously severe, and perhaps what maddened him more than anything else was the fact that, in spite of his self-esteem he realized the truth of the criticism. If his books had been less successful, or if he had been newer as an author, he might possibly have set himself out to profit by the keen thrusts given him by the Argus. He might have remembered that although Tennyson struck back at Christopher North, calling him rusty, crusty, and musty, yet the poet eliminated from later editions all blemishes which musty Christopher had pointed out.

Streeter resolved to strike back with something more tangible than a sarcastic verse. He quite admitted, even to himself, that a critic had every right to criticise—that was what he was for—but he claimed that a man who pretended to be an author's friend and who praised his books to his face, had no right to go behind his back and pen a criticism so scathing as that which appeared in the Argus: for Streeter knew that Alfred Davison had written the criticism in the Argus, and Davison had posed as his friend; and had pretended as well, that he had a great admiration for Streeter's books.

As Streeter walked down the Boulevard des Italiens, he saw, seated in front of a café, the man whom he hoped to meet: and furthermore, he was pleased to see that the man had a friend with him. The recognition of author and critic was mutual.

"Hallo, Streeter," cried Davison; "when did you come over?"

"I left London yesterday," answered Streeter.

"Then sit down and have something with us," said Davison, cordially. "Streeter, this is my friend Harmon. He is an exile and a resident in Paris, and, consequently, likes to meet his countrymen."

"In that case," said Streeter, "he is probably well acquainted with the customs of the place?"

"Rather!" returned Davison; "he has become so much of a Frenchman—he has been so contaminated, if I may put it that way—that I believe quite recently he was either principal or second in a duel. By the way, which was it, Harmon?"

"Merely a second," answered the other.

"I don't believe in duelling myself," continued Davison: "it seems to me an idiotic custom, and so futile."

"I don't agree with you," replied Streeter, curtly; "there is no reason why a duel should be futile, and there seem to be many reasons why a duel might be fought. There are many things, worse than crimes, which exist in all countries, and for which there is no remedy except calling a man out; misdemeanors, if I may so term them, that the law takes no cognisance of; treachery, for instance;—a person pretending to be a man's friend, and then the first chance he gets, stabbing him in the back."

Harmon nodded his approval of these sentiments, while Davison said jauntily:

"Oh, I don't know about that! It seems to me these things, which I suppose undoubtedly exist, should not be made important by taking much notice of them. What will you have to drink, Streeter?"

"Bring me a liqueur of brandy," said Streeter to the garçon who stood ready to take the order.

When the waiter returned with a small glass, into which he poured the brandy with the deftness of a Frenchman, filling it so that not a drop more could be added, and yet without allowing the glass to overflow, Streeter pulled out his purse.

"No, no!" cried Davison; "you are not going to pay for this—you are drinking with me."

"I pay for my own drinks," said Streeter, surlily.

"Not when I invite you to drink with me," protested the critic. "I pay for this brandy."

"Very well, take it, then!" said Streeter, picking up the little glass and dashing the contents in the face of Davison.

Davison took out his handkerchief.

"What the devil do you mean by that, Streeter?" he asked, as the color mounted to his brow.

Streeter took out his card and pencilled a word or two on the pasteboard.

"There," he said, "is my Paris address. If you do not know what I mean by that, ask your friend here; he will inform you."

And with that the novelist arose, bowed to the two, and departed.

When he returned to his hotel, after a stroll along the brilliantly- lighted Boulevards, he found waiting for him Mr. Harmon and a Frenchman.

"I had no idea you would come so soon," said Streeter, "otherwise I would not have kept you waiting."

"It does not matter," replied Harmon; "we have not waited long. Affairs of this kind require prompt action. An insult lasts but twenty-four hours, and my friend and principal has no desire to put you to the inconvenience of repeating your action of this evening. We are taking it for granted that you have a friend prepared to act for you; for your conduct appeared to be premeditated."

"You are quite right," answered Streeter; "I have two friends to whom I shall be pleased to introduce you. Come this way, if you will be so kind."

The preliminaries were speedily arranged, and the meeting was to take place next morning at daylight, with pistols.

Now that everything was settled, the prospect did not look quite so pleasant to Streeter as it had done when he left London. Davison had asked for no explanation; but that, of course, could be accounted for, because this critical sneak must be well aware of the reason for the insult. Still, Streeter had rather expected that he would perhaps have simulated ignorance, and on receiving enlightenment might have avoided a meeting to apologizing.

Anyhow, Streeter resolved to make a night of it. He left his friends to arrange for a carriage, and see to all that was necessary, while he donned his war-paint and departed for a gathering to which he had been invited, and where he was to meet many of his countrymen and countrywomen, in a fashionable part of Paris.

His hostess appeared to be overjoyed at seeing him.

"You are so late," she said, "that I was afraid something had occurred to keep you from coming altogether."

"Nothing could have prevented me from coming," said Streeter, gallantly, "where Mrs. Woodford is hostess!"

"Oh, that is very nice of you, Mr. Streeter!" answered the lady; "but I must not stand here talking with you, for I have promised to introduce you to Miss Neville, who wishes very much to meet you. She is a great admirer of yours, and has read all your books."

"There are not very many of them," said Streeter, with a laugh; "and such as they are, I hope Miss Neville thinks more of them than I do myself."

"Oh, we all know how modest authors are!" replied his hostess, leading him away to be introduced.

Miss Neville was young and pretty, and she was evidently pleased to meet the rising young author.

"I have long wanted to see you," she said, "to have a talk with you about your books."

"You are very kind," said Streeter, "but perhaps we might choose something more profitable to talk about?"

"I am not so sure of that. Doubtless you have been accustomed to hear only the nice things people say about you. That is the misfortune of many authors."

"It is a misfortune," answered Streeter.

"What a writer needs is somebody to tell him the truth."

"Ah!" said Miss Neville, "that is another thing I am not so sure about. Mrs. Woodford has told you, I suppose, that I have read all your books? Did she add that I detested them?"

Even Streeter was not able to conceal the fact that this remark caused him some surprise. He laughed uneasily, and said:

"On the contrary, Mrs. Woodford led me to believe that you had liked them."

The girl leaned back in her chair, and looked at him with half-closed eyes.

"Of course," she said, "Mrs. Woodford does not know. It is not likely that I would tell her I detested your books while I asked for an introduction to you. She took it for granted that I meant to say pleasant things to you, whereas I had made up my mind to do the exact reverse. No one would be more shocked than Mrs. Woodford—unless, perhaps, it is yourself—if she knew I was going to speak frankly with you."

"I am not shocked," said the young man, seriously; "I recognize that there are many things in my books that are blemishes."

"Of course you don't mean that," said the frank young woman; "because if you did you would not repeat the faults in book after book."

"A man can but do his best," said Streeter, getting annoyed in spite of himself, for no man takes kindly to the candid friend. "A man can but do his best, as Hubert said, whose grandsire drew a longbow at Hastings."

"Yes," returned Miss Neville, "a man can but do his best, although we should remember that the man who said that, said it just before he was defeated. What I feel is that you are not doing your best, and that you will not do your best until some objectionable person like myself has a good serious talk with you."

"Begin the serious talk," said Streeter; "I am ready and eager to listen."

"Did you read the review of your latest book which appeared in the Argus?"

"Did I?" said Streeter, somewhat startled—the thought of the meeting that was so close, which he had forgotten for the moment, flashing over him. "Yes, I did; and I had the pleasure of meeting the person who wrote it this evening."

Miss Neville almost jumped in her chair.

"Oh, I did not intend you to know that!" she said. "Who told you? How did you find out that I wrote reviews for the Argus?"

"You!" cried Streeter, astonished in his turn. "Do you mean to say that you wrote that review?"

Miss Neville sank back in her chair with a sigh.

"There!" she said, "my impetuosity has, as the Americans say, given me away. After all, you did not know I was the writer!"

"I thought Davison was the writer. I had it on the very best authority."

"Poor Davison!" said Miss Neville, laughing, "why, he is one of the best and staunchest friends you have: and so am I, for that matter— indeed, I am even more your friend than Mr. Davison; for I think you can do good work, while Mr. Davison is foolish enough to believe you are doing it."

At this point in the conversation Streeter looked hurriedly at his watch.

"Ah! I see," said Miss Neville; "this conversation is not to your taste. You are going to plead an appointment—as if anyone could have an appointment at this hour in the morning!"

"Nevertheless," said Streeter, "I have; and I must bid you good-bye. But I assure you that my eyes have been opened, and that I have learned a lesson to-night which I will not soon forget. I hope I may have the pleasure of meeting you again, and continuing this conversation. Perhaps some time I may tell you why I have to leave."

Streeter found his friends waiting for him. He knew it was no use trying to see Davison before the meeting. There was a long drive ahead of them, and it was grey daylight when they reached the ground, where they found the other party waiting.

Each man took his place and the pistol that was handed to him. When the word "Fire!" was given, Streeter dropped his hand to his side. Davison stood with his pistol still pointed, but he did not fire.

"Why don't you shoot, George?" said Davison.

Harmon, at this point, rebuked his principal, and said he must have no communication with the other except through a second.

"Oh!" said Davison, impatiently, "I don't pretend to know the rules of this idiotic game!"

Streeter stepped forward.

"I merely wished to give you the opportunity of firing at me if you cared to do so," he said; "and now I desire to apologize for my action at the café. I may say that what I did was done under a misapprehension. Anything that I can do to make reparation I am willing to do."

188

"Oh, that's all right!" said Davison; "nothing more need be said. I am perfectly satisfied. Let us get back to the city; I find it somewhat chilly out here."

"And yet," said Harmon, with a sigh, "Englishmen have the cheek to talk of the futility of French duels!"

CRANDALL'S CHOICE.

John Crandall sat at his office desk and thought the situation over. Everybody had gone and he was in the office alone. Crandall was rather tired and a little sleepy, so he was inclined to take a gloomy view of things. Not that there was anything wrong with his business; in fact, it was in a first-rate condition so far as it went, but it did not go far enough; that was what John thought as he brooded over his affairs. He was making money, of course, but the trouble was that he was not making it fast enough.

As he thought of these things John gradually and imperceptibly went to sleep, and while he slept he dreamt a dream. It would be quite easy to pretend that the two persons who came to him in the vision, actually entered the office and that he thought them regular customers or something of that sort, while at the end of the story, when everybody was bewildered, the whole matter might be explained by announcing the fact that it was all a dream, but this account being a true and honest one, no such artifice will be used and at the very beginning the admission is made that John was the victim of a vision.

In this dream two very beautiful ladies approached him. One was richly dressed and wore the most dazzling jewelry. The other was clad in plain attire. At first, the dreaming Mr. Crandall thought, or dreamt he thought, that the richly dressed one was the prettier. She was certainly very attractive, but, as she came closer, John imagined that much of her beauty was artificial. He said to himself that she painted artistically perhaps, but at any rate she laid it on rather thick.

About the other there was no question. She was a beauty, and what loveliness she possessed was due to the bounties of Providence and not to the assistance of the chemist. She was the first to speak.

"Mr. Crandall," she said, in the sweetest of voices, "we have come here together so that you may choose between us. Which one will you have?"

"Bless me," said Crandall, so much surprised at the unblushing proposal that he nearly awoke himself, "bless me, don't you know that I am married?"

"Oh, that doesn't matter," answered the fair young lady, with the divinest of smiles.

"Doesn't it?" said Mr. Crandall. "If you had the pleasure of meeting Mrs. Crandall I think you would find that it did—very much indeed."

"But we are not mortals; we are spirits."

"Oh, are you? Well, of course that makes a difference," replied Mr. Crandall much relieved, for he began to fear from the turn the conversation had taken that he was in the presence of two writers of modern novels.

"This lady," continued the first speaker, "is the spirit of wealth. If you choose her you will be a very rich man before you die."

"Oh, ho!" cried Crandall. "Are you sure of that?"

"Quite certain."

"Well, then I won't be long making my choice. I choose her, of course."

"But you don't know who I am. Perhaps when you know, you may wish to reverse your decision."

"I suppose you are the spirit of power or of fame or something of that sort. I am not an ambitious person; money is good enough for me."

"No, I am the spirit of health. Think well before you make your choice. Many have rejected me, and afterwards, have offered all their possessions fruitlessly, hoping to lure me to them."

"Ah," said Mr. Crandall, with some hesitation. "You are a very pleasant young person to have around the house. But why cannot I have both of you? How does that strike you?"

"I am very sorry, but I am not permitted to give you the choice of both."

"Why is that? Many people are allowed to choose both."

"I know that; still we must follow our instructions."

"Well, if that is the case, without wishing to offend you in the least, I think I will stand by my first choice. I choose wealth."

As he said this the other lady advanced toward him and smiled somewhat triumphantly as she held out her hand. Crandall grasped it and the first spirit sighed. Just as the spirit of wealth seemed about to speak, there was a shake at the office door, and Mr. John Crandall saw the spirits fade away. He rubbed his eyes and said to himself: "By George! I have been asleep. What a remarkably vivid dream that was."

As he yawned and stretched his arms above his head, the impatient rattle at the door told him that at least was not a part of the dream.

He arose and unlocked the door.

"Hello, Mr. Bullion," he said, as that solid man came in. "You're late, aren't you."

"Why, for that matter, so are you. You must have been absorbed in your accounts or you would have heard me sooner. I thought I would have to shake the place down."

"Well, you know, the policeman sometimes tries the door and I thought at first it was he. Won't you sit down?"

"Thanks! Don't care if I do. Busy tonight?"

"Just got through."

"Well, how are things going?"

"Oh, slowly as usual. Slowly because we have not facilities enough, but we've got all the work we can do."

"Does it pay you for what work you do?"

"Certainly. I'm not in this business as a philanthropist, you know."

"No. I didn't suppose you were. Now, see here, Crandall, I think you have a good thing of it here and one of the enterprises that if extended would develop into a big business."

192

"I know it. But what am I to do? I've practically no capital to enlarge the business, and I don't care to mortgage what I have and pay a high rate of interest when, just at the critical moment, we might have a commercial crisis and I would then lose everything."

"Quite right; quite right, and a safe principle. Well, that's what I came to see you about. I have had my eye on you and this factory for some time. Now, if you want capital I will furnish it on the condition that an accountant of mine examines the books and finds everything promising a fair return for enlarging the business. Of course I take your word for the state of affairs all right enough, but business is business, you know, and besides I want to get an expert opinion on how much enlargement it will stand. I suppose you could manage a manufactory ten or twenty times larger as easily as you do this one."

"Quite," said Mr. Crandall.

"Then what do you say to my coming round to-morrow at 9 with my man?"

"That would suit me all right."

Mr. John Crandall walked home a very much elated man that night.

"Well, doctor," said the patient in a very weak voice, "what is the verdict!"

"It is just as I said before. You will have to take a rest. You know I predicted this breakdown."

"Can't you give me something that will fix me up temporarily? It is almost imperative that I should stay on just now."

"Of course it is. It has been so for the last five years. You forget that in that time you have been fixed up temporarily on several occasions. Now, I will get you 'round so that you can travel in a few days and then I insist on a sea voyage or a quiet time somewhere on the continent. You will have to throw off business cares entirely. There are no ifs or buts about it."

"Look here, doctor. I don't see how I am to leave at this time. I have been as bad as this a dozen times before. You know that. I'm just a little fagged out and when I go back to the office I can take things easier. You see, we have a big South American contract on hand that I am very anxious about. New business, you know."

"I suppose you could draw your cheque for a pretty large amount, Mr. Crandall."

"Yes, I can. If money can bridge the thing over, I will arrange it."

"Well, money can't. What I wanted to say was that if, instead of having a large sum in the bank, you had overdrawn your account about as much as the bank would stand, would you be surprised if your cheque were not honored?"

"No, I wouldn't."

"Well, that is your state physically. You've overdrawn your vitality account. You've got to make a deposit. You must take a vacation."

"Any other time, doctor. I'll go sure, as soon as this contract is off. Upon my word I will. You needn't shake your head. A vacation just now would only aggravate the difficulty. I wouldn't have a moment's peace knowing this South American business might be bungled. I'd worry myself to death."

The funeral of Mr. Crandall was certainly one of the most splendid spectacles the city had seen for many a day. The papers all spoke highly of the qualities of the dead manufacturer, whose growth had been typical of the growth of the city. The eloquent minister spoke of the inscrutable ways of Providence in cutting off a man in his prime, and in the very height of his usefulness.

THE FAILURE OF BRADLEY.

The skater lightly laughs and glides,

Unknowing that beneath the ice

On which he carves his fair device

A stiffened corpse in silence glides.

It glareth upward at his play;

Its cold, blue, rigid fingers steal

Beneath the tracings of his heel.

It floats along and floats away.

—Unknown Poem.

"If I only had the courage," said Bradley, as he looked over the stone parapet of the embankment at the dark waters of the Thames as they flashed for a moment under the glitter of the gaslight and then disappeared in the black night to flash again farther down.

"Very likely I would struggle to get out again the moment I went over," he muttered to himself. "But if no help came it would all be done with, in a minute. Two minutes perhaps. I'll warrant those two minutes would seem an eternity. I would see a hundred ways of making a living, if I could only get out again. Why can't I see one now while I am out. My father committed suicide, why shouldn't I? I suppose it runs in the family. There seems to come a time when it is the only way out. I wonder if he hesitated? I'm a coward, that's the trouble."

After a moment's hesitation the man slowly climbed on the top of the stone wall and then paused again. He looked with a shudder at the gloomy river.

"I'll do it," he cried aloud, and was about to slide down, when a hand grasped his arm and a voice said:

"What will you do?"

In the light of the gas-lamp Bradley saw a man whose face seemed familiar and although he thought rapidly, "Where have I seen that man before?" he could not place him.

"Nothing," answered Bradley sullenly.

"That's right," was the answer. "I'd do nothing of that kind, if I were you."

"Of course you wouldn't. You have everything that I haven't—food, clothes, shelter. Certainly you wouldn't. Why should you?"

"Why should you, if it comes to that?"

"Because ten shillings stands between me and a job. That's why, if you want to know. There's eight shillings railway fare, a shilling for something to eat to-night and a shilling for something in the morning. But I haven't the ten shillings. So that's why."

"If I give you the ten shillings what assurance have I that you will not go and get drunk on it?"

"None at all. I have not asked you for ten shillings, nor for one. I have simply answered your question."

"That is true. I will give you a pound if you will take it, and so if unfortunately you spent half of it in cheering yourself, you will still have enough left to get that job. What is the job?"

"I am a carpenter."

"You are welcome to the pound."

"I will take it gladly. But, mind you, I am not a beggar. I will take it if you give me your address, so that I may send it back to you when I earn it."

By this time Bradley had come down on the pavement. The other man laughed quietly.

"I cannot agree to that. You are welcome to the money. More if you like. I merely doubled the sum you mentioned to provide for anything unseen."

"Unless you let me return it, I will not take the money."

"I have perfect confidence in your honesty. If I had not, I would not offer the money. I cannot give you my address, or, rather, I will not. If you will pay the pound to some charity or will give it to someone who is in need, I am more than satisfied. If you give it to the right man and tell him to do the same, the pound will do more good than ever it will in my pocket or in my usual way of spending it."

"But how are you to know I will do that?"

"I am considered rather a good judge of men. I am certain you will do what you say."

"I'll take the money. I doubt if there is anyone in London to-night who needs it much worse than I do."

Bradley looked after the disappearing figure of the man who had befriended him.

"I have seen that man somewhere before," he said to himself. But in that he was wrong. He hadn't.

Wealth is most unevenly and most unfairly divided. All of us admit that, but few of us agree about the remedy. Some of the best minds of the century have wrestled with this question in vain. "The poor ye have always with you" is as true to-day as it was 1800 years ago. Where so many are in doubt, it is perhaps a comfort to meet men who have no uncertainty as to the cause and the remedy. Such a body of men met in a back room off Soho Square.

"We are waiting for you, Bradley," said the chairman, as the carpenter took his place and the doors were locked. He looked better than he had done a year before on the Thames embankment.

"I know I'm late, but I couldn't help it. They are rushing things at the exhibition grounds. The time is short now, and they are beginning to be anxious for fear everything will not be ready in time."

"That's it," said one of the small group, "we are slaves and must be late or early as our so-called masters choose."

"Oh, there is extra pay," said Bradley with a smile, as he took a seat.

"Comrades," said the chairman, rapping on the desk, "we will now proceed to business. The secret committee has met and made a resolution. After the lots are drawn it will be my task to inform the man chosen what the job is. It is desirable that as few as possible, even among ourselves, should know who the man is, who has drawn the marked paper. Perhaps it may be my own good fortune to be the chosen man. One of the papers is marked with a cross. Whoever draws that paper is to communicate with me at my room within two days. He is to come alone. It is commanded by the committee that no man is to look at his paper until he leaves this room and then to examine it in secret. He is bound by his oath to tell no one at any time whether or not he is the chosen man."

The papers were put into a hat and each man in the room drew one. The chairman put his in his pocket, as did the others. The doors were unlocked and each man went to his home, if he had one.

Next evening Bradley called at the room of the chairman and said: "There is the marked paper I drew last night."

The exhibition building was gay with bunting and was sonorous with the sounds of a band of music. The machinery that would not stop for six months was still motionless, for it was to be started in an hour's time by His Highness. His Highness and suite had not yet arrived but the building was crowded by a well-dressed throng of invited guests—the best in the land as far as fame, title or money was concerned. Underneath the grand stand where His Highness and the distinguished guests were to make speeches and where the finger of nobility was to press the electric button, Bradley walked anxiously about, with the same haggard look on his face that was there the night he thought of slipping into the Thames. The place underneath was a wilderness of beams and braces. Bradley's wooden tool chest stood on the ground against one of the timbers. The foremen came through and struck a beam or a brace here and there.

"Everything is all right," he said to Bradley. "There will be no trouble, even if it was put up in a hurry, and in spite of the strain that will be on it to-day."

Bradley was not so sure of that, but he said nothing. When the foreman left him alone, he cautiously opened the lid of his tool chest and removed the carpenter's apron which covered something in the bottom. This something was a small box with a clockwork arrangement and a miniature uplifted hammer that hung like the sword of Damocles over a little copper cap. He threw the apron over it again, closed the lid of the chest, leaned against one of the timbers, folded his arms and waited.

Presently there was a tremendous cheer and the band struck up. "He is coming," said Bradley to himself, closing his lips tighter. "Carpenter," cried the policeman putting in his head through the little wooden door at the foot of the stage, "come here, quick. You can get a splendid sight of His Highness as he comes up the passage." Bradley walked to the opening and gazed at the distinguished procession coming toward him. Suddenly he grasped the arm of the policeman like a vice.

"Who is that man in the robes—at the head of the procession?"

"Don't you know? That is His Highness."

Bradley gasped for breath. He recognized His Highness as the man he had met on the embankment.

"Thank you," he said to the policeman, who looked at him curiously. Then he went under the grand stand among the beams and braces and leaned against one of the timbers with knitted brows.

After a few moments he stepped to his chest, pulled off the apron and carefully lifted out the machine. With a quick jerk he wrenched off the little hammer and flung it from him. The machinery inside whirred for a moment with a soft purr like a clock running down. He opened the box and shook out into his apron a substance like damp sawdust. He seemed puzzled for a moment what to do with it. Finally he took it out and scattered it along the grass-grown slope of a railway cutting. Then he returned to his tool chest, took out a chisel and grimly felt its edge with his thumb.

It was admitted on all hands that His Highness never made a better speech in his life than on the occasion of the opening of that exhibition. He touched lightly on the country's unexampled prosperity, of which the marvelous collection within those walls was an indication. He alluded to the general contentment that reigned among the classes to whose handiwork was due the splendid examples of human skill there exhibited. His Highness was thankful that peace and contentment reigned over the happy land and he hoped they would long continue so to reign. Then there were a good many light touches of humor in the discourse— touches that are so pleasing when they come from people in high places. In fact, the chairman said at the club afterwards (confidentially, of course) that the man who wrote His Highness's speeches had in that case quite outdone himself.

The papers had very full accounts of the opening of the exhibition next morning, and perhaps because these graphic articles occupied so much space, there was so little room for the announcement about the man who committed suicide. The papers did not say where the body was found, except that it was near the exhibition buildings, and His Highness never knew that he made that excellent speech directly over the body of a dead man.

RINGAMY'S CONVERT.

Mr. Johnson Ringamy, the author, sat in his library gazing idly out of the window. The view was very pleasant, and the early morning sun brought out in strong relief the fresh greenness of the trees that now had on their early spring suits of foliage. Mr. Ringamy had been a busy man, but now, if he cared to take life easy, he might do so, for few books had had the tremendous success of his latest work. Mr. Ringamy was thinking about this, when the door opened, and a tall, intellectual-looking young man entered from the study that communicated with the library. He placed on the table the bunch of letters he had in his hand, and, drawing up a chair, opened a blank notebook that had, between the leaves, a lead pencil sharpened at both ends.

"Good morning, Mr. Scriver," said the author, also hitching up his chair towards the table. He sighed as he did so, for the fair spring prospect from the library window was much more attractive than the task of answering an extensive correspondence.

"Is there a large mail this morning, Scriver?"

"A good-sized one, sir. Many of them, however, are notes asking for your autograph."

"Enclose stamps, do they?"

"Most of them, sir; those that did not, I threw in the waste basket."

"Quite right. And as to the autographs you might write them this afternoon, if you have time."

"I have already done so, sir. I flatter myself that even your most intimate friend could not tell my version of your autograph from your own."

As he said this, the young man shoved towards the author a letter which he had written, and Mr. Ringamy looked at it critically.

"Very good, Scriver, very good indeed. In fact, if I were put in the witness-box I am not sure that I would be able to swear that this was not my signature. What's this you have said in the body of the letter about sentiment? Not making me write anything sentimental, I hope. Be careful, my boy, I don't want the newspapers to get hold of anything that they could turn into ridicule. They are too apt to do that sort of thing if they get half a chance."

"Oh, I think you will find that all right," said the young man; "still I thought it best to submit it to you before sending it off. You see the lady who writes has been getting up a 'Ringamy Club' in Kalamazoo, and she asks you to give her an autographic sentiment which they will cherish as the motto of the club. So I wrote the sentence, 'All classes of labor should have equal compensation.' If that won't do, I can easily change it.'

"Oh, that will do first rate—first rate."

"Of course it is awful rot, but I thought it would please the feminine mind."

"Awful what did you say, Mr. Scriver?"

"Well, slush—if that expresses it better. Of course, you don't believe any such nonsense."

Mr. Johnson Ringamy frowned as he looked at his secretary.

"I don't think I understand you," he said, at last.

"Well, look here, Mr. Ringamy, speaking now, not as a paid servant to his master, but——"

"Now, Scriver, I won't have any talk like that. There is no master or servant idea between us. There oughtn't to be between anybody. All men are free and equal."

"They are in theory, and in my eye, as I might say if I wanted to make it more expressive."

"Scriver, I cannot congratulate you on your expressive language, if I may call it so. But we are wandering from the argument. You were going to say that speaking as——Well, go on."

"I was going to say that, speaking as one reasonably sensible man to

202

another, without any gammon about it; don't you think it is rank nonsense to hold that one class of labor should be as well compensated as another. Honestly now?"

The author sat back in his chair and gazed across the table at his secretary. Finally, he said:

"My dear Scriver, you can't really mean what you say. You know that I hold that all classes of labor should have exactly the same compensation. The miner, the blacksmith, the preacher, the postal clerk, the author, the publisher, the printer—yes, the man who sweeps out the office, or who polishes boots, should each share alike, if this world were what it should be—yes, and what it will be. Why, Scriver, you surely couldn't have read my book——"

"Read it? why, hang it, I wrote it."

"You wrote it? The deuce you did! I always thought I was the author of ——"

"So you are. But didn't I take it all down in shorthand, and didn't I whack it out on the type-writer, and didn't I go over the proof sheets with you. And yet you ask me if I have read it!"

"Oh, yes, quite right, I see what you mean. Well, if you paid as much attention to the arguments as you did to the mechanical production of the book, I should think you would not ask if I really meant what I said."

"Oh, I suppose you meant it all right enough—in a way—in theory, perhaps, but——"

"My dear sir, allow me to say that a theory which is not practical, is simply no theory at all. The great success of 'Gazing Upward,' has been due to the fact that it is an eminently practical work. The nationalization of everything is not a matter of theory. The ideas advocated in that book, can be seen at work at any time. Look at the Army, look at the Post Office."

"Oh, that's all right, looking at things in bulk. Let us come down to practical details. Detail is the real test of any scheme. Take this volume, 'Gazing Upward.' Now, may I ask how much this book has netted you up to date?"

"Oh, I don't know exactly. Somewhere in the neighborhood of £20,000."

"Very well then. Now let us look for a moment at the method by which that book was produced. You walked up and down this room with your hands behind your back, and dictated chapter after chapter, and I sat at this table taking it all down in shorthand. Then you went out and took the air while I industriously whacked it out on the type-writer."

"I wish you wouldn't say 'whacked,' Scriver. That's twice you've used it."

"All right:—typographical error—For 'whacked' read 'manipulated.' Then you looked over the type-written pages, and I erased and wrote in and finally got out a perfect copy. Now I worked as hard—probably harder—than you did, yet the success of that book was entirely due to you, and not to me. Therefore it is quite right that you should get £20,000 and that I should get two pounds a week. Come now, isn't it? Speaking as a man of common sense."

"Speaking exactly in that way I say no it is not right. If the world were properly ruled the compensation of author and secretary would have been exactly the same."

"Oh, well, if you go so far as that," replied the Secretary, "I have nothing more to say."

The author laughed, and the two men bent their energies to the correspondence. When the task was finished, Scriver said:

"I would like to get a couple of days off, Mr. Ringamy. I have some private business to attend to."

"When could you get back?"

"I'll report to you on Thursday morning."

"Very well, then. Not later than Thursday. I think I'll take a couple of days off myself."

On Thursday morning Mr. Johnson Ringamy sat in his library looking out of the window, but the day was not as pleasant as when he last gazed at the hills, and the woods, and green fields. A wild spring storm lashed the landscape, and rattled the raindrops against the pane. Mr. Ringamy waited for some time and then opened the study door and looked in. The little room was empty. He rang the bell, and the trim servant-girl appeared.

"Has Mr. Scriver come in yet?"

"No, sir, he haven't."

"Perhaps the rain has kept him."

"Mr. Scriver said that when you come back, sir, there was a letter on the table as was for you."

"Ah, so there is. Thank you, that will do."

The author opened the letter and read as follows:

"*MY DEAR MR. RINGAMY,—Your arguments the other day fully convinced me that you were right, and I was wrong* ("Ah! I thought they would," *murmured the author*). *I have therefore taken a step toward putting your theories into practice. The scheme is an old one in commercial life, but new in its present application, so much so that I fear it will find no defenders except yourself, and I trust that now when I am far away* ("Dear me, what does this mean!" *cried the author*) *you will show any doubters that I acted on the principles which will govern the world when the theories of 'Gazing Upward' are put into practice. For fear that all might not agree with you at present, I have taken the precaution of going to that undiscovered country, from whose bourne no extradition treaty forces the traveler to return—sunny Spain. You said you could not tell my rendition of your signature from your own. Neither could the bank cashier. My exact mutation of your signature has enabled me to withdraw £10,000 from your bank account. Half the profits, you know. You can send future accumulations, for the book will continue to sell, to the address of*

"*ADAM SCRIVER.*

"*Poste Restant, Madrid, Spain*"

Mr. Ringamy at once put the case in the hands of the detectives, where it still remains.

A SLIPPERY CUSTOMER.

When John Armstrong stepped off the train at the Union Station, in Toronto, Canada, and walked outside, a small boy accosted him.

"Carry your valise up for you, sir?"

"No, thank you," said Mr. Armstrong.

"Carry it up for ten cents, sir?"

"No."

"Take it up for five cents, sir?"

"Get out of my way, will you?"

The boy got out of the way, and John Armstrong carried the valise himself.

There was nearly half a million dollars in it, so Mr. Armstrong thought it best to be his own porter.

In the bay window of one of the handsomest residences in Rochester, New York, sat Miss Alma Temple, waiting for her father to come home from the bank. Mr. Horace Temple was one of the solid men of Rochester, and was president of the Temple National Bank. Although still early in December, the winter promised to be one of the most severe for many years, and the snow lay crisp and hard on the streets, but not enough for sleighing. It was too cold for snow, the weatherwise said. Suddenly Miss Alma drew back from the window with a quick flush on her face that certainly was not caused by the coming of her father. A dapper young man sprang lightly up the steps, and pressed the electric button at the door. When the young man entered the room a moment later Miss Alma was sitting demurely by the open fire. He advanced quickly toward her, and took both her outstretched hands in his. Then, furtively looking around the room, he greeted her still more affectionately, in a manner that the chronicler of these incidents, is not bound to particularize. However, the fact may be mentioned that whatever resistance the young woman thought fit to offer was of the faintest and most futile kind, and so it will be understood, at the beginning, that these two young persons had a very good understanding with each other.

"You seem surprised to see me," he began.

"Well, Walter, I understood that you left last time with some energetically expressed resolutions never to darken our doors again."

"Well, you see, my dear, I am sometimes a little hasty; and, in fact, the weather is so dark nowadays, anyhow, that a little extra darkness does not amount to much, and so I thought I would take the risk of darkening them once more."

"But I also understood that my father made you promise, or that you promised voluntarily, not to see me again without his permission?"

"Not voluntarily. Far from it. Under compulsion, I assure you. But I didn't come to see you at all. That's where you are mistaken. The seeing you is merely an accident, which I have done my best to avoid. Fact! The girl said, 'Won't you walk into the drawing-room,' and naturally I did so. Never expected to find you here. I thought I saw a young lady at the window as I came up, but I got such a momentary glimpse that I might have been mistaken."

"Then I will leave you and not interrupt——"

"Not at all. Now I beg of you not to leave on my account, Alma. You know I would not put you to any trouble for the world."

"You are very kind, I am sure, Mr. Brown."

"I am indeed, Miss Temple. All my friends admit that. But now that you are here—by the way, I came to see Mr. Temple. Is he at home?"

"I am expecting him every moment."

"Oh, well, I'm disappointed; but I guess I will bear up for awhile— until he comes, you know."

"I thought your last interview with him was not so pleasant that you would so soon seek another."

"The fact is, Alma, we both lost our tempers a bit, and no good ever comes of that. You can't conduct business in a heat, you know."

"Oh, then the asking of his daughter's hand was business—a mere business proposition, was it?"

"Well, I confess he put it that way—very strongly, too. Of course, with me there would have been pleasure mixed with it if he had—but he didn't. See here, Alma—tell me frankly (of course he talked with you about it) what objection he has to me anyhow."

"I suppose you consider yourself such a desirable young man that it astonishes you greatly that any person should have any possible objection to you?"

"Oh, come now, Alma; don't hit a fellow when he's down, you know. I don't suppose I have more conceit than the average young man; but then, on the other hand, I am not such a fool, despite appearances, as not to know that I am considered by some people as quite an eligible individual. I am not a pauper exactly, and your father knows that. I don't think I have many very bad qualities. I don't get drunk; I don't —oh, I could give quite a list of the things I don't do."

"You are certainly frank enough, my eligible young man. Still you must not forget that my papa is considered quite an eligible father-in-law, if it comes to that."

"Why, of course, I admit it. How could it be otherwise when he has such a charming daughter?"

"You know I don't mean that, Walter. You were speaking of wealth and so was I. Perhaps we had better change the subject."

"By the way, that reminds me of what I came to see you about. What do——"

"To see me? I thought you came to see my father."

208

"Oh, yes—certainly—I did come to see him, of course, but in case I saw you, I thought I would ask you for further particulars in the case. I have asked you the question but you have evaded the answer. You did not tell me why he is so prejudiced against me. Why did he receive me in such a gruff manner when I spoke to him about it? It is not a criminal act to ask a man for his daughter. It is not, I assure you. I looked up the law on the subject, and a young friend of mine, who is a barrister, says there is no statute in the case made and provided. The law of the State of New York does not recognize my action as against the peace and prosperity of the commonwealth. Well, he received me as if I had been caught robbing the bank. Now I propose to know what the objection is. I am going to hear——"

"Hush! Here is papa now."

Miss Alma quickly left the room, and met her father in the hall. Mr. Brown stood with his hands in his pockets and his back to the fire. He heard the gruff voice of Mr. Temple say, apparently in answer to some information given him by his daughter: "Is he? What does he want?"

There was a moment's pause, and then the same voice said:

"Very well, I will see him in the library in a few minutes."

Somehow the courage of young Mr. Brown sank as he heard the banker's voice, and the information he had made up his mind to demand with some hauteur, he thought he would ask, perhaps, in a milder manner.

Mr. Brown brightened up as the door opened, but it was not Miss Alma who came in. The servant said to him:

"Mr. Temple is in the library, sir. Will you come this way!"

He followed and found the banker seated at his library table, on which he had just placed some legal-looking papers, bound together with a thick rubber band. It was evident that his work did not stop when he left the bank. Young Brown noticed that Mr. Temple looked careworn and haggard, and that his manner was very different from what it had been on the occasion of the last interview.

"Good evening, Mr. Brown. I am glad you called. I was on the point of writing to you, but the subject of our talk the other night was crowded from my mind by more important matters."

Young Mr. Brown thought bitterly that there ought not to be matters more important to a father than his daughter's happiness, but he had the good sense not to say so.

"I spoke to you on that occasion with a—in a manner that was—well, hardly excusable, and I wish to say that I am sorry I did so. What I had to state might have been stated with more regard for your feelings."

"Then may I hope, Mr. Temple, that you have changed your mind with——"

"No, sir. What I said then—that is, the substance of what I said, not the manner of saying it—I still adhere to."

"May I ask what objection you have to me?"

"Certainly. I have the same objection that I have to the majority of the society young men of the present day. If I make inquiries about you, what do I find? That you are a noted oarsman—that you have no profession—that your honors at college consisted in being captain of the football team, and——"

"No, no, the baseball club."

"Same thing, I suppose."

"Quite different, I assure you, Mr. Temple."

"Well, it is the same to me at any rate. Now, in my time young men had a harder row to hoe, and they hoed it. I am what they call a self-made man and probably I have a harsher opinion of the young men of the present day than I should have. But if I had a son I would endeavor to have him know how to do something, and then I would see that he did it."

"I am obliged to you for stating your objection, Mr. Temple. I have taken my degree in Harvard law school, but I have never practiced, because, as the little boy said, I didn't have to. Perhaps if some one had spoken to me as you have done I would have pitched in and gone to work. It is not too late yet. Will you give me a chance? The position of cashier in your bank, for instance?"

The effect of these apparently innocent words on Mr. Temple was startling. He sprang to his feet and brought down his clenched fist on the table with a vehemence that made young Mr. Brown jump. "What do you mean, sir?" he cried, sternly. "What do you mean by saying such a thing?"

"Why, I—I—I—mean——" stammered Brown, but he could get no further. He thought the old man had suddenly gone crazy. He glared across the library table at Brown as if the next instant he would spring at his throat. Then the haggard look came into his face again, he passed his hand across his brow, and sank into his chair with a groan.

"My dear sir," said Brown, approaching him, "what is the matter? Is there anything I can——"

"Sit down, please," answered the banker, melancholy. "You will excuse me I hope, I am very much troubled. I did not intend to speak of it, but some explanation is due to you. A month from now, if you are the kind of man that most of your fellows are, you will not wish to marry my daughter. There is every chance that at that time the doors of my bank will be closed."

"You astonish me, sir. I thought——"

"Yes, and so every one thinks. I have seldom in my life trusted the wrong man, but this time I have done so, and the one mistake seems likely to obliterate all that I have succeeded in doing in a life of hard work."

"If I can be of any financial assistance I will be glad to help you."

"How much?"

"Well, I don't know—50,000 dollars perhaps or——"

"I must have 250,000 dollars before the end of this month."

"Two hundred and fifty thousand!"

"Yes, sir. William L. Staples, the cashier of our bank, is now in Canada with half a million of the bank funds. No one knows it but myself and one or two of the directors. It is generally supposed that he has gone to Washington on a vacation."

"But can't you put detectives on his track?"

"Certainly. Then the theft would be made public at once. The papers would be full of it. There might be a run on the bank, and we would have to close the doors the next day. To put the detectives on his track would merely mean bringing disaster on our own heads. Staples is quite safe, and he knows it. Thanks to an idiotic international arrangement he is as free from danger of arrest in Canada as you are here. It is impossible to extradite him for stealing."

"But I think there is a law against bringing stolen money into Canada."

"Perhaps there is. It would not help us at the present moment. We must compromise with him, if we can find him in time. Of course, even if the bank closed, we would pay everything when there was time to realize. But that is not the point. It would mean trouble and disaster, and would probably result in other failures all through one man's rascality."

"Then it all resolves itself to this. Staples must be found quietly and negotiated with. Mr. Temple, let me undertake the finding of him, and the negotiating, also, if you will trust me."

"Do you know him?"

"Never saw him in my life."

"Here is his portrait. He is easily recognized from that. You couldn't mistake him. He is probably living at Montreal under an assumed name. He may have sailed for Europe. You will say nothing of this to anybody?"

"Certainly not. I will leave on to-night's train for Montreal, or on the first train that goes."

Young Mr. Brown slipped the photograph into his pocket and shook hands with the banker. Somehow his confident, alert bearing inspired the old man with more hope than he would have cared to admit, for, as a general thing, he despised the average young man.

"How long can you hold out if this does not become public?"

"For a month at least; probably for two or three."

"Well, don't expect to hear from me too soon. I shall not risk writing. If there is anything to communicate, I will come myself."

"It is very good of you to take my trouble on your shoulders like this. I am very much obliged to you."

"I am not a philanthropist, Mr. Temple," replied young Brown.

When young Mr. Brown stepped off the train at the Central Station in Toronto, a small boy accosted him.

"Carry your valise up for you, sir?"

"Certainly," said Brown, handing it to him.

"How much do I owe you?" he asked at the lobby of the hotel.

"Twenty-five cents," said the boy promptly, and he got it.

Brown registered on the books of the hotel as John A. Walker, of Montreal.

Mr. Walter Brown, of Rochester, was never more discouraged in his life than at the moment he wrote on the register the words, "John A. Walker, Montreal." He had searched Montreal from one end to the other, but had found no trace of the man for whom he was looking. Yet, strange to say, when he raised his eyes from the register they met the face of William L. Staples, ex-cashier. It was lucky for Brown that Staples was looking at the words he had written, and not at himself, or he would have noticed Brown's involuntary start of surprise, and flush of pleasure. It was also rather curious that Mr. Brown had a dozen schemes in his mind for getting acquainted with Staples when he met him, and yet that the first advance should be made by Staples himself.

"You are from Montreal," said Mr. Staples, alias John Armstrong.

"That's my town," said Mr. Brown.

"What sort of a place is it in winter? Pretty lively?"

"Oh, yes. Good deal of a winter city, Montreal is. How do you mean, business or sport?"

"Well, both. Generally where there's lots of business there's lots of fun."

"Yes, that's so," assented Brown. He did not wish to prolong the conversation. He had some plans to make, so he followed his luggage up to his room. It was evident that he would have to act quickly. Staples was getting tired of Toronto.

Two days after Brown had his plans completed. He met Staples one evening in the smoking-room of the hotel.

"Think of going to Montreal?" asked Brown.

"I did think of it. I don't know, though. Are you in business there?"

"Yes. If you go, I could give you some letters of introduction to a lot of fellows who would show you some sport, that is, if you care for snow-shoeing, toboganning, and the like of that."

"I never went in much for athletics," said Staples.

"I don't care much for exertion myself," answered Brown. "I come up here every winter for some ice-yachting. That's my idea of sport. I own one of the fastest ice-boats on the bay. Ever been out?"

"No, I haven't. I've seen them at it a good deal. Pretty cold work such weather as we've been having, isn't it?"

"I don't think so. Better come out with me tomorrow?"

"Well, I don't care if I do."

The next day and the next they spun around the bay on the ice-boat. Even Staples, who seemed to be tired of almost everything, liked the swiftness and exhilaration of the iceboat.

214

One afternoon, Brown walked into the bar of the hotel, where he found Staples standing.

"See here, Armstrong." he cried, slapping that gentleman on the shoulder. "Are you in for a bit of sport? It's a nice moonlight night, and I'm going to take a spin down to Hamilton to meet some chaps, and we can come back on the iceboat, or if you think it too late, you can stay over, and come back on the train."

"Hamilton? That's up the lake, isn't it?"

"Yes, just a nice run from here. Come along—I counted on you."

An hour later they were skimming along the frozen surface of the lake.

"Make yourself warm and snug," said Brown. "That's what the buffalo robes are for. I must steer, so I have to keep in the open. If I were you I'd wrap up in those robes and go to sleep. I'll wake you when we're there."

"All right," answered Staples. "That's not a bad idea."

"General George Washington!" said young Brown to himself. "This is too soft a snap altogether. I'm going to run him across the lake like a lamb. Before he opens his eyes we'll have skimmed across the frozen lake, and he'll find himself in the States again when he wakes up. The only thing now to avoid are the air-holes and ice-hills, and I'm all right."

He had been over the course before and knew pretty well what was ahead of him. The wind was blowing stiffly straight up the lake and the boat silently, and swifter than the fastest express, was flying from Canada and lessening the distance to the American shore.

"How are you getting along, Walker," cried Staples, rousing himself up. "First rate," answered Brown. "We'll soon be there, Staples."

That unfortunate slip of the tongue almost cost young Mr. Brown his life. He had been, thinking of the man under his own name, and the name had come out unconsciously. He did not even notice it himself in time to prepare, and the next instant the thief flung himself upon him and jammed his head against the iron rod that guided the rudder, with such a force that the rudder stayed in its place and the boat flew along the ice without a swerve.

"You scoundrel!" roared the bank-robber. "That's your game, is it? By the gods, I'll teach you a lesson in the detective business!"

Athlete as young Brown was, the suddenness of the attack, and the fact that Staples clutched both hands round his neck and had his knee on his breast, left him as powerless as an infant. Even then he did not realize what had caused the robber to guess his position.

"For God's sake, let me up!" gasped Brown. "We'll be into an air-hole and drowned in a moment."

"I'll risk it, you dog! till I've choked the breath out of your body." Brown wriggled his head away from the rudder iron, hoping that the boat would slew around, but it kept its course. He realized that if he was to save his life he would have to act promptly. He seemed to feel his tongue swell in his parched mouth. His strength was gone and his throat was in an iron vice. He struck out wildly with his feet and one fortunate kick sent the rudder almost at right angles.

Instantly the boat flashed around into the wind. Even if a man is prepared for such a thing, it takes all his nerve and strength to keep him on an iceboat. Staples was not prepared. He launched head first into space and slid for a long distance on the rough ice. Brown was also flung on the ice and lay for a moment gasping for breath. Then he gathered himself together, and slipping his hand under his coat, pulled out his revolver. He thought at first that Staples was shamming, but a closer examination of him showed that the fall on the ice had knocked him senseless.

There was only one thing that young Mr. Brown was very anxious to know. He wanted to know where the money was. He had played the part of private detective well in Toronto, after the very best French style, and had searched the room of Staples in his absence, but he knew the money was not there nor in his valise. He knew equally well that the funds were in some safe deposit establishment in the city, but where he could not find out. He had intended to work on Staples' fears of imprisonment when once he had him safe on the other side of the line. But now that the man was insensible, he argued that it was a good time to find whether or not he had a record of the place of deposit in his pocket-book. He found no such book in his pockets. In searching, however, he heard the rustling of paper apparently in the lining of his coat. Then he noticed how thickly it was padded. The next moment he had it ripped open, and a glance showed him that it was lined with bonds. Both coat and vest were padded in this way—the vest being filled with Bank of England notes, so the chances were that Staples had meditated a tour in Europe. The robber evidently put no trust in Safe Deposits nor banks. Brown flung the thief over on his face, after having unbuttoned coat and vest, doubled back his arms and pulled off these garments. His own, Brown next discarded, and with some difficulty got them on the fallen man and then put on the clothes of mammon.

"This is what I call rolling in wealth," said Brown to himself. He admitted that he felt decidedly better after the change of clothing, cold as it was.

Buttoning his own garments on the prostrate man, Brown put a flask of liquor to his lips and speedily revived him. Staples sat on the ice in a dazed manner, and passed his hand across his brow. In the cold gleam of the moonlight he saw the shining barrel of Brown's revolver "covering" him.

"It's all up, Mr. Staples. Get on board the iceboat."

"Where are you going to take me to?"

"I'll let you go when we come to the coast if you tell me where the money is."

"You know you are guilty of the crime of kidnapping," said Mr. Staples, apparently with the object of gaining time. "So you are in some danger of the law yourself."

"That is a question that can be discussed later on. You came voluntarily, don't forget that fact. Where's the money?"

"It is on deposit in the Bank of Commerce."

"Well, here's paper and a stylographic pen, if the ink isn't frozen— no, it's all right—write a cheque quickly for the amount payable to bearer. Hurry up, or the ink will freeze."

There was a smile of satisfaction on the face of Staples as he wrote the check.

"There," he said, with a counterfeited sigh. "That is the amount."

The check was for 480,000 dollars.

When they came under the shadow of the American coast, Brown ordered his passenger off.

"You can easily reach land from here, and the walk will do you good. I'm going further up the lake."

When Staples was almost at the land he shouted through the clear night air: "Don't spend the money recklessly when you get it, Walker."

"I'll take care of it, Staples," shouted back young Brown.

Young Mr. Brown sprang lightly up the steps of the Temple mansion, Rochester, and pressed the electric button.

"Has Mr. Temple gone to the bank yet?" he asked the servant.

"No, sir; he is in the library."

"Thank you. Don't trouble. I know the way."

Mr. Temple looked around as the young man entered, and, seeing who it was, sprang to his feet with a look of painful expectancy on his face. "There's a little present for you," said Mr. Brown, placing a package on the table. "Four hundred and seventy-eight thousand: Bank of England notes and United States bonds." The old man grasped his hand, strove to speak, but said nothing.

People wondered why young Mr. and Mrs. Brown went to Toronto on their wedding tour in the depth of winter. It was so very unusual, don't you know.

THE SIXTH BENCH.

She was in earnest; he was not. When that state of things exists anything may happen. The occurrence may be commonplace, comic, or tragic, depending on the temperament and experience of the woman. In this instance the result was merely an appointment—which both of them kept.

Hector McLane came to Paris with noble resolutions, a theory of color, and a small allowance. Paris played havoc with all of these. He was engaged to a nice girl at home, who believed him destined to become a great painter; a delusion which McLane shared.

He entered with great zest into the life of a Parisian art student, but somehow the experience did not equal his anticipations. What he had read in books—poetry and prose—had thrown a halo around the Latin Quarter, and he was therefore disappointed in finding the halo missing. The romance was sordid and mercenary, and after a few months of it he yearned for something better.

In Paris you may have nearly everything—except the something better. It exists, of course, but it rarely falls in the way of the usually impecunious art student. Yet it happened that, as luck was not against the young man, he found it when he had abandoned the search for it.

McLane's theory was that art had become too sombre. The world was running overmuch after the subdued in color. He wanted to be able to paint things as they are, and was not to be deterred if his pictures were called gaudy. He obtained permission to set up his easel in the Church of Notre Dame, and in the dim light there, he endeavored to place on canvas some semblance of the splendor of color that came through the huge rose window high above him. He was discouraged to see how opaque the colors in the canvas were as compared with the translucent hues of the great window. As he leaned back with a sigh of defeat, his wandering eyes met, for one brief instant, something more beautiful than the stained glass, as the handiwork of God must always be more beautiful than the handiwork of man. The fleeting glimpse was of a melting pair of dark limpid eyes, which, meeting his, were instantly veiled, and then he had a longer view of the sweet face they belonged to. It was evident that the young girl had been admiring his work, which was more than he could hope to have the professor at Julien's do.

Lack of assurance was never considered, even by his dearest friend, to be among McLane's failings. He rose from his painting stool, bowed and asked her if she would not sit down for a moment; she could see the— the— painting so much better. The girl did not answer, but turned a frightened look upon him, and fled under the wing of her kneeling duenna, who had not yet finished her devotions. It was evident that the prayers of the girl had been briefer than those of the old woman in whose charge she was. Where the need is greatest the prayer is often the shortest. McLane had one more transitory glimpse of those dark eyes as he held open the swinging door. The unconscious woman and the conscious girl passed out of the church.

This was how it began.

The painting of the colored window of Notre Dame now occupied almost all the time at the disposal of Hector McLane. No great work is ever accomplished without unwearied perseverance. It was remarkable that the realization of this truth came upon him just after he had definitely made up his mind to abandon the task. Before he allowed the swinging door to close he had resolved to pursue his study in color. It thus happened, incidentally, that he saw the young girl again, always at the same hour, and always with the same companion. Once he succeeded, unnoticed by the elder, in slipping a note into her hand, which he was pleased and flattered to see she retained and concealed. Another day he had the joy of having a few whispered words with her in the dim shadow of one of the gigantic pillars. After that, progress was comparatively easy.

Her name was Yvette, he learned, and he was amused to find with what expert dexterity a perfectly guileless and innocent little creature such as she was, managed to elude the vigilance of the aged and experienced woman who had her in charge. The stolen interviews usually took place in the little

220

park behind Notre Dame. There they sat on the bench facing the fountain, or walked up and down on the crunching gravel under the trees. In the afternoons they walked in the secluded part of the park, in the shadow of the great church. It was her custom to send him dainty little notes telling him when she expected to be in the park, giving the number of the bench, for sometimes the duenna could not be eluded, and was seated there with Yvette. On these occasions McLane had to content himself with gazing from afar.

She was so much in earnest that the particular emotion which occupied the place of conscience in McLane's being, was troubled. He thought of the nice girl at home, and fervently hoped nothing of this would ever reach her ears. No matter how careful a man is, chance sometimes plays him a scurvy trick. McLane remembered instances, and regretted the world was so small. Sometimes a cry of recognition from one on the pavement to a comrade in the park, shouted through the iron railings, sent a shiver through McLane. Art students had an uncomfortable habit of roaming everywhere, and they were boisterous in hailing an acquaintance. Besides, they talked, and McLane dreaded having his little intrigue the joke of the school. At any moment an objectionable art student might drop into the park to sketch the fountain, or the nurses and children, or the back of the cathedral at one end of the park, or even the low, gloomy, unimposing front of the Morgue at the other.

He was an easy-going young fellow, who hated trouble, and perhaps, knowing that the inevitable day of reckoning was approaching, this accounted for the somewhat tardy awakening of his conscience.

He sometimes thought it would be best simply to leave Paris without any explanation, but he remembered that she knew his address, having written to him often, and that by going to the school she could easily find out where his home was. So if there was to be a scene it was much better that it should take place in Paris, rather than where the nice girl lived.

He nerved himself up many times to make the explanation and bring down the avalanche, but when the time came he postponed it. But the inevitable ultimately arrives. He had some difficulty at first in getting her to understand the situation clearly, but when he at last succeeded there was

221

no demonstration. She merely kept her eyes fixed on the gravel and gently withdrew her hand from his. To his surprise she did not cry, nor even answer him, but walked silently to and fro with downcast eyes in the shadow of the church. No one, he said, would ever occupy the place in his heart that she held. He was engaged to the other girl, but he had not known what love was until he met Yvette. He was bound to the other girl by ties he could not break, which was quite true, because the nice girl had a rich father. He drew such a pathetic picture of the loveless life he must in the future lead, that a great wave of self-pity surged up within him and his voice quavered. He felt almost resentful that she should take the separation in such an unemotional manner. When a man gets what he most desires he is still unsatisfied. This was exactly the way he had hoped she would take it.

All things come to an end, even explanations.

"Well, good-bye, Yvette," he said, reaching out his hand. She hesitated an instant, then without looking up, placed her small palm in his.

They stood thus for a moment under the trees, while the fountain beside them plashed and trickled musically. The shadow of the church was slowly creeping towards them over the gravel. The park was deserted, except by themselves. She tried gently to withdraw her hand, which he retained.

"Have you nothing to say to me, Yvette?" he asked, with a touch of reproach in his voice.

She did not answer. He held her fingers, which were slipping from his grasp, and the shadow touched her feet.

"Yvette, you will at least kiss me goodbye?"

She quickly withdrew her hand from his, shook her head and turned away. He watched her until she was out of sight, and then walked slowly towards his rooms on the Boulevard St. Germain. His thoughts were not comfortable. He was disappointed in Yvette. She was so clever, so witty, that he had at least expected she would have said something cutting, which he felt he thoroughly deserved. He had no idea she could be so heartless. Then his thoughts turned to the nice girl at home. She, too, had elements in her character that were somewhat bewildering to an honest young man. Her letters for a long time had been infrequent and unsatisfactory. It couldn't be possible that she had heard anything. Still, there is nothing so easy as point-blank denial, and he would see to that when he reached home.

An explanation awaited him at his rooms on the Boulevard. There was a foreign stamp on the envelope, and it was from the nice girl. There had been a mistake, she wrote, but happily she had discovered it before it was too late. She bitterly reproached herself, taking three pages to do it in, and on the fourth page he gathered that she would be married by the time he had the letter. There appeared to be no doubt that the nice girl fully realized how basely she had treated a talented, hard- working, aspiring, sterling young man, but the realization had not seemingly postponed the ringing of the wedding-bells to any appreciable extent.

Young McLane crushed the letter in his hand and used strong language, as, indeed, he was perfectly justified in doing. He laughed a hard dry laugh at the perfidy of woman. Then his thoughts turned towards Yvette. What a pity it was she was not rich! Like so many other noble, talented men, he realized he could not marry a poor woman. Suddenly it occurred to him that Yvette might not be poor. The more he pondered over the matter the more astonished he was that he had ever taken her poverty for granted. She dressed richly, and that cost money in Paris. He remembered that she wore a watch which flashed with jewels on the one occasion when he had seen it for a moment. He wished he had postponed his explanation for one more day; still, that was something easily remedied. He would tell her he had thrown over the other girl for her sake. Like a pang there came to him the remembrance that he did not know her address, nor even her family name. Still, she would be sure to visit the little park, and he would haunt it until she came. The haunting would give additional point to his story of consuming love. Anyhow, nothing could be done that night.

In the morning he was overjoyed to receive a letter from Yvette, and he was more than pleased when he read its contents. It asked for one more meeting behind the church.

"I could not tell you to-day," she wrote, "all I felt. To-morrow you *shall know, if you meet me. Do not fear that I will reproach you. You will receive this letter in the morning. At twelve o'clock I shall be waiting for you on the sixth bench on the row south of the fountain— the sixth bench—the farthest from the church."*

"YVETTE."

McLane was overjoyed at his good luck. He felt that he hardly merited it. He was early at the spot, and sat down on the last bench of the row facing the fountain. Yvette had not yet arrived, but it was still half an hour before the time. McLane read the morning paper and waited. At last the bells all around him chimed the hour of twelve. She had not come. This was unusual, but always possible. She might not have succeeded in getting away. The quarter and then the half hour passed before McLane began to suspect that he had been made the victim of a practical joke. He dismissed the thought; such a thing was so unlike her. He walked around the little park, hoping he had mistaken the row of benches. She was not there. He read the letter again. It was plain enough—the sixth bench. He counted the benches beginning at the church. One—two—three—four—five. There were only five benches in the row.

As he gazed stupidly at the fifth bench a man beside him said—"That is the bench, sir."

"What do you mean?" cried McLane, turning toward him, astonished at the remark.

"It was there that the young girl was found dead this morning— poisoned, they say."

McLane stared at him—and then he said huskily—

"Who—was she?"

"Nobody knows that—yet. We will soon know, for everybody, as you see, is going into the Morgue. She's the only one on the bench to-day. Better go before the crowd gets greater. I have been twice."

224

McLane sank on the seat and drew his hand across his forehead.

He knew she was waiting for him on the sixth bench—the furthest from the church!

THE STRONG ARM

CHAPTER I. — THE BEAUTIFUL JAILER OF GUDENFELS

The aged Emir Soldan sat in his tent and smiled; the crafty Oriental smile of an experienced man, deeply grounded in the wisdom of this world. He knew that there was incipient rebellion in his camp; that the young commanders under him thought their leader was becoming too old for the fray; caution overmastering courage. Here were these dogs of unbelievers setting their unhallowed feet on the sacred soil of Syria, and the Emir, instead of dashing against them, counselled coolness and prudence. Therefore impatience disintegrated the camp and resentment threatened discipline. When at last the murmurs could be no longer ignored the Emir gathered his impetuous young men together in his tent, and thus addressed them.

"It may well be that I am growing too old for the active field; it may be that, having met before this German boar who leads his herd of swine, I am fearful of risking my remnant of life against him, but I have ever been an indulgent general, and am now loath to let my inaction stand against your chance of distinction. Go you therefore forth against him, and the man who brings me this boar's head shall not lack his reward."

The young men loudly cheered this decision and brandished their weapons aloft, while the old man smiled upon them and added:

"When you are bringing confusion to the camp of the unbelievers, I shall remain in my tent and meditate on the sayings of the Prophet, praying him to keep you a good spear's length from the German's broad sword, which he is the habit of wielding with his two hands."

The young Saracens went forth with much shouting, a gay prancing of the horses underneath them and a marvellous flourishing of spears above them, but they learned more wisdom in their half hour's communion with the German than the Emir, in a long life of counselling, had been able to bestow upon them. The two-handed sword they now met for the first time, and the acquaintance brought little joy to them. Count Herbert, the leader of the invaders, did no shouting, but reserved his breath for other purposes. He spurred his horse among them, and his foes went down around him as a thicket melts away before the well-swung axe of a stalwart woodman. The Saracens had little fear of death, but mutilation was another thing, for they knew that they would spend eternity in Paradise, shaped as they had left this earth, and while a spear's thrust or a wound from an arrow, or even the gash left by a short sword may be concealed by celestial robes, how is a man to comport himself in the Land of the Blest who is compelled to carry his head under his arm, or who is split from crown to midriff by an outlandish weapon that falls irresistible as the wrath of Allah! Again and again they threw themselves with disastrous bravery against the invading horde, and after each encounter they came back with lessened ranks and a more chastened spirit than when they had set forth. When at last, another counsel of war was held, the young men kept silence and waited for the smiling Emir to speak.

"If you are satisfied that there are other things to think of in war than the giving and taking of blows I am prepared to meet this German, not on his own terms but on my own. Perhaps, however, you wish to try conclusions with him again?"

The deep silence which followed this inquiry seemed to indicate that no such desire animated the Emir's listeners, and the old man smiled benignly upon his audience and went on.

"There must be no more disputing of my authority, either expressed or by implication. I am now prepared to go forth against him taking with me forty lancers."

Instantly there was a protest against this; the number was inadequate, they said.

"In his fortieth year our Prophet came to a momentous decision," continued the Emir, unheeding the interruption, "and I take a spear with me for every year of the Prophet's life, trusting that Allah will add to our number, at the prophet's intervention, should such an augmentation prove necessary. Get together then the forty oldest men under my command. Let them cumber themselves with nothing in the way of offence except one tall

230

spear each, and see that every man is provided with water and dates for twenty days' sustenance of horse and man in the desert."

The Emir smiled as he placed special emphasis on the word "oldest," and the young men departed abashed to obey his orders.

Next morning Count Herbert von Schonburg saw near his camp by the water-holes a small group of horsemen standing motionless in the desert, their lances erect, butt downward, resting on the sand, the little company looking like an oasis of leafless poplars. The Count was instantly astride his Arab charger, at the head of his men, ready to meet whatever came, but on this occasion the enemy made no effort to bring on a battle, but remained silent and stationary, differing greatly from the hordes that had preceded it.

"Well," cried the impatient Count, "if Mahomet will not come to the mountain, the mountain for once will oblige him."

He gave the word to charge, and put spurs to his horse, causing instant animation in the band of Saracens, who fled before him as rapidly as the Germans advanced. It is needless to dwell on the project of the Emir, who simply followed the example of the desert mirages he had so often witnessed in wonder. Never did the Germans come within touch of their foes, always visible, but not to be overtaken. When at last Count Herbert was convinced that his horses were no match for the fleet steeds of his opponents he discovered that he and his band were hopelessly lost in the arid and pathless desert, the spears of the seemingly phantom host ever quivering before him in the tremulous heated air against the cloudless horizon. Now all his energies were bent toward finding the way that led to the camp by the water-holes, but sense of locality seemed to have left him, and the ghostly company which hung so persistently on his flanks gave no indication of direction, but merely followed as before they had fled. One by one the Count's soldiers succumbed, and when at last the forty spears hedged him round the Emir approached a prisoner incapable of action. The useless sword which hung from his saddle was taken, and water was given to the exhausted man and his dying horse.

When the Emir Soldan and his forty followers rode into camp with their prisoner there was a jubilant outcry, and the demand was made that the foreign dog be instantly decapitated, but the Emir smiled and, holding up his hand, said soothingly:

"Softly, softly, true followers of the only Prophet. Those who neglected to remove his head while his good sword guarded it, shall not now possess themselves of it, when that sword is in my hands."

And against this there could be no protest, for the prisoner belonged to the Emir alone, and was to be dealt with as the captor ordained.

When the Count had recovered speech, and was able to hold himself as a man should, the Emir summoned him, and they had a conference together in Soldan's tent.

"Western barbarian," said the Emir, speaking in that common tongue made up of languages Asiatic and European, a strange mixture by means of which invaders and invaded communicated with each other, "who are you and from what benighted land do you come?"

"I am Count Herbert von Schonburg. My castle overlooks the Rhine in Germany."

"What is the Rhine? A province of which you are the ruler?"

"No, your Highness, it is a river; a lordly stream that never diminishes, but flows unceasingly between green vine-clad hills; would that I had some of the vintage therefore to cheer me in my captivity and remove the taste of this brackish water!"

"In the name of the Prophet, then, why did you leave it?"

"Indeed, your Highness, I have often asked myself that question of late and found but insufficient answer."

"If I give you back your sword, which not I, but the demon Thirst captured from you, will you pledge me your word that you will draw it no more against those of my faith, but will return to your own land, safe escort being afforded you to the great sea where you can take ship?"

"As I have fought for ten years, and have come no nearer Jerusalem than where I now stand, I am content to give you my word in exchange for my sword, and the escort you promise."

And thus it came about that Count Herbert von Schonburg, although still a young man, relinquished all thought of conquering the Holy Land, and found himself one evening, after a long march, gazing on the placid bosom of the broad Rhine, which he had not seen since he bade good-bye to it, a boy of twenty-one, then as warlike and ambitious, as now, he was peace loving and tired of strife. The very air of the Rhine valley breathed rest and quiet, and Herbert, with a deep sigh, welcomed the thought of a life passed in comforting uneventfulness.

"Conrad," he said to his one follower, "I will encamp here for the night. Ride on down the Rhine, I beg of you, and cross the river where you may, that you may announce my coming some time before I arrive. My father is an old man, and I am the last of the race, so I do not wish to come unexpectedly on him; therefore break to him with caution the fact that I am in the neighbourhood, for hearing nothing from me all these years it is like to happen he believes me dead."

Conrad rode down the path by the river and disappeared while his master, after seeing to the welfare of his horse, threw himself down in a thicket and slept the untroubled sleep of the seasoned soldier. It was daylight when he was awakened by the tramp of horses. Starting to his feet, he was confronted by a grizzled warrior with half a dozen men at his back, and at first the Count thought himself again a prisoner, but the friendliness of the officer soon set all doubts at rest.

"Are you Count Herbert von Schonburg?" asked the intruder.

"Yes. Who are you?"

"I am Richart, custodian of Castle Gudenfels, and commander of the small forces possessed by her Ladyship, Countess von Falkenstein. I have to acquaint you with the fact that your servant and messenger has been captured. Your castle of Schonburg is besieged, and Conrad, unaware, rode straight into custody. This coming to the ears of my lady the Countess, she directed me to intercept you if possible, so that you might not share the fate of your servant, and offer to you the hospitality of Gudenfels Castle until such time as you had determined what to do in relation to the siege of your own."

"I give my warmest thanks to the Countess for her thoughtfulness. Is her husband the Count then dead?"

"It is the young Countess von Falkenstein whose orders I carry. Her father and mother are both dead, and her Ladyship, their only child, now holds Gudenfels."

"What, that little girl? She was but a child when I left the Rhine."

"Her Ladyship is a woman of nineteen now."

"And how long has my father been besieged?"

"Alas! it grieves me to state that your father, Count von Schonburg, has also passed away. He has been dead these two years."

The young man bowed his head and crossed himself. For a long time he rode in silence, meditating upon this unwelcome intelligence, grieved to think that such a desolate home-coming awaited him.

"Who, then, holds my castle against the besiegers?"

"The custodian Heinrich has stubbornly stood siege since the Count, your father, died, saying he carries out the orders of his lord until the return of the son."

"Ah! if Heinrich is in command then is the castle safe," cried the young man, with enthusiasm. "He is a born warrior and first taught me the use of the broad-sword. Who besieges us? The Archbishop of Mayence? He was ever a turbulent prelate and held spite against our house."

Richart shifted uneasily in his saddle, and for the moment did not answer. Then he said, with hesitation:

"I think the Archbishop regards the siege with favour, but I know little of the matter. My Lady, the Countess, will possess you with full information."

234

Count Herbert looked with astonishment upon the custodian of Castle Gudenfels. Here was a contest going on at his very doors, even if on the opposite side of the river, and yet a veteran knew nothing of the contest. But they were now at the frowning gates of Castle Gudenfels, with its lofty square pinnacled tower, and the curiosity of the young Count was dimmed by the admiration he felt for this great stronghold as he gazed upward at it. An instant later he with his escort passed through the gateway and stood in the courtyard of the castle. When he had dismounted the Count said to Richart:

"I have travelled far, and am not in fit state to be presented to a lady. Indeed, now that I am here, I dread the meeting. I have seen nothing of women for ten years, and knew little of them before I left the Rhine. Take me, I beg of you, to a room where I may make some preparation other than the camp has heretofore afforded, and bring me, if you can, a few garments with which to replenish this faded, torn and dusty apparel."

"My Lord, you will find everything you wish in the rooms allotted to you. Surmising your needs, I gave orders to that effect before I left the castle."

"That was thoughtful of you, Richart, and I shall not forget it."

The Custodian without replying led his guest up one stair and then another. The two traversed a long passage until they came to an open door. Richart standing aside, bowed low, and entreated his lordship to enter. Count Herbert passed into a large room from which a doorway led into a smaller apartment which the young man saw was fitted as a bedroom. The rooms hung high over the Rhine, but the view of the river was impeded by the numerous heavy iron bars which formed a formidable lattice-work before the windows. The Count was about to thank his conductor for providing so sumptuously for him, but, turning, he was amazed to see Richart outside with breathless eagerness draw shut the strong door that led to the passage from which he had entered, and a moment later, Herbert heard the ominous sound of stout bolts being shot into their sockets. He stood for a moment gazing blankly now at the bolted door, now at the barred window, and then slowly there came to him the knowledge which would have enlightened a more suspicious man long before—that he was a prisoner in the grim fortress of Gudenfels. Casting his mind backward over the events of the morning, he now saw a dozen sinister warnings that had heretofore escaped him. If a friendly invitation had been intended, what need of the numerous guard of armed men sent to escort him? Why had Richart hesitated when certain questions were asked him? Count Herbert paced up and down the long room, reviewing with clouded brow the events of the past few hours, beginning with the glorious freedom of the open hillside in the early dawn and ending with these impregnable stone walls that now environed him. He was a man slow to anger, but resentment once aroused, burned in his heart with a steady fervour that was unquenchable. He stopped at last in his aimless pacing, raised his clinched fist toward the timbered ceiling, and cursed the Countess von Falkenstein. In his striding to and fro the silence had been broken by the clank of his sword on the stone floor, and he now smiled grimly as he realised that they had not dared to deprive him of his formidable weapon; they had caged the lion from the distant desert without having had the courage to clip his claws. The Count drew his broadsword and swung it hissing through the air, measuring its reach with reference to the walls on either hand, then, satisfying himself that he had free play, he took up a position before the door and stood there motionless as the statue of a war-god. "Now, by the Cross I fought for," he muttered to himself, "the first man who sets foot across this threshold enters the chamber of death."

He remained thus, leaning with folded arms on the hilt of his long sword, whose point rested on the flags of the floor, and at last his patience was rewarded. He heard the rattle of the bolts outside, and a tense eagerness thrilled his stalwart frame. The door came cautiously inward for a space of perhaps two feet and was then brought to a stand by the tightening links of a stout chain, fastened one end to the door, the other to the outer wall. Through the space that thus gave a view of the wide outer passage the Count saw Richart stand with pale face, well back at a safe distance in the centre of the hall. Two men-at-arms held a position behind their master.

"My Lord," began Richart in trembling voice, "her Ladyship, the Countess, desires——"

"Open the door, you cringing Judas!" interrupted the stern command of the count; "open the door and set me as free as your villainy found me. I hold no parley with a traitor."

"My Lord, I implore you to listen. No harm is intended you, and my Lady, the Countess, asks of you a conference touching——"

The heavy sword swung in the air and came down upon the chain with a force that made the stout oaken door shudder. Scattering sparks cast a momentary glow of red on the whitened cheeks of the startled onlookers. The edge of the sword clove the upper circumference of an iron link, leaving the severed ends gleaming like burnished silver, but the chain still held. Again and again the sword fell, but never twice in the same spot, anger adding strength to the blows, but subtracting skill.

"My Lord! my Lord!" beseeched Richart, "restrain your fury. You cannot escape from this strong castle even though you sever the chain."

"I'll trust my sword for that," muttered the prisoner between his set teeth.

There now rang out on the conflict a new voice; the voice of a woman, clear and commanding, the tones instinct with that inborn quality of imperious authority which expects and usually obtains instant obedience.

"Close the door, Richart," cried the unseen lady. The servitor made a motion to obey, but the swoop of the sword seemed to paralyse him where he stood. He cast a beseeching look at his mistress, which said as plainly as words: "You are ordering me to my death." The Count, his weapon high in mid-air, suddenly swerved it from its course, for there appeared across the opening a woman's hand and arm, white and shapely, fleecy lace falling away in dainty folds from the rounded contour of the arm. The small, firm hand grasped bravely the almost severed chain and the next instant the door was drawn shut, the bolts clanking into their places. Count Herbert, paused, leaning on his sword, gazing bewildered at the closed door.

"Ye gods of war!" he cried; "never have I seen before such cool courage as that!"

For a long time the Count walked up and down the spacious room, stopping now and then at the window to peer through the iron grille at the rapid current of the river far below, the noble stream as typical of freedom as were the bars that crossed his vision, of captivity. It seemed that the authorities of the castle had abandoned all thought of further communication with their truculent prisoner. Finally he entered the inner room and flung himself down, booted and spurred as he was, upon the couch, and, his sword for a bedmate, slept. The day was far spent when he awoke, and his first sensation was that of gnawing hunger, for he was a healthy man. His next, that he had heard in his sleep the cautious drawing of bolts, as if his enemies purposed to project themselves surreptitiously in upon him, taking him at a disadvantage. He sat upright, his sword ready for action, and listened intently. The silence was profound, and as the Count sat breathless, the stillness seemed to be emphasised rather than disturbed by a long-drawn sigh which sent a thrill of superstitious fear through the stalwart frame of the young man, for he well knew that the Rhine was infested with spirits animated by evil intentions toward human beings, and against such spirits his sword was but as a willow wand. He remembered with renewed awe that this castle stood only a few leagues above the Lurlei rocks where a nymph of unearthly beauty lured men to their destruction, and the knight crossed himself as a protection against all such. Gathering courage from this devout act, and abandoning his useless weapon, he tiptoed to the door that led to the larger apartment, and there found his worst anticipations realised. With her back against the closed outer door stood a Siren of the Rhine, and, as if to show how futile is the support of the Evil One in a crisis, her very lips were pallid with fear and her blue eyes were wide with apprehension, as they met those of the Count von Schonburg. Her hair, the colour of ripe yellow wheat, rose from her smooth white forehead and descended in a thick braid that almost reached to the floor. She was dressed in the humble garb of a serving maiden, the square bit of lace on her crown of fair hair and the apron she wore, as spotless as new fallen snow. In her hand she held a tray which supported a loaf of bread and a huge flagon brimming with wine. On seeing the Count, her quick breathing stopped for the moment and she dropped a low courtesy.

"My Lord," she said, but there came a catch in her throat, and she could speak no further.

238

Seeing that he had to deal with no spirit, but with an inhabitant of the world he knew and did not fear, there arose a strange exultation in the heart of the Count as he looked upon this fair representative of his own country. For ten years he had seen no woman, and now a sudden sense of what he had lost overwhelmed him, his own breath coming quicker as the realisation of this impressed itself upon him. He strode rapidly toward her, and she seemed to shrink into the wall at his approach, wild fear springing into her eyes, but he merely took the laden tray from her trembling hands and placed it upon a bench. Then raising the flagon to his lips, he drank a full half of its contents before withdrawing it. A deep sigh of satisfaction followed, and he said, somewhat shamefacedly:

"Forgive my hurried greed, maiden, but the thirst of the desert seems to be in my throat, and the good wine reminds me that I am a German."

"It was brought for your use," replied the girl, demurely, "and I am gratified that it meets your commendation, my Lord."

"And so also do you, my girl. What is your name and who are you?"

"I am called Beatrix, my Lord, a serving-maid of this castle, the daughter of the woodman Wilhelm, and, alas! that it should be so, for the present your jailer."

"If I quarrelled as little with my detention, as I see I am like to do with my keeper, I fear captivity would hold me long in thrall. Are the men in the castle such cravens then that they bestow so unwelcome a task upon a woman?"

"The men are no cravens, my Lord, but this castle is at war with yours, and for each man there is a post. A woman would be less missed if so brave a warrior as Count von Schonburg thought fit to war upon us."

"But a woman makes war upon me, Beatrix. What am I to do? Surrender humbly?"

"Brave men have done so before now and will again, my Lord, where women are concerned. At least," added Beatrix, blushing and casting down her eyes, "I have been so informed."

"And small blame to them," cried the count, with enthusiasm. "I swear to you, my girl, that if women warriors were like the woodman's daughter, I would cast away all arms except these with which to enclasp her."

And he stretched out his hands, taking a step nearer, while she shrank in alarm from him.

"My Lord, I am but an humble messenger, and I beg of you to listen to what I am asked to say. My Lady, the Countess, has commissioned me to tell you that—"

A startling malediction of the Countess that accorded ill with the scarlet cross emblazoned on the young man's breast, interrupted the girl.

"I hold no traffic with the Countess," he cried. "She has treacherously laid me by the heels, coming as I did from battling for the Cross that she doubtless professes to regard as sacred."

"It was because she feared you, my Lord. These years back tales of your valour in the Holy Land have come to the Rhine, and now you return to find your house at war with hers. What was she to do? The chances stood even with only your underling in command; judge then what her fate must be with your strong sword thrown in the balance against her. All's fair in war, said those who counselled her. What would you have done in such an extremity, my Lord?"

"What would I have done? I would have met my enemy sword in hand and talked with him or fought with him as best suited his inclination."

"But a lady cannot meet you, sword in hand, my Lord."

The Count paused in the walk he had begun when the injustice of his usage impressed itself once more upon him. He looked admiringly at the girl.

"That is most true, Beatrix. I had forgotten. Still, I should not have been met with cozenry. Here came I from starvation in the wilderness, thirst in the desert, and from the stress of the battle-field, back to mine own land with my heart full of yearning love for it and for all within its boundaries. I came even from prison, captured in fair fight, by an untaught heathen, whose men lay slain by my hand, yet with the nobility of a true warrior, he asked neither ransom nor hostage, but handed back my sword, saying, 'Go in peace.' That in a heathen land! but no sooner does my foot rest on this Christian soil than I am met by false smiles and lying tongues, and my welcome to a neighbour's house is the clank of the inthrust bolt."

"Oh, it was a shameful act and not to be defended," cried the girl, with moist eyes and quivering lip, the sympathetic reverberation of her voice again arresting the impatient steps of the young man, causing him to pause and view her with a feeling that he could not understand, and which he found some difficulty in controlling. Suddenly all desire for restraint left him, he sprang forward, clasped the girl in his arms and drew her into the middle of the room, where she could not give the signal that might open the door.

"My Lord! my Lord!" she cried in terror, struggling without avail to free herself.

"You said all's fair in war and saying so, gave but half the proverb, which adds, all's fair in love as well, and maiden, nymph of the woodland, so rapidly does a man learn that which he has never been taught, I proclaim with confidence that I love thee."

"A diffident and gentle lover you prove yourself!" she gasped with rising indignation, holding him from her.

"Indeed, my girl, there was little of diffidence or gentleness in my warring, and my wooing is like to have a touch of the same quality. It is useless to struggle for I have thee firm, so take to yourself some of that gentleness you recommend to me."

He strove to kiss her, but Beatrix held her head far from him, her open palm pressed against the red cross that glowed upon his breast, keeping him thus at arm's length.

"Count von Schonburg, what is the treachery of any other compared with yours? You came heedlessly into this castle, suspecting as you say,

241

no danger: I came within this room to do you service, knowing my peril, but trusting to the honour of a true soldier of the Cross, and this is my reward! First tear from your breast this sacred emblem, valorous assaulter of a defenceless woman, for it should be worn by none but stainless gentlemen."

Count Herbert's arms relaxed, and his hands dropped listless to his sides.

"By my sword," he said, "they taught you invective in the forest. You are free. Go."

The girl made no motion to profit by her newly acquired liberty, but stood there, glancing sideways at him who scowled menacingly at her.

When at last she spoke, she said, shyly: "I have not yet fulfilled my mission."

"Fulfil it then in the fiend's name and begone."

"Will you consent to see my Lady the Countess?"

"No."

"Will you promise not to make war upon her if you are released?"

"No."

"If, in spite of your boorishness, she sets you free, what will you do?"

"I will rally my followers to my banner, scatter the forces that surround my castle, then demolish this prison trap."

"Am I in truth to carry such answers to the Countess?"

"You are to do as best pleases you, now and forever."

"I am but a simple serving-maid, and know nothing of high questions of state, yet it seems to me such replies do not oil prison bolts, and believe me, I grieve to see you thus detained."

"I am grateful for your consideration. Is your embassy completed?"

The girl, her eyes on the stone floor, paused long before replying, then

242

said, giving no warning of a change of subject, and still not raising her eyes to his:

"You took me by surprise; I am not used to being handled roughly; you forget the distance between your station and mine, you being a noble of the Empire, and I but a serving-maid; if, in my anger, I spoke in a manner unbecoming one so humble, I do beseech that your Lordship pardon me."

"Now by the Cross to which you appealed, how long will you stand chattering there? Think you I am made of adamant, and not of flesh and blood? My garments are tattered at best, I would in woman's company they were finer, and this cross of Genoa red hangs to my tunic, but by a few frail threads. Beware, therefore, that I tear it not from my breast as you advised, and cast it from me."

Beatrix lifted one frightened glance to the young man's face and saw standing on his brow great drops of sweat. His right hand grasped the upper portion of the velvet cross, partly detached from his doublet, and he looked loweringly upon her. Swiftly she smote the door twice with her hand and instantly the portal opened as far as the chain would allow it. Count Herbert noticed that in the interval, three other chains had been added to the one that formerly had baffled his sword. The girl, like a woodland pigeon, darted underneath the lower chain, and although the prisoner took a rapid step forward, the door, with greater speed, closed and was bolted.

The Count had requested the girl to be gone, and surely should have been contented now that she had withdrawn herself, yet so shifty a thing is human nature, that no sooner were his commands obeyed than he began to bewail their fulfilment. He accused himself of being a double fool, first, for not holding her when he had her; and secondly, having allowed her to depart, he bemoaned the fact that he had acted rudely to her, and thus had probably made her return impossible. His prison seemed inexpressibly dreary lacking her presence. Once or twice he called out her name, but the echoing empty walls alone replied.

For the first time in his life the heavy sleep of the camp deserted him, and in his dreams he pursued a phantom woman, who continually dissolved in his grasp, now laughingly, now in anger.

The morning found him deeply depressed, and he thought the unaccustomed restraints of a prison were having their effect on the spirits of a man heretofore free. He sat silently on the bench watching the door.

At last, to his great joy, he heard the rattle of bolts being withdrawn. The door opened slowly to the small extent allowed by the chains, but no one entered and the Count sat still, concealed from the view of whoever stood without.

"My Lord Count," came the sweet tones of the girl and the listener with joy, fancied he detected in it a suggestion of apprehension, doubtless caused by the fact that the room seemed deserted. "My Lord Count, I have brought your breakfast; will you not come and receive it?"

Herbert rose slowly and came within range of his jailer's vision. The girl stood in the hall, a repast that would have tempted an epicure arrayed on the wooden trencher she held in her hands.

"Beatrix, come in," he said.

"I fear that in stooping, some portion of this burden may fall. Will you not take the trencher?"

The young man stepped to the opening and, taking the tray from her, placed it on the bench as he had previously done; then repeated his invitation.

"You were displeased with my company before, my Lord, and I am loath again to offend."

"Beatrix, I beg you to enter. I have something to say to you."

"Stout chains bar not words, my Lord. Speak and I shall listen."

"What I have to say, is for your ear alone."

"Then are the conditions perfect for such converse, my Lord. No guard stands within this hall."

The Count sighed deeply, turned and sat again on the bench, burying his face in his hands. The maiden having given excellent reasons why she should not enter, thus satisfying her sense of logic, now set logic at defiance, slipped under the lowest chain and stood within the room, and, so that there might be no accusation that she did things by halves, closed the door leaning her back against it. The knight looked up at her and saw that she too had rested but indifferently. Her lovely eyes half veiled, showed traces of weeping, and there was a wistful expression in her face that touched him tenderly, and made him long for her; nevertheless he kept a rigid government upon himself, and sat there regarding her, she flushing, slightly under his scrutiny, not daring to return his ardent gaze.

"Beatrix," he said slowly, "I have acted towards you like a boor and a ruffian, as indeed I am; but let this plead for me, that I have ever been used to the roughness of the camp, bereft of gentler influences. I ask your forgiveness."

"There is nothing to forgive. You are a noble of the Empire, and I but a lowly serving-maid."

"Nay, that cuts me to the heart, and is my bitterest condemnation. A true man were courteous to high and low alike. Now, indeed, you overwhelm me with shame, maiden of the woodlands."

"Such was not my intention, my Lord. I hold you truly noble in nature as well as in rank, otherwise I stood not here."

"Beatrix, does any woodlander come from the forest to the castle walls and there give signal intended for you alone?"

"Oh, no, my Lord."

"Perhaps you have kindly preference for some one within this stronghold?"

"You forget, my Lord, that the castle is ruled by a lady, and that the preference you indicate would accord ill with her womanly government."

"In truth I know little of woman's rule, but given such, I suppose the case would stand as you say. The Countess then frowns upon lovers' meetings."

"How could it be otherwise?"

"Have you told her of—of yesterday?"

"You mean of your refusal to come to terms with her? Yes, my Lord."

"I mean nothing of the kind, Beatrix."

"No one outside this room has been told aught to your disadvantage, my Lord," said the girl blushing rose-red.

"Then she suspects nothing?"

"Suspects nothing of what, my Lord?"

"That I love you, Beatrix."

The girl caught her breath, and seemed about to fly, but gathering courage, remained, and said speaking hurriedly and in some confusion: "As I did not suspect it myself I see not how my Lady should have made any such surmise, but indeed it may be so, for she chided me bitterly for remaining so long with you, and made me weep with her keen censure; yet am I here now against her express wish and command, but that is because of my strong sympathy for you and my belief that the Countess has wrongfully treated you."

"I care nothing for the opinion of that harridan, except that it may bring harsh usage to you; but Beatrix, I have told you bluntly of my love for you, answer me as honestly."

"My Lord, you spoke just now of a woodlander—"

"Ah, there is one then. Indeed, I feared as much, for there can be none on all the Rhine as beautiful or as good as you."

"There are many woodlanders, my Lord, and many women more beautiful than I. What I was about to say was that I would rather be the wife of the poorest forester, and lived in the roughest hut on the hillside, than dwell otherwise in the grandest castle on the Rhine."

"Surely, surely. But you shall dwell in my castle of Schonburg as my

246

most honoured wife, if you but will it so."

"Then, my Lord, I must bid you beware of what you propose. Your wife must be chosen from the highest in the land, and not from the lowliest. It is not fitting that you should endeavour to raise a serving-maid to the position of Countess von Schonburg. You would lose caste among your equals, and bring unhappiness upon us both."

Count Herbert grasped his sword and lifting it, cried angrily: "By the Cross I serve, the man who refuses to greet my wife as he would greet the Empress, shall feel the weight of this blade."

"You cannot kill a whisper with a sword, my Lord."

"I can kill the whisperer."

"That can you not, my Lord, for the whisperer will be a woman."

"Then out upon them, we will have no traffic with them. I have lived too long away from the petty restrictions of civilisation to be bound down by them now, for I come from a region where a man's sword and not his rank preserved his life." As he spoke he again raised his huge weapon aloft, but now held it by the blade so that it stood out against the bright window like a black cross of iron, and his voice rang forth defiantly: "With that blade I won my honour; by the symbol of its hilt I hope to obtain my soul's salvation, on both united I swear to be to you a true lover and a loyal husband."

With swift motion the girl covered her face with her hands and Herbert saw the crystal drops trickle between her fingers. For long she could not speak and then mastering her emotion, she said brokenly:

"I cannot accept, I cannot now accept. I can take no advantage of a helpless prisoner. At midnight I shall come and set you free, thus my act may atone for the great wrong of your imprisonment; atone partially if not wholly. When you are at liberty, if you wish to forget your words, which I can never do, then am I amply repaid that my poor presence called them forth. If you remember them, and demand of the Countess that I stand as hostage for peace, she is scarce likely to deny you, for she loves not war. But know that nothing you have said is to be held against you, for I would have you leave this castle as free as when you entered it. And now, my Lord, farewell."

Before the unready man could make motion to prevent her, she had opened the door and was gone, leaving it open, thus compelling the prisoner to be his own jailer and close it, for he had no wish now to leave the castle alone when he had been promised such guidance.

The night seemed to Count Herbert the longest he had ever spent, as he sat on the bench, listening for the withdrawing of the bolts; if indeed they were in their sockets, which he doubted. At last the door was pushed softly open, and bending under the chain, he stood in the outside hall, peering through the darkness, to catch sight of his conductor. A great window of stained glass occupied the southern end of the hall, and against it fell the rays of the full moon now high in the heavens, filling the dim and lofty apartment with a coloured radiance resembling his visions of the half tones of fairyland. Like a shadow stood the cloaked figure of the girl, who timidly placed her small hand in his great palm, and that touch gave a thrill of reality to the mysticism of the time and the place. He grasped it closely, fearing it might fade away from him as it had done in his dream. She led him silently by another way from that by which he had entered, and together they passed through a small doorway that communicated with a narrow circular stair which wound round and round downwards until they came to another door at the bottom, which let them out in the moonlight at the foot of a turret.

"Beatrix," whispered the young man, "I am not going to demand you of the Countess. I shall not be indebted to her for my wife. You must come with me now."

"No, no," cried the girl shrinking from him, "I cannot go with you thus surreptitiously, and no one but you and me must ever learn that I led you from the castle. You shall come for me as a lord should for his lady, as if he thought her worthy of him."

"Indeed, that do I. Worthy? It is I who am unworthy, but made more worthy I hope in that you care for me."

From where they stood the knight saw the moonlight fall on his own castle of Schonburg, the rays seeming to transform the grey stone into the whitest of marble, the four towers standing outlined against the blue of the cloudless sky. The silver river of romance, flowed silently at its feet reflecting again the snowy purity of the reality in an inverted quivering watery vision. All the young man's affection for the home he had not seen for years seemed to blend with his love for the girl standing there in the moonlight. Gently he drew her to him, and kissed her unresisting lips.

"Woodland maiden," he said tenderly, "here at the edge of the forest is your rightful home and not in this grim castle, and here will I woo thee again, being now a free man."

"Indeed," said the girl with a laugh in which a sob and a sigh intermingled, "it is but scanty freedom I have brought to you; an exchange of silken fetters for iron chains."

His arms still around her, he unloosed the ribbon that held in thrall the thick braid of golden hair, and parting the clustering strands speedily encompassed her in a cloak of misty fragrance that seemed as unsubstantial as the moonlight that glittered through its meshes. He stood back the better to admire the picture he seemed to have created.

"My darling," he cried, "you are no woodland woman, but the very spirit of the forest herself. You are so beautiful, I dare not leave you here to the mercies of this demon, who, finding me gone, may revenge herself on you. If before she dared to censure you, what may she not do now that you have set me free? Curse her that she stands for a moment between my love and me."

He raised his clenched fist and shook it at the tower above him, and seemed about to break forth in new maledictions against the lady, when Beatrix, clasping her hands cried in terror:

"No, no, Herbert, you have said enough. How can you pretend to love me when implacable hatred lies so near to your affection. You must forgive the Countess. Oh, Herbert, Herbert, what more could I do to atone? I have withdrawn my forces from around your castle; I have set you free and your path to Schonburg lies unobstructed. Even now your underling, thinking himself victorious, is preparing an expedition against me, and nothing but your word stands, between me and instant attack. Ponder, I beseech of you, on my position. War, not of my seeking, was bequeathed to me, and a woman who cannot fight must trust to her advisers, and thus may do what her own heart revolts against. They told me that if I made you prisoner I could stop the war, and thus I consented to that act of treachery for which you so justly condemn me."

"Beatrix," cried her amazed lover, "what madness has come over you?"

"No madness touched me, Herbert, until I met you, and I sometimes think that you have brought back with you the eastern sorcery of which I have heard—at least such may perhaps make excuse for my unmaidenly behaviour. Herbert, I am Beatrix of Gudenfels, Countess von Falkenstein, who is and ever will be, if you refuse to pardon her, a most unhappy woman."

"No woodland maiden, but the Countess! The Countess von Falkenstein!" murmured her lover more to himself than to, his eager listener, the lines on his perplexed brow showing that he was endeavouring to adjust the real and the ideal in his slow brain.

"A Countess, Herbert, who will joyfully exchange the privileges of her station for the dear preference shown to the serving-maid."

A smile came to the lips of Von Schonburg as he held out his hands, in which the Countess placed her own.

"My Lady Beatrix," he said, "how can I refuse my pardon for the first encroachment on my liberty, now that you have made me your prisoner for life?"

"Indeed, my captured lord," cried the girl, "you are but now coming to a true sense of your predicament. I marvelled that you felt so resentful about the first offence, when the second was so much more serious. Am I then forgiven for both?"

It seemed that she was, and the Count insisted on returning to his captivity, and coming forth the next day, freed by her commands, whereupon,

250

in the presence of all her vassals, he swore allegiance to her with such deference that her advisers said to her that she must now see they had been right in counselling his imprisonment. Prison, they said, had a wonderfully quieting effect upon even the most truculent, the Count being quickly subdued when he saw his sword-play had but little effect on the chain. The Countess graciously acknowledged that events had indeed proved the wisdom of their course, and said it was not to be wondered at that men should know the disposition of a turbulent man, better than an inexperienced woman could know it.

And thus was the feud between Gudenfels and Schonburg happily ended, and Count Herbert came from the Crusades to find two castles waiting for him instead of one as he had expected, with what he had reason to prize above everything else, a wife as well.

CHAPTER II. — THE REVENGE OF THE OUTLAW

The position of Count Herbert when, at the age of thirty-one he took up his residence in the ancient castle of his line, was a most enviable one. His marriage with Beatrix, Countess von Falkenstein, had added the lustre of a ruling family to the prestige of his own, and the renown of his valour in the East had lost nothing in transit from the shores of the Mediterranean to the banks of the Rhine. The Counts of Schonburg had ever been the most conservative in counsel and the most radical in the fray, and thus Herbert on returning, found himself, without seeking the honor, regarded by common consent as leader of the nobility whose castles bordered the renowned river. The Emperor, as was usually the case when these imperial figure-heads were elected by the three archbishops and their four colleagues, was a nonentity, who made no attempt to govern a turbulent land that so many were willing to govern for him. His majesty left sword and sceptre to those who cared for such baubles, and employed himself in banding together the most notable company of meistersingers that Germany had ever listened to. But although harmony reigned in Frankfort, the capital, there was much lack of it along the Rhine, and the man with the swiftest and heaviest sword, usually accumulated the greatest amount of property, movable and otherwise.

Among the truculent nobles who terrorised the country side, none was held In greater awe than Baron von Wiethoff, whose Schloss occupied a promontory Some distance up the stream from Castle Schonburg, on the same side of the river. Public opinion condemned the Baron, not because he exacted tribute from the merchants who sailed down the Rhine, for such collections were universally regarded as a legitimate source of revenue, but because he was in the habit of killing the goose that laid the golden egg, which action was looked upon with disfavour by those who resided between Schloss Wiethoff and Cologne, as interfering with their right to exist, for a merchant, although well-plucked, is still of advantage to those in whose hands he falls, if life and some of his goods are left to him. Whereas, when cleft from scalp to midriff by the Baron's long sword, he became of no value either to himself or to others. While many nobles were satisfied with levying a scant five or ten per cent on a voyager's belongings, the Baron rarely rested contented until he had acquired the full hundred, and, the merchant objecting, von Wiethoff would usually order him hanged or decapitated, although at times when he was in good humour he was wont to confer honour upon the trading classes by despatching the grumbling seller of goods with his own weapon, which created less joy in the commercial community than the Baron seemed to expect. Thus navigation on the swift current of the Rhine began to languish, for there was little profit in the transit of goods from Mayence to Cologne if the whole consignment stood in jeopardy and the owner's life as well, so the merchants got into the habit of carrying their gear overland on the backs of mules, thus putting the nobility to great inconvenience in scouring the forests, endeavouring to intercept the caravans. The nobility, with that stern sense of justice which has ever characterised the higher classes, placed the blame of this diversion of traffic from its natural channel not upon the merchants but upon the Baron, where undoubtedly it rightly belonged, and although, when they came upon an overland company which was seeking to avoid them, they gathered in an extra percentage of the goods to repay in a measure the greater difficulty they had in their woodland search, they always informed the merchants with much politeness, that, when river traffic was resumed, they would be pleased to revert to the original exaction, which the traders, not without reason pointed out was of little avail to them as long as Baron von Wiethoff was permitted to confiscate the whole.

In their endeavours to resuscitate the navigation interests of the Rhine, several expeditions had been formed against the Baron, but his castle was strong, and there were so many conflicting interests among those who attacked him that he had always come out victorious, and after each onslaught the merchants suffered more severely than before.

Affairs were in this unsatisfactory condition when Count Herbert of Schonburg returned from the Holy Land, the fame of his deeds upon him, and married Beatrix of Gudenfels. Although the nobles of the Upper Rhine held aloof from all contest with the savage Baron of Schloss Wiethoff, his exactions not interfering with their incomes, many of those further down the river offered their services to Count Herbert, if he would consent to lead them against the Baron, but the Count pleaded that he was still a stranger in his own country, having so recently returned from his ten contentious years in Syria, therefore he begged time to study the novel conditions confronting him before giving an answer to their proposal.

The Count learned that the previous attacks made upon Schloss Wiethoff had been conducted with but indifferent generalship, and that failure had been richly earned by desertions from the attacking force, each noble thinking himself justified in withdrawing himself and his men, when offended, or when the conduct of affairs displeased him, so von Schonburg informed the second deputation which waited on him, that he was more accustomed to depend on himself than on the aid of others, and that if any quarrel arose between Castle Schonburg and Schloss Wiethoff, the Count would endeavour to settle the dispute with his own sword, which reply greatly encouraged the Baron when he heard of it, for he wished to try conclusions with the newcomer, and made no secret of his disbelief in the latter's Saracenic exploits, saying the Count had returned when there was none left of the band he took with him, and had, therefore, with much wisdom, left himself free from contradiction.

There was some disappointment up and down the Rhine when time passed and the Count made no warlike move. It was well known that the Countess was much averse to war, notwithstanding the fact that she was indebted to war for her stalwart husband, and her peaceful nature was held to excuse the non-combative life lived by the Count, although there were others who gave it as their opinion that the Count was really afraid of the Baron, who daily became more and more obnoxious as there seemed to be less and less to fear. Such boldness did the Baron achieve that he even organised a slight raid upon the estate of Gudenfels which belonged to the Count's wife, but still Herbert of Schonburg did not venture from the security of his castle, greatly to the disappointment and the disgust of his neighbours, for there are on earth no people who love a fight more dearly than do those who reside along the banks of the placid Rhine.

At last an heir was born to Castle Schonburg, and the rejoicings throughout all the district governed by the Count were general and enthusiastic. Bonfires were lit on the heights and the noble river glowed red under the illumination at night. The boy who had arrived at the castle was said to give promise of having all the beauty of his mother and all the strength of his father, which was admitted by everybody to be a desirable combination, although some shook their heads and said they hoped that with strength there would come greater courage than the Count appeared to possess. Nevertheless, the Count had still some who believed in him, notwithstanding his long period of inaction, and these said that on the night the boy was born, and word was brought to him in the great hall that mother and child were well, the cloud that had its habitual resting-place on the Count's brow lifted and his lordship took down from its place his great broadsword, rubbed from its blade the dust and the rust that had collected, swung the huge weapon hissing through the air, and heaved a deep sigh, as one who had come to the end of a period of restraint.

The boy was just one month old on the night that there was a thunderous knocking at the gate of Schloss Wiethoff. The Baron hastily buckled on his armour and was soon at the head of his men eager to repel the invader. In a marvellously short space of time there was a contest in progress at the gates which would have delighted the heart of the most quarrelsome noble from Mayence to Cologne. The attacking party which appeared in large force before the gate, attempted to batter in the oaken leaves of the portal, but the Baron was always prepared for such visitors, and the heavy timbers that were heaved against the oak made little impression, while von Wiethoff roared defiance from the top of the wall that surrounded the castle and what was more to the purpose, showered down stones and arrows on the besiegers, grievously thinning their ranks. The Baron, with creditable ingenuity, had constructed above the inside of the gate a scaffolding, on the top of which was piled a mountain of huge stones. This scaffold was arranged in such a way that a man pulling a lever caused it to collapse, thus piling the stones instantly against the inside of the gate, rendering it impregnable against assault by battering rams. The Baron was always jubilant when his neighbours attempted to force the gate, for he was afforded much amusement at small expense to himself, and he cared little for the damage the front door received, as he had built his castle not for ornament but for his own protection. He was a man with an amazing vocabulary, and as he stood on the wall shaking his mailed fist at the intruders he poured forth upon them invective more personal than complimentary.

While thus engaged, rejoicing over the repulse of the besiegers, for the attack was evidently losing its vigour, he was amazed to note a sudden illumination of the forest-covered hill which he was facing. The attacking party rallied with a yell when the light struck them, and the Baron, looking hastily over his shoulder to learn the source of the ruddy glow on the trees, saw with dismay that his castle was on fire and that Count Herbert followed by his men had possession of the battlements to the rear, while the courtyard swarmed with soldiers, who had evidently scaled the low wall along the river front from rafts or boats.

"Surrender!" cried Count Herbert, advancing along the wall. "Your castle is taken, and will be a heap of ruins within the hour."

"Then may you be buried beneath them," roared the Baron, springing to the attack.

Although the Baron was a younger man than his antagonist, it was soon proven that his sword play was not equal to that of the Count, and the broadsword fight on the battlements in the light of the flaming stronghold, was of short duration, watched breathlessly as it was by men of both parties above and below. Twice the Baron's guard was broken, and the third time, such was the terrific impact of iron on iron, that the Baron's weapon was struck from his benumbed hands and fell glittering through the air to the ground outside the walls. The Count paused in his onslaught, refraining from striking a disarmed man, but again demanding his submission. The Baron cast one glance at his burning house, saw that it was doomed, then, with a movement as reckless as it was unexpected, took the terrific leap from the wall top to the ground, alighting on his feet near his fallen sword which he speedily recovered. For an instant the Count hovered on the brink to follow him, but the swift thought of his wife and child restrained him, and he feared a broken limb in the fall, leaving him thus at the mercy of his enemy. The moment for decision was short enough, but the years of regret for this

256

hesitation were many and long. There were a hundred men before the walls to intercept the Baron, and it seemed useless to jeopardise life or limb in taking the leap, so the Count contented himself by giving the loud command: "Seize that man and bind him."

It was an order easy to give and easy to obey had there been a dozen men below as brave as their captain, or even one as brave, as stalwart and as skilful; but the Baron struck sturdily around him and mowed his way through the throng as effectually as a reaper with a sickle clears a path for himself in the standing corn. Before Herbert realised what was happening, the Baron was safe in the obscurity of the forest.

The Count of Schonburg was not a man to do things by halves, even though upon the occasion of this attack he allowed the Baron to slip through his fingers. When the ruins of the Schloss cooled, he caused them to be removed and flung stone by stone into the river, leaving not a vestige of the castle that had so long been a terror to the district, holding that if the lair were destroyed the wolf would not return. In this the Count proved but partly right. Baron von Wiethoff renounced his order, and became an outlaw, gathering round him in the forest all the turbulent characters, not in regular service elsewhere, publishing along the Rhine by means of prisoners he took and then released that as the nobility seemed to object to his preying upon the merchants, he would endeavour to amend his ways and would harry instead such castles as fell into his hands. Thus Baron von Wiethoff became known as the Outlaw of the Hundsrück, and being as intrepid as he was merciless, soon made the Rhenish nobility withdraw attention from other people's quarrels in order to bestow strict surveillance upon their own. It is possible that if the dwellers along the river had realised at first the kind of neighbour that had been produced by burning out the Baron, they might, by combination have hunted him down in the widespread forests of the Hundsrück, but as the years went on, the Outlaw acquired such knowledge of the interminable mazes of this wilderness, that it is doubtful whether all the troops in the Empire could have brought his band to bay. The outlaws always fled before a superior force, and always massacred an inferior one, and like the lightning, no man could predict where the next stroke would fall. On one occasion he even threatened the walled town of Coblentz, and the citizens compounded with him, saying they had no quarrel with any but the surrounding nobles, which expression the thrifty burghers regretted when Count Herbert marched his men through their streets and for every coin they, had paid the Outlaw, exacted ten.

The boy of Castle Schonburg was three years old, when he was allowed to play on the battlements, sporting with a wooden sword and imagining himself as great a warrior as his father had ever been. He was a brave little fellow whom nothing could frighten but the stories his nurse told him of the gnomes and goblins who infested the Rhine, and he longed for the time when he would be a man and wear a real sword. One day just before he had completed his fourth year, a man came slinking out of the forest to the foot of the wall, for the watch was now slack as the Outlaw had not been heard of for months, and then was far away in the direction of Mayence. The nurse was holding a most absorbing conversation with the man-at-arms, who should, instead, have been pacing up and down the terrace while she should have been watching her charge. The man outside gave a low whistle which attracted the attention of the child and then beckoned him to come further along the wall until he had passed the west tower.

"Well, little coward," said the man, "I did not think you would have the courage to come so far away from the women."

"I am not a coward," answered the lad, stoutly, "and I do not care about the women at all."

"Your father was a coward."

"He is not. He is the bravest man in the world."

"He did not dare to jump off the wall after the Baron."

"He will cut the Baron in pieces if he ever comes near our castle."

"Yet he dared not jump as the Baron did."

"The Baron was afraid of my father; that's why he jumped."

"Not so. It was your father who feared to follow him, though he had a sword and the Baron had none. You are all cowards in Castle Schonburg. I don't believe you have the courage to jump even though I held out my arms to catch you, but if you do I will give you the sword I wear."

The little boy had climbed on the parapet, and now stood hovering on the brink of the precipice, his childish heart palpitating through fear of the chasm before him, yet beneath its beatings was an insistent command to prove his impugned courage. For some moments there was deep silence, the man below gazing aloft and holding up his hands. At last he lowered his outstretched arms and said in a sneering tone:

"Good-bye, craven son of a craven race. You dare not jump."

The lad, with a cry of despair, precipitated himself into the empty air and came fluttering down like a wounded bird, to fall insensible into the arms that for the moment saved him from death or mutilation. An instant later there was a shriek from the negligent nurse, and the man-at-arms ran along the battlements, a bolt on his cross-bow which he feared to launch at the flying abductor, for in the speeding of it he might slay the heir of Schonburg. By the time the castle was aroused and the gates thrown open to pour forth searchers, the man had disappeared into the forest, and in its depths all trace of young Wilhelm was lost. Some days after, the Count von Schonburg came upon the deserted camp of the outlaws, and found there evidences, not necessary to be here set down, that his son had been murdered. Imposing secrecy on his followers, so that the Countess might still retain her unshaken belief that not even an outlaw would harm a little child, the Count returned to his castle to make preparations for a complete and final campaign of extinction against the scourge of the Hundsrück, but the Outlaw had withdrawn his men far from the scene of his latest successful exploit and the Count never came up with him.

Years passed on and the silver came quickly to Count Herbert's hair, he attributing the change to the hardships endured in the East, but all knowing well the cause sprang from his belief in his son's death. The rapid procession of years made little impression on the beauty of the Countess, who, although grieving for the absence of her boy, never regarded him as lost but always looked for his return. "If he were dead," she often said to her husband, "I should know it in my heart; I should know the day, the hour and the moment."

This belief the Count strove to encourage, although none knew better than he how baseless it was. Beatrix, with a mother's fondness, kept little Wilhelm's room as it had been when he left it, his toys in their places, and his bed prepared for him, allowing no one else to share the task she had allotted to herself. She seemed to keep no count of the years, nor to realise that if her son returned he would return as a young man and not as a child. To the mind of Beatrix he seemed always her boy of four.

When seventeen years had elapsed after the abduction of the heir of Schonburg, there came a rumour that the Outlaw of Hundsrück was again at his depredations in the neighbourhood of Coblentz. He was at this time a man of forty-two, and if he imagined that the long interval had led to any forgetting on the part of the Count von Schonburg, a most unpleasant surprise awaited him. The Count divided his forces equally between his two castles of Schonburg and Gudenfels situated on the west bank and the east bank respectively. If either castle were attacked, arrangements were made for getting word to the other, when the men in that other would cross the Rhine and fall upon the rear of the invaders, hemming them thus between two fires. The Count therefore awaited with complacency whatever assault the Outlaw cared to deliver.

It was expected that the attack would be made in the night, which was the usual time selected for these surprise parties that kept life from stagnating along the Rhine, but to the amazement of the Count the onslaught came in broad daylight, which seemed to indicate that the Outlaw had gathered boldness with years. The Count from the battlements scanned his opponents and saw that they were led, not by the Outlaw in person, but by a young man who evidently held his life lightly, so recklessly did he risk it. He was ever in the thick of the fray, dealing sword strokes with a lavish generosity which soon kindled a deep respect for him in the breasts of his adversaries. The Count had not waited for the battering in of his gates but had sent out his men to meet the enemy in the open, which was rash generalship, had he not known that the men of Gudenfels were hurrying round to the rear of the outlaws. Crossbowmen lined the battlements ready to cover the retreat of the defenders of the castle, should they meet a reverse, but now they stood in silence, holding their shafts, for in the mêslée there was a danger of destroying friend as well as foe. But in spite of the superb leadership of the young captain, the outlaws, seemingly panic-stricken, when there was no particular reason, deserted their commander in a body and fled in spite of his frantic efforts to rally them. The young man found himself surrounded, and, after a brave defence, overpowered. When the Gudenfels men came up, there was none to oppose them, the leader of the enemy being within the gates of Schonburg, bound, bleeding and a prisoner. The attacking outlaws were nowhere to be seen.

The youthful captive, unkempt as he was, appeared in the great hall of the castle before its grey-headed commander, seated in his chair of state.

"You are the leader of this unwarranted incursion?" said the Count, sternly, as he looked upon the pinioned lad.

"Warranted or unwarranted, I was the leader."

"Who are you?"

"I am Wilhelm, only son of the Outlaw of Hundsrück."

"The only son," murmured the Count, more to himself than to his auditors, the lines hardening round his firm mouth. For some moments there was a deep silence in the large room, then the Count spoke in a voice that had no touch of mercy in it:

"You will be taken to a dungeon and your wounds cared for. Seven days from now, at this hour, you will appear again before me, at which time just sentence will be passed upon you, after I hear what you have to say in your own defence."

"You may hear that now, my Lord. I besieged your castle and would perhaps have taken it, had I not a pack of cowardly dogs at my heels. I am now in your power, and although you talk glibly of justice, I know well what I may expect at your hands. Your delay of a week is the mere pretence of a

261

hypocrite, who wishes to give colour of legality to an act already decided upon. I do not fear you now, and shall not fear you then, so spare your physicians unnecessary trouble, and give the word to your executioner."

"Take him away, attend to his wounds, and guard him strictly. Seven days from now when I call for him; see to it that you can produce him."

Elsa, niece of the Outlaw, watched anxiously for the return of her cousin from the long prepared for expedition. She had the utmost confidence in his bravery and the most earnest belief in his success, yet she watched for the home-coming of the warriors with an anxious heart. Perhaps a messenger would arrive telling of the capture of the castle; perhaps all would return with news of defeat, but for what actually happened the girl was entirely unprepared. That the whole company, practically unscathed, should march into camp with the astounding news that their leader had been captured and that they had retreated without striking a blow on his behalf, seemed to her so monstrous, that her first thought was fear of the retribution which would fall on the deserters when her uncle realised the full import of the tidings. She looked with apprehension at his forbidding face and was amazed to see something almost approaching a smile part his thin lips.

"The attack has failed, then. I fear I sent out a leader incompetent and too young. We must make haste to remove our camp or the victorious Count, emboldened by success, may carry the war into the forest." With this amazing proclamation the Outlaw turned and walked to his hut followed by his niece, bewildered as one entangled in the mazes of a dream. When they were alone together, the girl spoke.

"Uncle, has madness overcome you?"

"I was never saner than now, nor happier, for years of waiting are approaching their culmination."

"Has, then, all valour left your heart?"

"Your question will be answered when next I lead my band."

"When next you lead it? Where will you lead it?"

262

"Probably in the vicinity of Mayence, toward which place we are about to journey."

"Is it possible that you retreat from here without attempting the rescue of your son, now in the hands of your lifelong enemy?"

"All things are possible in an existence like ours. The boy would assault the castle; he has failed and has allowed himself to be taken. It is the fortune of war and I shall not waste a man in attempting his rescue."

Elsa stood for a moment gazing in dismay at her uncle, whose shifty eyes evaded all encounter with hers, then she strode to the wall, took down a sword and turned without a word to the door. The Outlaw sprang between her and the exit.

"What are you about to do?" he cried.

"I am about to rally all who are not cowards round me, then at their head, I shall attack Castle Schonburg and set Wilhelm free or share his fate."

The Outlaw stood for a few moments, his back against the door of the hut, gazing in sullen anger at the girl, seemingly at a loss to know how she should be dealt with. At last his brow cleared and he spoke: "Is your interest in Wilhelm due entirely to the fact that you are cousins?"

A quick flush overspread the girl's fair cheeks with colour and her eyes sought the floor of the hut. The point of the sword she held lowered until it rested on the stone flags, and she swayed slightly, leaning against its hilt, while the keen eyes of her uncle regarded her critically. She said in a voice little above a whisper, contrasting strongly with her determined tone of a moment before:

"My interest is due to our relationship alone."

"Has no word of love passed between you?"

"Oh, no, no. Why do you ask me such a question?"

"Because on the answer given depends whether or not I shall entrust you with knowledge regarding him. Swear to me by the Three Kings of Cologne that you will tell to none what I will now impart to you."

"I swear," said Elsa, raising her right hand, and holding aloft the sword with it.

"Wilhelm is not my son, nor is he kin to either of us, but is the heir of the greatest enemy of our house, Count Herbert of Schonburg. I lured him from his father's home as a child and now send him back as a man. Some time later I shall acquaint the Count with the fact that the young man he captured is his only son."

The girl looked at her uncle, her eyes wide with horror.

"It is your purpose then that the father shall execute his own son?"

The Outlaw shrugged his shoulders.

"The result lies not with me, but with the Count. He was once a crusader and the teaching of his master is to the effect that the measure he metes to others, the same shall be meted to him, if I remember aright the tenets of his faith. Count Herbert wreaking vengeance upon my supposed son, is really bringing destruction upon his own, which seems but justice. If he show mercy to me and mine, he is bestowing the blessed balm thereof on himself and his house. In this imperfect world, few events are ordered with such admirable equity as the capture of young Lord Wilhelm, by that haughty and bloodthirsty warrior, his father. Let us then await with patience the outcome, taking care not to interfere with the designs of Providence."

"The design comes not from God but from the evil one himself."

"It is within the power of the Deity to overturn even the best plans of the fiend, if it be His will. Let us see to it that we do not intervene between two such ghostly potentates, remembering that we are but puny creatures, liable to err."

"The plot is of your making, secretly held, all these years, with unrelenting malignity. The devil himself is not wicked enough to send an innocent, loyal lad to his doom in his own mother's house, with his father as his executioner. Oh, uncle, uncle, repent and make reparation before it is too late."

"Let the Count repent and make reparation. I have now nothing to do with the matter. As I have said, if the Count is merciful, he is like to be glad of it later in his life; if he is revengeful, visiting the sin of the father on the son, innocent, I think you called him, then he deserves what his own hand deals out to himself. But we have talked too much already. I ask you to remember your oath, for I have told you this so that you will not bring ridicule upon me by a womanish appeal to my own men, who would but laugh at you in any case and think me a dotard in allowing women overmuch to say in the camp. Get you back to your women, for we move camp instantly. Even if I were to relent, as you term it, the time is past, for Wilhelm is either dangling from the walls of Castle Schonburg or he is pardoned, and all that we could do would be of little avail. Prepare you then instantly for our journey."

Elsa, with a sigh, went slowly to the women's quarters, her oath, the most terrible that may be taken on the Rhine, weighing heavily upon her. Resolving not to break it, yet determined in some way to save Wilhelm, the girl spent the first part of the journey in revolving plans of escape, for she found as the cavalcade progressed that her uncle did not trust entirely to the binding qualities of the oath she had taken, but had her closely watched as well. As the expedition progressed farther and farther south in the direction of Mayence, vigilance was relaxed, and on the evening of the second day, when a camp had been selected for the night, Elsa escaped and hurried eastward through the forest until she came to the Rhine, which was to be her guide to the castle of Schonburg. The windings of the river made the return longer than the direct journey through the wilderness had been, and in addition to this, Elsa was compelled to circumambulate the numerous castles, climbing the hills to avoid them, fearing capture and delay, so it was not until the sun was declining on the sixth day after the assault on the castle that she stood, weary and tattered and unkempt, before the closed gates of Schonburg, and beat feebly with her small hand against the oak, crying for admittance. The guard of the gate, seeing through the small lattice but a single dishevelled woman standing there, anticipating treachery, refused to open the little door in the large leaf until his captain was summoned, who, after some parley, allowed the girl to enter the courtyard.

"What do you want?" asked the captain, curtly.

She asked instead of answered:

"Is your prisoner still alive?"

"The son of the Outlaw? Yes, but he would be a confident prophet who would predict as much for him at this hour to-morrow."

"Take me, I beg of you, to the Countess."

"That is as it may be. Who are you and what is your business with her?"

"I shall reveal myself to her Ladyship, and to her will state the object of my coming."

"Your object is plain enough. You are some tatterdemalion of the forest come to beg the life of your lover, who hangs to-morrow, or I am a heathen Saracen."

"I do beseech you, tell the Countess that a miserable woman craves permission to speak with her."

What success might have attended her petition is uncertain, but the problem was solved by the appearance of the Countess herself on the terrace above them, which ran the length of the castle on its western side. The lady leaned over the parapet and watched with evident curiosity the strange scene in the courtyard below, the captain and his men in a ring around the maiden of the forest, who occupying the centre of the circle, peered now in one face, now in another, as if searching for some trace of sympathy in the stolid countenances of the warriors all about her. Before the captain could reply, his lady addressed him.

"Whom have you there, Conrad?"

It seemed as if the unready captain would get no word said, for again before he had made answer the girl spoke to the Countess.

"I do implore your Ladyship to grant me speech with you."

The Countess looked down doubtfully upon the supplicant, evidently prejudiced by her rags and wildly straying hair. The captain cleared his throat and opened his mouth, but the girl eagerly forestalled him.

"Turn me not away, my Lady, because I come in unhandsome guise, for I have travelled far through forest and over rock, climbing hills and skirting the river's brink to be where I am. The reluctant wilderness, impeding me, has enviously torn my garments, leaving me thus ashamed before you, but, dear Lady, let not that work to my despite. Grant my petition and my prayer shall ever be that the dearest wish of your own heart go not unsatisfied."

"Alas!" said the Countess, with a deep sigh, "my dearest wish gives little promise of fulfilment."

Conrad, seeing that the lady thought of her lost son, frowned angrily, and in low growling tones bade the girl have a care what she said, but Elsa was not to be silenced and spoke impetuously.

"Oh, Countess, the good we do often returns to us tenfold; mercy calls forth mercy. An acorn planted produces an oak; cruelty sown leaves us cruelty to reap. It is not beyond imagination that the soothing of my bruised heart may bring balm to your own."

"Take the girl to the east room, Conrad, and let her await me there," said the Countess.

"With a guard, your Ladyship?"

"Without a guard, Conrad."

"Pardon me, my Lady, but I distrust her. She may have designs against you."

The Countess had little acquaintance with fear. She smiled at the anxious captain and said:

"Her only desire is to reach my heart, Conrad."

"God grant it may not be with a dagger," grumbled the captain, as he made haste to obey the commands of the lady.

When the Countess entered the room in which Elsa stood, her first question was an inquiry regarding her visitor's name and station, the telling of which seemed but an indifferent introduction for the girl, who could not help noting that the Countess shrank, involuntarily from her when she heard the Outlaw mentioned.

"Our house has little cause to confer favour on any kin of the Outlaw of Hundsrück," the lady said at last.

"I do not ask for favour, my Lady. I have come to give your revenge completeness, if it is revenge you seek. The young man now imprisoned in Schonburg is so little esteemed by my uncle that not a single blow has been struck on his behalf. If the Count thinks to hurt the Outlaw by executing Wilhelm, he will be gravely in error, for my uncle and his men regard the captive so lightly that they have gone beyond Mayence without even making an effort toward his rescue. As for me, my uncle bestows upon me such affection as he is capable of, and would be more grieved should I die, than if any other of his kin were taken from him. Release Wilhelm and I will gladly take his place, content to receive such punishment as his Lordship, the Count, considers should be imposed on a relative of the Outlaw."

"What you ask is impossible. The innocent should not suffer for the guilty."

"My Lady, the innocent have suffered for others since the world began, and will continue to do so till it ends. Our only hope of entering Heaven comes through Him who was free from sin being condemned in our stead. I do beseech your Ladyship to let me take the place of Wilhelm."

"You love this young man," said the Countess, seating herself, and regarding the girl with the intent interest which women, whose own love affair has prospered, feel when they are confronted with an incident that reminds them of their youth.

"Not otherwise than as a friend and dear companion, my Lady," replied Elsa, blushing. "When he was a little boy and I a baby, he carried me about in his arms, and since that time we have been comrades together."

"Comradeship stands for much, my girl," said the Countess, in kindly manner, "but it rarely leads one friend willingly to accept death for another. I have not seen this young man whom you would so gladly liberate; the dealing with prisoners is a matter concerning my husband alone; I never interfere, but if I should now break this rule because you have travelled so far, and are so anxious touching the prisoner's welfare, would you be willing to accept my conditions?"

"Yes, my Lady, so that his life were saved."

"He is a comely young man doubtless, and there are some beautiful women within this castle; would it content you if he were married to one of my women, and so escaped with life?"

A sudden pallor overspread the girl's face, and she clasped her hands nervously together. Tears welled into her eyes, and she stood thus for a few moments unable to speak. At last she murmured, with some difficulty:

"Wilhelm can care nothing for any here, not having beheld them, and it would be wrong to coerce a man in such extremity. I would rather die for him, that he might owe his life to me."

"But he would live to marry some one else."

"If I were happy in heaven, why should I begrudge Wilhelm's happiness on earth?"

"Ah, why, indeed, Elsa? And yet you disclaim with a sigh. Be assured that I shall do everything in my power to save your lover, and that not at the expense of your own life or happiness. Now come with me, for I would have you arrayed in garments more suited to your youth and your beauty, that you may not be ashamed when you meet this most fascinating prisoner, for such he must be, when you willingly risk so much for his sake."

The Countess, after conducting the girl to the women's apartments, sought her husband, but found to her dismay that he showed little sign of concurrence with her sympathetic views regarding the fate of the prisoner. It was soon evident to her that Count Herbert had determined upon the young man's destruction, and that there was some concealed reason for this obdurate conclusion which the Count did not care to disclose. Herbert von Schonburg was thoroughly convinced that his son was dead, mutilated beyond recognition by the Outlaw of Hundsrück, yet this he would not tell to Beatrix, his wife, who cherished the unshaken belief that the boy still lived and would be restored to her before she died. The Count for years had waited for his revenge, and even though his wife now pleaded that he forego it, the Master of Schonburg was in no mind to comply, though he said little in answer to her persuading. The incoming of Elsa to the castle merely convinced him that some trick was meditated on the part of the Outlaw, and the sentimental consideration urged by the Countess had small weight with him. He gave a curt order to his captain to double his guards around the stronghold, and relax no vigilance until the case of the prisoner had been finally dealt with. He refused permission for Elsa to see her cousin, even in the presence of witnesses, as he was certain that her coming was for the purpose of communicating to him some message from the Outlaw, the news of whose alleged withdrawal he did not believe.

"With the country at peace, the Outlaw has instigated, and his son has executed, an attack upon this castle. The penalty is death. To-morrow I shall hear what he has to say in his defence, and shall deliver judgment, I hope, justly. If his kinswoman wishes to see him, she may come to his trial, and then will be in a position to testify to her uncle that sentence has been pronounced in accordance with the law that rules the Rhine provinces. If she has communication to make to her cousin, let it be made in the Judgment Hall in the presence of all therein."

The Countess, with sinking heart, left her husband, having the tact not to press upon him too strongly the claims of mercy as well as of justice. She knew that his kind nature would come to the assistance of her own suing, and deeply regretted that the time for milder influences to prevail was so short. In a brief conference with Elsa, she endeavoured to prepare the girl's mind for a disastrous ending of her hopes.

Some minutes before the hour set for Wilhelm's trial, the Countess Beatrix, followed by Elsa, entered the Judgment Hall to find the Count seated moodily in the great chair at one end of the long room, in whose ample inclosure many an important state conference had been held, each of the forefathers of the present owner being seated in turn as president of the assemblage. Some thought of this seemed to oppress the Count's mind, for seated here with set purpose to extinguish his enemy's line, the remembrance that his own race died with him was not likely to be banished. The Countess brought Elsa forward and in a whisper urged her to plead for her kinsman before his judge. The girl's eloquence brought tears to the eyes of Beatrix, but the Count's impassive face was sphinx-like in its settled gloom. Only once during the appeal did he speak, and that was when Elsa offered herself as a sacrifice to his revenge, then he said, curtly:

"We do not war against women. You are as free to go as you were to come, but you must not return."

A dull fear began to chill the girl's heart and to check her earnest pleading: She felt that her words were making no impression on the silent man seated before her, and this knowledge brought weak hesitation to her tongue and faltering to her speech. In despair she wrung her hands and cried: "Oh, my Lord, my Lord, think of your own son held at the mercy of an enemy. Think of him as a young man just the age of your prisoner, at a time when life is sweetest to him! Think, think, I beg of you———"

The Count roused himself like a lion who had been disturbed, and cried in a voice that resounded hoarsely from the rafters of the arched roof, startling the Countess with the unaccustomed fierceness of its tone:

"Yes, I will think of him—of my only son in the clutch of his bitter foe, and I thank you for reminding me of him, little as I have for these long years needed spur to my remembrance. Bring in the prisoner."

When Wilhelm was brought in, heavy manacles on his wrists, walking between the men who guarded him, Elsa looked from judge to culprit, and her heart leaped with joy. Surely such blindness could not strike this whole concourse that some one within that hall would not see that, here confronted, stood father and son, on the face of one a frown of anger, on the face of the other a frown of defiance, expressions almost identical, the only difference being the thirty years that divided their ages. For a few moments the young man did not distinguish Elsa in the throng, then a glad cry of recognition escaped him, and the cloud cleared from his face as if a burst of sunshine had penetrated the sombre-coloured windows and had thrown its illuminating halo around his head. He spoke impetuously, leaning forward:

"Elsa, Elsa, how came you here?" then, a shadow of concern crossing his countenance, "you are not a prisoner, I trust?"

"No, no, Wilhelm, I am here to beseech the clemency of the Count—"

"Not for me!" exclaimed the prisoner, defiantly, drawing himself up proudly: "not for me, Elsa. You must never ask favour from a robber and a coward like, Count von Schonburg, brave only in his own Judgment Hall."

"Oh, Wilhelm, Wilhelm, have a care what you say, or you will break my heart. And your proclamation is far from true. The Count is a brave man who has time and again proved himself so, and my only hope is that he will prove as merciful as he is undoubtedly courageous. Join your prayers with mine, Wilhelm, and beg for mercy rather than justice."

"I beg from no man, either mercy or justice. I am here, my Lord Count, ready to receive whatever you care to bestow, and I ask you to make the waiting brief for the sake of the women present, for I am I sure the beautiful, white-haired lady there dislikes this traffic in men's lives as much as does my fair-haired cousin."

"Oh, my lord Count, do not heed what he says; his words but show the recklessness of youth; hold them not against him."

"Indeed I mean each word I say, and had I iron in my hand instead of round my wrists, his Lordship would not sit so calmly facing me."

Elsa, seeing how little she had accomplished with either man began to weep helplessly, and the Count, who had not interrupted the colloquy, listening unmoved to the contumely heaped upon him by the prisoner, now said to the girl:

"Have you finished your questioning?"

Receiving no answer, he said to the prisoner after a pause:

"Why did you move against this castle?"

"Because I hoped to take it, burn it, and hang or behead its owner."

"Oh, Wilhelm, Wilhelm!" wailed the girl.

"And, having failed, what do you expect?"

"To be hanged, or beheaded, depending on whether your Lordship is the more expert with a cord or with an axe."

"You called me a coward, and I might have retorted that in doing so you took advantage of your position as prisoner, but setting that aside, and speaking as man to man, what ground have you for such an accusation?"

"We cannot speak as man to man, for I am bound and you are free, but touching the question of your cowardice, I have heard it said by those who took part in the defence of my father's castle, when you attacked it and destroyed it, commanding a vastly superior force, my father leaped from the wall and dared you to follow him. For a moment, they told me, it seemed that you would accept the challenge, but you contented yourself with calling on others to do what you feared to do yourself, and thus my father, meeting no opposition from a man of his own rank, was compelled to destroy the unfortunate serfs who stood in his way and, so cut out a path to safety. In refusing to accept the plunge he took, you branded yourself a coward, and once a coward always a coward."

"Oh, Wilhelm," cried Elsa, in deep distress at the young man's lack of diplomacy, while she could not but admire his ill-timed boldness, "speak not so to the Count, for I am sure what you say is not true."

"Indeed," growled Captain Conrad, "the young villain is more crafty than we gave him credit for. Instead of a rope he will have a challenge from the Count, and so die honourably like a man, in place of being strangled like the dog he is."

"Dear Wilhelm, for my sake, do not persist in this course, but throw yourself on the mercy of the Count. Why retail here the irresponsible gossip of a camp, which I am sure contains not a word of truth, so far as the Count is concerned."

Herbert of Schonburg held up his hand for silence, and made confession with evident difficulty.

"What the young man says with harshness is true in semblance, if not strictly so in action. For the moment, thinking of my wife and child, I hesitated, and when the hesitation was gone the opportunity was gone with it. My punishment has been severe; by that moment's cowardice, I am now a childless man, and therefore perhaps value my life less highly than I held it at the time we speak of. Hear then, your sentence: You will be taken to the top of the wall, the iron removed from your wrists, and your sword placed in your hand. You will then leap from that wall, and if you are unhurt, I will leap after you. Should your sword serve you as well as your father's served him, you will be free of the forest, and this girl is at liberty to accompany you. I ask her now to betake herself to the field outside the gate, there to await the result of our contest."

At this there was an outcry on the part of Countess Beatrix, who protested against her husband placing himself in this unnecessary jeopardy, but the Count was firm and would permit no interference with his sentence. Elsa was in despair at the unaccountable blindness of all concerned, not knowing that the Count was convinced his son was dead, and that the Countess thought continually of her boy as a child of four, taking no account of the years that had passed, although her reason, had she applied reason to that which touched her affections only, would have told her, he must now be a stalwart young man and not the little lad she had last held in her arms. For a moment Elsa wavered in her allegiance to the oath she had taken, but she saw against the wall the great crucifix which had been placed there by the first crusader who had returned to the castle from the holy wars and she breathed a prayer as she passed it, that the heir of this stubborn house might not be cut off in his youth through the sightless rancour that seemed to pervade it.

The Count tried to persuade his weeping wife not to accompany him to the walls, but she would not be left behind, and so, telling Conrad to keep close watch upon her, in case that in her despair she might attempt to harm herself, his lordship led the way to the battlements.

Wilhelm, at first jubilant that he was allowed to take part in a sword contest rather than an execution, paused for a moment as he came to the courtyard, and looked about him in a dazed manner, once or twice drawing his hand across his eyes, as if to perfect his vision. Some seeing him thus stricken silent and thoughtful, surmised that the young man was like to prove more courageous in word than in action; others imagined that the sudden coming from the semi-gloom of the castle interior into the bright light dazzled him. The party climbed the flight of stone steps which led far upward to the platform edged by the parapet from which the spring was to be made. The young man walked up and down the promenade, unheeding those around him, seeming like one in a dream, groping for something he failed to find. The onlookers watched him curiously, wondering at his change of demeanour.

Suddenly he dropped his sword on the stones at his feet, held up his hands and cried aloud:

"I have jumped from here before—when I was a lad—a baby almost—I remember it all now—where am I—when was I here before—where is my wooden sword—and where is Conrad, who made it—Conrad, where are you?"

The captain was the first to realise what had happened. He stepped hurriedly forward, scrutinising his late prisoner, the light of recognition, in his eyes.

"It is the young master," he shouted. "My Lord Count, this is no kinsman of the Outlaw, but your own son, a man grown."

The Count stood amazed, as incapable of motion as a statue of stone; the countess, gazing with dreamy eyes, seemed trying to adjust her inward vision of the lad of four with the outward reality of the man of twenty-one. In the silence rose the clear sweet voice of Elsa without the walls, her face upturned like a painting of the Madonna, her hands clasped in front of her.

"Dear Virgin Mother in Heaven, I thank thee that my prayer was not unheard, and bear me witness that I have kept my oath—I have kept my oath, and may Thy intervention show a proud and sinful people the blackness of revenge."

Count Herbert, rousing himself from his stupor, appealed loudly to the girl.

"Woman, is this indeed my son, and, if so, why did you not speak before we came to such extremity?"

"I cannot answer. I have sworn an oath. If you would learn who stands beside you, send a messenger to the Outlaw, saying you have killed him, as indeed you purposed doing," then stretching out her arms, she said, with faltering voice: "Wilhelm, farewell," and turning, fled toward the forest.

"Elsa, Elsa, come back!" the young man cried, foot on the parapet, but the girl paid no heed to his commanding summons, merely waving her hand without looking over her shoulder.

"Elsa!"

The name rang out so thrillingly strange that its reverberation instantly arrested the flying footsteps of the girl. Instinctively she knew it was the voice of a man falling rapidly through the air. She turned in time to see Wilhelm strike the ground, the impetus precipitating him prone on his face, where he lay motionless. The cry of horror from the battlements was echoed by her own as she sped swiftly toward him. The young man sprang to his feet as she approached and caught her breathless in his arms.

"Ah, Elsa," he said, tenderly, "forgive me the fright I gave you, but I knew of old your fleetness of foot, and if the forest once encircled you, how was I ever to find you?"

The girl made no effort to escape from her imprisonment, and showed little desire to exchange the embrace she endured for that of the forest.

"Though I should blush to say it, Wilhelm, I fear I am easily found, when you are the searcher."

"Then let old Schloss Schonburg claim you, Elsa, that the walls which beheld a son go forth, may see a son and daughter return."

276

CHAPTER III. — A CITY OF FEAR

The Countess Beatrix von Schonburg warmly welcomed her lost son and her newly-found daughter. The belief of Beatrix in Wilhelm's ultimate return had never wavered during all the long years of his absence, and although she had to translate her dream of the child of four into a reality that included a stalwart young man of twenty-one, the readjustment was speedily accomplished. Before a week had passed it seemed to her delighted heart that the boy had never left the castle. The Countess had liked Elsa from the first moment when she saw her, ragged, unkempt and forlorn, among the lowering, suspicious men-at-arms in the courtyard, and now that she knew the dangers and the privations the girl had braved for the sake of Wilhelm, the affectionate heart of Beatrix found ample room for the motherless Elsa.

With the Count, the process of mental reconstruction was slower, not only on account of his former conviction that his son was dead, but also because of the deep distrust in which he held the Outlaw. He said little, as was his custom, but often sat with brooding brows, intently regarding his son, gloomy doubt casting a shadow over his stern countenance. Might not this be a well-laid plot on the part of the Outlaw to make revenge complete by placing a von Weithoff in the halls of Schonburg as master of that ancient stronghold? The circumstances in which identity was disclosed, although sufficient to convince every one else in the castle, appeared at times to the Count but the stronger evidence of the Outlaw's craft and subtlety. If the young man were actually the son of von Weithoff, then undoubtedly the Outlaw had run great risk of having him hanged forthwith, but on the other hand, the prize to be gained, comprising as it did two notable castles and two wide domains, was a stake worth playing high for, and a stake which appealed strongly to a houseless, landless man, with not even a name worth leaving to his son. Thus, while the Countess lavished her affection on young Wilhelm, noticing nothing of her husband's distraction in this excessive happiness, Count Herbert sat alone in the lofty Knight's Hall, his elbows resting on the table before him, his head buried in his hands, ruminating on the strange transformation that had taken place, endeavouring to weigh the evidence pro and con with the impartial mind of an outsider, becoming the more bewildered the deeper he penetrated into the mystery.

It was in this despondent attitude that Elsa found him a few days after the leap from the wall that had caused her return to Schonburg, a willing captive. The Count did not look up when she entered, and the girl stood for a few moments in silence near him. At last she spoke in a low voice, hesitating slightly, nevertheless going with incisive directness into the very heart of the problem that baffled Count Herbert.

"My Lord, you do not believe that Wilhelm is indeed your son."

The master of Schonburg raised his head slowly and looked searchingly into the frank face of the girl, gloomy distrust reflected from his own countenance.

"Were you sent by your uncle to allay my suspicion?

"No, my Lord. I thought that a hint of the truth being given, Nature would come to the assistance of mutual recognition. Such has been the case between my lady and her son, but I see that you are still unconvinced."

"For my sins, I know something of the wickedness of this world, a knowledge from which her purity has protected the Countess. You believe that Wilhelm is my son?"

"I have never said so, my Lord."

"What you did say was that you had taken an oath. You are too young and doubtless too innocent to be a party to any plot, but you may have been the tool of an unscrupulous man, who knew the oath would be broken when the strain of a strong affection was brought to bear upon it."

"Yet, my Lord, I kept my oath, although I saw my—my—"

The girl hesitated and blushed, but finally spoke up bravely:

"I saw my lover led to his destruction. If Wilhelm is my cousin, then did his father take a desperate chance in trusting first, to my escape from the

278

camp, and second to my perjury. You endow him with more than human foresight, my Lord."

"He builded on your love for Wilhelm, which he had seen growing under his eye before either you or the lad had suspicion of its existence. I know the man, and he is a match for Satan, his master."

"But Satan has been discomfited ere now by the angels of light, and even by holy men, if legend tells truly. I have little knowledge of the world, as you have said, but the case appears to me one of the simplest. If my uncle wished the bitterest revenge on you, what could be more terrible than cause you to be the executioner of your own son? The vengeance, however, to be complete, depends on his being able to place before you incontrovertible proof that you were the father of the victim. Send, therefore, a messenger to him, one from Gudenfels, who knows nothing of what has happened in this castle of Schonburg, and who is therefore unable to disclose, even if forced to confess, that Wilhelm is alive. Let the messenger inform my uncle that his son is no more, which is true enough, and then await the Outlaw's reply. And meanwhile let me venture to warn you, my Lord, that it would be well to conceal your disbelief from Wilhelm, for he is high-spirited, and if he gets but an inkling that you distrust him, he will depart; for not all your possessions will hold your son if he once learns that you doubt him, so you are like to find yourself childless again, if your present mood masters you much longer."

The Count drew a deep sigh, then roused himself and seemed to shake off the influence that enchained him.

"Thank you, my girl," he cried, with something of the old ring in his voice, "I shall do as you advise, and if this embassy results as you say, you will ever find your staunchest friend in me."

He held out his hand to Elsa, and departed to his other castle of Gudenfels on the opposite side of the Rhine. From thence he sent a messenger who had no knowledge of what was happening in Schonburg.

When at last the messenger returned from the Outlaw's camp, he brought with him a wailing woman and grim tidings that he feared to deliver.

Thrice his lordship demanded his account, the last time with such sternness that the messenger quailed before him.

"My Lord," he stammered at last, "a frightful thing has taken place—would that I had died before it was told to me. The young man your lordship hanged was no other than——'

"Well, why do you pause? You were going to say he was my own son. What proof does the Outlaw offer that such was indeed the case?"

"Alas! my Lord, the proof seems clear enough. Here with me is young Lord Wilhelm's nurse, whose first neglect led to his abduction, and who fled to the forest after him, and was never found. She followed him to the Outlaw's camp, and was there kept prisoner by him until she was at last given charge of the lad, under oath that she would teach him to forget who he was, the fierce Outlaw threatening death to both woman and child were his orders disobeyed. She has come willingly with me hoping to suffer death now that one she loved more than son has died through her first fault."

Then to the amazement of the pallid messenger the Count laughed aloud and called for Wilhelm, who, when he was brought, clasped the trembling old woman in his arms, overjoyed to see her again and eager to learn news of the camp. How was the stout Gottlieb? Had the messenger seen Captain Heinrich? and so on.

"Indeed, my young Lord," answered the overjoyed woman "there was such turmoil in the camp that I was glad to be quit of it with unbroken bones. When the Outlaw proclaimed that you were hanged, there was instant rebellion among his followers, who thought that your capture was merely a trick to be speedily amended, being intended to form a laughing matter to your discomfiture when you returned. They swore they would have torn down Schonburg with their bare hands rather than have left you in jeopardy, had they known their retreat imperilled your life."

"The brave lads!" cried the young man in a glow of enthusiasm, "and here have I been maligning them for cowards! What was the outcome?"

"That I do not know, my Lord, being glad to escape from the ruffians with unfractured head."

The result of the embassy was speedily apparent at Schonburg. Two days later, in the early morning, the custodians at the gate were startled by the shrill Outlaw yell, which had on so many occasions carried terror with it into the hearts of Rhine strongholds.

"Come out, Hangman of Schonburg!" they shouted, "come out, murderer of a defenceless prisoner. Come out, before we drag you forth, for the rope is waiting for your neck and the gallows tree is waiting for the rope."

Count Herbert was first on the battlements, and curtly he commanded his men not to launch bolt at the invaders, knowing the outlaws mistakenly supposed him to be the executioner of their former comrade. A moment later young Wilhelm himself appeared on the wall above the gate, and, lifting his arms above his head raised a great shout of joy at seeing there collected his old companions, calling this one or that by name as he recognised them among the seething, excited throng. There was an instant's cessation of the clamour, then the outlaws sent forth a cheer that echoed from all the hills around. They brandished their weapons aloft, and cheered again and again, the garrison of the castle, now bristling along the battlements, joining in the tumult with strident voices. Gottlieb advanced some distance toward the gate, and holding up his hand for silence addressed Wilhelm.

"Young master," he cried, "we have deposed von Weithoff, and would have hanged him, but that he escaped during the night, fled to Mayence and besought protection of the Archbishop. If you will be our leader we will sack Mayence and hang the Archbishop from his own cathedral tower."

"That can I hardly do, Gottlieb, as a messenger has been sent to the Archbishop asking him to come to Schonburg and marry Elsa to me. He might take our invasion as an unfriendly act and refuse to perform the ceremony."

Gottlieb scratched his head as one in perplexity, seeing before him a question of etiquette that he found difficult to solve. At last he said:

"What need of Archbishop? You and Elsa have been brought up among us, therefore confer honour on our free company by being married by our own Monk who has tied many a knot tight enough to hold the most wayward of our band. The aisles of the mighty oaks are more grand than the cathedral at Mayence or the great hall of Schonburg."

"Indeed I am agreed, if Elsa is willing. We will be married first in the forest and then by the Archbishop in the great hall of Schonburg."

"In such case there will be delay, for now that I bethink me, his Lordship of Mayence has taken himself to Frankfort, where he is to meet the Archbishops of Treves and Cologne who will presently journey to the capital We were thinking of falling upon his reverence of Cologne as he passed up the river, unless he comes with an escort too numerous for us, which, alas! is most likely, so suspicious has the world grown."

"You will be wise not to meddle with the princes of the Church, be their escorts large or small."

"Then, Master Wilhelm, be our leader, for we are likely to get into trouble unless a man of quality is at our head."

Wilhelm breathed a deep sigh and glanced sideways at his father, who stood some distance off, leaning on his two-handed sword, a silent spectator of the meeting.

"The free life of the forest is no more for me, Gottlieb. My duty is here in the castle of my forefathers, much though I grieve to part with you."

This decision seemed to have a depressing effect on the outlaws within hearing. Gottlieb retired, and the band consulted together for a time, then their spokesman again advanced.

"Some while since," he began in dolorous tone, "we appealed to the Emperor to pardon us, promising in such case to quit our life of outlawry and take honest service with those nobles who needed stout blades, but his Majesty sent reply that if we came unarmed to the capital and tendered submission, he would be graciously pleased to hang a round dozen of us to be selected by him, scourge the rest through the streets of Frankfort and so bestow his clemency on such as survived. This imperial tender we did not accept, as there was some uncertainty regarding whose neck should feel the rope and whose back the scourge. While all were willing to admit that more than a dozen of us sorely needed hanging, yet each man seemed loath to claim precedence over his neighbour in wickedness, and desired, in some sort, a voice in the selection of the victims. But if you will accept our following, Master Wilhelm, we will repair at once to Frankfort and make submission to his Majesty the Emperor. The remnant being well scourged, will then return to Schonburg to place themselves under your command."

"Are you willing then to hang for me, Gottlieb?"

"I hanker not after the hanging, but if hang we must, there is no man I would rather hang for than Wilhelm, formerly of the forest, but now, alas! of Schonburg. And so say they all without dissent, therefore the unanimity must needs include the eleven other danglers."

"Then draw nigh, all of you, to the walls and hear my decision."

Gottlieb waving his arms, hailed the outlaws trooping to the walls, and, his upraised hand bringing silence, Wilhelm spoke:

"Such sacrifice as you propose, I cannot accept, yet I dearly wish to lead a band of men like you. Elsa and I shall be married by our ancient woodland father in the forest and then by the Abbot of St. Werner in the hall of Schonburg. We will make our wedding journey to Frankfort, and you shall be our escort and our protectors."

There was for some moments such cheering at this that the young man was compelled to pause in his address, and then as the outcry was again and again renewed, he looked about for the cause and saw that Elsa and his mother had taken places on the balcony which overlooked the animated scene. The beautiful girl had been recognised by the rebels and she waved her hand in response to their shouting.

"We will part company," resumed Wilhelm, "as near Frankfort as it is safe for you to go, and my wife and I, accompanied by a score of men from this castle, will enter the capital. I will beg your complete pardon from his

Majesty and if at first it is refused, I think Elsa will have better success with the Empress, who may incline her imperial husband toward clemency. All this I promise, providing I receive the consent and support of my father, and I am not likely to be refused, for he already knows the persuasive power of my dear betrothed when she pleads for mercy."

"My consent and support I most willingly bestow," said the Count, with a fervour that left no doubt of his sincerity.

The double marriage was duly solemnised, and Wilhelm, with his newly-made wife, completed their journey to Frankfort, escorted until almost within sight of the capital by five hundred and twenty men, but they entered the gates of the city accompanied by only the score of Schonburg men, the remaining five hundred concealing themselves in the rough country, as they well knew how to do.

Neither Wilhelm nor Elsa had ever seen a large city before, and silence fell upon them as they approached the western gate, for they were coming upon a world strange to them, and Wilhelm felt an unaccustomed elation stir within his breast, as if he were on the edge of some adventure that might have an important bearing on his future. Instead of passing peaceably through the gate as he had expected, the cavalcade was halted after the two had ridden under the gloomy stone archway, and the portcullis was dropped with a sudden clang, shutting out the twenty riders who followed. One of several officers who sat on a stone bench that fronted the guard-house within the walls, rose and came forward.

"What is your name and quality?" he demanded, gruffly.

"I am Wilhelm, son of Count von Schonberg."

"What is your business here in Frankfort?"

"My business relates to the emperor, and is not to be delivered to the first underling who has the impudence to make inquiry," replied Wilhelm in a haughty tone, which could scarcely be regarded, in the circumstances, as diplomatic.

Nevertheless, the answer did not seem to be resented, but rather appeared to have a subduing effect on the questioner, who turned, as if for further instruction, to another officer, evidently his superior in rank. The latter now rose, came forward, doffing his cap, and said:

"I understand your answer better than he to whom it was given, my Lord."

"I am glad there is one man of sense at a gate of the capital," said Wilhelm, with no relaxation of his dignity, but nevertheless bewildered at the turn the talk had taken, seeing there was something underneath all this which he did not comprehend, yet resolved to carry matters with a high hand until greater clearness came to the situation.

"Will you order the portcullis raised and permit my men to follow me?"

"They are but temporarily detained until we decide where to quarter them, my Lord. You know," he added, lowering his voice, "the necessity for caution. Are you for the Archbishop of Treves, of Cologne, or of Mayence?"

"I am from the district of Mayence, of course."

"And are you for the archbishop?"

"For the archbishop certainly. He would have honoured me by performing our marriage ceremony had he not been called by important affairs of state to the capital, as you may easily learn by asking him, now that he is within these walls."

The officer bowed low with great obsequiousness and said:

"Your reply is more than sufficient, my Lord, and I trust you will pardon the delay we have caused you. The men of Mayence are quartered in the Leinwandhaus, where room will doubtless be made for your followers.

"It is not necessary for me to draw upon the hospitality of the good Archbishop, as I lodge in my father's town house near the palace, and there is room within for the small escort I bring."

Again the officer bowed to the ground, and the portcullis being by this time raised, the twenty horsemen came clattering under the archway, and

285

thus, without further molestation, they arrived at the house of the Count von Schonburg.

"Elsa," said Wilhelm, when they were alone in their room, "there is something wrong in this city. Men look with fear one upon another, and pass on hurriedly, as if to avoid question. Others stand in groups at the street corners and speak in whispers, glancing furtively over their shoulders."

"Perhaps that is the custom in cities," replied Elsa.

"I doubt it. I have heard that townsmen are eager for traffic, inviting all comers to buy, but here most of the shops are barred, and no customers are solicited. They seem to me like people under a cloud of fear. What can it be?"

"We are more used to the forest path than to city streets, Wilhelm. They will all become familiar to us in a day or two, yet I feel as if I could not get a full breath in these narrow streets and I long for the trees already, but perhaps content will come with waiting."

"'Tis deeper than that. There is something ominous in the air. Noted you not the questioning at the gate and its purport? They asked me if I favoured Treves, or Cologne, or Mayence, but none inquired if I stood loyal to the Emperor, yet I was entering his capital city of Frankfort."

"Perhaps you will learn all from the Emperor when you see him," ventured Elsa.

"Perhaps," said Wilhelm.

The chamberlain of the von Schonburg household, who had supervised the arrangements for the reception of the young couple, waited upon his master in the evening and informed him that the Emperor would not be visible for some days to come.

"He has gone into retreat, in the cloisters attached to the cathedral, and it is the imperial will that none disturb him on worldly affairs. Each day at the hour when the court assembles at the palace, the Emperor hears exhortation from the pious fathers in the Wahlkapelle of the cathedral; the chapel in which emperors are elected; these exhortations pertaining to the ruling of the land, which his majesty desires to govern justly and well.

"An excellent intention," commented the young man, with suspicion of impatience in his tone, "but meanwhile, how are the temporal affairs of the country conducted?"

"The Empress Brunhilda is for the moment the actual head of the state. Whatever act of the ministers receives her approval, is sent by a monk to the Emperor, who signs any document so submitted to him."

"Were her majesty an ambitious woman, such transference of power might prove dangerous."

"She is an ambitious woman, but devoted to her husband, who, it perhaps may be whispered, is more monk than king," replied the chamberlain under his breath. "Her majesty has heard of your lordship's romantic adventures and has been graciously pleased to command that you and her ladyship, your wife, be presented to her to-morrow in presence of the court."

"This is a command which it will be a delight to obey. But tell me, what is wrong in this great town? There is a sinister feeling in the air; uneasiness is abroad, or I am no judge of my fellow-creatures."

"Indeed, my Lord, you have most accurately described the situation. No man knows what is about to happen. The gathering of the Electors is regarded with the gravest apprehension. The Archbishop of Mayence, who but a short time since crowned the Emperor at the great altar of the cathedral, is herewith a thousand men at his back. The Count Palatine of the Rhine is also within these walls with a lesser entourage. It is rumoured that his haughty lordship, the Archbishop of Treves, will reach Frankfort to-morrow, to be speedily followed by that eminent Prince of the Church, the Archbishop of Cologne. Thus there will be gathered in the capital four Electors, a majority of the college, a conjunction that has not occurred for centuries, except on the death of an emperor, necessitating the nomination and election of his successor."

"But as the Emperor lives and there is no need of choosing another, wherein lies the danger?

"The danger lies in the fact that the college has the power to depose as well as to elect."

"Ah! And do the Electors threaten to depose?"

"No. Treves is much too crafty for any straight-forward statement of policy. He is the brains of the combination, and has put forward Mayence and the Count Palatine as the moving spirits, although it is well known that the former is but his tool and the latter is moved by ambition to have his imbecile son selected emperor."

"Even if the worst befall, it seems but the substitution of a weak-minded man for one who neglects the affairs of state, although I should think the princes of the Church would prefer a monarch who is so much under the influence of the monks."

"The trouble is deeper than my imperfect sketch of the situation would lead you to suppose, my Lord. The Emperor periodically emerges from his retirement, promulgates some startling decree, unheeding the counsel of any adviser, then disappears again, no man knowing what is coming next. Of such a nature was his recent edict prohibiting the harrying of merchants going down the Rhine and the Moselle, which, however just in theory, is impracticable, for how are the nobles to reap revenue if such practices are made unlawful? This edict has offended all the magnates of both rivers, and the archbishops, with the Count Palatine, claim that their prerogatives have been infringed, so they come to Frankfort ostensibly to protest, while the Emperor in his cloister refuses to meet them. The other three Electors hold aloof, as the edict touches them not, but they form a minority which is powerless, even if friendly to the Emperor. Meanwhile his majesty cannot be aroused to an appreciation of the crisis, but says calmly that if it is the Lord's will he remain emperor, emperor he will remain."

"Then at its limit, chamberlain, all we have to expect is a peaceful deposition and election?"

"Not so, my lord. The merchants of Frankfort are fervently loyal, to the Emperor, who, they say, is the first monarch to give forth a just law for their protection. At present the subtlety of Treves has nullified all combined action on their part, for he has given out that he comes merely to petition his over-lord, which privilege is well within his right, and many citizens actually believe him, but others see that a majority of the college will be within these walls before many days are past, and that the present Emperor may be legally deposed and another legally chosen. Then if the citizens object, they are rebels, while at this moment if they fight for the Emperor they are patriots, so you see the position is not without its perplexities, for the citizens well know that if they were to man the walls and keep out Treves and Cologne, the Emperor himself would most likely disclaim their interference, trusting as he does so entirely in Providence that a short time since he actually disbanded the imperial troops, much to the delight of the archbishops, who warmly commended his action. And now, my Lord, if I may venture to tender advice unasked, I would strongly counsel you to quit Frankfort as soon as your business here is concluded, for I am certain that a change of government is intended. All will be done promptly, and the transaction will be consummated before the people are aware that such a step is about to be taken. The Electors will meet in the Wahlzimmer or election room of the Romer and depose the Emperor, then they will instantly select his successor, adjourn to the Wahlkapelle and elect him. The Palatine's son is here with his father, and will be crowned at the high altar by the Archbishop of Mayence. The new Emperor will dine with the Electors in the Kaisersaal and immediately after show himself on the balcony to the people assembled in the Romerberg below. Proclamation of his election will then be made, and all this need not occupy more than two hours. The Archbishop of Mayence already controls the city gates, which since the disbanding of the imperial troops have been unguarded, and none can get in or out of the city without that potentate's permission. The men of Mayence are quartered in the centre of the town, the Count Palatine's troops are near the gate. Treves and Cologne will doubtless command other positions, and thus between them they will control the city. Numerous as the merchants and their dependents are, they will have no chance against the disciplined force of the Electors, and the streets of Frankfort are like to run with blood, for the nobles are but too eager to see a sharp check given to the rising pretensions of the mercantile classes, who having heretofore led peaceful lives, will come out badly in combat, despite their numbers; therefore I beg of you, my Lord, to withdraw with her Ladyship before this hell's caldron is uncovered."

"Your advice is good, chamberlain, in so far as it concerns my wife, and I will beg of her to retire to Schonburg, although I doubt if she will obey, but, by the bones of Saint Werner which floated against the current of the Rhine in this direction, if there must be a fray, I will be in the thick of it."

"Remember, my Lord, that your house has always stood by the Archbishop of Mayence."

"It has stood by the Emperor as well, chamberlain."

The Lady Elsa was amazed by the magnificence of the Emperor's court, when, accompanied by her husband, she walked the length of the great room to make obeisance before the throne. At first entrance she shrank timidly, closer to the side of Wilhelm, trembling at the ordeal of passing, simply costumed as she now felt herself to be, between two assemblages of haughty knights and high-born dames, resplendent in dress, with the proud bearing that pertained to their position in the Empire. Her breath came and went quickly, and she feared that all courage would desert her before she traversed the seemingly endless lane, flanked by the nobility of Germany, which led to the royal presence. Wilhelm, unabashed, holding himself the equal of any there, was not to be cowed by patronising glance, or scornful gaze. The thought flashed through his mind:

"How can the throne fall, surrounded as it is by so many supporters?"

But when the approaching two saw the Empress, all remembrance of others faded from their minds. Brunhilda was a woman of superb stature. She stood alone upon the dais which supported the vacant throne, one hand resting upon its carven arm. A cloak of imperial ermine fell gracefully from her shapely shoulders and her slightly-elevated position on the platform added height to her goddess-like tallness, giving her the appearance of towering above every other person in the room, man or woman. The excessive pallor of her complexion was emphasised by the raven blackness of her wealth of hair, and the sombre midnight of her eyes; eyes with slumbering fire in them, qualified by a haunted look which veiled their burning intensity. Her brow was too broad and her chin too firm for a painter's ideal of beauty; her commanding presence giving the effect of majesty rather than of loveliness. Deep lines of care marred the marble of her forehead, and Wilhelm said to himself:

"Here is a woman going to her doom; knowing it; yet determined to show no sign of fear and utter no cry for mercy."

Every other woman there had eyes of varying shades of blue and gray, and hair ranging from brown to golden yellow; thus the Empress stood before them like a creature from another world.

Elsa was about to sink in lowly courtesy before the queenly woman when the Empress came forward impetuously and kissed the girl on either cheek, taking her by the hand.

"Oh, wild bird of the forest," she cried, "why have you left the pure air of the woods, to beat your innocent wings in this atmosphere of deceit! And you, my young Lord, what brings you to Frankfort in these troublous times? Have you an insufficiency of lands or of honours that you come to ask augmentation of either?"

"I come to ask nothing for myself, your Majesty."

"But to ask, nevertheless," said Brunhilda, with a frown.

"Yes, your Majesty."

"I hope I may live to see one man, like a knight of old, approach the foot of the throne without a request on his lips. I thought you might prove an exception, but as it is not so, propound your question?"

"I came to ask if my sword, supplemented by the weapons of five hundred followers, can be of service to your Majesty."

The Empress seemed taken aback by the young man's unexpected reply, and for some moments she gazed at him searchingly in silence.

At last she said:

"Your followers are the men of Schonburg and Gudenfels, doubtless?"

291

"No, your Majesty. Those you mention, acknowledge my father as their leader. My men were known as the Outlaws of the Hundsrück, who have deposed von Weithoff, chosen me as their chief, and now desire to lead honest lives."

The dark eyes of the Empress blazed again.

"I see, my Lord, that you have quickly learned the courtier's language. Under proffer of service you are really demanding pardon for a band of marauders."

Wilhelm met unflinchingly the angry look of this imperious woman, and was so little a courtier that he allowed a frown to add sternness to his brow.

"Your Majesty puts it harshly," he said, "I merely petition for a stroke of the pen which will add half a thousand loyal men to the ranks of the Emperor's supporters."

Brunhilda pondered on this, then suddenly seemed to arrive at a decision. Calling one of the ministers of state to her side, she said, peremptorily:

"Prepare a pardon for the Outlaws of the Hundsrück. Send the document at once to the Emperor for signature, and then bring it to me in the Red Room."

The minister replied with some hesitation:

"I should have each man's name to inscribe on the roll, otherwise every scoundrel in the Empire will claim protection under the edict."

"I can give you every man's name," put in Wilhelm, eagerly.

"It is not necessary," said the Empress.

"Your Majesty perhaps forgets," persisted the minister, "that pardon has already been proffered by the Emperor under certain conditions that commended themselves to his imperial wisdom, and that the clemency so graciously tendered was contemptuously refused."

At this veiled opposition all the suspicion in Brunhilda's nature turned from Wilhelm to the high official, and she spoke to him in the tones of one accustomed to prompt obedience.

"Prepare an unconditional pardon, and send it immediately to the Emperor without further comment, either to him or to me."

The minister bowed low and retired. The Empress dismissed the court, detaining Elsa, and said to Wilhelm:

"Seek us half an hour later in the Red Room. Your wife I shall take with me, that I may learn from her own lips the adventures which led to your recognition as the heir of Schonburg, something of which I have already heard. And as for your outlaws, send them word if you think they are impatient to lead virtuous lives, which I take leave to doubt, that before another day passes they need fear no penalty for past misdeed, providing their future conduct escapes censure."

"They are one and all eager to retrieve themselves in your Majesty's eyes!"

"Promise not too much, my young Lord, for they may be called upon to perform sooner than they expect," said Brunhilda, with a significant glance at Wilhelm.

The young man left the imperial presence, overjoyed to know that his mission had been successful.

CHAPTER IV. — THE PERIL OF THE EMPEROR

Wilhelm awaited with impatience the passing of the half hour the Empress had fixed as the period of his probation, for he was anxious to have the signed pardon for the outlaws actually in his hand, fearing the intrigues of the court might at the last moment bring about its withdrawal.

When the time had elapsed he presented himself at the door of the Red Room and was admitted by the guard. He found the Empress alone, and she advanced toward him with a smile on her face, which banished the former hardness of expression.

"Forgive me," she said, "my seeming discourtesy in the Great Hall. I am surrounded by spies, and doubtless Mayence already knows that your outlaws have been pardoned, but that will merely make him more easy about the safety of his cathedral town, especially as he holds Baron von Weithoff their former leader. I was anxious that it should also be reported to him that I had received you somewhat ungraciously. Your wife is to take up her abode in the palace, as she refuses to leave Frankfort if you remain here. She tells me the outlaws are brave men."

"The bravest in the world, your Majesty."

"And that they will follow you unquestioningly."

"They would follow me to the gates of—" He paused, and added as if in afterthought—"to the gates of Heaven."

The lady smiled again.

"From what I have heard of them," she said, "I feared their route lay in another direction, but I have need of reckless men, and although I hand you their pardon freely, it is not without a hope that they will see fit to earn it."

"Strong bodies and loyal souls, we belong to your Majesty. Command and we will obey, while life is left us."

"Do you know the present situation of the Imperial Crown, my Lord?"

"I understand it is in jeopardy through the act of the Electors, who, it is thought, will depose the Emperor and elect a tool of their own. I am also aware that the Imperial troops have been disbanded, and that there will be four thousand armed and trained men belonging to the Electors within the walls of Frankfort before many days are past."

"Yes. What can five hundred do against four thousand?"

"We could capture the gates and prevent the entry of Treves and Cologne."

"I doubt that, for there are already two thousand troops obeying Mayence and the Count Palatine now in Frankfort. I fear we must meet strength by craft. The first step is to get your five hundred secretly into this city. The empty barracks stand against the city wall; if you quartered your score of Schonburg men there, they could easily assist your five hundred to scale the wall at night, and thus your force would be at hand concealed in the barracks without knowledge of the archbishops. Treves and his men will be here to-morrow, before it would be possible for you to capture the gates, even if such a design were practicable. I am anxious above all things to avoid bloodshed, and any plan you have to propose must be drafted with that end in view."

"I will ride to the place where my outlaws are encamped on the Rhine, having first quartered the Schonburg men in the barracks with instructions regarding our reception. If the tales which the spies tell the Archbishop of Mayence concerning my arrival and reception at court lead his lordship to distrust me, he will command the guards at the gate not to re-admit me. By to-morrow morning, or the morning after at latest, I expect to occupy the barracks with five hundred and twenty men, making arrangement meanwhile for the quiet provisioning of the place. When I have consulted Gottlieb, who is as crafty as Satan himself, I shall have a plan to lay before your Majesty."

Wilhelm took leave of the Empress, gave the necessary directions to the men he left behind him, and rode through the western gate unmolested and unquestioned. The outlaws hailed him that evening with acclamations that re-echoed from the hills which surrounded them, and their cheers redoubled when Wilhelm presented them with the parchment which made them once more free citizens of the Empire. That night they marched in, five companies, each containing a hundred men, and the cat's task of climbing the walls of Frankfort in the darkness before the dawn, merely gave a pleasant fillip to the long tramp. Daylight, found them sound asleep, sprawling on the floors of the huge barracks.

When Wilhelm explained the situation to Gottlieb the latter made light of the difficulty, as his master expected he would.

"'Tis the easiest thing in the world," he said.

"There are the Mayence men quartered in the Leinwandhaus. The men of Treves are here, let us say, and the men of Cologne there. Very well, we divide our company into four parties, as there is also the Count Palatine to reckon with. We tie ropes round the houses containing these sleeping men, set fire to the buildings all at the same time, and, pouf! burn the vermin where they lie. The hanging of the four Electors after, will be merely a job for a dozen of our men, and need not occupy longer than while one counts five score."

Wilhelm laughed.

"Your plan has the merit of simplicity, Gottlieb, but it does not fall in with the scheme of the Empress, who is anxious that everything be accomplished legally and without bloodshed. But if we can burn them, we can capture them, imprisonment being probably more to the taste of the vermin, as you call them, than cremation, and equally satisfactory to us. Frankfort prison is empty, the Emperor having recently liberated all within it. The place will amply accommodate four thousand men. Treves has arrived to-day with much pomp, and Cologne will be here to-morrow. To-morrow night the Electors hold their first meeting in the election chamber of the Romer. While they are deliberating, do you think you and your five hundred could lay four thousand men by the heels and leave each bound and gagged in the city prison with good strong bolts shot in on them?"

"Look on it as already done, my Lord. It is a task that requires speed, stealth and silence, rather than strength. The main point is to see that no alarm is prematurely given, and that no fugitive from one company escape to give warning to the others. We fall upon sleeping men, and if some haste is used, all are tied and gagged before they are full awake."

"Very well. Make what preparations are necessary, as this venture may be wrecked through lack of a cord or a gag, so see that you have everything at hand, for we cannot afford to lose a single trick. The stake, if we fail, is our heads."

Wilhelm sought the Empress to let her know that he had got his men safely housed in Frankfort, and also to lay before her his plan for depositing the Electors' followers in prison.

Brunhilda listened to his enthusiastic recital in silence, then shook her head slowly.

"How can five hundred men hope to pinion four thousand?" she asked. "It needs but one to make an outcry from an upper window, and, such is the state of tension in Frankfort at the present moment that the whole city will be about your ears instantly, thus bringing forth with the rest the comrades of those you seek to imprison."

"My outlaws are tigers, your Majesty. The Electors' men will welcome prison, once the Hundsrückers are let loose on them."

"Your outlaws may understand the ways of the forest, but not those of a city."

"Well, your Majesty, they have sacked Coblentz, if that is any recommendation for them."

The reply of the Empress seemed irrelevant.

"Have you ever seen the hall in which the Emperors are nominated—or deposed?" she asked.

"No, your Majesty."

"Then follow me."

The lady led him along a passage that seemed interminable, then down a narrow winding stair, through a vaulted tunnel, the dank air of which struck so cold and damp that the young man felt sure it was subterranean; lastly up a second winding stair, at the top of which, pushing aside some hanging tapestry, they stood within the noble chamber known as the Wahlzimmer. The red walls were concealed by hanging tapestry, the rich tunnel groining of the roof was dim in its lofty obscurity. A long table occupied the centre of the room, with three heavily-carved chairs on either side, and one, as ponderous as a throne, at the head.

"There," said the Empress, waving her hand, "sit the seven Electors when a monarch of this realm is to be chosen. There, to-morrow night will sit a majority of the Electoral College. In honour of this assemblage I have caused these embroidered webs to be hung round the walls, so you see, I, too, have a plan. Through this secret door which the Electors know nothing of, I propose to admit a hundred of your men to be concealed behind the tapestry. My plan differs from yours in that I determine to imprison four men, while you would attempt to capture four thousand; I consider therefore that my chances of success, compared with yours, are as a thousand to one. I strike at the head; you strike at the body. If I paralyse the head, the body is powerless."

Wilhelm knit his brows, looked around the room, but made no reply.

"Well," cried the Empress, impatiently, "I have criticised your plan; criticise mine if you find a flaw in it."

"Is it your Majesty's intention to have the men take their places behind the hangings before the archbishops assemble?"

"Assuredly."

"Then you will precipitate a conflict before all the Electors are here, for it is certain that the first prince to arrive will have the place thoroughly searched for spies. So momentous a meeting will never be held until all fear of eavesdroppers is allayed."

"That is true, Wilhelm," said the Empress with a sigh, "then there is nothing left but your project; which I fear will result in a mêlée and frightful slaughter."

"I propose, your Majesty, that we combine the two plans. We will imprison as many as may be of the archbishops' followers and then by means of the secret stairway surround their lordships."

"But they will, in the silence of the room, instantly detect the incoming of your men."

"Not so, if the panel which conceals the stair, work smoothly. My men are like cats, and their entrance and placement will not cause the most timid mouse to cease nibbling."

"The panel is silent enough, and it may be that your men will reach their places without betraying their presence to the archbishops, but it would be well to instruct your leaders that in case of discovery they are to rush forward, without waiting for your arrival or mine, hold the door of the Wahlzimmer at all hazards, and see that no Elector escapes. I am firm in my belief that once the persons of the archbishops are secured, this veiled rebellion ends, whether you imprison your four thousand or not, for I swear by my faith that if their followers raise a hand against me, I will have the archbishops slain before their eyes, even though I go down in disaster the moment after."

The stern determination of the Empress would have inspired a less devoted enthusiast than Wilhelm. He placed his hand on the hilt of his sword.

"There will be no disaster to the Empress," he said, fervently.

They retired into the palace by the way they came, carefully closing the concealed panel behind them.

As Wilhelm passed through the front gates of the Palace to seek Gottlieb at the barracks, he pondered over the situation and could not conceal from himself the fact that the task he had undertaken was almost impossible of accomplishment. It was an unheard of thing that five hundred men should overcome eight times their number and that without raising a disturbance in so closely packed a city as Frankfort, where, as the Empress had said, the state of tension was already extreme. But although he found that the pessimism of the Empress regarding his project was affecting his own belief in it, he set his teeth resolutely and swore that if it failed it would not be through lack of taking any precaution that occurred to him.

At the barracks he found Gottlieb in high feather. The sight of his cheerful, confident face revived the drooping spirits of the young man.

"Well, master," he cried, the freedom of outlawry still in the abruptness of his speech, "I have returned from a close inspection of the city."

"A dangerous excursion," said Wilhelm. "I trust no one else left the barracks."

"Not another man, much as they dislike being housed, but it was necessary some one should know where our enemies are placed. The Archbishop of Treves, with an assurance that might have been expected of him, has stalled his men in the cathedral, no less, but a most excellent place for our purposes. A guard at each door, and there you are.

"Ah, he has selected the cathedral not because of his assurance, but to intercept any communication with the Emperor, who is in the cloisters attached to it, and doubtless his lordship purposes to crown the new emperor before daybreak at the high altar. The design of the archbishop is deeper than appears on the surface, Gottlieb. His men in the cathedral gives him possession of the Wahlkapelle where emperors are elected, after having been nominated in the Wahlzimmer. His lordship has a taste for doing things legally. Where are the men of Cologne?"

"In a church also; the church of St. Leonhard on the banks of the Main. That is as easily surrounded and is as conveniently situated as if I had selected it myself. The Count Palatine's men are in a house near the northern gate, a house which has no back exit, and therefore calls but for the closing of a street. Nothing could be better."

"But the Drapers' Hall which holds the Mayence troops, almost adjoins the cathedral. Is there not a danger in this circumstance that a turmoil in the one may be heard in the other?"

"No, because we have most able allies."

"What? the townsmen? You have surely taken none into your confidence, Gottlieb?"

"Oh, no, my Lord. Our good copartners are none other than the archbishops themselves. It is evident they expect trouble to-morrow, but none to-night. Orders have been given that all their followers are to get a good night's rest, each man to be housed and asleep by sunset. The men of both Treves and Cologne are tired with their long and hurried march and will sleep like the dead. We will first attack the men of Mayence surrounding the Leinwandhaus, and I warrant you that no matter what noise there is, the Treves people will not hear. Then being on the spot, we will, when the Mayence soldiers are well bound, tie up those in the cathedral. I purpose if your lordship agrees to leave our bound captives where they are, guarded by a sufficient number of outlaws, in case one attempts to help the other, until we have pinioned those of Cologne and the Count Palatine. When this is off our minds we can transport all our prisoners to the fortress at our leisure."

Thus it was arranged, and when night fell on the meeting of the Electors, so well did Gottlieb and his men apply themselves to the task that before an hour had passed the minions of the Electors lay packed in heaps in the aisles and the rooms where they lodged, to be transported to the prison at the convenience of their captors.

Many conditions favoured the success of the seemingly impossible feat. Since the arrival of the soldiery there had been so many night brawls in the streets that one more or less attracted little attention, either from the military or from the civilians. The very boldness and magnitude of the scheme was an assistance to it. Then the stern cry of "In the name of the Emperor!" with which the assaulters once inside cathedral, church or house, fell upon their victims, deadened opposition, for the common soldiers, whether enlisted by Treves, Cologne, or Mayence, knew that the Emperor was over all, and they had no inkling of the designs of their immediate masters. Then, as Gottlieb had surmised, the extreme fatigue of the followers of Treves and Cologne, after their toilsome march from their respective cities, so overcame them that many went to sleep when being conveyed from church and cathedral to prison. There was some resistance on the part of officers, speedily quelled by the victorious woodlanders, but aside from this there were few heads broken, and the wish of the Empress for a bloodless conquest was amply fulfilled.

Two hours after darkness set in, Gottlieb, somewhat breathless, saluted his master at the steps of the palace and announced that the followers of the archbishops and the Count Palatine were behind bars in the Frankfort prison, with a strong guard over them to discourage any attempt at jailbreaking. When Wilhelm led his victorious soldiery silently up the narrow secret stair, pushed back, with much circumspection and caution, the sliding panel, listened for a moment to the low murmur of their lordships' voices, waited until each of his men had gone stealthily behind the tapestry, listened again and still heard the drone of speech, he returned as he came, and accompanied by a guard of two score, escorted the Empress to the broad public stairway that led up one flight to the door of the Wahlzimmer. The two sentinels at the foot of the stairs crossed their pikes to bar the entrance of Brunhilda, but they were overpowered and gagged so quickly and silently that their two comrades at the top had no suspicion of what was going forward until they had met a similar fate. The guards at the closed door, more alert, ran forward, only to be carried away with their fellow-sentinels. Wilhelm, his sword drawn, pushed open the door and cried, in a loud voice:

"My Lords, I am commanded to announce to you that her Majesty the Empress honours you with her presence."

It would have been difficult at that moment to find four men in all Germany more astonished than were the Electors. They saw the young man who held open the door, bow low, then the stately lady so sonorously announced come slowly up the hall and stand silently before them. Wilhelm closed the door and set his back against it, his naked sword still in his right hand. Three of the Electors were about to rise to their feet, but a motion of the hand by the old man of Treves, who sat the head of the table, checked them.

"I have come," said the Empress in a low voice, but distinctly heard in the stillness of the room, "to learn why you are gathered here in Frankfort and in the Wahlzimmer, where no meeting has taken place for three hundred years, except on the death of an emperor."

"Madame," said the Elector of Treves, leaning back in his chair and placing the tips of his fingers together before him, "all present have the right to assemble in this hall unquestioned, with the exception of yourself and the young man who erroneously styled you Empress, with such unnecessary flourish, as you entered. You are the wife of our present Emperor, but under the Salic law no woman can occupy the German throne. If flatterers have misled you by bestowing a title to which you have no claim, and if the awe inspired by that spurious appellation has won your admission past ignorant guards who should have prevented your approach, I ask that you will now withdraw, and permit us to resume deliberations that should not have been interrupted."

"What is the nature of those deliberations, my Lord?"

"The question is one improper for you to ask. To answer it would be to surrender our rights as Electors of the Empire. It is enough for you to be assured, madame, that we are lawfully assembled, and that our purposes are strictly legal."

"You rest strongly on the law, my Lord, so strongly indeed that were I a suspicious person I might surmise that your acts deserved strict scrutiny. I will appeal to you, then, in the name of the law. Is it the law of this realm that he who directly or indirectly conspires against the peace and comfort of his emperor is adjudged a traitor, his act being punishable by death?"

"The law stands substantially as you have cited it, madame, but its bearing upon your presence in this room is, I confess, hidden from me."

"I shall endeavour to enlighten you, my Lord. Are you convened here to further the peace and comfort of his Majesty the Emperor?"

"We devoutly trust so, madame. His Majesty is so eminently fitted for a cloister, rather than for domestic bliss or the cares of state, that we hope to pleasure him by removing all barriers in his way to a monastery."

"Then until his Majesty is deposed you are, by your own confession, traitors."

"Pardon me, madame, but the law regarding traitors which you quoted with quite womanly inaccuracy, and therefore pardonable, does not apply to eight persons within this Empire, namely, the seven Electors and the Emperor himself."

"I have been unable to detect the omission you state, my Lord. There are no exceptions, as I read the law."

"The exceptions are implied, madame, if not expressly set down, for it would be absurd to clothe Electors with a power in the exercise of which they would constitute themselves traitors. But this discussion is as painful as it is futile, and therefore it must cease. In the name of the Electoral College here in session assembled, I ask you to withdraw, madame."

"Before obeying your command, my Lord Archbishop, there is another point which I wish to submit to your honourable body, so learned in the law. I see three vacant chairs before me, and I am advised that it is illegal to depose an emperor unless all the members of the college are present and unanimous."

"Again you have been misinformed. A majority of the college elects; a majority can depose, and in retiring to private life, madame, you have the consolation of knowing that your intervention prolonged your husband's term of office by several minutes. For the third time I request you to leave this room, and if you again refuse I shall be reluctantly compelled to place you under arrest. Young man, open the door and allow this woman to pass through."

"I would have you know, my Lord," said Wilhelm, "that I am appointed commander of the imperial forces, and that I obey none but his Majesty the Emperor."

"I understood that the Emperor depended upon the Heavenly Hosts," said the Archbishop, with the suspicion of a smile on his grim lips.

"It does not become a prince of the Church to sneer at Heaven or its power," said the Empress, severely.

"Nothing was further from my intention, madame, but you must excuse me if I did not expect to see the Heavenly Hosts commanded by a young man so palpably German. Still all this is aside from the point. Will you retire, or must I reluctantly use force?"

"I advise your lordship not to appeal to force."

The old man of Treves rose slowly to his feet, an ominous glitter in his eyes. He stood for some minutes regarding angrily the woman before him, as if to give her time to reconsider her stubborn resolve to hold her ground. Then raising his voice the Elector cried:

"Men of Treves! enter!"

While one might count ten, dense silence followed this outcry, the seated Electors for the first time glancing at their leader with looks of apprehension.

"Treves! Treves! Treves!"

That potent name reverberated from the lips of its master, who had never known its magic to fail in calling round him stout defenders, and who could not yet believe that its power should desert him at this juncture. Again there was no response.

"As did the prophet of old, ye call on false gods."

The low vibrant voice of the Empress swelled like the tones of a rich organ as the firm command she had held over herself seemed about to depart.

"Lord Wilhelm, give them a name, that carries authority in its sound."

Wilhelm strode forward from the door, raised his glittering sword high above his head and shouted:

"THE EMPEROR! Cheer, ye woodland wolves!"

With a downward sweep of his sword, he cut the two silken cords which, tied to a ring near the door, held up the tapestry. The hangings fell instantly like the drop curtain of a theatre, its rustle overwhelmed in the vociferous yell that rang to the echoing roof.

"Forward! Close up your ranks!"

With simultaneous movement the men stepped over the folds on the floor and stood shoulder to shoulder, an endless oval line of living warriors, surrounding the startled group in the centre of the great hall.

"Aloft, rope-men."

Four men, with ropes wound round their bodies, detached themselves from the circle, and darting to the four corners of the room, climbed like squirrels until they reached the tunnelled roofing, where, making their way to the centre with a dexterity that was marvellous, they threw their ropes over the timbers and came spinning down to the floor, like gigantic spiders, each suspended on his own line. The four men, looped nooses in hand, took up positions behind the four Electors, all of whom were now on their feet. Wilhelm saluted the Empress, bringing the hilt of his sword to his forehead, and stepped back.

The lady spoke:

"My Lords, learned in the law, you will perhaps claim with truth that there is no precedent for hanging an Electoral College, but neither is there precedent for deposing an Emperor. It is an interesting legal point on which we shall have definite opinion pronounced in the inquiry which will follow the death of men so distinguished as yourselves, and if it should be held that I have exceeded my righteous authority in thus pronouncing sentence upon you as traitors, I shall be nothing loath to make ample apology to the state."

"Such reparation will be small consolation to us, your Majesty," said the Archbishop of Cologne, speaking for the first time. "My preference is for an ante-mortem rather than a post-mortem adjustment of the law. My colleague of Treves, in the interests of a better understanding, I ask you to destroy the document of deposition, which you hold in your hand, and which I beg to assure her Majesty, is still unsigned."

The trembling fingers of the Archbishop of Treves proved powerless to tear the tough parchment, so he held it for a moment until it was consumed in the flame of a taper which stood on the table.

"And now, your Majesty, speaking entirely for myself, I give you my word as a prince of the Church and a gentlemen of the Empire, that my vote as an Elector will always be against the deposition of the Emperor, for I am convinced that imperial power is held in firm and capable hands."

The great prelate of Cologne spoke as one making graceful concession to a lady, entirely uninfluenced by the situation in which he so unexpectedly found himself. A smile lit up the face of the Empress as she returned his deferential bow.

"I accept your word with pleasure, my Lord, fully assured that, once given, it will never be tarnished by any mental reservation."

"I most cordially associate myself with my brother of Cologne and take the same pledge," spoke up his Lordship of Mayence.

The Count Palatine of the Rhine moistened his dry lips and said:

"I was misled by ambition, your Majesty, and thus in addition to giving you my word, I crave your imperial pardon as well."

The Archbishop of Treves sat in his chair like a man collapsed. He had made no movement since the burning of the parchment. All eyes were turned upon him in the painful stillness. With visible effort he enunciated in deep voice the two words: "And I."

The face of the Empress took on a radiance that had long been absent from it.

"It seems, my Lords, that there has been merely a slight misunderstanding, which a few quiet words and some legal instruction has entirely dissipated. To seal our compact, I ask you all to dine with me to-morrow night, when I am sure it will afford intense gratification to prelates so pious as yourselves to send a message to his Majesty the Emperor, informing him that his trust in Providence has not been misplaced."

CHAPTER V. — THE NEEDLE DAGGER

Wilhelm Von Schonburg, Commander of the Imperial Forces at Frankfort, applied himself to the task of building up an army round his nucleus of five hundred with all the energy and enthusiasm of youth. He first put parties of trusty men at the various city gates so that he might control, at least in a measure, the human intake and output of the city. The power which possession of the gates gave him he knew to be more apparent than real, for Frankfort was a commercial city, owing its prosperity to traffic, and any material interference with the ebb or flow of travel had a depressing influence on trade. If the Archbishops meant to keep their words given to the Empress, all would be well, but of their good faith Wilhelm had the gravest doubts. It would be impossible to keep secret the defeat of their Lordships, when several thousands of their men lay immured in the city prison. The whole world would thus learn sooner or later that the great Princes of the Church had come to shear and had departed shorn; and this blow to their pride was one not easily forgiven by men so haughty and so powerful as the prelates of Treves, Mayence and Cologne. Young as he was, Wilhelm's free life in the forest, among those little accustomed to control the raw passions of humanity, had made him somewhat a judge of character, and he had formed the belief that the Archbishop of Cologne, was a gentleman, and would keep his word, that the Archbishop of Treves would have no scruple in breaking his, while the Archbishop of Mayence would follow the lead of Treves. This suspicion he imparted to the Empress Brunhilda, but she did not agree with him, believing that all three, with the Count Palatine, would hereafter save their heads by attending strictly to their ecclesiastical business, leaving the rule of the Empire in the hands which now held it.

"Cologne will not break the pledge he has given me," she said; "of that I am sure. Mayence is too great an opportunist to follow an unsuccessful leader; and the Count Palatine is too great a coward to enter upon such a dangerous business as the deposing of an emperor who is my husband. Besides, I have given the Count Palatine a post at Court which requires his constant presence in Frankfort, and so I have him in some measure a prisoner. The Electors are powerless if even one of their number is a defaulter, so what can Treves do, no matter how deeply his pride is injured, or how bitterly he thirsts for revenge? His only resource is boldly to raise the flag of rebellion and march his troops on Frankfort. He is too crafty a man to take such risk or to do anything so open. For this purpose he must set about the collection of an army secretly, while we may augment the Imperial troops in the light of day. So, unless he strikes speedily, we will have a force that will forever keep him in awe."

This seemed a reasonable view, but it only partly allayed the apprehensions of Wilhelm. He had caught more than one fierce look of hatred directed toward him by the Archbishop of Treves, since the meeting in the Wahlzimmer, and the regard of his Lordship of Mayence had been anything but benign. These two dignitaries had left Frankfort together, their way lying for some distance in the same direction. Wilhelm liberated their officers, and thus the two potentates had scant escort to their respective cities. Their men he refused to release, which refusal both Treves and Mayence accepted with bad grace, saying the withholding cast an aspersion on their honour. This example was not followed by the suave Archbishop of Cologne, who departed some days after his colleagues. He laughed when Wilhelm informed him that his troops would remain in Frankfort, and said he would be at the less expense in his journey down the Rhine, as his men were gross feeders.

Being thus quit of the three Archbishops, the question was what to do with their three thousand men. It was finally resolved to release them by detachments, drafting into the Imperial army such as were willing so to serve and take a special oath of allegiance to the Emperor, allowing those who declined to enlist to depart from the city in whatever direction pleased them, so that they went away in small parties. It was found, however, that the men cared little for whom they fought, providing the pay was good and reasonably well assured. Thus the Imperial army received many recruits and the country round Frankfort few vagrants.

The departed Archbishops made no sign, the Count Palatine seemed engrossed with his duties about the Court, the army increased daily and life went on so smoothly that Wilhelm began to cease all questioning of the future, coming at last to believe that the Empress was right in her estimate of the situation. He was in this pleasing state of mind when an incident occurred which would have caused him greater anxiety than it did had he been better acquainted with the governing forces of his country. On arising one morning he found on the table of his room a parchment, held in place by a long thin dagger of peculiar construction. His first attention was given to the weapon and not to the scroll. The blade was extremely thin and sharp at the point, and seemed at first sight to be so exceedingly frail as to be of little service in actual combat, but a closer examination proved that it was practically unbreakable, and of a temper so fine that nothing made an impression on its keen edge. Held at certain angles, the thin blade seemed to disappear altogether and leave the empty hilt in the hand. The hilt had been treated as if it were a crucifix, and in slightly raised relief there was a figure of Christ, His outstretched arms extending along the transverse guard. On the opposite side of the handle were the sunken letters "S. S. G. G."

Wilhelm fingered this dainty piece of mechanism curiously, wondering where it was made. He guessed Milan as the place of its origin, knowing enough of cutlery to admire the skill and knowledge of metallurgy that had gone to its construction, and convinced as he laid it down that it was foreign. He was well aware that no smith in Germany could fashion a lancet so exquisitely tempered. He then turned his attention to the document which had been fastened to the table by this needle-like stiletto. At the top of the parchment were the same letters that had been cut in the handle of the dagger.

S. S. G. G.

First warning. Wear this dagger thrust into your doublet over the heart, and allow him who accosts you, fearing nothing if your heart be true and loyal. In strict silence safety lies.

Wilhelm laughed.

"It is some lover's nonsense of Elsa's," he said to himself. "'If your heart be true and loyal,' that is a woman's phrase and nothing else."

Calling his wife, he held out the weapon to her and said:

"Where did you get this, Elsa? I would be glad to know who your

310

armourer is, for I should dearly love to provide my men with weapons of such temper."

Elsa looked alternately at the dagger and at her husband, bewildered.

"I never saw it before, nor anything like it," she replied. "Where did you find it? It is so frail it must be for ornament merely."

"Its frailness is deceptive. It is a most wonderful instrument, and I should like to know where it comes from. I thought you had bought it from some armourer and intended me to wear it as a badge of my office. Perhaps it was sent by the Empress. The word 'loyalty' seems to indicate that, though how it got into this room and on this table unknown to me is a mystery."

Elsa shook her head as she studied the weapon and the message critically.

"Her Majesty is more direct than this would indicate. If she had aught to say to you she would say it without ambiguity. Do you intend to wear the dagger as the scroll commands?"

"If I thought it came from the Empress I should, not otherwise."

"You may be assured some one else has sent it. Perhaps it is intended for me," and saying this Elsa thrust the blade of the dagger through the thick coil of her hair and turned coquettishly so that her husband might judge of the effect.

"Are you ambitious to set a new fashion to the Court, Elsa?" asked Wilhelm, smiling.

"No; I shall not wear it in public, but I will keep the dagger if I may."

Thus the incident passed, and Wilhelm gave no more thought to the mysterious warning. His duties left him little time for meditation during the day, but as he returned at night from the barracks his mind reverted once more to the dagger, and he wondered how it came without his knowledge into his private room. His latent suspicion of the Archbishops became aroused again, and he pondered on the possibility of an emissary of theirs placing the document on his table. He had given strict instructions that

311

if any one supposed to be an agent of their lordships presented himself at the gates he was to be permitted to enter the city without hindrance, but instant knowledge of such advent was to be sent to the Commander, which reminded him that he had not seen Gottlieb that day, this able lieutenant having general charge of all the ports. So he resolved to return to the barracks and question his underling regarding the recent admittances. Acting instantly on this determination, he turned quickly and saw before him a man whom he thought he recognised by his outline in the darkness as von Brent, one of the officers of Treves whom he had released, and who had accompanied the Archbishop on his return to that city. The figure, however, gave him no time for a closer inspection, and, although evidently taken by surprise, reversed his direction, making off with speed down the street. Wilhelm, plucking sword from scabbard, pursued no less fleetly. The scanty lighting of the city thoroughfares gave advantage to the fugitive, but Wilhelm's knowledge of the town was now astonishingly intimate, considering the short time he had been a resident, and his woodlore, applied to the maze of tortuous narrow alleys made him a hunter not easily baffled. He saw the flutter of a cloak as its wearer turned down a narrow lane, and a rapid mental picture of the labyrinth illuminating his mind, Wilhelm took a dozen long strides to a corner and there stood waiting. A few moments later a panting man with cloak streaming behind him came near to transfixing himself on the point of the Commander's sword. The runner pulled himself up with a gasp and stood breathless and speechless.

"I tender you good-evening, sir," said Wilhelm, civilly, "and were I not sure of your friendliness, I should take it that you were trying to avoid giving me salutation."

"I did not recognise you, my Lord, in the darkness."

The man breathed heavily, which might have been accounted for by his unaccustomed exertion.

"'Tis strange, then, that I should have recognised you, turning unexpectedly as I did, while you seemingly had me in your eye for some time before."

"Indeed, my Lord, and that I had not. I but just emerged from this crooked lane, and seeing you turn so suddenly, feared molestation, and so took to my heels, which a warrior should be shamed to confess, but I had no wish to be embroiled in a street brawl."

"Your caution does you credit, and should commend you to so peacefully-minded a master as his Lordship of Treves, who, I sincerely trust, arrived safely in his ancient city."

"He did, my Lord."

"I am deeply gratified to hear it, and putting my knowledge of his lordship's methods in conjunction with your evident desire for secrecy, I should be loath to inquire into the nature of the mission that brings you to the capital so soon after your departure from it."

"Well, my Lord," said von Brent, with an attempt at a laugh, "I must admit that it was my purpose to visit Frankfort with as little publicity as possible. You are mistaken, however, in surmising that I am entrusted with any commands from my lord, the Archbishop, who, at this moment, is devoting himself with energy to his ecclesiastical duties and therefore has small need for a soldier. This being the case, I sought and obtained leave of absence, and came to Frankfort on private affairs of my own. To speak truth, as between one young man and another, not to be further gossiped about, while, stationed here some days ago, I became acquainted with a girl whom I dearly wish to meet again, and this traffic, as you know, yearns not for either bray of trumpet or rattle of drum."

"The gentle power of love," said Wilhelm in his most affable tone, "is a force few of us can resist. Indeed, I am myself not unacquainted with its strength, and I must further congratulate you on your celerity of conquest, for you came to Frankfort in the morning, and were my guest in the fortress in the evening, so you certainly made good use of the brief interval. By what gate did you enter Frankfort?"

"By the western gate, my Lord."

"This morning?"

"No, my Lord. I entered but a short time since, just before the gates were closed for the night."

"Ah! that accounts for my hearing no report of your arrival, for it is my wish, when distinguished visitors honour us with their presence, that I may be able to offer them every courtesy."

Von Brent laughed, this time with a more genuine ring to his mirth.

"Seeing that your previous hospitality included lodging in the city prison, my Lord, as you, a moment ago, reminded me, you can scarcely be surprised that I had no desire to invite a repetition of such courtesy, if you will pardon the frank speaking of a soldier."

"Most assuredly. And to meet frankness with its like, I may add that the city prison still stands intact. But I must no longer delay an impatient lover, and so, as I began, I give you a very good evening, sir."

Von Brent returned the salutation, bowing low, and Wilhelm watched him retrace his steps and disappear in the darkness. The Commander, returning his blade to its scabbard, sought Gottlieb at the barracks.

"Do you remember von Brent, of Treves' staff?"

"That hangdog-looking officer? Yes, master. I had the pleasure of knocking him down in the Cathedral before pinioning him."

"He is in Frankfort to-night, and said he entered by the western gate just before it was closed."

"Then he is a liar," commented Gottlieb, with his usual bluntness.

"Such I strongly suspect him to be. Nevertheless, here he is, and the question I wish answered is, how did he get in?"

"He must have come over the wall, which can hardly be prevented if an incomer has a friend who will throw him a rope."

"It may be prevented if the walls are efficiently patrolled. See instantly to that, Gottlieb, and set none but our own woodlanders on watch."

314

Several days passed, and Wilhelm kept a sharp lookout for von Brent, or any other of the Archbishop's men, but he saw none such, nor could he learn that the lieutenant had left the city. He came almost to believe that the officer had spoken the truth, when distrust again assailed him on finding in the barracks a second document almost identical with the first, except that it contained the words, "Second warning," and the dirk had been driven half its length into the lid of the desk. At first he thought it was the same parchment and dagger, but the different wording showed him that at least the former was not the same. He called Gottlieb, and demanded to know who had been allowed to pass the guards and enter that room. The honest warrior was dismayed to find such a thing could have happened, and although he was unable to read the lettering, he turned the missive over and over in his hand as if he expected close scrutiny to unravel the skein. He then departed and questioned the guards closely, but was assured that no one had entered except the Commander.

"I cannot fathom it," he said on returning to his master, "and, to tell truth, I wish we were well back in the forest again, for I like not this mysterious city and its ways. We have kept this town as close sealed as a wine butt, yet I dare swear that I have caught glimpses of the Archbishop's men, flitting here and there like bats as soon as darkness gathers. I have tried to catch one or two of them to make sure, but I seem to have lost all speed of foot on these slippery stones, and those I follow disappear as if the earth swallowed them."

"Have you seen von Brent since I spoke to you about him?"

"I thought so, Master Wilhelm, but I am like a man dazed in the mazes of an evil dream, who can be certain of nothing. I am afraid of no man who will stand boldly up to me, sword in hand, with a fair light on both of us, but this chasing of shadows with nothing for a pike to pierce makes a coward of me."

"Well, the next shadow that follows me will get my blade in its vitals, for I think my foot is lighter than yours, Gottlieb. There is no shadow in this town that is not cast by a substance, and that substance will feel a sword thrust if one can but get within striking distance. Keep strict watch and we

315

will make a discovery before long, never fear. Do you think the men we have enlisted from the Archbishop's company are trying to play tricks with us? Are they to be trusted?"

"Oh, they are stout rascals with not enough brains among them all to plan this dagger and parchment business, giving little thought to anything beyond eating and drinking, and having no skill of lettering."

"Then we must look elsewhere for the explanation. It may be that your elusive shadows will furnish a clue."

On reaching his own house Wilhelm said carelessly to his wife, whom he did not wish to alarm unnecessarily:

"Have you still in your possession that dagger which I found on my table?"

"Yes, it is here. Have you found an owner for it or learned how it came there?"

"No. I merely wished to look at it again."

She gave it to him, and he saw at once that it was a duplicate of the one he had hidden under his doublet. The mystery was as far from solution as ever, and the closest examination of the weapon gave no hint pertaining to the purport of the message. Yet it is probable that Wilhelm was the only noble in the German Empire who was ignorant of the significance of the four letters, and doubtless the senders were amazed at his temerity in nonchalantly ignoring the repeated warnings, which would have brought pallor to the cheeks of the highest in the land. Wilhelm had been always so dependent on the advice of Gottlieb that it never occurred to him to seek explanation from any one else, yet in this instance Gottlieb, from the same cause of woodland training, was as ignorant as his master.

It is possible that the two warnings might have made a greater impression on the mind of the young man were it not that he was troubled about his own status in the Empire. There had been much envy in the Court at the elevation of a young man practically unknown, to the position of commander-in-chief of the German army, and high officials had gone so far as to protest against what they said was regarded as a piece of unaccountable favouritism. The Empress, however, was firm, and for a time comment seemed to cease, but it was well known that Wilhelm had no real standing, unless his appointment was confirmed by the Emperor, and his commission made legal by the royal signature. It became known, or, at least, was rumoured that twice the Empress had sent this document to her husband and twice it had been returned unsigned. The Emperor went so far as to refuse to see his wife, declining to have any discussion about the matter, and Wilhelm well knew that every step he took in the fulfilment of his office was an illegal step, and if a hint of this got to the ears of the Archbishops they would be more than justified in calling him to account, for every act he performed relating to the army after he knew that his monarch had refused to sanction his nomination was an act of rebellion and usurpation punishable by death. The Empress was well aware of the jeopardy in which her attaché stood, but she implored him not to give up the position, although helpless to make his appointment regular. She hoped her husband's religious fervour would abate and that he would deign to bestow some attention upon earthly things, allowing himself to be persuaded of the necessity of keeping up a standing army, commanded by one entirely faithful to him. Wilhelm himself often doubted the wisdom of his interference, which had allowed the throne to be held by a man who so neglected all its duties that intrigues and unrest were honeycombing the whole fabric of society, beginning at the top and working its way down until now even the merchants were in a state of uncertainty, losing faith in the stability of the government. The determined attitude of Wilhelm, the general knowledge that he came from a family of fighters, and the wholesome fear of the wild outlaws, under his command, did more than anything else to keep down open rebellion in Court and to make the position of the Empress possible. It was believed that Wilhelm would have little hesitation in obliterating half the nobility of the Court, or the whole of it for that matter, if but reasonable excuse were given him for doing so, and every one was certain that his cut-throats, as they were called, would obey any command he liked to give, and would delight in whatever slaughter ensued. The Commander held aloof from the Court, although, because of his position, he had a room in the palace which no one but the monarch and the chief officer of the army might enter, yet he rarely occupied this apartment, using, instead, the suite at the barracks.

Some days after the second episode of the dagger he received a summons from the Empress commanding his instant presence at the palace. On arriving at the Court, he found Brunhilda attended by a group of nobles, who fell back as the young commander approached. The Empress smiled as he bent his knee and kissed her hand, but Wilhelm saw by the anxiety in her eye that something untoward had happened, guessing that his commission was returned for the third time unsigned from the Emperor, and being correct in his surmise.

"Await me in the Administration Room of the Army," said the Empress. "I will see you presently. You have somewhat neglected that room of late, my Lord."

"I found I could more adequately fulfil your Majesty's command and keep in closer touch with the army by occupying my apartments at the barracks."

"I trust, then, that you will have a good report to present to me regarding the progress of my soldiers," replied the Empress, dismissing him with a slight inclination of her head.

Wilhelm left the audience chamber and proceeded along the corridor with which his room was connected. The soldier at the entrance saluted him, and Wilhelm entered the Administration Chamber. It was a large room and in the centre of it stood a large table. After closing the door Wilhelm paused in his advance, for there in the centre of the table, buried to its very hilt through the planks, was a duplicate of the dagger he had concealed inside his doublet. It required some exertion of Wilhelm's great strength before he dislodged the weapon from the timber into which it had been so fiercely driven. The scroll it affixed differed from each of the other two. It began with the words, "Final warning," and ended with "To Wilhelm of Schonburg, so-called Commander of the Imperial forces," as if from a desire on the part of the writer that there should be no mistake regarding the destination of the missive. The young man placed the knife on the parchment and stood looking at them both until

318

the Empress was announced. He strode forward to meet her and conducted her to a chair, where she seated herself, he remaining on his feet.

"I am in deep trouble," she began, "the commission authorising you to command the Imperial troops has been returned for the third time unsigned; not only that, but the act authorising the reconstruction of the army, comes back also without the Emperor's signature."

Wilhelm remained silent, for he well knew that the weakness of their position was the conduct of the Emperor, and this was an evil which he did not know how to remedy.

"When he returned both documents the first time," continued the Empress, "I sent to him a request for an interview that I might explain the urgency and necessity of the matter. This request was refused, and although I know of course that my husband might perhaps be called eccentric, still he had never before forbade my presence. This aroused my suspicion."

"Suspicion of what, your Majesty?" inquired Wilhelm.

"My suspicion that the messages I sent him have been intercepted."

"Who would dare do such a thing, your Majesty?" cried Wilhelm in amazement.

"Where large stakes are played for, large risks must be taken," went on the lady. "I said nothing at the time, but yesterday I sent to him two acts which he himself had previously sanctioned, but never carried out; these were returned to me to-day unsigned, and now I fear one of three things. The Emperor is ill, is a prisoner, or is dead."

"If it is your Majesty's wish," said Wilhelm, "I will put myself at the head of a body of men, surround the cathedral, search the cloisters, and speedily ascertain whether the Emperor is there or no."

"I have thought of such action," declared the Empress, "but I dislike to take it. It would bring me in conflict with the Church, and then there is always the chance that the Emperor is indeed within the cloisters, and that, of his own free will, he refuses to sign the documents I have sent to him. In such case what excuse could we give for our interference? It might precipitate the very crisis we are so anxious to avoid."

The Empress had been sitting by the table with her arm resting upon it, her fingers toying unconsciously with the knife while she spoke, and now as her remarks reached their conclusion her eyes fell upon its hilt and slender blade. With an exclamation almost resembling a scream the Empress sprang to her feet and allowed the dagger to fall clattering on the floor.

"Where did that come from?" she cried. "Is it intended for me?" and she shook her trembling hands as if they had touched a poisonous scorpion.

"Where it comes from I do not know, but it is not intended for your Majesty, as this scroll will inform you."

Brunhilda took the parchment he offered and held it at arm's length from her, reading its few words with dilated eyes, and Wilhelm was amazed to see in them the fear which they failed to show when she faced the three powerful Archbishops. Finally the scroll fluttered from her nerveless fingers to the floor and the Empress sank back in her chair.

"You have received two other warnings then?" she said in a low voice.

"Yes, your Majesty. What is their meaning?"

"They are the death warrants of the Fehmgerichte, a dread and secret tribunal before which even emperors quail. If you obey this mandate you will never be seen on earth again; if you disobey you will be secretly assassinated by one of these daggers, for after ignoring the third warning a hundred thousand such blades are lying in wait for your heart, and ultimately one of them will reach it, no matter in what quarter of Germany you hide yourself."

"And who are the members of this mysterious association, your Majesty?

"That, you can tell as well as I, better perhaps, for you may be a member while I cannot be. Perhaps the soldier outside this door belongs to the Fehmgerichte, or your own Chamberlain, or perhaps your most devoted lieutenant, the lusty Gottlieb."

"That, your Majesty, I'll swear he is not, for he was as amazed as I when he saw the dagger at the barracks."

Brunhilda shook her head.

"You cannot judge from pretended ignorance," she said, "because a member is sworn to keep all secrets of the holy Fehm from wife and child, father and mother, sister and brother, fire and wind; from all that the sun shines on and the rain wets, and from every being between heaven and earth. Those are the words of the oath."

Wilhelm found himself wondering how his informant knew so much about the secret court if all those rules were strictly kept, but he naturally shrank from any inquiry regarding the source of her knowledge. Nevertheless her next reply gave him an inkling of the truth.

"Who is the head of this tribunal?" he asked.

"The Emperor is the nominal head, but my husband never approved of the Fehmgerichte; originally organised to redress the wrongs of tyranny, it has become a gigantic instrument of oppression. The Archbishop of Cologne is the actual president of the order, not in his capacity as an elector, nor as archbishop, but because he is Duke of Westphalia, where this tragic court had its origin."

"Your Majesty imagines then, that this summons comes from the Archbishop of Cologne?"

"Oh, no. I doubt if he has any knowledge of it. Each district has a freigraf, or presiding judge, assisted by seven assessors, or freischoffen, who sit in so called judgment with him, but literally they merely record the sentence, for condemnation is a foregone conclusion."

"Is the sentence always death?"

"Always, at this secret tribunal; a sentence of death immediately carried out. In the open Fehmic court, banishment, prison, or other penalty may be inflicted, but you are summoned to appear before the secret tribunal."

"Does your Majesty know the meaning of these cabalistic letters on the dagger's hilt and on the parchment?"

"The letters 'S. S. G. G.' stand for Strick, Stein, Gras, Grün: Strick meaning, it is said, the rope which hangs you; Stein, the stone at the head of your grave, and Gras, Grün, the green grass covering it."

"Well, your Majesty," said Wilhelm, picking up the parchment from the floor and tearing it in small pieces, "if I have to choose between the rope and the dagger, I freely give my preference to the latter. I shall not attend this secret conclave, and if any of its members think to strike a dagger through my heart, he will have to come within the radius of my sword to do so."

"God watch over you," said the Empress fervently, "for this is a case in which the protection of an earthly throne is of little avail. And remember, Lord Wilhelm, trust not even your most intimate friend within arm's length of you. The only persons who may not become members of this dread order are a Jew, an outlaw, an infidel, a woman, a servant, a priest, or a person excommunicated."

Wilhelm escorted the Empress to the door of the red room, and there took leave of her; he being unable to suggest anything that might assuage her anxiety regarding her husband, she being unable to protect him from the new danger that threatened. Wilhelm was as brave as any man need be, and in a fair fight was content to take whatever odds came, but now he was confronted by a subtle invisible peril, against which ordinary courage was futile. An unaccustomed shiver chilled him as the palace sentinel, in the gathering gloom of the corridor, raised his hand swiftly to his helmet in salute. He passed slowly down the steps of the palace into the almost deserted square in front of it, for the citizens of Frankfort found it expedient to get early indoors when darkness fell. The young man found himself glancing furtively from right to left, starting at every shadow and scrutinising every passerby who was innocently hurrying to his own home. The name "Fehmgerichte" kept repeating itself in his brain like an incantation. He took the middle of the square and hesitated when he came to the narrow street down which his way lay. At the street corner he paused, laid his hand on the hilt of his sword and drew a deep breath.

"Is it possible," he muttered to himself, "that I am afraid? Am I at heart a coward? By the cross which is my protection," he cried, "if they wish to try their poniarding, they shall have an opportunity!"

And drawing his sword he plunged into the dark and narrow street, his footsteps ringing defiantly in the silence on the stone beneath him as he strode resolutely along. He passed rapidly through the city until he came to the northern gate. Here accosting his warders and being assured that all was well, he took the street which, bending like a bow, followed the wall until it came to the river. Once or twice he stopped, thinking himself followed, but the darkness was now so impenetrable that even if a pursuer had been behind him he was safe from detection if he kept step with his victim and paused when he did. The street widened as it approached the river, and Wilhelm became convinced that some one was treading in his footsteps. Clasping his sword hilt more firmly in his hand he wheeled about with unexpectedness that evidently took his follower by surprise, for he dashed across the street and sped fleetly towards the river. The glimpse Wilhelm got of him in the open space between the houses made him sure that he was once more on the track of von Brent, the emissary of Treves. The tables were now turned, the pursuer being the pursued, and Wilhelm set his teeth, resolved to put a sudden end to this continued espionage. Von Brent evidently remembered his former interception, and now kept a straight course. Trusting to the swiftness of his heels, he uttered no cry, but directed all his energies toward flight, and Wilhelm, equally silent, followed as rapidly.

Coming to the river, von Brent turned to the east, keeping in the middle of the thoroughfare. On the left hand side was a row of houses, on the right flowed the rapid Main. Some hundreds of yards further up there were houses on both sides of the street, and as the water of the river flowed against the walls of the houses to the right, Wilhelm knew there could be no escape that way. Surmising that his victim kept the middle of the street in order to baffle the man at his heels, puzzling him as to which direction the fugitive intended to bolt, Wilhelm, not to be deluded by such a device, ran close to the houses on the left, knowing that if von Brent turned to the right he would be speedily stopped by the Main. The race promised to reach a sudden conclusion, for

Wilhelm was perceptibly gaining on his adversary, when coming to the first house by the river the latter swerved suddenly, jumped to a door, pushed it open and was inside in the twinkling of an eye, but only barely in time to miss the sword thrust that followed him. Quick as thought Wilhelm placed his foot in such a position that the door could not be closed. Then setting his shoulder to the panels, he forced it open in spite of the resistance behind it. Opposition thus overborne by superior strength, Wilhelm heard the clatter of von Brent's footsteps down the dark passage, and next instant the door was closed with a bang, and it seemed to the young man that the house had collapsed upon him. He heard his sword snap and felt it break beneath him, and he was gagged and bound before he could raise a hand to help himself. Then when it was too late, he realised that he had allowed the heat and fervour of pursuit to overwhelm his judgment, and had jumped straight into the trap prepared for him. Von Brent returned with a lantern in his hand and a smile on his face, breathing quickly after his exertions. Wilhelm, huddled in a corner, saw a dozen stalwart ruffians grouped around him, most of them masked, but two or three with faces bare, their coverings having come off in the struggle. These slipped quickly out of sight, behind the others, as if not wishing to give clue for future recognition.

"Well, my Lord," said von Brent, smiling, "you see that gagging and binding is a game that two may play at."

There was no reply to this, first, because Wilhelm was temporarily in a speechless condition, and, second, because the proposition was not one to be contradicted.

"Take him to the Commitment Room," commanded von Brent.

Four of the onlookers lifted Wilhelm and carried him down a long stairway, across a landing and to the foot of a second flight of steps, where he was thrown into a dark cell, the dimensions of which he could not estimate. When the door was closed the prisoner lay with his head leaning against it, and for a time the silence was intense. By and by he found that by turning his head so that his ear was placed against the panel of the door, he heard distinctly the footfalls outside, and even a shuffling sound near him, which seemed to indicate that a man was on guard at the other side of the oak. Presently some one approached, and in spite of the low tones used, Wilhelm not only heard what was being said, but recognised the voice of von Brent, who evidently was his jailer.

"You have him safely then?"

"Gagged and bound, my Lord."

"Is he disarmed?"

"His sword was broken under him, my Lord, when we fell upon him."

"Very well. Remove the gag and place him with No. 13. Bar them in and listen to their conversation. I think they have never met, but I want to be sure of it."

"Is there not a chance that No. 13 may make himself known, my Lord?"

"No matter if he does. In fact, it is my object to have No. 13 and No. 14 known to each other, and yet be not aware that we have suspicion of their knowledge."

When the door of the cell was opened four guards came in. It was manifest they were not going to allow Wilhelm any chance to escape, and were prepared to overpower him should he attempt flight or resistance. The gag was taken from his mouth and the thongs which bound his legs were untied, and thus he was permitted to stand on his feet. Once outside his cell he saw that the subterranean region in which he found himself was of vast extent, resembling the crypt of a cathedral, the low roof being supported by pillars of tremendous circumference. From the direction in which he had been carried from the foot of the stairs he surmised, and quite accurately, that this cavern was under the bed of the river. Those who escorted him and those whom he met were masked. No torches illuminated the gloom of this sepulchral hall, but each individual carried, attached in some way to his belt, a small horn lantern, which gave for a little space around a dim uncertain light, casting weird shadows against the pillars of the cavern. Once or twice they met a man clothed in an apparently seamless cloak of black cloth, that covered the head and extended to the feet. Two holes in front of the face allowed a momentary glimpse of a pair of flashing eyes as the yellow light from the lanterns smote them. These grim figures were presumably persons of importance, for the guards stopped, and saluted, as each one approached, not going forward until he had silently passed them. When finally the door of the cell they sought was reached, the guards drew back the bolts, threw it open, and pushed Wilhelm into the apartment that had been designated for him. Before closing the door, however, one of the guards placed a lantern on the floor so that the fellow-prisoners might have a chance of seeing each other. Wilhelm beheld, seated on a pallet of straw, a man well past middle-age, his face smooth-shaven and of serious cast, yet having, nevertheless, a trace of irresolution in his weak chin. His costume was that of a mendicant monk, and his face seemed indicative of the severity of monastic rule. There was, however, a serenity of courage in his eye which seemed to betoken that he was a man ready to die for his opinions, if once his wavering chin allowed him to form them. Wilhelm remembering that priests were not allowed to join the order of the Fehmgerichte reflected that here was a man who probably, from his fearless denunciations of the order, had brought down upon himself the hatred of the secret tribunal, whose only penalty was that of death. The older man was the first to speak.

"So you also are a victim of the Fehmgerichte?"

"I have for some minutes suspected as much," replied von Schonburg.

"Were you arrested and brought here, or did you come here willingly?"

"Oh, I came here willingly enough. I ran half a league in my eagerness to reach this spot and fairly jumped into it," replied Wilhelm, with a bitter laugh.

"You were in such haste to reach this spot?" said the old man, sombrely, "what is your crime?"

"That I do not know, but I shall probably soon learn when I come before the court."

"Are you a member of the order, then?"

"No, I am not."

"In that case, it will require the oaths of twenty-one members to clear you, therefore, if you have not that many friends in the order I look upon you as doomed."

"Thank you. That is as God wills."

"Assuredly, assuredly. We are all in His hands," and the good man devoutly crossed himself.

"I have answered your questions," said Wilhelm, "answer you some of mine. Who are you?"

"I am a seeker after light."

"Well, there it is," said Wilhelm, touching the lantern with his foot as he paced up and down the limits of the cell.

"Earthly light is but dim at best, it is the light of Heaven I search after."

"Well, I hope you may be successful in finding it. I know of no place where it is needed so much as here."

"You speak like a scoffer. I thought from what you said of God's will, that you were a religious man."

"I am a religious man, I hope, and I regret if my words seem lightly spoken."

"What action of man, think you then, is most pleasing to God?"

"That is a question which you, to judge by your garb, are more able to answer than I."

"Nay, nay, I want your opinion."

"Then in my opinion, the man most pleasing to God is he who does his duty here on earth."

"Ah! right, quite right," cried the older man, eagerly. "But there lies the core of the whole problem. What is duty; that is what I have spent my life trying to learn."

"Then at a venture I should say your life has been a useless one. Duty is as plain as the lighted lantern there before us. If you are a priest, fulfil your priestly office well; comfort the sick, console the dying, bury the dead. Tell your flock not to speculate too much on duty, but to try and accomplish the work in hand."

"But I am not a priest," faltered the other, rising slowly to his feet.

"Then if you are a soldier, strike hard for your King. Kill the man immediately before you, and if, instead, he kills you, be assured that the Lord will look after your soul when it departs through the rent thus made in your body."

"There is a ring of truth in that, but it sounds worldly. How can we tell that such action is pleasing to God? May it not be better to depend entirely on the Lord, and let Him strike your blows for you?"

"Never! What does He give you arms for but to protect your own head, and what does He give you swift limbs for if not to take your body out of reach when you are threatened with being overmatched? God must despise such a man as you speak of, and rightly so. I am myself a commander of soldiers, and if I had a lieutenant who trusted all to me and refused to strike a sturdy blow on his own behalf I should tear his badge from him and have him scourged from out the ranks."

"But may we not, by misdirected efforts, thwart the will of God?"

"Oh! the depths of human vanity! Thwart the will of God? What, a puny worm like you? You amaze me, sir, with your conceit, and I lose the respect for you which at first your garb engendered in my mind. Do your work manfully, and flatter not yourself that your most strenuous efforts are able to cross the design of the Almighty. My own poor belief is that He has patience with any but a coward and a loiterer."

The elder prisoner staggered into the centre of the room and raised his hands above his head.

328

"Oh, Lord, have mercy upon me," he cried. "Thou who hast brought light to me in this foul dungeon which was refused to me in the radiance of Thy Cathedral. Have mercy on me, oh, Lord, the meanest of Thy servants—a craven Emperor."

"The Emperor!" gasped Wilhelm, the more amazed because he had his Majesty in mind when he spoke so bitterly of neglected duty, unconsciously blaming his sovereign rather than his own rashness for the extreme predicament in which he found himself.

Before either could again speak the door suddenly opened wide, and a deep voice solemnly enunciated the words:

"Wilhelm of Schonburg, pretended Commander of his Majesty's forces, you are summoned to appear instantly before the court of the Holy Fehm, now in session and awaiting you."

CHAPTER VI. — THE HOLY FEHM

When the spokesman of the Fehmgerichte had finished his ominous summons, his attendants crowded round Wilhelm swiftly and silently as if to forestall any attempt at resistance either on his part or on the part of the Emperor. They hurried their victim immediately out of the cell and instantly barred the door on the remaining prisoner. First they crossed the low-roofed, thickly-pillared great hall, passing through a doorway at which two armed men stood guard, masked, as were all the others. The Judgment Hall of the dread Fehmgerichte was a room of about ten times the extent of the cell Wilhelm had just left, but still hardly of a size that would justify the term large. The walls and vaulted roof were of rough stone, and on the side opposite the entrance had been cut deeply the large letters S. S. G. G. A few feet distant from this lettered wall stood a long table, and between the wall and the table sat seven men. The Freigraf, as Wilhelm surmised him to be, occupied in the centre of this line a chair slightly more elevated than those of the three who sat on either hand. Seven staples had been driven into the interstices of the stones above the heads of the Court and from each staple hung a lighted lantern, which with those at the belts of the guard standing round, illuminated the dismal chamber fairly well. To the left of the Court was a block draped in black and beside it stood the executioner with his arms resting on the handle of his axe. In the ceiling above his head was an iron ring and from this ring depended a rope, the noose of which dangled at the shoulder of the headsman, for it was the benevolent custom of the Court to allow its victim a choice in the manner of his death. It was also a habit of the judges of this Court to sit until the sentence they had pronounced was carried out, and thus there could be no chance of mistake or rescue. No feature of any judge was visible except the eyes through the holes pierced for the purposes of vision in the long black cloaks which completely enveloped their persons.

As Wilhelm was brought to a stand before this assemblage, the Freigraf nodded his head and the guards in silence undid the thongs which pinioned together wrists and elbows, leaving the prisoner absolutely unfettered.—This done, the guard retreated backwards to the opposite wall, and Wilhelm stood alone before the seven sinister doomsmen. He expected that his examination, if the Court indulged in any such, would be begun by the Freigraf, but this was not the case. The last man to the left in the row had a small bundle of documents on the table before him. He rose to his feet, bowed low to his brother judges, and then with less deference to the prisoner. He spoke in a voice lacking any trace of loudness, but distinctly heard in every corner of the room because of the intense stillness. There was a sweet persuasiveness in the accents he used, and his sentences resembled those of a lady anxious not to give offence to the person addressed.

"Am I right in supposing you to be Wilhelm, lately of Schonburg, but now of Frankfort?"

"You are right."

"May I ask if you are a member of the Fehmgerichte?"

"I am not. I never heard of it until this afternoon."

"Who was then your informant regarding the order?"

"I refuse to answer."

The examiner inclined his head gracefully as if, while regretting the decision of the witness, he nevertheless bowed to it.

"Do you acknowledge his lordship the Archbishop of Mayence as your over lord?"

"Most assuredly."

"Have you ever been guilty of an act of rebellion or insubordination against his lordship?"

"My over-lord, the Archbishop of Mayence, has never preferred a request to me which I have refused."

"Pardon me, I fear I have not stated my proposition with sufficient clearness, and so you may have misunderstood the question. I had in my

331

mind a specific act, and so will enter into further detail. Is it true that in the Wahlzimmer you entered the presence of your over-lord with a drawn sword in your hand, commanding a body of armed men lately outlaws of the Empire, thus intimidating your over-lord in the just exercise of his privileges and rights as an Elector?"

"My understanding of the Feudal law," said Wilhelm, "is that the commands of an over-lord are to be obeyed only in so far as they do not run counter to orders from a still higher authority."

"Your exposition of the law is admirable, and its interpretation stands exactly as you have stated it. Are we to understand then that you were obeying the orders of some person in authority who is empowered to exercise a jurisdiction over his lordship the Archbishop, similar to that which the latter in his turn claims over you?"

"That is precisely what I was about to state."

"Whose wishes were you therefore carrying out?

"Those of his Majesty the Emperor."

The examiner bowed with the utmost deference when the august name was mentioned.

"I have to thank you in the name of the Court," he went on, "for your prompt and comprehensive replies, which have thus so speedily enabled us to come to a just and honourable verdict, and it gives me pleasure to inform you that the defence you have made is one that cannot be gainsaid, and, therefore, with the exception of one slight formality, there is nothing more for us to do but to set you at liberty and ask pardon for the constraint we regret having put upon you, and further to request that you take oath that neither to wife nor child, father nor mother, sister nor brother, fire nor wind, will you reveal anything that has happened to you; that you will conceal it from all that the sun shines on and from all that the rain wets, and from every being between heaven and earth. And now before our doors are thus opened I have to beg that you will favour the Court with the privilege of examining the commission that his Majesty the Emperor has signed."

"You cannot expect me to carry my commission about on my person, more especially as I had no idea I should be called upon to undergo examination upon it."

"Such an expectation would certainly be doomed to disappointment, but you are doubtless able to tell us where the document lies, and I can assure you that, wherever it is placed, an emissary of this order will speedily fetch it, whether, it is concealed in palace or in hut. Allow me to ask you then, where this commission is?"

"I cannot tell you."

"Do you mean you cannot, or you will not?"

"Take it whichever way you please, it is a matter of indifference to me."

The examiner folded his arms under his black cloak and stood for some moments in silence, looking reproachfully at the prisoner. At last he spoke in a tone which seemed to indicate that he was pained at the young man's attitude:

"I sincerely trust I am mistaken in supposing that you refuse absolutely to assist this Court in the securing of a document which not only stands between you and your liberty, but also between you and your death."

"Oh, a truce to this childish and feigned regret," cried Wilhelm with rude impatience. "I pray you end the farce with less of verbiage and of pretended justice. You have his Majesty here a prisoner. You have, through my own folly, my neck at the mercy of your axe or your rope. There stands the executioner eager for his gruesome work. Finish that which you have already decided upon, and as sure as there is a God in heaven there will be quick retribution for the crimes committed in this loathsome dungeon."

The examiner deplored the introduction of heat into a discussion that required the most temperate judgment.

"But be assured," he said, "that the hurling of unfounded accusations against this honourable body will not in the least prejudice their members in dealing with your case."

"I know it," said Wilhelm with a sneering laugh.

"We have been informed that no such commission exists, that the document empowering you to take instant command of the Imperial troops rests in the hands of the wife of his Majesty the Emperor and is unsigned."

"If you know that, then why do you ask me so many questions about it?"

"In the sincere hope that by the production of the document itself, you may be able to repudiate so serious an accusation. You admit then that you have acted without the shelter of a commission from his Majesty?"

"I admit nothing."

The examiner looked up and down the row of silent figures as much as to say, "I have done my best; shall any further questions be put?" There being no response to this the examiner said, still without raising his voice:

"There is a witness in this case, and I ask him to stand forward."

A hooded and cloaked figure approached the table.

"Are you a member of the Fehmgerichte?"

"I am."

"In good and honourable standing?"

"In good and honourable standing."

"You swear by the order to which you belong that the evidence you give shall be truth without equivocation and without mental reservation?"

"I swear it."

"Has the prisoner a commission signed by the Emperor empowering him to command the Imperial troops?"

"He has not, and never has had such a commission. A document was made out and sent three times to his Majesty for signature; to-day it was returned for the third time unsigned."

"Prisoner, do you deny that statement?"

"I neither deny nor affirm."

Wilhelm was well aware that his fate was decided upon. Even if he had appeared before a regularly constituted court of the Empire instead of at the bar of an underground secret association, the verdict must inevitably have gone against him, so long as the Emperor's signature was not appended to the document which would have legalised his position.

"It would appear then," went on the examiner, "that in the action you took against your immediate over-lord, the Archbishop of Mayence, you were unprotected by the mandate of the Emperor. Freigraf and Freischoffen have heard question and answer. With extreme reluctance I am compelled to announce to this honourable body, that nothing now remains except to pronounce the verdict."

With this the examiner sat down, and for a few moments there was silence, then the Freigraf enunciated in a low voice the single word:

"Condemned."

And beginning at the right hand, each member of the Court pronounced the word "Condemned."

Wilhelm listened eagerly to the word, expecting each moment to hear the voice of one or other of the Archbishops, but in this he was disappointed. The low tone universally used by each speaker gave a certain monotony of sound which made it almost impossible to distinguish one voice from another. This evident desire for concealment raised a suspicion in the young man's mind that probably each member of the Court did not know who his neighbours were. When the examiner at the extreme left had uttered the word "Condemned" the Freigraf again spoke:

"Is there any reason why the sentence just pronounced be not immediately carried out?"

The examiner again rose to his feet and said quietly, but with great respect:

"My Lord, I ask that this young man be not executed immediately, but on the contrary, be taken to his cell, there to be held during the pleasure of the Court."

There seemed to be a murmured dissent to this, but a whispered explanation passed along the line and the few that had at first objected, nodded their heads in assent.

"Our rule cannot be set aside," said the Freigraf, "unless with unanimous consent. Does any member demur?"

No protests being made the Freigraf ordered Wilhelm to be taken to a cell, which was accordingly done.

The young man left alone in the darkness felt a pleasure in being able to stretch his arms once more, and he paced up and down the narrow limits of his cell, wondering what the next move would be in this mysterious drama. In the Judgment Chamber he had abandoned all hope, and had determined that when the order was given to seize him he would pluck the dagger of the order from the inside of his doublet, and springing over the table, kill one or more of these illegal judges before he was overpowered. The sudden change in tactics persuaded him that something else was required of him rather than the death which seemed so imminent. It was palpable that several members of the Court at least were unacquainted with the designs of the master mind which was paramount in his prosecution. They had evinced surprise when the examiner had demanded postponement of the execution. There was something behind all this that betrayed the crafty hand of the Archbishop of Treves. He was not long left in doubt. The door of the cell opened slowly and the pale rays of a lantern illuminated the blackness which surrounded him. The young man stopped in his walk and awaited developments. There entered to him one of the cloak-enveloped figures, who might, or might not, be a member of the Holy Court. Wilhelm thought that perhaps his visitor was the examiner, but the moment the silence was broken, in spite of the fact that the speaker endeavoured to modulate his tones as the others had done, the young man knew the incomer was not the person who had questioned him.

"We are somewhat loth," the intruder began, "to cut short the career of one so young as you are, and one who gives promise of becoming a notable captain."

"What have you seen of me," inquired Wilhelm, "that leads you to suppose I have the qualities of a capable officer in me?"

The other did not reply for a moment or two; then he said slowly:

"I do not say that I have seen anything to justify such a conclusion, but I have heard of your action in the Wahlzimmer, and by the account given, I judge you to be a young man of resource."

"I am indebted to you for the good opinion you express. It is quite in your power to set me free, and then the qualities you are kind enough to commend, may have an opportunity for development."

"Alas!" said the visitor, "it is not in my power to release you; that lies entirely with yourself."

"You bring comforting news. What is the price?"

"You are asked to become a member of the Fehmgerichte."

"I should suppose that to be easily accomplished, as I am now a partaker of its hospitality. What else?"

"The remaining proviso is that you take service, with his lordship, the Archbishop of Treves, and swear entire allegiance to him."

"I am already in the service of the Emperor."

"It has just been proven that you are not."

"How could the Archbishop expect faithful service from me, if I prove traitor to the one I deem my master?"

"The Archbishop will probably be content to take the risk of that."

"Are you commissioned to speak for the Archbishop?"

"I am."

"Are you one of the Archbishop's men?"

"My disposition towards him is friendly; I cannot say that I am one of his men."

"Granting, then, that I took service with the Archbishop to save my life, what would he expect me to do?"

"To obey him in all things."

"Ah, be more explicit, as the examiner said. I am not a man to enter into a bargain blindly. I must know exactly what is required of me."

"It is probable that your first order would be to march your army from Frankfort to Treves. Would the men follow you, do you think?"

"Undoubtedly. The men will follow wherever I choose to lead them. Another question. What becomes of the Emperor in case I make this bargain?"

"That question it is impossible at the present moment, to answer. The Court of the Holy Fehm is now awaiting my return, and when I take my place on the bench the Emperor will be called upon to answer for his neglect of duty."

"Nevertheless you may hazard a guess regarding his fate."

"I hazard this guess then, that his fate will depend largely upon himself, just as your fate depends upon yourself."

"I must see clearly where I am going, therefore I request you to be more explicit. What will the Court demand of the Emperor that he may save his life?"

"You are questioning me touching the action of others; therefore, all I can do is merely to surmise. My supposition is that if the Emperor promises to abdicate he will be permitted to pass unscathed from the halls of the Fehmgerichte."

"And should he refuse?"

"Sir, I am already at the end of my patience through your numerous questions," and as the voice rose in something approaching anger, Wilhelm seemed to recognise its ring. "I came here, not to answer your questions, but to have you answer mine. What is your decision?"

"My decision is that you are a confessed traitor; die the death of such!"

Wilhelm sprang forward and buried the dagger of the Fehmgerichte into the heart of the man before him. His action was so unexpected that the victim could make no motion to defend himself. So truly was the fierce blow dealt that the doomed man, without a cry or even a groan, sank in his death collapse at the young man's feet in a heap on the floor.

Wilhelm, who thought little of taking any man's life in a fair fight, shuddered as he gazed at the helpless bundle at his feet; a moment before, this uncouth heap stood erect, a man like himself, conversing with him, then the swift blow and the resulting huddle of clay.

"Oh, God above me, Over-lord of all, I struck for my King, yet I feel myself an assassin. If I am, indeed, a murderer in Thy sight, wither me where I stand, and crush me to the ground, companion to this dead body."

For a few moments Wilhelm stood rigid, his face uplifted, listening to the pulsations in his own throat and the strident beatings of his own heart. No bolt from heaven came to answer his supplication. Stooping, he, with some difficulty, drew the poniard from its resting-place. The malignant ingenuity of its construction had caused its needle point to penetrate the chain armour, while its keen double edge cut link after link of the hard steel as it sunk into the victim's breast. The severed ends of the links now clutched the blade as if to prevent its removal. Not a drop of blood followed its exit, although it had passed directly through the citadel of life itself. Again concealing the weapon within his doublet, a sudden realisation of the necessity for speed overcame the assaulter. He saw before him a means of escape. He had but to don the all-concealing cloak and walk out of this subterranean charnel house by the way he had entered it, if he could but find the foot of the stairs, down which they had carried him. Straightening out the body he pulled the cloak free from it, thus exposing the face to the yellow light of the lantern. His heart stood still as he saw that the man he had killed was no other than that exalted Prince of the Church, the venerable Archbishop of Treves. He drew the body to the pallet of straw in the corner of the cell, and there, lying on its face, he left it. A moment later he was costumed as a high priest of the order of the Fehmgerichte. Taking the lantern in his hand he paused before the closed door. He could not remember whether or not he had heard the bolts shot after the Archbishop had entered. Conning rapidly in his mind the startling change in the situation, he stood there until he had recovered command of himself, resolved that if possible no mistake on his part should now mar his chances of escape, and in this there was no thought of saving his own life, but merely a determination to get once more into the streets of Frankfort, rally his men, penetrate into these subterranean regions, and rescue the Emperor alive. He pushed with all his might against the door, and to his great relief the heavy barrier swung slowly round on its hinges. Once outside he pushed it shut again, and was startled by two guards springing to his assistance, one of them saying:

"Shall we thrust in the bolts, my Lord?"

"Yes," answered Wilhelm in the low tone which all, costumed as he was, had used. He turned away but was dismayed to find before him two brethren of the order arrayed in like manner to himself, who had evidently been waiting for him.

"What is the result of the conference? Does he consent?"

Rapidly Wilhelm had to readjust events in his own mind to meet this unexpected emergency.

"No," he replied slowly, "he does not consent, at least, not just at the moment. He has some scruples regarding his loyalty to the Emperor."

"Those scruples will be speedily removed then, when we remove his Majesty. The other members of the Court are but now awaiting us in the Judgment Chamber. Let us hasten there, and make a quick disposal of the Emperor."

Wilhelm saw that there was no possibility of retreat. Any attempt at flight would cause instant alarm and the closing of the exits, then both the Emperor and himself would be caught like rats in a trap, yet there was almost

340

equal danger in entering the Council Chamber. He had not the remotest idea which seat at the table he should occupy, and he knew that a mistake in placing himself would probably lead to discovery. He lagged behind, but the others persistently gave him precedence, which seemed to indicate that they knew the real quality of the man they supposed him to be. He surmised that his seat was probably that of the Freigraf in the centre, but on crossing the threshold past the saluting guards, he saw that the Freigraf occupied the elevated seat, having at his left three Freischoffen, while the remaining seats at his right were unoccupied. It was a space of extreme anxiety when his two companions stopped to allow him to go first. He dared not take the risk of placing himself wrongly at the board. There was scant time for consideration, and Wilhelm speedily came to a decision. It was merely one risk to take where several were presented, and he chose that which seemed to be the safest. Leaning towards his companions he said quietly:

"I beg of you, be seated. I have a few words to address to the Holy Court."

The two inclined their heads in return, and one of them in passing him murmured the scriptural words, "The first shall be last," which remark still further assisted in reversing Wilhelm's former opinion and convinced him that the identity of the Archbishop was known to them. When they were seated, the chair at the extreme right was the only one vacant, and Wilhelm breathed easier, having nothing further to fear from that source, if he could but come forth scatheless from his speech.

"I have to acquaint the Court of the Holy Fehm," he said, speaking audibly, but no more, "that my mission to the cell of the prisoner who has just left us, resulted partly in failure and partly in success. The young man has some hesitation in placing himself in open opposition to the Emperor. I therefore suggest that we go on with our deliberations, leaving the final decision of his case until a later period."

To this the Court unanimously murmured the word: "Agreed," and Wilhelm took his place at the table.

"Bring in prisoner No. 13," said the Freigraf, and a few moments later the Emperor of Germany stood before the table.

He regarded the dread tribunal with a glance of haughty scorn while countenance and demeanour exhibited a dignity which Wilhelm had fancied was lacking during their interview in the cell.

The examiner rose to his feet and in the same suave tones he had used in questioning Wilhelm, propounded the usual formal interrogatory regarding name and quality. When he was asked:

"Are you a member of the Holy Order of the Fehmgerichte?" the Emperor's reply seemed to cause some consternation among the judges.

"I am not only a member of the Fehmgerichte, but by its constitution, I am the head of it, and I warn you that any action taken by this Court without my sanction, is, by the statutes of the order, illegal."

The examiner paused in his questioning apparently taken aback by this assertion, and looked towards the Freigraf as if awaiting a decision before proceeding further.

"We acknowledge freely," said the Freigraf, "that you are the figure-head of the order, and that in all matters pertaining to a change of constitution your consent would probably be necessary, but stretching your authority to its utmost limit, it does not reach to the Courts of the Holy Fehm, which have before now sat in judgment on the highest in the land. For more than a century the position of the Emperor as head of the Fehmgerichte has been purely nominal, and I know of no precedent where the ruler of the land has interfered with the proceedings of the secret Court. We avow allegiance to the actual head of the order, who is the Duke of Westphalia."

"Is the Duke of Westphalia here present?"

"That is a question improper for you to ask."

"If the Duke of Westphalia is one of the members of this Court, I command him by the oath which he took at his installation, to descend from his place and render his seat to me, the head of this order."

"The nominal head," corrected the Freigraf.

"The actual head," persisted the prisoner. "The position remained nominal only because the various occupants did not choose to exercise the authority vested in them. It is my pleasure to resume the function which has too long remained in abeyance, thus allowing inferior officers to pretend to a power which is practical usurpation, and which, according to the constitution of our order, is not to be tolerated. Disobey at your peril. I ask the Archbishop of Cologne, Duke of Westphalia, as the one, high vassal of the Empire, as the other, my subordinate in the Fehmgerichte, to stand forth and salute his chief."

Wilhelm's heart beat rapidly underneath his black cloak as he saw this spectacle of helpless prisoner defying a power, which, in its sphere of action, was almost omnipotent. It was manifest that the Emperor's trenchant sentences had disturbed more than one member of the convention, and even the Freigraf glanced in perplexity towards the supposed Archbishop of Treves as if for a hint anent the answer that should be given. As if in response to the silent appeal, Wilhelm rose slowly to his feet, while the examiner seated himself.

"It is my privilege," he began, "on behalf of my fellow members, to inform the prisoner that the Court of the Holy Fehm has ever based its action on the broad principles of eternal justice."

A sarcastic smile wreathed the lips of the Emperor at this. Wilhelm went on unheeding.

"A point of law has been raised by the prisoner, which, I think, at least merits our earnest consideration, having regard for the future welfare of this organisation, and being anxious not to allow any precedent to creep in, which may work to the disadvantage of those who follow us. In order that our deliberations may have that calm impartiality which has ever distinguished them, I ask unanimous consent to my suggestion that the prisoner be taken back to his cell until we come to a decision regarding the matter in dispute."

This proposition being agreed to without a dissenting voice, the prisoner was removed from the room and the eyes of all the judges were turned towards Wilhelm. The Freigraf was the first to break the silence.

"Although I have agreed to the removal of the prisoner," he said, "yet I see not the use of wasting so many words on him. While there is undoubted wisdom in winning to our side the man who controls the army, there seems to me little to gain in prolonging discussion with the Emperor, who is a nonentity at best, and has no following. The path to the throne must be cleared, and there is but one way of doing it."

"Two, I think," murmured Wilhelm.

"What other than by this prisoner's death?"

"His abdication would suffice."

"But, as you know, he has already refused to abdicate."

"Ah, that was before he saw the executioner standing here. I think he is now in a condition to reconsider his determination. Thus we will avoid discussion of the knotty points which he raised, and which I, for one, would prefer to see remain where they are. The moment he consents to abdicate, the commander of the forces is willing to swear allegiance to us. It must not be forgotten that even if we execute these two men we have still the troops who hold the city of Frankfort to reckon with, and although their leader may have disappeared, the young man has some sturdy lieutenants who will give us trouble."

"What do you propose?" asked the Freigraf.

"If the colleague at my left will accompany me, we will visit the prisoner and may have some proposals to submit to you on our return."

This being acceded to, the two left the Judgment Chamber and proceeded slowly to the cell of No. 13. On the way thither Wilhelm said to his companion:

"As the prisoner may be on his guard if we enter together, I prefer to sound him first alone, and at the proper moment, if you stay outside the door of the cell, I shall summon you to enter."

This meeting the sanction of Wilhelm's companion, the young man

344

entered the cell alone, carefully closing the door behind him.

"Your Majesty," he whispered, "the situation is extremely critical, and I entreat you to maintain silence while I make explanation to you. I am Wilhelm, the loyal commander of the Imperial forces, your Majesty's most devoted servant."

"Are you then," said the amazed monarch, "also a member of the Fehmgerichte? I thought you came here as a prisoner, and, like myself, a victim."

Wilhelm drew off over his head the cloak which enveloped him, leaving his limbs free, standing thus in his own proper person before the Emperor.

"I was, indeed, a prisoner, and was visited in my cell by the Archbishop of Treves. It was in his robe that I emerged from my cell undetected, hoping to escape and bring rescue to your Majesty, but other brethren were awaiting me outside, and I found myself compelled to sit in the Court before which you made such an able defence."

"It was you, then, who proposed that I should be taken back to my cell?"

"Yes, your Majesty. And now a colleague remains outside this door, who waits, expecting a summons to enter, but first I came to give warning to your Majesty that you may make no outcry, if you should see what appears to be two brothers of the order struggling together."

"I shall keep strict silence. Is the Archbishop of Treves then a prisoner in your cell?"

"He is, I assure you, a fast prisoner."

"You propose that I should don the cloak of the incomer, and that thus we make our escape together. We must be in haste, then, for if the Archbishop releases himself from his bonds, he may produce such an uproar in his cell that suspicion will be aroused."

"The bonds in which I left the Archbishop of Treves will hold him firm until we are outside this nest of vipers. And now, your Majesty, I beg you to put on this cloak which I have been wearing, which will leave me free speedily to overpower our visitor."

The Emperor arrayed himself and stood, as he was fully entitled to do, a fully costumed member of the Fehmgerichte. Wilhelm opened the door and said softly:

"Enter, brother, that I may learn if the arrangements just made are confirmed by your wisdom."

The light within had been placed at the further end of the cell, and the visitor's own lantern gave but scant illumination. The moment the door was firmly closed Wilhelm sprang upon him and bore him to the ground. If the assaulted man attempted to make any sound, it was muffled by the folds of his own cloak. A moment later, however, Wilhelm got a firm grip on his bare throat, and holding him thus, pulled away his disguise from him, revealing the pallid face of the Archbishop of Mayence. The young man plucked the dagger from the inside of his doublet and placed it at the breast of the prostrate man.

"If you make the slightest sound," he whispered, "I shall bury this dagger in your heart. It is the weapon of the Fehmgerichte and you know it will penetrate chain armour."

It was evident that the stricken Archbishop was much too frightened to do anything to help himself, and Wilhelm unbuckling his own empty sword-belt, proceeded to tie his trembling limbs. The Emperor whispered:

"The cords which bound me are still here, as well as the gag which silenced me."

Wilhelm put those instruments of tyranny to immediate use, and shortly the Archbishop was a helpless silent heap in the further corner of the room. Wilhelm and the Emperor each with a lantern, and each indistinguishable from other members of the secret organisation, pushed open the door and emerged from the cell. Closing the door again, Wilhelm said to the guard:

"Bolt this portal firmly and allow no one to enter who does not give you this password."

The young man stooped and whispered into the ear of the guard the word "Elsa." The two fugitives then walked slowly along the great hall, the young man peering anxiously to his right for any sign of the stairway by which he had descended. They passed numerous doors, all closed, and at last Wilhelm began to wonder if one of these covered the exit which he sought. Finally they came to the end of the large hall without seeing trace of any outlet, and Wilhelm became conscious of the fact that getting free from this labyrinth was like to prove more difficult than the entering had been. Standing puzzled, not knowing where next to turn, aware that precious time was being wasted fruitlessly, Wilhelm saw a man masked and accoutred as a guard approach them.

"Is there anything in which I can pleasure your Lordships?" he asked deferentially.

"Yes," said Wilhelm, "we desire to have a breath of fresh air; where is the exit?"

"If your Lordship has the password, you may go out by the entrance in the city. If you have not the word, then must you use the exit without the wall, which is a long walk from here."

"That does not matter," replied Wilhelm, "it is the country air we wish to breathe."

"I cannot leave my post, but I shall get one who will guide you."

So saying, the man left them for several anxious minutes, going into a room that apparently was used as guard-house, and reappearing with a man who rubbed his eyes sleepily, as if newly awakened. Then the first guard drew bolts from a stout door and pulled it open, revealing a dark chasm like the entrance to a cell. Both Wilhelm and the Emperor viewed this black enigma with deep suspicion, but their guide with his lantern plunged into it and they followed, after which the door was closed and barred behind them.

It was, indeed, as the first man had said, a long walk, as Wilhelm knew it must be if it extended under the western gate and out into the country. The passage was so narrow that two could not walk abreast, and frequently the arched ceiling was so low that the guide ahead warned them to stoop as they came on. At last he reached the foot of a stairway, and was about to mount when Wilhelm said to him:

"Stand here till we return. Allow no one to pass who does not give you this word," and again he whispered the word "Elsa" in the man's ear.

To the dismay of Wilhelm, the Emperor addressed the guard:

"Are there many prisoners within?"

"There are two only," replied the man, "numbers 13 and 14. I helped to carry No. 14 down the stair, and am glad his sword broke beneath him as he fell, for, indeed, we had trouble enough with him as it was."

Here Wilhelm took the liberty of touching the Emperor on the arm as if to warn him that such discourse was untimely and dangerous. With beating heart the young man led the way up the stairs, and at the top of the second flight, came into what seemed to be the vestibule of a house, in which, on benches round the wall, there sat four men seemingly on guard, who immediately sprang to their feet when they saw the ghostly apparitions before them.

"Unbar the door," said Wilhelm, quietly, in the tone of one whose authority is not to be disputed. "Close it after us and allow none to enter or emerge who does not give you the word 'Elsa.'"

This command was so promptly obeyed that Wilhelm could scarcely believe they had won so easily to the outer air. The house stood alone on the bank of the river at the end of a long garden which extended to the road. Facing the thoroughfare and partly concealing the house from any chance straggler was a low building which Wilhelm remembered was used as a wayside drinking-place, in which wine, mostly of a poor quality, was served to thirsty travellers. The gate to the street appeared deserted, but as the two approached by the walk leading from the house, a guard stood out from the shadow of the wall, scrutinised for a moment their appearance, then saluting, held the gate open for them.

Once on the road, the two turned towards the city, whose black wall barred their way some distance ahead, and whose towers and spires stood out dimly against the starlit sky. A great silence, broken only by the soothing murmur of the river, lay on the landscape. Wilhelm cast a glance aloft at the star-sprinkled dome of heaven, and said:

"I judge it to be about an hour after midnight."

"It may be so," answered the Emperor, "I have lost all count of time."

"Has your Majesty been long in prison?"

"That I do not know. I may have lain there two days or a dozen. I had no means of measuring the length of my imprisonment."

"May I ask your Majesty in what manner you were lured into the halls of the Fehmgerichte?"

"It was no lure. While I lay asleep at night in the cloisters by the Cathedral I was bound and gagged, carried through the dark streets helpless on a litter and finally flung into the cell in which you found me."

"May I further inquire what your Majesty's intentions are regarding the fulfilment of the duties imposed upon you by your high office?"

There was a long pause before the Emperor replied, then he said:

"Why do you ask?"

"Because, your Majesty, I have on several occasions imperilled my life for an Emperor who does not rule, who has refused even to sign my commission as officer of his troops."

"Your commission was never sent to me."

"I beg your Majesty's pardon, but it was sent three times to you in the cloisters of the Cathedral, and returned three times unsigned."

"Then it is as I suspected," returned the Emperor, "the monks must have connived at my capture. I have pleasure in confirming your appointment. I am sure that the command could not be in more capable hands. And in further reply to your question, if God permits me to see the light of day, I shall be an emperor who rules."

"It delights my heart to hear you say so. And now I ask, as a favour, that you allow me to deal untrammelled with the Fehmgerichte."

"I grant that most willingly."

By this time they were almost under the shadow of the great wall of the city, and Wilhelm, stopping, said to the Emperor:

"I think it well that we now divest ourselves of these disguises."

They had scarcely thrown their cloaks behind the bushes at the side of the road when they were accosted by the guard at the top of the wall.

"Halt! Who approaches the gate?"

Wilhelm strode forward.

"Is Gottlieb at the guard-house or at the barracks?" he asked.

"He is at the guard-house," replied the sentinel, recognising the questioner.

"Then arouse him immediately, and open the gates."

"Gottlieb," said Wilhelm, when once within the walls, "take a score of men with you and surround the first house on the margin of the river up this street. I shall accompany you so that there may be no mistake. Send another score under a trusty leader to the house which stands alone outside of the gates also on the margin of the stream. Give orders that the men are to seize any person who attempts to enter or to come out; kill if necessary, but let none escape you. Let a dozen men escort me to the Palace."

Having seen the Emperor safely housed in the Palace, Wilhelm returned quickly to the place where Gottlieb and his score held guard over the town entrance of the cellars he had quitted.

"Gottlieb, are you fully awake?" asked Wilhelm.

"Oh, yes, master; awake and ready for any emergency."

"Then send for some of your most stalwart sappers with tools to break through a stone wall, and tell them to bring a piece of timber to batter in this door."

When the men arrived three blows from the oaken log sent the door shattering from its hinges. Wilhelm sprang at once over the prostrate portal, but not in time to prevent the flight of the guard down the stairway. Calling the sappers to the first landing, and pointing to the stone wall on the right:

"Break through that for me," he cried.

"Master," expostulated Gottlieb, "if you break through that wall I warn you that the river will flow in."

"Such is my intention, Gottlieb, and a gold piece to each man who works as he has never wrought before."

For a few moments there was nothing heard but the steady ring of iron on stone as one by one the squares were extracted, the water beginning to ooze in as the energetic sappers reached the outer course. At last the remaining stones gave way, carried in with a rush by the torrent.

"Save yourselves!" cried Wilhelm, standing knee deep in the flood and not stepping out until each man had passed him. There was a straining crash of rending timber, and Gottlieb, dashing down, seized his master by the arm, crying:

"My Lord, my Lord, the house is about to fall!"

With slight loss of time commander and lieutenant stood together in the street and found that the latter's panic was unwarranted, for the house, although it trembled dangerously and leaned perceptibly toward the river, was stoutly built of hewn stone. Grey daylight now began to spread over the city, but still Wilhelm stood there listening to the inrush of the water.

"By the great wine tub of Hundsrück!" exclaimed Gottlieb in amazement, "that cellar is a large one. It seems to thirst for the whole flood of the Main."

"Send a messenger," cried Wilhelm, "to the house you are guarding

351

outside the gates and discover for me whether your men have captured any prisoners."

It was broad daylight when the messenger returned, and the torrent down the stair had become a rippling surface of water at the level of the river, showing that all the cavern beneath was flooded.

"Well, messenger, what is your report?" demanded his commander.

"My Lord, the officer in charge says that a short time ago the door of the house was blown open as if by a strong wind; four men rushed out and another was captured in the garden; all were pinioned and gagged, as you commanded."

"Are the prisoners men of quality or common soldiers?"

"Common soldiers, my Lord."

"Very well; let them be taken to the prison. I will visit them later in the day."

As Wilhelm, thoroughly fatigued after a night so exciting, walked the streets of Frankfort toward his home the bells of the city suddenly began to ring a merry peal, and, as if Frankfort had become awakened by the musical clangor, windows were raised and doors opened, while citizens inquired of each other the meaning of the clangor, a question which no one seemed prepared to answer.

Reaching his own house, Wilhelm found Elsa awaiting him with less of anxiety on her face than he had expected.

"Oh, Wilhelm!" she cried, "what a fright you gave me, and not until I knew where you were, did any peace come to my heart."

"You knew where I was?" said Wilhelm in amazement. "Where was I, then?"

"You were with the Emperor, of course. That is why the bells are ringing; the Emperor has returned, as you know, and is resolved to take his proper place at the head of the state, much to the delight of the Empress, I can assure you. But what an anxious time we spent until shortly after midnight, when the Emperor arrived and told us you had been with him."

"How came you to be at the Palace?"

"It happened in this way. You had hardly left the court last night when his lordship the Archbishop of Cologne came and seemed anxious about the welfare of the Emperor."

"The Archbishop of Cologne! Is he still there or did he go elsewhere?"

"He is still there, and was there when the Emperor came in. Why do you ask so eagerly? Is there anything wrong?"

"Not so far as the Archbishop is concerned, apparently. He has kept his word and so there is one less high office vacant. Well, what did the Archbishop say?"

"He wished to see you, and so the Empress sent for you, but search as we would, you were nowhere to be found. On hearing this I became alarmed and went at once to the Palace. The Archbishop seemed in deep trouble, but he refused to tell the Empress the cause of it, and so increased our anxiety. However, all was right when the Emperor came, and now they are ringing the bells, for he is to appear before the people on the balcony of the Romer, as if he were newly crowned. We must make haste if we are to see him."

Wilhelm escorted his wife to the square before the Romer, but so dense was the cheering crowd that it was impossible for him to force a way through. They were in time to see the Emperor appear on the balcony, and Wilhelm, raising his sword aloft, shouted louder than any in that throng, Elsa herself waving a scarf above her head in the enthusiasm of the moment.

THE COUNT'S APOLOGY

The fifteen nobles, who formed the Council of State for the Moselle Valley, stood in little groups in the Rittersaal of Winneburg's Castle, situated on a hill-top in the Ender Valley, a league or so from the waters of the Moselle. The nobles spoke in low tones together, for a greater than they were present, no other than their over-lord, the Archbishop of Treves, who, in his stately robes of office, paced up and down the long room, glancing now and then through the narrow windows which gave a view down the Ender Valley.

There was a trace of impatience in his Lordship's bearing, and well there might be, for here was the Council of State in assemblage, yet their chairman was absent, and the nobles stood there helplessly, like a flock of sheep whose shepherd is missing. The chairman was the Count of Winneburg, in whose castle they were now collected, and his lack of punctuality was thus a double discourtesy, for he was host as well as president.

Each in turn had tried to soothe the anger of the Archbishop, for all liked the Count of Winneburg, a bluff and generous-hearted giant, who would stand by his friends against all comers, was the quarrel his own or no. In truth little cared the stalwart Count of Winneburg whose quarrel it was so long as his arm got opportunity of wielding a blow in it. His Lordship of Treves had not taken this championship of the absent man with good grace, and now strode apart from the group, holding himself haughtily; muttering, perhaps prayers, perhaps something else.

When one by one the nobles had arrived at Winneburg's Castle, they were informed that its master had gone hunting that morning, saying he would return in time for the mid-day meal, but nothing had been heard of him since, although mounted messengers had been sent forth, and the great bell in the southern tower had been set ringing when the Archbishop arrived. It was the general opinion that Count Winneburg, becoming interested in the chase, had forgotten all about the Council, for it was well known that the Count's body was better suited for athletic sports or warfare than was his mind for the consideration of questions of State, and the nobles, themselves of similar calibre, probably liked him none the less on that account.

Presently the Archbishop stopped in his walk and faced the assemblage. "My Lords," he said, "we have already waited longer than the utmost stretch of courtesy demands. The esteem in which Count Winneburg holds our deliberations is indicated by his inexcusable neglect of a duty conferred upon him by you, and voluntarily accepted by him. I shall therefore take my place in his chair, and I call upon you to seat yourselves at the Council table."

Saying which the Archbishop strode to the vacant chair, and seated himself in it at the head of the board. The nobles looked one at the other with some dismay, for it was never their intention that the Archbishop should preside over their meeting, the object of which was rather to curb that high prelate's ambition, than to confirm still further the power he already held over them.

When, a year before, these Councils of State had been inaugurated, the Archbishop had opposed them, but, finding that the Emperor was inclined to defer to the wishes of his nobles, the Lord of Treves had insisted upon his right to be present during the deliberations, and this right the Emperor had conceded. He further proposed that the meeting should be held at his own castle of Cochem, as being conveniently situated midway between Coblentz and Treves, but to this the nobles had, with fervent unanimity, objected. Cochem Castle, they remembered, possessed strong walls and deep dungeons, and they had no desire to trust themselves within the lion's jaws, having little faith in his Lordship's benevolent intentions towards them.

The Emperor seemed favourable to the selection of Cochem as a convenient place of meeting, and the nobles were nonplussed, because they could not give their real reason for wishing to avoid it, and the Archbishop continued to press the claims of Cochem as being of equal advantage to all.

"It is not as though I asked them to come to Treves," said the Archbishop, "for that would entail a long journey upon those living near the Rhine, and in going to Cochem I shall myself be called upon to travel as far as those who come from Coblentz."

The Emperor said:

"It seems a most reasonable selection, and, unless some strong objection be urged, I shall confirm the choice of Cochem."

The nobles were all struck with apprehension at these words, and knew not what to say, when suddenly, to their great delight, up spoke the stalwart Count of Winneburg.

"Your Majesty," he said, "my Castle stands but a short league from Cochem, and has a Rittersaal as large as that in the pinnacled palace owned by the Archbishop. It is equally convenient for all concerned, and every gentleman is right welcome to its hospitality. My cellars are well filled with good wine, and my larders are stocked with an abundance of food. All that can be urged in favour of Cochem applies with equal truth to the Schloss Winneburg. If, therefore, the members of the Council will accept of my roof, it is theirs."

The nobles with universal enthusiasm cried:

"Yes, yes; Winneburg is the spot."

The Emperor smiled, for he well knew that his Lordship of Treves was somewhat miserly in the dispensing of his hospitality. He preferred to see his guests drink the wine of a poor vintage rather than tap the cask which contained the yield of a good year. His Majesty smiled, because he imagined his nobles thought of the replenishing of their stomachs, whereas they were concerned for the safety of their necks; but seeing them unanimous in their choice, he nominated Schloss Winneburg as the place of meeting, and so it remained.

When, therefore, the Archbishop of Treves set himself down in the ample chair, to which those present had, without a dissenting vote, elected Count Winneburg, distrust at once took hold of them, for they were ever jealous of the encroachments of their over-lord. The Archbishop glared angrily around him, but no man moved from where he stood.

"I ask you to be seated. The Council is called to order."

Baron Beilstein cleared his throat and spoke, seemingly with some hesitation, but nevertheless with a touch of obstinacy in his voice:

"May we beg a little more time for Count Winneburg? He has doubtless gone farther afield than he intended when he set out. I myself know something of the fascination of the chase, and can easily understand that it wipes out all remembrance of lesser things."

"Call you this Council a lesser thing?" demanded the Archbishop. "We have waited an hour already, and I shall not give the laggard a moment more."

"Indeed, my Lord, then I am sorry to hear it. I would not willingly be the man who sits in Winneburg's chair, should he come suddenly upon us."

"Is that a threat?" asked the Archbishop, frowning.

"It is not a threat, but rather a warning. I am a neighbour of the Count, and know him well, and whatever his virtues may be, calm patience is not one of them. If time hangs heavily, may I venture to suggest that your Lordship remove the prohibition you proclaimed when the Count's servants offered us wine, and allow me to act temporarily as host, ordering the flagons to be filled, which I think will please Winneburg better when he comes, than finding another in his chair."

"This is no drunken revel, but a Council of State," said the Archbishop sternly; "and I drink no wine when the host is not here to proffer it.

"Indeed, my Lord," said Beilstein, with a shrug of the shoulders, "some of us are so thirsty that we care not who makes the offer, so long as the wine be sound."

What reply the Archbishop would have made can only be conjectured, for at that moment the door burst open and in came Count Winneburg, a head and shoulders above any man in that room, and huge in proportion.

"My Lords, my Lords," he cried, his loud voice booming to the rafters, "how can I ask you to excuse such a breach of hospitality. What! Not a single flagon of wine in the room? This makes my deep regret almost unbearable. Surely, Beilstein, you might have amended that, if only for the sake of an old and constant comrade. Truth, gentlemen, until I heard the bell of the castle toll, I had no thought that this was the day of our meeting, and then, to my despair, I found myself an hour away, and have ridden hard to be among you."

Then, noticing there was something ominous in the air, and an unaccustomed silence to greet his words, he looked from one to the other, and his eye, travelling up the table, finally rested upon the Archbishop in his chair. Count Winneburg drew himself up, his ruddy face colouring like fire. Then, before any person could reach out hand to check him, or move lip in counsel, the Count, with a fierce oath, strode to the usurper, grasped him by the shoulders, whirled his heels high above his head, and flung him like a sack of corn to the smooth floor, where the unfortunate Archbishop, huddled in a helpless heap, slid along the polished surface as if he were on ice. The fifteen nobles stood stock-still, appalled at this unexpected outrage upon their overlord. Winneburg seated himself in the chair with an emphasis that made even the solid table rattle, and bringing down his huge fist crashing on the board before him, shouted:

"Let no man occupy my chair, unless he has weight enough to remain there."

Baron Beilstein, and one or two others, hurried to the prostrate Archbishop and assisted him to his feet.

"Count Winneburg," said Beilstein, "you can expect no sympathy from us for such an act of violence in your own hall."

"I want none of your sympathy," roared the angry Count. "Bestow it on the man now in your hands who needs it. If you want the Archbishop of Treves to act as your chairman, elect him to that position and welcome. I shall have no usurpation in my Castle. While I am president I sit in the chair, and none other."

There was a murmur of approval at this, for one and all were deeply suspicious of the Archbishop's continued encroachments.

His Lordship of Treves once more on his feet, his lips pallid, and his face colourless, looked with undisguised hatred at his assailant. "Winneburg," he said slowly, "you shall apologise abjectly for this insult, and that in presence of the nobles of this Empire, or I will see to it that not one stone of this castle remains upon another."

"Indeed," said the Count nonchalantly, "I shall apologise to you, my Lord, when you have apologised to me for taking my place. As to the castle, it is said that the devil assisted in the building of it, and it is quite likely that through friendship for you, he may preside over its destruction."

The Archbishop made no reply, but, bowing haughtily to the rest of the company, who looked glum enough, well knowing that the episode they had witnessed meant, in all probability, red war let loose down the smiling valley of the Moselle, left the Rittersaal.

"Now that the Council is duly convened in regular order," said Count Winneburg, when the others had seated themselves round his table, "what questions of state come up for discussion?"

For a moment there was no answer to this query, the delegates looking at one another speechless. But at last Baron Beilstein shrugging his shoulder, said drily:

"Indeed, my Lord Count, I think the time for talk is past, and I suggest that we all look closely to the strengthening of our walls, which are likely to be tested before long by the Lion of Treves. It was perhaps unwise, Winneburg, to have used the Archbishop so roughly, he being unaccustomed to athletic exercise; but, let the consequences be what they may, I, for one, will stand by you."

"And I; and I; and I; and I," cried the others, with the exception of the Knight of Ehrenburg, who, living as he did near the town of Coblentz, was learned in the law, and not so ready as some of his comrades to speak first and think afterwards.

"My good friends," cried their presiding officer, deeply moved by this token of their fealty, "what I have done I have done, be it wise or the reverse, and the results must fall on my head alone. No words of mine can remove the dust of the floor from the Archbishop's cloak, so if he comes, let him come. I will give him as hearty a welcome as it is in my power to render. All I ask is fair play, and those who stand aside shall see a good fight. It is not right that a hasty act of mine should embroil the peaceful country side, so if Treves comes on I shall meet him alone here in my castle. But, nevertheless, I thank you all for your offers of help; that is all, except the Knight of Ehrenburg, whose tender of assistance, if made, has escaped my ear."

The Knight of Ehrenburg had, up to that moment, been studying the texture of the oaken table on which his flagon sat. Now he looked up and spoke slowly.

"I made no proffer of help," he said, "because none will be needed, I believe, so far as the Archbishop of Treves is concerned. The Count a moment ago said that all he wanted was fair play, but that is just what he has no right to expect from his present antagonist. The Archbishop will make no attempt on this castle; he will act much more subtly than that. The Archbishop will lay the redress of his quarrel upon the shoulders of the Emperor, and it is the oncoming of the Imperial troops you have to fear, and not an invasion from Treves. Against the forces of the Emperor we are powerless, united or divided. Indeed, his Majesty may call upon us to invest this castle, whereupon, if we refuse, we are rebels who have broken our oaths."

"What then is there left for me to do?" asked the Count, dismayed at the coil in which he had involved himself.

"Nothing," advised the Knight of Ehrenburg, "except to apologise abjectly to the Archbishop, and that not too soon, for his Lordship may refuse to accept it. But when he formally demands it, I should render it to him on his own terms, and think myself well out of an awkward position."

The Count of Winneburg rose from his seat, and lifting his clinched fist high above his head, shook it at the timbers of the roof.

"That," he cried, "will I never do, while one stone of Winneburg stands upon another."

At this, those present, always with the exception of the Knight of

360

Ehrenburg, sprang to their feet, shouting:

"Imperial troops or no, we stand by the Count of Winneburg!"

Some one flashed forth a sword, and instantly a glitter of blades was in the air, while cheer after cheer rang to the rafters. When the uproar had somewhat subsided, the Knight of Ehrenburg said calmly:

"My castle stands nearest to the capital, and will be the first to fall, but, nevertheless, hoping to do my shouting when the war is ended, I join my forces with those of the rest of you."

And amidst this unanimity, and much emptying of flagons, the assemblage dissolved, each man with his escort taking his way to his own stronghold, perhaps to con more soberly, next day, the problem that confronted him. They were fighters all, and would not flinch when the pinch came, whatever the outcome.

Day followed day with no sign from Treves. Winneburg employed the time in setting his house in order to be ready for whatever chanced, and just as the Count was beginning to congratulate himself that his deed was to be without consequences, there rode up to his castle gates a horseman, accompanied by two lancers, and on the newcomer's breast were emblazoned the Imperial arms. Giving voice to his horn, the gates were at once thrown open to him, and, entering, he demanded instant speech with the Count.

"My Lord, Count Winneburg," he said, when that giant had presented himself, "His Majesty the Emperor commands me to summon you to the court at Frankfort."

"Do you take me as prisoner, then?" asked the Count.

"Nothing was said to me of arrest. I was merely commissioned to deliver to you the message of the Emperor."

"What are your orders if I refuse to go?"

A hundred armed men stood behind the Count, a thousand more were within call of the castle bell; two lances only were at the back of the messenger; but the strength of the broadcast empire was betokened by the symbol on his breast.

"My orders are to take back your answer to his Imperial Majesty," replied the messenger calmly.

The Count, though hot-headed, was no fool, and he stood for a moment pondering on the words which the Knight of Ehrenburg had spoken on taking his leave:

"Let not the crafty Archbishop embroil you with the Emperor."

This warning had been the cautious warrior's parting advice to him.

"If you will honour my humble roof," said the Count slowly, "by taking refreshment beneath it, I shall be glad of your company afterwards to Frankfort, in obedience to his Majesty's commands."

The messenger bowed low, accepted the hospitality, and together they made way across the Moselle, and along the Roman road to the capital.

Within the walls of Frankfort the Count was lodged in rooms near the palace, to which his conductor guided him, and, although it was still held that he was not a prisoner, an armed man paced to and fro before his door all night. The day following his arrival, Count Winneburg was summoned to the Court, and in a large ante-room found himself one of a numerous throng, conspicuous among them all by reason of his great height and bulk.

The huge hall was hung with tapestry, and at the further end were heavy curtains, at each edge of which stood half-a-dozen armoured men, the detachments being under command of two gaily-uniformed officers. Occasionally the curtains were parted by menials who stood there to perform that duty, and high nobles entered, or came out, singly and in groups. Down the sides of the hall were packed some hundreds of people, chattering together for the most part, and gazing at those who passed up and down the open space in the centre.

The Count surmised that the Emperor held his Court in whatever apartment was behind the crimson curtains. He felt the eyes of the multitude upon him, and shifted uneasily from one foot to another, cursing his ungainliness, ashamed of the tingling of the blood in his cheeks. He was out of plaice in this laughing, talking crowd, experiencing the sensations of an uncouth rustic suddenly thrust into the turmoil of a metropolis, resenting bitterly the supposed sneers that were flung at him. He suspected that the whispering and the giggling were directed towards himself, and burned to draw his sword and let these popinjays know for once what a man could do. As a matter of fact it was a buzz of admiration at his stature which went up when he entered, but the Count had so little of self-conceit in his soul that he never even guessed the truth.

Two nobles passing near him, he heard one of them say distinctly:

"That is the fellow who threw the Archbishop over his head," while the other, glancing at him, said:

"By the Coat, he seems capable of upsetting the three of them, and I, for one, wish more power to his muscle should he attempt it."

The Count shrank against the tapestried walls, hot with anger, wishing himself a dwarf that he might escape the gaze of so many inquiring eyes. Just as the scrutiny was becoming unbearable, his companion touched him on the elbow, and said in a low voice:

"Count Winneburg, follow me."

He held aside the tapestry at the back of the Count, and that noble, nothing loth, disappeared from view behind it.

Entering a narrow passage-way, they traversed it until they came to a closed door, at each lintel of which stood a pikeman, fronted with a shining breastplate of metal. The Count's conductor knocked gently at the closed door, then opened it, holding it so that the Count could pass in, and when he had done so, the door closed softly behind him. To his amazement, Winneburg saw before him, standing at the further end of the small room, the Emperor Rudolph, entirely alone. The Count was about to kneel awkwardly, when his liege strode forward and prevented him.

"Count Winneburg," he said, "from what I hear of you, your elbow-joints are more supple than those of your knees, therefore let us be thankful that on this occasion there is no need to use either. I see you are under the mistaken impression that the Emperor is present. Put that thought from your mind, and regard me simply as Lord Rudolph—one gentleman wishing to have some little conversation with another."

"Your Majesty—" stammered the Count.

"I have but this moment suggested that you forget that title, my Lord. But, leaving aside all question of salutation, let us get to the heart of the matter, for I think we are both direct men. You are summoned to Frankfort because that high and mighty Prince of the Church, the Archbishop of Treves, has made complaint to the Emperor against you alleging what seems to be an unpardonable indignity suffered by him at your hands."

"Your Majesty—my Lord, I mean," faltered the Count. "The indignity was of his own seeking; he sat down in my chair, where he had no right to place himself, and I—I—persuaded him to relinquish his position."

"So I am informed—that is to say, so his Majesty has been informed," replied Rudolph, a slight smile hovering round his finely chiselled lips. "We are not here to comment upon any of the Archbishop's delinquencies, but, granting, for the sake of argument, that he had encroached upon your rights, nevertheless, he was under your roof, and honestly, I fail to see that you were justified in cracking his heels against the same."

"Well, your Majesty—again I beg your Majesty's pardon—"

"Oh, no matter," said the Emperor, "call me what you like; names signify little."

"If then the Emperor," continued the Count, "found an intruder sitting on his throne, would he like it, think you?"

"His feeling, perhaps, would be one of astonishment, my Lord Count, but speaking for the Emperor, I am certain that he would never lay hands on the usurper, or treat him like a sack of corn in a yeoman's barn."

The Count laughed heartily at this, and was relieved to find that this quitted him of the tension which the great presence had at first inspired.

"Truth to tell, your Majesty, I am sorry I touched him. I should have requested him to withdraw, but my arm has always been more prompt in action than my tongue, as you can readily see since I came into this room."

"Indeed, Count, your tongue does you very good service," continued the Emperor, "and I am glad to have from you an expression of regret. I hope, therefore, that you will have no hesitation in repeating that declaration to the Archbishop of Treves."

"Does your Majesty mean that I am to apologise to him?"

"Yes," answered the Emperor.

There was a moment's pause, then the Count said slowly:

"I will surrender to your Majesty my person, my sword, my castle, and my lands. I will, at your word, prostrate myself at your feet, and humbly beg pardon for any offence I have committed against you, but to tell the Archbishop I am sorry when I am not, and to cringe before him and supplicate his grace, well, your Majesty, as between man and man, I'll see him damned first."

Again the Emperor had some difficulty in preserving that rigidity of expression which he had evidently resolved to maintain.

"Have you ever met a ghost, my Lord Count?" he asked.

Winneburg crossed himself devoutly, a sudden pallor sweeping over his face.

"Indeed, your Majesty, I have seen strange things, and things for which there was no accounting; but it has been usually after a contest with the wine flagon, and at the time my head was none of the clearest, so I could not venture to say whether they were ghosts or no."

"Imagine, then, that in one of the corridors of your castle at midnight you met a white-robed transparent figure, through whose form your sword passed scathlessly. What would you do, my Lord?"

"Indeed, your Majesty, I would take to my heels, and bestow myself elsewhere as speedily as possible."

"Most wisely spoken and you, who are no coward, who fear not to face willingly in combat anything natural, would, in certain circumstances, trust to swift flight for your protection. Very well, my Lord, you are now confronted with something against which your stout arm is as unavailing as it would be if an apparition stood in your path. There is before you the spectre of subtlety. Use arm instead of brain, and you are a lost man.

"The Archbishop expects no apology. He looks for a stalwart, stubborn man, defying himself and the Empire combined. You think, perhaps, that the Imperial troops will surround your castle, and that you may stand a siege. Now the Emperor would rather have you fight with him than against him, but in truth there will be no contest. Hold to your refusal, and you will be arrested before you leave the precincts of this palace. You will be thrown into a dungeon, your castle and your lands sequestered; and I call your attention to the fact that your estate adjoins the possessions of the Archbishop at Cochem, and Heaven fend me for hinting that his Lordship casts covetous eyes over his boundary; yet, nevertheless, he will probably not refuse to accept your possessions in reparation for the insult bestowed upon him. Put it this way if you like. Would you rather pleasure me or pleasure the Archbishop of Treves?"

"There is no question as to that," answered the Count.

"Then it will please me well if you promise to apologise to his Lordship the Archbishop of Treves. That his Lordship will be equally pleased, I very much doubt."

"Will your Majesty command me in open Court to apologise?"

"I shall request you to do so. I must uphold the Feudal law."

"Then I beseech your Majesty to command me, for I am a loyal subject, and will obey."

"God give me many such," said the Emperor fervently, "and bestow upon me the wisdom to deserve them!"

He extended his hand to the Count, then touched a bell on the table beside him. The officer who had conducted Winneburg entered silently, and acted as his guide back to the thronged apartment they had left. The Count saw that the great crimson curtains were now looped up, giving a view of the noble interior of the room beyond, thronged with the notables of the Empire. The hall leading to it was almost deserted, and the Count, under convoy of two lancemen, himself nearly as tall as their weapons, passed in to the Throne Room, and found all eyes turned upon him.

He was brought to a stand before an elevated dais, the centre of which was occupied by a lofty throne, which, at the moment, was empty. Near it, on the elevation, stood the three Archbishops of Treves, Cologne, and Mayence, on the other side the Count Palatine of the Rhine with the remaining three Electors. The nobles of the realm occupied places according to their degree.

As the stalwart Count came in, a buzz of conversation swept over the hall like a breeze among the leaves of a forest. A malignant scowl darkened the countenance of the Archbishop of Treves, but the faces of Cologne and Mayence expressed a certain Christian resignation regarding the contumely which had been endured by their colleague. The Count stood stolidly where he was placed, and gazed at the vacant throne, turning his eyes neither to the right nor the left.

Suddenly there was a fanfare of trumpets, and instant silence smote the assembly. First came officers of the Imperial Guard in shining armour, then the immediate advisers and councillors of his Majesty, and last of all, the Emperor himself, a robe of great richness clasped at his throat, and trailing behind him; the crown of the Empire upon his head. His face was pale and stern, and he looked what he was, a monarch, and a man. The Count rubbed his eyes, and could scarcely believe that he stood now in the presence of one who had chatted amiably with him but a few moments before.

The Emperor sat on his throne and one of his councillors whispered for some moments to him; then the Emperor said, in a low, clear voice, that penetrated to the farthest corner of the vast apartment:

"Is the Count of Winneburg here?"

"Yes, your Majesty."

"Let him stand forward."

The Count strode two long steps to the front, and stood there, red-faced and abashed. The officer at his side whispered:

"Kneel, you fool, kneel."

And the Count got himself somewhat clumsily down upon his knees, like an elephant preparing to receive his burden. The face of the Emperor remained impassive, and he said harshly:

"Stand up."

The Count, once more upon his feet, breathed a deep sigh of satisfaction at finding himself again in an upright posture.

"Count of Winneburg," said the Emperor slowly, "it is alleged that upon the occasion of the last meeting of the Council of State for the Moselle valley, you, in presence of the nobles there assembled, cast a slight upon your overlord, the Archbishop of Treves. Do you question the statement?"

The Count cleared his throat several times, which in the stillness of that vaulted room sounded like the distant booming of cannon.

"If to cast the Archbishop half the distance of this room is to cast a slight upon him, I did so, your Majesty."

There was a simultaneous ripple of laughter at this, instantly suppressed when the searching eye of the Emperor swept the room.

"Sir Count," said the Emperor severely, "the particulars of your outrage are not required of you; only your admission thereof. Hear, then, my commands. Betake yourself to your castle of Winneburg, and hold yourself there in readiness to proceed to Treves on a day appointed by his Lordship the Archbishop, an Elector of this Empire, there to humble yourself before him, and crave his pardon for the offence you have committed. Disobey at your peril."

Once or twice the Count moistened his dry lips, then he said:

"Your Majesty, I will obey any command you place upon me."

"In that case," continued the Emperor, his severity visibly relaxing, "I can promise that your over-lord will not hold this incident against you. Such, I understand, is your intention, my Lord Archbishop?" and the Emperor turned toward the Prince of Treves.

The Archbishop bowed low, and thus veiled the malignant hatred in his eyes. "Yes, your Majesty," he replied, "providing the apology is given as publicly as was the insult, in presence of those who were witnesses of the Count's foolishness."

"That is but a just condition," said the Emperor. "It is my pleasure that the Council be summoned to Treves to hear the Count's apology. And now, Count of Winneburg, you are at liberty to withdraw."

The Count drew his mammoth hand across his brow, and scattered to the floor the moisture that had collected there. He tried to speak, but apparently could not, then turned and walked resolutely towards the door. There was instant outcry at this, the Chamberlain of the Court standing in stupefied amazement at a breach of etiquette which exhibited any man's back to the Emperor; but a smile relaxed the Emperor's lips, and he held up his hand.

"Do not molest him," he said, as the Count disappeared. "He is unused to the artificial manners of a Court. In truth, I take it as a friendly act, for I am sure the valiant Count never turned his back upon a foe," which Imperial witticism was well received, for the sayings of an Emperor rarely lack applause.

The Count, wending his long way home by the route he had come, spent the first half of the journey in cursing the Archbishop, and the latter half in thinking over the situation. By the time he had reached his castle he had formulated a plan, and this plan he proceeded to put into execution on receiving the summons of the Archbishop to come to Treves on the first day of the following month and make his apology, the Archbishop, with characteristic penuriousness, leaving the inviting of the fifteen nobles, who formed the Council, to Winneburg, and thus his Lordship of Treves was saved the expense of sending special messengers to each. In case Winneburg neglected to summon the whole Council, the Archbishop added to his message, the statement that he would refuse to receive the apology if any of the nobles were absent.

Winneburg sent messengers, first to Beilstein, asking him to attend at Treves on the second day of the month, and bring with him an escort of at least a thousand men. Another he asked for the third, another for the fourth, another for the fifth, and so on, resolved that before a complete quorum was present, half of the month would be gone, and with it most of the Archbishop's provender, for his Lordship, according to the laws of hospitality, was bound to entertain free of all charge to themselves the various nobles and their followings.

On the first day of the month Winneburg entered the northern gate of Treves, accompanied by two hundred horsemen and eight hundred foot soldiers. At first, the officers of the Archbishop thought that an invasion was contemplated, but Winneburg suavely explained that if a thing was worth doing at all, it was worth doing well, and he was not going to make any hole-and-corner affair of his apology. Next day Beilstein came along accompanied by five hundred cavalry, and five hundred foot soldiers.

The Chamberlain of the Archbishop was in despair at having to find quarters for so many, but he did the best he could, while the Archbishop was enraged to observe that the nobles did not assemble in greater haste, but each as he came had a plausible excuse for his delay. Some had to build bridges, sickness had broken out in another camp, while a third expedition had lost its way and wandered in the forest.

The streets of Treves each night resounded with songs of revelry, varied by the clash of swords, when a party of the newcomers fell foul of a squad of the town soldiers, and the officers on either side had much ado to keep the peace among their men. The Archbishop's wine cups were running dry, and the price of provisions had risen, the whole surrounding country being placed under contribution for provender and drink. When a week had elapsed the Archbishop relaxed his dignity and sent for Count Winneburg.

"We will not wait for the others," he said. "I have no desire to humiliate you unnecessarily. Those who are here shall bear witness that you have apologised, and so I shall not insist on the presence of the laggards, but will receive your apology to-morrow at high noon in the great council chamber."

"Ah, there speaks a noble heart, ever thinking generously of those who despitefully use you, my Lord Archbishop," said Count Winneburg. "But no, no, I cannot accept such a sacrifice. The Emperor showed me plainly the enormity of my offence. In the presence of all I insulted you, wretch that I am, and in the presence of all shall I abase myself."

"But I do not seek your abasement," protested the Archbishop, frowning.

"The more honour, then, to your benevolent nature," answered the Count, "and the more shameful would it be of me to take advantage of it. As I stood a short time since on the walls, I saw coming up the river the banners of the Knight of Ehrenburg. His castle is the furthest removed from Treves, and so the others cannot surely delay long. We will wait, my Lord Archbishop, until all are here. But I thank you just as much for your generosity as if I were craven enough to shield myself behind it."

The Knight of Ehrenburg in due time arrived, and behind him his thousand men, many of whom were compelled to sleep in the public buildings, for all the rooms in Treves were occupied. Next day the Archbishop summoned the assembled nobles and said he would hear the apology in their presence. If the others missed it, it was their own fault—they should have been in time.

"I cannot apologise;" said the Count, "until all are here. It was the Emperor's order, and who am I to disobey my Emperor? We must await their coming with patience, and, indeed, Treves is a goodly town, in which all of us find ourselves fully satisfied."

"Then, my blessing on you all," said the Archbishop in a sour tone

371

most unsuited to the benediction he was bestowing. "Return, I beg of you, instantly, to your castles. I forego the apology."

"But I insist on tendering it," cried the Count, his mournful voice giving some indication of the sorrow he felt at his offence if it went unrequited. "It is my duty, not only to you, my Lord Archbishop, but also to his Majesty the Emperor."

"Then, in Heaven's name get on with it and depart. I am willing to accept it on your own terms, as I have said before."

"No, not on my own terms, but on yours. What matters the delay of a week or two? The hunting season does not begin for a fortnight, and we are all as well at Treves as at home. Besides, how could I ever face my Emperor again, knowing I had disobeyed his commands?"

"I will make it right with the Emperor," said the Archbishop.

The Knight of Ehrenburg now spoke up, calmly, as was his custom:

"'Tis a serious matter," he said, "for a man to take another's word touching action of his Majesty the Emperor. You have clerks here with you; perhaps then you will bid them indite a document to be signed by yourself absolving my friend, the Count of Winneburg, from all necessity of apologising, so that should the Emperor take offence at his disobedience, the parchment may hold him scathless."

"I will do anything to be quit of you," muttered the Archbishop more to himself than to the others.

And so the document was written and signed. With this parchment in his saddle-bags the Count and his comrades quitted the town, drinking in half flagons the health of the Archbishop, because there was not left in Treves enough wine to fill the measures to the brim.

CONVERTED

In the ample stone-paved courtyard of the Schloss Grunewald, with its mysterious bubbling spring in the centre, stood the Black Baron beside his restive horse, both equally eager to be away. Round the Baron were grouped his sixteen knights and their saddled chargers, all waiting the word to mount. The warder was slowly opening the huge gates that hung between the two round entrance towers of the castle, for it was the Baron's custom never to ride out at the head of his men until the great leaves of the strong gate fell full apart, and showed the green landscape beyond. The Baron did not propose to ride unthinkingly out, and straightway fall into an ambush.

He and his sixteen knights were the terror of the country-side, and many there were who would have been glad to venture a bow shot at him had they dared. There seemed to be some delay about the opening of the gates, and a great chattering of underlings at the entrance, as if something unusual had occurred, whereupon the rough voice of the Baron roared out to know the cause that kept him waiting, and every one scattered, each to his own affair, leaving only the warder, who approached his master with fear in his face.

"My Lord," he began, when the Baron had shouted what the devil ailed him, "there has been nailed against the outer gate; sometime in the night, a parchment with characters written thereon."

"Then tear it down and bring it to me," cried the Baron. "What's all this to-do about a bit of parchment?"

The warder had been loath to meddle with it, in terror of that witchcraft which he knew pertained to all written characters; but he feared the Black Baron's frown even more than the fiends who had undoubtedly nailed the documents on the gate, for he knew no man in all that well-cowed district would have the daring to approach the castle even in the night, much less meddle with the gate or any other belonging of the Baron von Grunewald; so, breathing a request to his patron saint (his neglect of whom he now remembered with remorse) for protection, he tore the document from its fastening and brought it, trembling, to the Baron. The knights crowded round as von Grunewald held the parchment in his hand, bending his dark brows upon it, for it conveyed no meaning to him. Neither the Baron nor his knights could read.

"What foolery, think you, is this?" he said, turning to the knight nearest him. "A Defiance?"

The knight shook his head. "I am no clerk," he answered.

For a moment the Baron was puzzled; then he quickly bethought himself of the one person in the castle who could read.

"Bring hither old Father Gottlieb," he commanded, and two of those waiting ran in haste towards the scullery of the place, from which they presently emerged dragging after them an old man partly in the habit of a monk and partly in that of a scullion, who wiped his hands on the coarse apron, that was tied around his waist, as he was hurried forward.

"Here, good father, excellent cook and humble servitor, I trust your residence with us has not led you to forget the learning you put to such poor advantage in the Monastery of Monnonstein. Canst thou construe this for us? Is it in good honest German or bastard Latin?"

"It is in Latin," said the captive monk, on glancing at the document in the other's hand.

"Then translate it for us, and quickly."

Father Gottlieb took the parchment handed him by the Baron, and as his eyes scanned it more closely, he bowed his head and made the sign of the cross upon his breast.

"Cease that mummery," roared the Baron, "and read without more waiting or the rod's upon thy back again. Who sends us this?"

"It is from our Holy Father the Pope," said the monk, forgetting his menial position for the moment, and becoming once more the scholar of the monastery. The sense of his captivity faded from him as he realised that the long arm of the Church had extended within the impregnable walls of that tyrannical castle.

"Good. And what has our Holy Father the Pope to say to us? Demands he the release of our excellent scullion, Father Gottlieb?"

The bent shoulders of the old monk straightened, his dim eye brightened, and his voice rang clear within the echoing walls of the castle courtyard.

"It is a ban of excommunication against thee, Lord Baron von Grunewald, and against all within these walls, excepting only those unlawfully withheld from freedom."

"Which means thyself, worthy Father. Read on, good clerk, and let us hear it to the end."

As the monk read out the awful words of the message, piling curse on curse with sonorous voice, the Baron saw his trembling servitors turn pale, and even his sixteen knights, companions in robbery and rapine, fall away from him. Dark red anger mounted to his temples; he raised his mailed hand and smote the reading monk flat across the mouth, felling the old man prone upon the stones of the court.

"That is my answer to our Holy Father the Pope, and when thou swearest to deliver it to him as I have given it to thee, the gates are open and the way clear for thy pilgrimage to Rome."

But the monk lay where he fell and made no reply.

"Take him away," commanded the Baron impatiently, whereupon several of the menials laid hands on the fallen monk and dragged him into the scullery he had left.

Turning to his men-at-arms, the Baron roared: "Well, my gentle wolves, have a few words in Latin on a bit of sheep-skin turned you all to sheep?"

"I have always said," spoke up the knight Segfried, "that no good came of captured monks, or meddling with the Church. Besides, we are noble all, and do not hold with the raising of a mailed hand against an unarmed man."

There was a low murmur of approval among the knights at Segfried's boldness.

"Close the gates," shouted the maddened Baron. Every one flew at the word of command, and the great oaken hinges studded with iron, slowly came together, shutting out the bit of landscape their opening had discovered. The Baron flung the reins on his charger's neck, and smote the animal on the flank, causing it to trot at once to its stable.

"There will be no riding to-day," he said, his voice ominously lowering. The stablemen of the castle came forward and led away the horses. The sixteen knights stood in a group together with Segfried at their head, waiting with some anxiety on their brows for the next move in the game. The Baron, his sword drawn in his hand, strode up and down before them, his brow bent on the ground, evidently struggling to get the master hand over his own anger. If it came to blows the odds were against him and he was too shrewd a man to engage himself single-handed in such a contest.

At length the Baron stopped in his walk and looked at the group. He said, after a pause, in a quiet tone of voice: "Segfried, if you doubt my courage because I strike to the ground a rascally monk, step forth, draw thine own good sword, our comrades will see that all is fair betwixt us, and in this manner you may learn that I fear neither mailed nor unmailed hand."

But the knight made no motion to lay his hand upon his sword, nor did he move from his place. "No one doubts your courage, my Lord," he said, "neither is it any reflection on mine that in answer to your challenge my sword remains in its scabbard. You are our overlord and it is not meet that our weapons should be raised against you."

"I am glad that point is firmly fixed in your minds. I thought a moment since that I would be compelled to uphold the feudal law at the peril of my own body. But if that comes not in question, no more need be said. Touching the unarmed, Segfried, if I remember aright you showed no such squeamishness at our sacking of the Convent of St. Agnes."

376

"A woman is a different matter, my Lord," said Segfried uneasily.

The Baron laughed and so did some of the knights, openly relieved to find the tension of the situation relaxing.

"Comrades!" cried the Baron, his face aglow with enthusiasm, all traces of his former temper vanishing from his brow. "You are excellent in a mêlée, but useless at the council board. You see no further ahead of you than your good right arms can strike. Look round you at these stout walls; no engine that man has yet devised can batter a breach in them. In our vaults are ten years' supply of stolen grain. Our cellars are full of rich red wine, not of our vintage, but for our drinking. Here in our court bubbles forever this good spring, excellent to drink when wine gives out, and medicinal in the morning when too much wine has been taken in." He waved his hand towards the overflowing well, charged with carbonic acid gas, one of the many that have since made this region of the Rhine famous. "Now I ask you, can this Castle of Grunewald ever be taken—excommunication or no excommunication?"

A simultaneous shout of "No! Never!" arose from the knights.

The Baron stood looking grimly at them for several moments. Then he said in a quiet voice, "Yes, the Castle of Grunewald can be taken. Not from without but from within. If any crafty enemy sows dissension among us; turns the sword of comrade against comrade; then falls the Castle of Grunewald! To-day we have seen how nearly that has been done. We have against us in the monastery of Monnonstein no fat-headed Abbot, but one who was a warrior before he turned a monk. 'Tis but a few years since, that the Abbot Ambrose stood at the right hand of the Emperor as Baron von Stern, and it is known that the Abbot's robes are but a thin veneer over the iron knight within. His hand, grasping the cross, still itches for the sword. The fighting Archbishop of Treves has sent him to Monnonstein for no other purpose than to leave behind him the ruins of Grunewald, and his first bolt was shot straight into our courtyard, and for a moment I stood alone, without a single man-at-arms to second me."

The knights looked at one another in silence, then cast their eyes to the stone-paved court, all too shamed-faced to attempt reply to what all knew was the truth. The Baron, a deep frown on his brow, gazed sternly at the chap-fallen group.... "Such was the effect of the first shaft shot by good Abbot Ambrose, what will be the result of the second?"

"There will be no second," said Segfried stepping forward. "We must sack the Monastery, and hang the Abbot and his craven monks in their own cords."

"Good," cried the Baron, nodding his head in approval, "the worthy Abbot, however, trusts not only in God, but in walls three cloth yards thick. The monastery stands by the river and partly over it. The besieged monks will therefore not suffer from thirst. Their larder is as amply provided as are the vaults of this castle. The militant Abbot understands both defence and sortie. He is a master of siege-craft inside or outside stone walls. How then do you propose to sack and hang, good Segfried?"

The knights were silent. They knew the Monastery was as impregnable as the castle, in fact it was the only spot for miles round that had never owned the sway of Baron von Grunewald, and none of them were well enough provided with brains to venture a plan for its successful reduction. A cynical smile played round the lips of their over-lord, as he saw the problem had overmatched them. At last he spoke.

"We must meet craft with craft. If the Pope's Ban cast such terror among my good knights, steeped to the gauntlets in blood, what effect, think you, will it have over the minds of devout believers in the Church and its power? The trustful monks know that it has been launched against us, therefore are they doubtless waiting for us to come to the monastery, and lay our necks under the feet of their Abbot, begging his clemency. They are ready to believe any story we care to tell touching the influence of such scribbling over us. You Segfried, owe me some reparation for this morning's temporary defection, and to you, therefore, do I trust the carrying out of my plans. There was always something of the monk about you, Segfried, and you will yet end your days sanctimoniously in a monastery, unless you are first hanged at Treves or knocked on the head during an assault.

"Draw, then, your longest face, and think of the time when you will be a monk, as Ambrose is, who, in his day, shed as much blood as ever you have done. Go to the Monastery of Monnonstein in most dejected fashion, and unarmed. Ask in faltering tones, speech of the Abbot, and say to him, as if he knew nought of it, that the Pope's Ban is on us. Say that at first I defied it, and smote down the good father who was reading it, but add that as the pious man fell, a sickness like unto a pestilence came over me and over my men, from which you only are free, caused, you suspect, by your loudly protesting against the felling of the monk. Say that we lie at death's door, grieving for our sins, and groaning for absolution. Say that we are ready to deliver up the castle and all its contents to the care of the holy Church, so that the Abbot but sees our tortured souls safely directed towards the gates of Paradise. Insist that all the monks come, explaining that you fear we have but few moments to live, and that the Abbot alone would be as helpless as one surgeon on a battle-field. Taunt them with fear of the pestilence if they hesitate, and that will bring them."

Segfried accepted the commission, and the knights warmly expressed their admiration of their master's genius. As the great red sun began to sink behind the westward hills that border the Rhine, Segfried departed on horseback through the castle gates, and journeyed toward the monastery with bowed head and dejected mien. The gates remained open, and as darkness fell, a lighted torch was thrust in a wrought iron receptacle near the entrance at the outside, throwing a fitful, flickering glare under the archway and into the deserted court. Within, all was silent as the ruined castle is to-day, save only the tinkling sound of the clear waters of the effervescing spring as it flowed over the stones and trickled down to disappear under the walls at one corner of the courtyard.

The Baron and his sturdy knights sat in the darkness, with growing impatience, in the great Rittersaal listening for any audible token of the return of Segfried and his ghostly company. At last in the still night air there came faintly across the plain a monkish chant growing louder and louder, until finally the steel-shod hoofs of Segfried's charger rang on the stones of the causeway leading to the castle gates. Pressed behind the two heavy open leaves of the gates stood the warder and his assistants, scarcely breathing, ready to close the gates sharply the moment the last monk had entered.

Still chanting, led by the Abbot in his robes of office, the monks slowly marched into the deserted courtyard, while Segfried reined his horse close inside the entrance. "Peace be upon this house and all within," said the deep voice of the Abbot, and in unison the monks murmured "Amen," the word echoing back to them in the stillness from the four grey walls.

Then the silence was rudely broken by the ponderous clang of the closing gates and the ominous rattle of bolts being thrust into their places with the jingle of heavy chains. Down the wide stairs from the Rittersaal came the clank of armour and rude shouts of laughter. Newly lighted torches flared up here and there, illuminating the courtyard, and showing, dangling against the northern wall a score of ropes with nooses at the end of each. Into the courtyard clattered the Baron and his followers. The Abbot stood with arms folded, pressing a gilded cross across his breast. He was a head taller than any of his frightened, cowering brethren, and his noble emaciated face was thin with fasting caused by his never-ending conflict with the world that was within himself. His pale countenance betokened his office and the Church; but the angry eagle flash of his piercing eye spoke of the world alone and the field of conflict.

The Baron bowed low to the Abbot, and said: "Welcome, my Lord Abbot, to my humble domicile! It has long been the wish of my enemies to stand within its walls, and this pleasure is now granted you. There is little to be made of it from without."

"Baron Grunewald," said the Abbot, "I and my brethren are come hither on an errand of mercy, and under the protection of your knightly word."

The Baron raised his eyebrows in surprise at this, and, turning to Segfried, he said in angry tones: "Is it so? Pledged you my word for the safety of these men?"

"The reverend Abbot is mistaken," replied the knight, who had not yet descended from his horse. "There was no word of safe conduct between us."

"Safe conduct is implied when an officer of the Church is summoned to administer its consolations to the dying," said the Abbot.

"All trades," remarked the Baron suavely, "have their dangers—yours among the rest, as well as ours. If my follower had pledged my word regarding your safety, I would now open the gates and let you free. As he has not done so, I shall choose a manner for your exit more in keeping with your lofty aspirations."

Saying this, he gave some rapid orders; his servitors fell upon the unresisting monks and bound them hand and foot. They were then conducted to the northern wall, and the nooses there adjusted round the neck of each. When this was done, the Baron stood back from the pinioned victims and addressed them:

"It is not my intention that you should die without having time to repent of the many wicked deeds you have doubtless done during your lives. Your sentence is that ye be hanged at cockcrow to-morrow, which was the hour when, if your teachings cling to my memory, the first of your craft turned traitor to his master. If, however, you tire of your all-night vigil, you can at once obtain release by crying at the top of your voices 'So die all Christians.' Thus you will hang yourselves, and so remove some responsibility from my perhaps overladen conscience. The hanging is a device of my own, of which I am perhaps pardonably proud, and it pleases me that it is to be first tried on so worthy an assemblage. With much labour we have elevated to the battlements an oaken tree, lopped of its branches, which will not burn the less brightly next winter in that it has helped to commit some of you to hotter flames, if all ye say be true. The ropes are tied to this log, and at the cry 'So die all Christians,' I have some stout knaves in waiting up above with levers, who will straightway fling the log over the battlements on which it is now poised, and the instant after your broken necks will impinge against the inner coping of the northern wall. And now good-night, my Lord Abbot, and a happy release for you all in the morning."

"Baron von Grunewald, I ask of you that you will release one of us who may thus administer the rites of the Church to his brethren and receive in turn the same from me."

"Now, out upon me for a careless knave!" cried the Baron. "I had forgotten that; it is so long since I have been to mass and such like ceremonies myself. Your request is surely most reasonable, and I like you the better that you keep up the farce of your calling to the very end. But think not that I am so inhospitable, as to force one guest to wait upon another, even in matters spiritual. Not so. We keep with us a ghostly father for such occasions, and use him between times to wait on us with wine and other necessaries. As soon as he has filled our flagons, I will ask good Father Gottlieb to wait upon you, and I doubt not he will shrive with any in the land, although he has been this while back somewhat out of practice. His habit is rather tattered and stained with the drippings of his new vocation, but I warrant you, you will know the sheep, even though his fleece be torn. And now, again, good-night, my Lord."

The Baron and his knights returned up the broad stairway that led to the Rittersaal. Most of the torches were carried with them. The defences of the castle were so strong that no particular pains were taken to make all secure, further than the stationing of an armed man at the gate. A solitary torch burnt under the archway, and here a guard paced back and forth. The courtyard was in darkness, but the top of the highest turrets were silvered by the rising moon. The doomed men stood with the halters about their necks, as silent as a row of spectres.

The tall windows of the Rittersaal, being of coloured glass, threw little light into the square, although they glowed with a rainbow splendour from the torches within. Into the silence of the square broke the sound of song and the clash of flagons upon the oaken table.

At last there came down the broad stair and out into the court a figure in the habit of a monk, who hurried shufflingly across the stones to the grim row of brown-robed men. He threw himself sobbing at the feet of the tall Abbot.

"Rise, my son, and embrace me," said his superior. When Father Gottlieb did so, the other whispered in his ear: "There is a time to weep and a time for action. Now is the time for action. Unloosen quickly the bonds around me, and slip this noose from my neck."

Father Gottlieb acquitted himself of his task as well as his agitation and trembling hands would let him.

"Perform a like service for each of the others," whispered the Abbot curtly. "Tell each in a low voice to remain standing just as if he were still bound. Then return to me."

When the monk had done what he was told, he returned to his superior.

"Have you access to the wine cellar?" asked the Abbot.

"Yes, Father."

"What are the strongest wines?"

"Those of the district are strong. Then there is a barrel or two of the red wine of Assmannshausen."

"Decant a half of each in your flagons. Is there brandy?"

"Yes, Father."

"Then mix with the two wines as much brandy as you think their already drunken palates will not detect. Make the potation stronger with brandy as the night wears on. When they drop off into their sodden sleep, bring a flagon to the guard at the gate, and tell him the Baron sends it to him."

"Will you absolve me, Father, for the—"

"It is no falsehood, Gottlieb. I, the Baron, send it. I came hither the Abbot Ambrose: I am now Baron von Stern, and if I have any influence with our mother Church the Abbot's robe shall fall on thy shoulders, if you but do well what I ask of you to-night. It will be some compensation for what, I fear, thou hast already suffered."

Gottlieb hurried away, as the knights were already clamouring for more wine. As the night wore on and the moon rose higher the sounds of revelry increased, and once there was a clash of arms and much uproar, which subsided under the over-mastering voice of the Black Baron. At last the Abbot, standing there with the rope dangling behind him, saw Gottlieb bring a huge beaker of liquor to the sentinel, who at once sat down on the stone bench under the arch to enjoy it.

Finally, all riot died away in the hall except one thin voice singing, waveringly, a drinking song, and when that ceased silence reigned supreme, and the moon shone full upon the bubbling spring.

Gottlieb stole stealthily out and told the Abbot that all the knights were stretched upon the floor, and the Baron had his head on the table, beside his overturned flagon. The sentinel snored upon the stone bench.

"I can now unbar the gate," said Father Gottlieb, "and we may all escape."

"Not so," replied the Abbot. "We came to convert these men to Christianity, and our task is still to do."

The monks all seemed frightened at this, and wished themselves once more within the monastery, able to say all's well that ends so, but none ventured to offer counsel to the gaunt man who led them. He bade each bring with him the cords that had bound him, and without a word they followed him into the Rittersaal, and there tied up the knights and their master as they themselves had been tied.

"Carry them out," commanded the Abbot, "and lay them in a row, their feet towards the spring and their heads under the ropes. And go you, Gottlieb, who know the ways of the castle, and fasten the doors of all the apartments where the servitors are sleeping."

When this was done, and they gathered once more in the moonlit courtyard, the Abbot took off his robes of office and handed them to Father Gottlieb, saying significantly: "The lowest among you that suffers and is true shall be exalted." Turning to his own flock, he commanded them to go in and obtain some rest after such a disquieting night; then to Gottlieb, when the monks had obediently departed: "Bring me, an' ye know where to find such, the apparel of a fighting man and a sword."

Thus arrayed, he dismissed the old man, and alone in the silence, with the row of figures like effigies on a tomb beside him, paced up and down through the night, as the moon dropped lower and lower, in the heavens.

384

There was a period of dark before the dawn, and at last the upper walls began to whiten with the coming day, and the Black Baron moaned uneasily in his drunken sleep. The Abbot paused in his walk and looked down upon them, and Gottlieb stole out from the shadow of the door and asked if he could be of service. He had evidently not slept, but had watched his chief, until he paused in his march.

"Tell our brothers to come out and see the justice of the Lord."

When the monks trooped out, haggard and wan, in the pure light of the dawn, the Abbot asked Gottlieb to get a flagon and dash water from the spring in the faces of the sleepers.

The Black Baron was the first to come to his senses and realise dimly, at first, but afterwards more acutely, the changed condition of affairs. His eye wandered apprehensively to the empty noose swaying slightly in the morning breeze above him. He then saw that the tall, ascetic man before him had doffed the Abbot's robes and wore a sword by his side, and from this he augured ill. At the command of the Abbot the monks raised each prostrate man and placed him against the north wall.

"Gottlieb," said, the Abbot slowly, "the last office that will be required of you. You took from our necks the nooses last night. Place them, I pray you, on the necks of the Baron and his followers."

The old man, trembling, adjusted the ropes.

"My Lord Abbot——" began the Baron.

"Baron von Grunewald," interrupted the person addressed, "the Abbot Ambrose is dead. He was foully assassinated last night. In his place stands Conrad von Stern, who answers for his deeds to the Emperor, and after him, to God."

"Is it your purpose to hang me, Baron?"

"Was it your purpose to have hanged us, my Lord?"

"I swear to heaven, it was not. 'Twas but an ill-timed pleasantry. Had I wished to hang you I would have done so last night."

"That seems plausible."

The knights all swore, with many rounded oaths, that their over-lord spoke the truth, and nothing was further from their intention than an execution.

"Well, then, whether you hang or no shall depend upon yourselves."

"By God, then," cried the Baron, "an' I have aught to say on that point, I shall hang some other day."

"Will you then, Baron, beg admittance to Mother Church, whose kindly tenets you have so long outraged?"

"We will, we do," cried the Baron fervently, whispering through his clenched teeth to Segfried, who stood next him: "Wait till I have the upper hand again." Fortunately the Abbot did not hear the whisper. The knights all echoed aloud the Baron's pious first remark, and, perhaps, in their hearts said "Amen" to his second.

The Abbot spoke a word or two to the monks, and they advanced to the pinioned men and there performed the rites sacred to their office and to the serious situation of the penitents. As the good brothers stood back, they begged the Abbot for mercy to be extended towards the new converts, but the sphinx-like face of their leader gave no indication as to their fate, and the good men began to fear that it was the Abbot's intention to hang the Baron and his knights.

"Now—brothers," said the Abbot, with a long pause before he spoke the second word, whereupon each of the prisoners heaved a sigh of relief, "I said your fate would depend on yourselves and on your good intent."

They all vociferously proclaimed that their intentions were and had been of the most honourable kind.

"I trust that is true, and that you shall live long enough to show your faith by your works. It is written that a man digged a pit for his enemy and

386

fell himself therein. It is also written that as a man sows, so shall he reap. If you meant us no harm then your signal shouted to the battlements will do you no harm."

"For God's sake, my Lord...." screamed the Baron. The Abbot, unheeding, raised his face towards the northern wall and shouted at the top of his voice:

"So die SUCH Christians!" varying the phrase by one word. A simultaneous scream rose from the doomed men, cut short as by a knife, as the huge log was hurled over the outer parapet, and the seventeen victims were jerked into the air and throttled at the coping around the inner wall.

Thus did the Abbot Ambrose save the souls of Baron von Grunewald and his men, at some expense to their necks.

AN INVITATION

The proud and warlike Archbishop Baldwin of Treves was well mounted, and, although the road by the margin of the river was in places bad, the august horseman nevertheless made good progress along it, for he had a long distance to travel before the sun went down. The way had been rudely constructed by that great maker of roads—the army—and the troops who had built it did not know, when they laboured at it, that they were preparing a path for their own retreat should disaster overtake them. The grim and silent horseman had been the brains, where the troops were the limbs; this thoroughfare had been of his planning, and over it, back into Treves, had returned a victorious, not a defeated, army. The iron hand of the Archbishop had come down on every truculent noble in the land, and every castle gate that had not opened to him through fear, had been battered in by force. Peace now spread her white wings over all the country, and where opposition to his Lordship's stubborn will had been the strongest, there was silence as well, with, perhaps, a thin wreath of blue smoke hovering over the blackened walls. The provinces on each bank of the Moselle from Treves to the Rhine now acknowledged Baldwin their over-lord—a suzerainty technically claimed by his Lordship's predecessors—but the iron Archbishop had changed the nominal into the actual, and it had taken some hard knocks to do it. His present journey was well earned, for he was betaking himself from his more formal and exacting Court at Treves to his summer palace at Cochem, there to rest from the fatigues of a campaign in which he had used not only his brain, but his good right arm as well.

The palace which was to be the end of his journey was in some respects admirably suited to its master, for, standing on an eminence high above Cochem, with its score of pinnacles glittering in the sun, it seemed, to one below, a light and airy structure; but it was in reality a fortress almost impregnable, and three hundred years later it sent into a less turbulent sphere the souls of one thousand six hundred Frenchmen before its flag was lowered to the enemy.

The personal appearance of the Archbishop and the smallness of his escort were practical illustrations of the fact that the land was at peace, and that he was master of it. His attire was neither clerical nor warlike, but rather that of a nobleman riding abroad where no enemy could possibly lurk. He was to all appearance unarmed, and had no protection save a light chain mail jacket of bright steel, which was worn over his vesture, and not concealed as was the custom. This jacket sparkled in the sun as if it were woven of fine threads strung with small and innumerable diamonds. It might ward off a dagger thrust, or turn aside a half-spent arrow, but it was too light to be of much service against sword or pike. The Archbishop was well mounted on a powerful black charger that had carried him through many a hot contest, and it now made little of the difficulties of the ill-constructed road, putting the other horses on their mettle to equal the pace set to them.

The escort consisted of twelve men, all lightly armed, for Gottlieb, the monk, who rode sometimes by the Archbishop's side, but more often behind him, could hardly be counted as a combatant should defence become necessary. When the Archbishop left Treves his oldest general had advised his taking an escort of a thousand men at least, putting it on the ground that such a number was necessary to uphold the dignity of his office; but Baldwin smiled darkly, and said that where he rode the dignity of the Electorship would be safe, even though none rode beside or behind him. Few dared offer advice to the Elector, but the bluff general persisted, and spoke of danger in riding down the Moselle valley with so small a following.

"Who is there left to molest me?" asked the Archbishop; and the general was forced to admit that there was none.

An army builds a road along the line of the least resistance; and often, when a promontory thrust its rocky nose into the river, the way led up the hill through the forest, getting back into the valley again as best it could. During these inland excursions, the monk, evidently unused to equestrianism, fell behind, and sometimes the whole troop was halted by command of its chief, until Gottlieb, clinging to his horse's mane, emerged from the thicket, the Archbishop curbing the impatience of his charger and watching, with a cynical smile curling his stern lips, the reappearance of the good father.

After one of the most laborious ascents and descents they had encountered that day, the Archbishop waited for the monk; and when he came up with his leader, panting and somewhat dishevelled, the latter said, "There appears to be a lesson in your tribulations which hereafter you may retail with profit to your flock, relating how a good man leaving the right and beaten path and following his own devices in the wilderness may bring discomfiture upon himself."

"The lesson it conveys to me, my Lord," said the monk, drily, "is that a man is but a fool to leave the stability of good stout sandals with which he is accustomed, to venture his body on a horse that pays little heed to his wishes."

"This is our last detour," replied the Elector; "there are now many miles of winding but level road before us, and you have thus a chance to retrieve your reputation as a horseman in the eyes of our troop."

"In truth, my Lord, I never boasted of it," returned the monk, "but I am right glad to learn that the way will be less mountainous. To what district have we penetrated?"

"Above us, but unseen from this bank of the river, is the castle of the Widow Starkenburg. Her days of widowhood, however, are nearly passed, for I intend to marry her to one of my victorious knights, who will hold the castle for me."

"The Countess of Starkenburg," said the monk, "must surely now be at an age when the thoughts turn toward Heaven rather than toward matrimony."

"I have yet to meet the woman," replied the Archbishop, gazing upward, "who pleads old age as an excuse for turning away from a suitable lover. It is thy misfortune, Gottlieb, that in choosing a woollen cowl rather than an iron head-piece, thou should'st thus have lost a chance of advancement. The castle, I am told, has well-filled wine vaults, and old age in wine is doubtless more to thy taste than the same quality in woman. 'Tis a pity thou art not a knight, Gottlieb."

"The fault is not beyond the power of our Holy Father to remedy by special dispensation," replied the monk, with a chuckle.

The Elector laughed silently, and looked down on his comrade in kindly fashion, shaking his head.

"The wines of Castle Starkenburg are not for thy appreciative palate, ghostly father. I have already selected a mate for the widow."

"And what if thy selection jumps not with her approval. They tell me the countess has a will of her own."

"It matters little to me, and I give her the choice merely because I am loth to war with a woman. The castle commands the river and holds the district. The widow may give it up peaceably at the altar, or forcibly at the point of the sword, whichever method most commends itself to her ladyship. The castle must be in the command of one whom I can trust."

The conversation here met a startling interruption. The Archbishop and his guard were trotting rapidly round a promontory and following a bend of the river, the nature of the country being such that it was impossible to see many hundred feet ahead of them. Suddenly, they came upon a troop of armed and mounted men, standing like statues before them. The troop numbered an even score, and completely filled the way between the precipice on their left and the stream on their right. Although armed, every sword was in its scabbard, with the exception of the long two-handed weapon of the leader, who stood a few paces in advance of his men, with the point of his sword resting on the ground. The black horse, old in campaigns, recognised danger ahead, and stopped instantly, without waiting for the drawing of the rein, planting his two forefeet firmly in front, with a suddenness of action that would have unhorsed a less alert rider. Before the archbishop could question the silent host that barred his way, their leader raised his long sword until it was poised perpendicularly in the air above his head, and, with a loud voice, in measured tones, as one repeats a lesson he has learned by rote, he cried, "My Lord Archbishop of Treves, the Countess Laurette von Starkenburg invites you to sup with her."

In the silence that followed, the leader's sword still remained uplifted untrembling in the air. Across the narrow gorge, from the wooded sides of the opposite mountains, came, with mocking cadence, the echo of the last words of the invitation, clear and distinct, as if spoken again by some one concealed in the further forest. A deep frown darkened the brow of the fighting archbishop.

"The Countess is most kind," he said, slowly. "Convey to her my respectful admiration, and express my deep regret that I am unable to accept her hospitality, as I ride to-night to my Castle at Cochem."

The leader of the opposing host suddenly lowered his upraised sword, as if in salute, but the motion seemed to be a preconcerted signal, for every man behind him instantly whipped blade from scabbard, and stood there with naked weapon displayed. The leader, raising his sword once more to its former position, repeated in the same loud and monotonous voice, as if the archbishop had not spoken. "My Lord Archbishop of Treves, the Countess Laurette von Starkenburg invites you to sup with her."

The intelligent war-horse, who had regarded the obstructing force with head held high, retreated slowly step by step, until now a considerable distance separated the two companies. The captain of the guard had seen from the first that attack or defence was equally useless, and, with his men, had also given way gradually as the strange colloquy went on. Whether any of the opposing force noticed this or not, they made no attempt to recover the ground thus almost imperceptibly stolen from them, but stood as if each horse were rooted to the spot.

Baldwin the Fighter, whose compressed lips showed how loth he was to turn his back upon any foe, nevertheless saw the futility of resistance, and in a quick, clear whisper, he said, hastily, "Back! Back! If we cannot fight them, we can at least out-race them."

The good monk had taken advantage of his privilege as a non-combatant to retreat well to the rear while the invitation was being given and declined, and in the succeeding flight found himself leading the van. The captain of the guard threw himself between the Starkenburg men and the prince of the Church, but the former made no effort at pursuit, standing motionless as they had done from the first until the rounding promontory hid them from view. Suddenly, the horse on which the monk rode stood stock still, and its worthy rider, with a cry of alarm, clinging to the animal's mane, shot over its head and came heavily to the ground. The whole flying troop came to a sudden halt, for there ahead of them was a band exactly similar in numbers and appearance to that from which they were galloping. It seemed as if the same company had been transported by magic over the promontory and placed across the way. The sun shone on the uplifted blade of the leader, reminding the archbishop of the flaming sword that barred the entrance of our first parents to Paradise.

The leader, with ringing voice, that had a touch of menace in it, cried:

"My Lord Archbishop of Treves, the Countess Laurette von Starkenburg invites you to sup with her."

"Trapped, by God!" muttered the Elector between his clinched teeth. His eyes sparkled with anger, and the sinister light that shot from them had before now made the Emperor quail. He spurred his horse toward the leader, who lowered his sword and bowed to the great dignitary approaching him.

"The Countess of Starkenburg is my vassal," cried the Archbishop. "You are her servant; and in much greater degree, therefore, are you mine. I command you to let us pass unmolested on our way; refuse at your peril."

"A servant," said the man, slowly, "obeys the one directly above him, and leaves that one to account to any superior authority. My men obey me; I take my orders from my lady the countess. If you, my Lord, wish to direct the authority which commands me, my lady the countess awaits your pleasure at her castle of Starkenburg."

"What are your orders, fellow?" asked the Archbishop, in a calmer tone.

"To convey your Lordship without scathe to the gates of Starkenburg."

"And if you meet resistance, what then?"

"The orders stand, my Lord."

"You will, I trust, allow this mendicant monk to pass peaceably on his way to Treves."

"In no castle on the Moselle does even the humblest servant of the

Church receive a warmer welcome than at Starkenburg. My lady would hold me to blame were she prevented from offering her hospitality to the mendicant."

"Does the same generous impulse extend to each of my followers?"

"It includes them all, my Lord."

"Very well. We will do ourselves the honour of waiting upon this most bountiful hostess."

By this time the troop which had first stopped the Archbishop's progress came slowly up, and the little body-guard of the Elector found themselves hemmed in with twenty men in the front and twenty at the rear, while the rocky precipice rose on one hand and the rapid river flowed on the other.

The cortège reformed and trotted gently down the road until it came to a by-way leading up the hill. Into this by-way the leaders turned, reducing their trot to a walk because of the steepness of the ascent. The Archbishop and his men followed, with the second troop of Starkenburg bringing up the rear. His Lordship rode at first in sullen silence, then with a quick glance of his eye he summoned the captain to his side. He slipped the ring of office from his finger and passed it unperceived into the officer's hand.

"There will be some confusion at the gate," he said, in a low voice. "Escape then if you can. Ride for Treves as you never rode before. Stop not to fight with any; everything depends on outstripping pursuit. Take what horses you need wherever you find them, and kill them all if necessary, but stop for nothing. This ring will be warrant for whatever you do. Tell my general to invest this castle instantly with ten thousand men and press forward the siege regardless of my fate. Tell him to leave not one stone standing upon another, and to hang the widow of Starkenburg from her own blazing timbers. Succeed, and a knighthood and the command of a thousand men awaits you."

"I will succeed or die, my Lord."

"Succeed and live," said the Archbishop, shortly.

As the horses slowly laboured up the zigzagging road, the view along the silvery Moselle widened and extended, and at last the strong grey walls of the castle came into sight, with the ample gates wide open. The horsemen in front drew up in two lines on each side of the gates without entering, and thus the Archbishop, at the head of his little band, slowly rode first under the archway into the courtyard of the castle.

On the stone steps that led to the principal entrance of the castle stood a tall, graceful lady, with her women behind her. She was robed in black, and the headdress of her snow-white hair gave her the appearance of a dignified abbess at her convent door. Her serene and placid face had undoubtedly once been beautiful; and age, which had left her form as straight and slender as one of her own forest pines, forgetting to place its customary burden upon her graceful shoulders, had touched her countenance with a loving hand. With all her womanliness, there was, nevertheless, a certain firmness in the finely-moulded chin that gave evidence of a line of ancestry that had never been too deferential to those in authority.

The stern Archbishop reined in his black charger when he reached the middle of the courtyard, but made no motion to dismount. The lady came slowly down the broad stone steps, followed by her feminine train, and, approaching the Elector, placed her white hand upon his stirrup, in mute acknowledgment of her vassalage.

"Welcome, prince of the Church and protector of our Faith," she said. "It is a hundred years since my poor house has sheltered so august a guest."

The tones were smooth and soothing as the scarcely audible plash of a distant fountain; but the incident she cited struck ominously on the Archbishop's recollection, rousing memory and causing him to dart a quick glance at the countess, in which was blended sharp enquiry and awakened foreboding; but the lady, unconscious of his scrutiny, stood with drooping head and downcast eyes, her shapely hand still on his stirrup-iron.

"If I remember rightly, madame, my august predecessor slept well beneath this roof."

"Alas, yes!" murmured the lady, sadly. "We have ever accounted it the greatest misfortune of our line, that he should have died mysteriously here. Peace be to his soul!"

"Not so mysteriously, madame, but that there were some shrewd guesses concerning his malady."

"That is true, my Lord," replied the countess, simply. "It was supposed that in his camp upon the lowlands by the river he contracted a fever from which he died."

"My journey by the Moselle has been of the briefest. I trust, therefore, I have not within me the seeds of his fatal distemper."

"I most devoutly echo that trust, my Lord, and pray that God, who watches over us all, may guard your health while sojourning here."

"Forgive me, madame, if, within the shadow of these walls, I say 'Amen' to your prayer with some emphasis."

The Countess Laurette contented herself with bowing low and humbly crossing herself, making no verbal reply to his Lordship's remark. She then beseeched the Archbishop to dismount, saying something of his need of rest and refreshment, begging him to allow her to be his guide to the Rittersaal.

When the Archbishop reached the topmost step that led to the castle door, he cast an eye, not devoid of anxiety, over the court-yard, to see how his following had fared. The gates were now fast closed, and forty horses were ranged with their tails to the wall, the silent riders in their saddles. Rapid as was his glance, it showed him his guard huddled together in the centre of the court, his own black charger, with empty saddle, the only living thing among them that showed no sign of dismay. Between two of the hostile horsemen stood his captain, with doublet torn and headgear awry, evidently a discomfited prisoner.

The Archbishop entered the gloomy castle with a sense of defeat tugging down his heart to a lower level than he had ever known it to reach before; for in days gone by, when fate had seemed to press against him, he had been in the thick of battle, and had felt an exultation in rallying his half-discouraged followers, who had never failed to respond to the call of a born leader of men. But here he had to encounter silence, with semi-darkness over his head, cold stone under foot, and round him the unaccustomed hiss of women's skirts.

The Countess conducted her guest through the lofty Knight's Hall, in which his Lordship saw preparations for a banquet going forward. An arched passage led them to a small room that seemed to be within a turret hanging over a precipice, as if it were an eagle's nest. This room gave an admirable and extended view over the winding Moselle and much of the surrounding country. On a table were flagons of wine and empty cups, together with some light refection, upon all of which the Archbishop looked with suspicious eye. He did not forget the rumoured poisoning of his predecessor in office. The countess asked him, with deference, to seat himself; then pouring out a cup of wine, she bowed to him and drank it. Turning to rinse the cup in a basin of water which a serving-woman held, she was interrupted by her guest, who now, for the first time, showed a trace of gallantry.

"I beg of you, madame," said the Archbishop, rising; and, taking the unwashed cup from her hand, he filled it with wine, drinking prosperity to herself and her home. Then, motioning her to a chair, he said seating himself: "Countess von Starkenburg, I am a man more used to the uncouth rigour of a camp than the dainty etiquette of a lady's boudoir. Forgive me, then, if I ask you plainly, as a plain man may, why you hold me prisoner in your castle."

"Prisoner, my lord?" echoed the lady, with eyebrows raised in amazement. "How poorly are we served by our underlings, if such a thought has been conveyed to your lordship's mind. I asked them to invite you hither with such deference as a vassal should hold toward an over-lord. I am grievously distressed to learn that my commands have been so ill obeyed."

"Your commands were faithfully followed, madame, and I have made no complaint regarding lack of deference, but when two-score armed men carry a respectful invitation to one having a bare dozen at his back, then all option vanishes, and compulsion takes its place."

"My lord, a handful of men were fit enough escort for a neighbouring baron should he visit us, but, for a prince of the Church, all my retainers are but scanty acknowledgment of a vassal's regard. I would they had been twenty thousand, to do you seemly honour."

"I am easily satisfied, madame, and had they been fewer I might have missed this charming outlook. I am to understand, then, that you have no demands to make of me; and that I am free to depart, accompanied by your good wishes."

"With my good wishes now and always, surely, my Lord. I have no demands to make—the word ill befits the lips of a humble vassal; but, being here——"

"Ah! But, being here——" interrupted the Archbishop, glancing keenly at her.

"I have a favour to beg of you. I wish to ask permission to build a castle on the heights above Trarbach, for my son."

"The Count Johann, third of the name?"

"The same, my Lord, who is honoured by your Lordship's remembrance of him."

"And you wish to place this stronghold between your castle of Starkenburg and my town of Treves? Were I a suspicious man, I might imagine you had some distrust of me."

"Not so, my lord. The Count Johann will hold the castle in your defence."

"I have ever been accustomed to look to my own defence," said the Archbishop, drily; adding, as if it were an afterthought, "with the blessing of God upon my poor efforts."

The faintest suspicion of a smile hovered for an instant on the lips of the countess, that might have been likened to the momentary passing of a gleam of sunshine over the placid waters of the river far below; for she well knew, as did all others, that it was the habit of the fighting Archbishop to smite sturdily first, and ask whatever blessing might be needed on the blow afterwards.

"The permission being given, what follows?"

"That you will promise not to molest me during the building."

"A natural corollary. 'Twould be little worth to give permission and then bring up ten thousand men to disturb the builders. That granted, remains there anything more?"

"I fear I trespass on your Lordship's patience but this is now the end. A strong house is never built with a weak purse. I do entreat your lordship to cause to be sent to me from your treasury in Treves thousand pieces of gold, that the castle may be a worthy addition to your province."

The Archbishop arose with a scowl on his face, and paced the narrow limits of the room like a caged lion. The hot anger mounted to his brow and reddened it, but he strode up and down until he regained control of himself, then spoke with a touch of hardness in his voice:

"A good fighter, madame, holds his strongest reserves to the last. You have called me a prince of the Church, and such I am. But you flatter me, madame; you rate me too high. The founder of our Church, when betrayed, was sold for silver, and for a lesser number of pieces than you ask in gold."

The lady, now standing, answered nothing to this taunt, but the colour flushed her pale cheeks.

"I am, then, a prisoner, and you hold me for ransom, but it will avail you little. You may close your gates and prevent my poor dozen of followers from escaping, but news of this outrage will reach Treves, and then, by God, your walls shall smoke for it. There will be none of the Starkenburgs left, either to kidnap or to murder future archbishops."

Still the lady stood silent and motionless as a marble statue. The Elector paced up and down for a time, muttering to himself, then smote his open palm against a pillar of the balcony, and stood gazing on the fair landscape of river and rounded hill spread below and around him. Suddenly he turned and looked at the Countess, meeting her clear, fearless grey eyes, noticing, for the first time, the resolute contour of her finely-moulded chin.

"Madame," he said, with admiration in his tone, "you are a brave woman."

"I am not so brave as you think me, my Lord," she answered, coldly. "There is one thing I dare not do. I am not brave enough to allow your Lordship to go free, if you refuse what I ask."

"And should I not relent at first, there are dungeons in Starkenburg where this proud spirit, with which my enemies say I am cursed, will doubtless be humbled."

"Not so, my Lord. You will be treated with that consideration which should be shown to one of your exalted station."

"Indeed! And melted thus by kindness, how long, think you, will the process take?"

"It will be of the shortest, my Lord, for if, as you surmise rumour should get abroad and falsely proclaim that the Archbishop lodges here against his will, there's not a flying baron or beggared knight in all the land but would turn in his tracks and cry to Starkenburg, 'In God's name, hold him, widow, till we get our own again!' Willingly would they make the sum I beg of you an annual tribute, so they might be certain your Lordship were well housed in this castle."

"Widow, there is truth in what you say, even if a woman hath spoken it," replied the Archbishop, with a grim smile on his lips and undisguised admiration gleaming from his dark eye. "This cowardly world is given to taking advantage of a man when opportunity offers. But there is one point you have not reckoned upon: What of my stout army lying at Treves?"

"What of the arch when the keystone is withdrawn? What of the sheep when the shepherd disappears? My Lord, you do yourself and your great military gifts a wrong. Through my deep regard for you I gave strict command that not even the meanest of your train should be allowed to wander till all were safe within these gates, for I well knew that, did but a whisper of my

400

humble invitation and your gracious acceptance of the same reach Treves, it might be misconstrued; and although some sturdy fellows would be true, and beat their stupid heads against these walls, the rest would scatter like a sheaf of arrows suddenly unloosed, and seek the strongest arm upraised in the mêlée sure to follow. Against your army, leaderless, I would myself march out at the head of my two-score men without a tremor at my heart; before that leader, alone and armyless, I bow my head with something more akin to fear than I have ever known before, and crave his generous pardon for my bold request."

The Archbishop took her unresisting hand, and, bending, raised it to his lips with that dignified courtesy which, despite his disclaimer, he knew well how, upon occasion, to display.

"Madame," he said, "I ask you to believe that your request was granted even before you marshalled such unanswerable arguments to stand, like armoured men, around it. There is a tern and stringent law of our great Church which forbids its servants suing for a lady's hand. Countess, I never felt the grasp of that iron fetter until now."

Thus came the strong castle above Trarbach to be builded, and that not at the expense of its owners.

THE ARCHBISHOP'S GIFT

Arras, blacksmith and armourer, stood at the door of his hut in the valley of the Alf, a league or so from the Moselle, one summer evening. He was the most powerful man in all the Alf-thal, and few could lift the iron sledge-hammer he wielded as though it were a toy. Arras had twelve sons scarce less stalwart than himself, some of whom helped him in his occupation of blacksmith and armourer, while the others tilled the ground near by, earning from the rich soil of the valley such sustenance as the whole family required.

The blacksmith thus standing at his door, heard, coming up the valley of the Alf, the hoof-beats of a horse, and his quick, experienced ear told him, though the animal was yet afar, that one of its shoes was loose. As the hurrying rider came within call, the blacksmith shouted to him in stentorian tones:

"Friend, pause a moment, until I fasten again the shoe on your horse's foot."

"I cannot stop," was the brief answer.

"Then your animal will go lame," rejoined the blacksmith.

"Better lose a horse than an empire," replied the rider, hurrying by.

"Now what does that mean?" said the blacksmith to himself as he watched the disappearing rider, while the click-clack of the loosened shoe became fainter and fainter in the distance.

Could the blacksmith have followed the rider into Castle Bertrich, a short distance further up the valley, he would speedily have learned the meaning of the hasty phrase the horseman had flung behind him as he rode past. Ascending the winding road that led to the gates of the castle as hurriedly as the jaded condition of his beast would permit, the horseman paused, unloosed the horn from his belt, and blew a blast that echoed from the wooded hills around. Presently an officer appeared above the gateway, accompanied by two or three armed men, and demanded who the stranger was and why he asked admission. The horseman, amazed at the officer's ignorance of heraldry that caused him to inquire as to his quality, answered with some haughtiness:

"Messenger of the Archbishop of Treves, I demand instant audience with Count Bertrich."

The officer, without reply, disappeared from the castle wall, and presently the great leaves of the gate were thrown open, whereupon the horseman rode his tired animal into the courtyard and flung himself off.

"My horse's shoe is loose," he said to the Captain. "I ask you to have your armourer immediately attend to it."

"In truth," replied the officer, shrugging his shoulders, "there is more drinking than fighting in Castle Bertrich; consequently we do not possess an armourer. If you want blacksmithing done you must betake yourself to armourer Arras in the valley, who will put either horse or armour right for you."

With this the messenger was forced to be content; and, begging the attendants who took charge of his horse to remember that it had travelled far and had still, when rested, a long journey before it, he followed the Captain into the great Rittersaal of the castle, where, on entering, after having been announced, he found the Count of Bertrich sitting at the head of a long table, holding in his hand a gigantic wine flagon which he was industriously emptying. Extending down each side of the table were many nobles, knights, and warriors, who, to judge by the hasty glance bestowed upon them by the Archbishop's messenger, seemed to be energetically following the example set them by their over-lord at the head. Count Bertrich's hair was unkempt, his face a purplish red, his eye bloodshot; and his corselet, open at the throat, showed the great bull-neck of the man, on whose gigantic frame constant dissipation seemed to have merely temporary effect.

"Well!" roared the nobleman, in a voice that made the rafters ring. "What would you with Count Bertrich?"

"I bear an urgent despatch to you from my Lord the Archbishop of Treves," replied the messenger.

"Then down on your knees and present it," cried the Count, beating the table with his flagon.

"I am Envoy of his Lordship of Treves," said the messenger, sternly.

"You told us that before," shouted the Count; "and now you stand in the hall of Bertrich. Kneel, therefore, to its master."

"I represent the Archbishop," reiterated the messenger, "and I kneel to none but God and the Emperor."

Count Bertrich rose somewhat uncertainly to his feet, his whole frame trembling with anger, and volleyed forth oaths upon threats. The tall nobleman at his right hand also rose, as did many of the others who sat at the table, and, placing his hand on the arm of his furious host, said warningly:

"My Lord Count, the man is right. It is against the feudal law that he should kneel, or that you should demand it. The Archbishop of Treves is your overlord, as well as ours, and it is not fitting that his messenger should kneel before us."

"That is truth—the feudal law," muttered others down each side of the table.

The enraged Count glared upon them one after another, partially subdued by their breaking away from him.

The Envoy stood calm and collected, awaiting the outcome of the tumult. The Count, cursing the absent Archbishop and his present guests with equal impartiality, sat slowly down again, and flinging his empty flagon at an attendant, demanded that it should be refilled. The others likewise resumed their seats; and the Count cried out, but with less of truculence in his tone:

"What message sent the Archbishop to Castle Bertrich?"

"My Lord, the Archbishop of Treves requires me to inform Count

Bertrich and the assembled nobles that the Hungarians have forced passage across the Rhine, and are now about to make their way through the defiles of the Eifel into this valley, intending to march thence upon Treves, laying that ancient city in ruin and carrying havoc over the surrounding country. His Lordship commands you, Count Bertrich, to rally your men about you and to hold the infidels in check in the defiles of the Eifel until the Archbishop comes, at the bead of his army, to your relief from Treves."

There was deep silence in the vast hall after this startling announcement. Then the Count replied:

"Tell the Archbishop of Treves that if the Lords of the Rhine cannot keep back the Hungarians, it is hardly likely that we, less powerful, near the Moselle, can do it."

"His Lordship urges instant compliance with his request, and I am to say that you refuse at your peril. A few hundred men can hold the Hungarians in check while they are passing through the narrow ravines of the Eifel, while as many thousands might not be successful against them should they once reach the open valleys of the Alf and the Moselle. His Lordship would also have you know that this campaign is as much in your own interest as in his, for the Hungarians, in their devastating march, spare neither high nor low."

"Tell his Lordship," hiccoughed the Count, "that I sit safely in my Castle of Bertrich, and that I defy all the Hungarians who were ever let loose to disturb me therein. If the Archbishop keeps Treves as tightly as I shall hold Castle Bertrich, there is little to fear from the invaders."

"Am I to return to Treves then with your refusal?" asked the Envoy.

"You may return to Treves as best pleases you, so that you rid us of your presence here, where you mar good company."

The Envoy, without further speech, bowed to Count Bertrich and also to the assembled nobles, passed silently out of the hall, once more reaching the courtyard of the castle, where he demanded that his horse be brought to him.

"The animal has had but scant time for feeding and rest," said the

Captain.

"'Twill be sufficient to carry us to the blacksmith's hut," answered the Envoy, as he put his foot in stirrup.

The blacksmith, still standing at the door of his smithy, heard, coming from the castle, the click of the broken shoe, but this time the rider drew up before him and said:

"The offer of help which you tendered me a little ago I shall now be glad to accept. Do your work well, smith, and know that in performing it, you are obliging an envoy of the Archbishop of Treves."

The armourer raised his cap at the mention of the august name, and invoked a blessing upon the head of that renowned and warlike prelate.

"You said something," spoke up the smith, "of loss of empire, as you rode by. I trust there is no disquieting news from Treves?"

"Disquieting enough," replied the messenger. "The Hungarians have crossed the Rhine, and are now making their way towards the defiles of the Eifel. There a hundred men could hold the infidels in check; but you breed a scurvy set of nobles in the Alf-thal, for Count Bertrich disdains the command of his over-lord to rise at the head of his men and stay the progress of the invader until the Archbishop can come to his assistance."

"Now, out upon the drunken Count for a base coward!" cried the armourer in anger. "May his castle be sacked and himself hanged on the highest turret, for refusing aid to his over-lord in time of need. I and my twelve sons know every rock and cave in the Eifel. Would the Archbishop, think you, accept the aid of such underlings as we, whose only commendation is that our hearts are stout as our sinews?"

"What better warranty could the Archbishop ask than that?" replied the Envoy. "If you can hold back the Hungarians for four or five days, then I doubt not that whatever you ask of the Archbishop will speedily be granted."

"We shall ask nothing," cried the blacksmith, "but his blessing, and be deeply honoured in receiving it."

Whereupon the blacksmith, seizing his hammer, went to the door of his hut, where hung part of a suit of armour, that served at the same time as a sign of his profession and as a tocsin. He smote the hanging iron with his sledge until the clangorous reverberation sounded through the valley, and presently there came hurrying to him eight of his stalwart sons, who had been occupied in tilling the fields.

"Scatter ye," cried the blacksmith, "over the land. Rouse the people, and tell them the Hungarians are upon us. Urge all to collect here at midnight, with whatever of arms or weapons they may possess. Those who have no arms, let them bring poles, and meanwhile your brothers and myself will make pike-heads for them. Tell them they are called to, action by a Lord from the Archbishop of Treves himself, and that I shall lead them. Tell them they fight for their homes, their wives, and their children. And now away."

The eight young men at once dispersed in various directions. The smith himself shod the Envoy's horse, and begged him to inform the Archbishop that they would defend the passes of the Eifel while a man of them remained alive.

Long before midnight the peasants came straggling to the smithy from all quarters, and by daylight the blacksmith had led them over the volcanic hills to the lip of the tremendous pass through which the Hungarians must come. The sides of this chasm were precipitous and hundreds of feet in height. Even the peasants themselves, knowing the rocks as they did, could not have climbed from the bottom of the pass to the height they now occupied. They had, therefore, no fear that the Hungarians could scale the walls and decimate their scanty band.

When the invaders appeared the blacksmith and his men rolled great stones and rocks down upon them, practically annihilating the advance guard and throwing the whole army into confusion. The week's struggle that followed forms one of the most exciting episodes in German history. Again and again the Hungarians attempted the pass, but nothing could withstand the avalanche of stones and rocks wherewith they were overwhelmed. Still, the devoted little band did not have everything its own way. They were so few—and they had to keep watch night and day—that ere the week was out many turned longing eyes towards the direction whence the Archbishop's army was expected to appear. It was not until the seventh day that help arrived, and then the Archbishop's forces speedily put to flight the now demoralised Hungarians, and chased them once more across the Rhine.

"There is nothing now left for us to do," said the tired blacksmith to his little following; "so I will get back to my forge and you to your farms."

And this without more ado they did, the cheering and inspiring ring of iron on anvil awakening the echoes of the Alf-thal once again.

The blacksmith and his twelve sons were at their noon-day meal when an imposing cavalcade rode up to the smithy. At the head was no other than the Archbishop himself, and the blacksmith and his dozen sons were covered with confusion to think that they had such a distinguished visitor without the means of receiving him in accordance with his station. But the Archbishop said:

"Blacksmith Arras, you and your sons would not wait for me to thank you; so I am now come to you that in presence of all these followers of mine I may pay fitting tribute to your loyalty and your bravery."

Then, indeed, did the modest blacksmith consider he had received more than ample compensation for what he had done, which, after all, as he told his neighbours, was merely his duty. So why should a man be thanked for it?

"Blacksmith," said the Archbishop, as he mounted his horse to return to Treves, "thanks cost little and are easily bestowed. I hope, however, to have a present for you that will show the whole country round how much I esteem true valour."

At the mouth of the Alf-thal, somewhat back from the small village of Alf and overlooking the Moselle, stands a conical hill that completely commands the valley. The Archbishop of Treves, having had a lesson regarding the dangers of an incursion through the volcanic region of the Eifel, put some hundreds of men at work on this conical hill, and erected on the top a strong castle, which was the wonder of the country. The year was nearing its end when this great stronghold was completed, and it began to be known throughout the land that the Archbishop intended to hold high revel there, and had invited to the castle all the nobles in the country, while the chief guest was no other than the Emperor himself. Then the neighbours of the blacksmith learned that a gift was about to be bestowed upon that stalwart man. He and his twelve sons received notification to attend at the castle, and to enjoy the whole week's festivity. He was commanded to come in his leathern apron, and to bring with him his huge sledge-hammer, which, the Archbishop said, had now become a weapon as honourable as the two-handed sword itself.

Never before had such an honour been bestowed upon a common man, and though the peasants were jubilant that one of their caste should be thus singled out to receive the favour of the famous Archbishop, and meet not only great nobles, but even the Emperor himself, still, it was gossiped that the Barons grumbled at this distinction being placed upon a serf like the blacksmith Arras, and none were so loud in their complaints as Count Bertrich, who had remained drinking in the castle while the blacksmith fought for the land. Nevertheless, all the nobility accepted the invitation of the powerful Archbishop of Treves, and assembled in the great room of the new castle, each equipped in all the gorgeous panoply of full armour. It had been rumoured among the nobles that the Emperor would not permit the Archbishop to sully the caste of knighthood by asking the Barons to recognise or hold converse with one in humble station of life. Indeed, had it been otherwise, Count Bertrich, with the Barons to back him, were resolved to speak out boldly to the Emperor, upholding the privileges of their class, and protesting against insult to it in presence of the blacksmith and his sons.

When all assembled in the great hall they found at the centre of the long side wall a magnificent throne erected, with a daïs in front of it, and on this throne sat, the Emperor in state, while at his right hand stood the lordly Archbishop of Treves. But what was more disquieting, they beheld also the blacksmith standing before the daïs, some distance in front of the Emperor, clad in his leathern apron, with his big brawny hands folded over the top of the handle of his huge sledge-hammer. Behind him were ranged his twelve sons. There were deep frowns on the brows of the nobles when they saw this, and, after kneeling and protesting their loyalty to the Emperor, they stood aloof and apart, leaving a clear space between themselves and the plebeian blacksmith on whom they cast lowering looks. When the salutations of the Emperor had been given, the Archbishop took a step forward on the daïs and spoke in a clear voice that could be heard to the furthermost corner of the room.

"My Lords," he said, "I have invited you hither that you may have the privilege of doing honour to a brave man. I ask you to salute the blacksmith Arras, who, when his country was in danger, crushed the invaders as effectually as ever his right arm, wielding sledge, crushed hot iron."

A red flush of confusion overspread the face of the blacksmith, but loud murmurs broke out among the nobility, and none stepped forward to salute him. One, indeed, stepped forward, but it was to appeal to the Emperor.

"Your Majesty," exclaimed Count Bertrich, "this is an unwarranted breach of our privileges. It is not meet that we, holding noble names, should be asked to consort with an untitled blacksmith. I appeal to your Majesty against the Archbishop under the feudal law."

All eyes turned upon the Emperor, who, after a pause, said:

"Count Bertrich is right, and I sustain his appeal."

An expression of triumph came into the red bibulous face of Count Bertrich, and the nobles shouted joyously:

"The Emperor, the Emperor!"

The Archbishop, however, seemed in no way non-plussed by his defeat, but, addressing the armourer, said:

"Advance, blacksmith, and do homage to your Emperor and mine."

When the blacksmith knelt before the throne, the Emperor, taking his jewelled sword from his side, smote the kneeling man lightly on his broad shoulders, saying:

"Arise, Count Arras, noble of the German Empire, and first Lord of the

410

Alf-thal."

The blacksmith rose slowly to his feet, bowed lowly to the Emperor, and backed to the place where he had formerly stood, again resting his hands on the handle of his sledge-hammer. The look of exultation faded from the face of Count Bertrich, and was replaced by an expression of dismay, for he had been until that moment, himself first Lord of the Alf-thal, with none second.

"My Lords," once more spoke up the Archbishop, "I ask you to salute Count Arras, first Lord of the Alf-thal."

No noble moved, and again Count Bertrich appealed to the Emperor.

"Are we to receive on terms of equality," he said, "a landless man; the count of a blacksmith's hut; a first lord of a forge? For the second time I appeal to your Majesty against such an outrage."

The Emperor replied calmly:

"Again I support the appeal of Count Bertrich."

There was this time no applause from the surrounding nobles, for many of them had some smattering idea of what was next to happen, though the muddled brain of Count Bertrich gave him no intimation of it.

"Count Arras," said the Archbishop, "I promised you a gift when last I left you at your smithy door. I now bestow upon you and your heirs forever this castle of Burg Arras, and the lands adjoining it. I ask you to hold it for me well and faithfully, as you held the pass of the Eifel. My Lords," continued the Archbishop, turning to the nobles, with a ring of menace in his voice, "I ask you to salute Count Arras, your equal in title, your equal in possessions, and the superior of any one of you in patriotism and bravery. If any noble question his courage, let him neglect to give Count of Burg Arras his title and salutation as he passes before him."

"Indeed, and that will not I," said the tall noble who had sat at Bertrich's right hand in his castle, "for, my Lords, if we hesitate longer, this doughty blacksmith will be Emperor before we know it." Then, advancing towards the ex-armourer, he said: "My Lord, Count of Burg Arras, it gives me pleasure to

411

salute you, and to hope that when Emperor or Archbishop are to be fought for, your arm will be no less powerful in a coat of mail than it was when you wore a leathern apron."

One by one the nobles passed and saluted as their leader had done. Count Bertrich hung back until the last, and then, as he passed the new Count of Burg Arras, he hissed at him, with a look of rage, the single word, "Blacksmith!"

The Count of Burg Arras, stirred to sudden anger, and forgetting in whose presence he stood, swung his huge sledge-hammer round his head, and brought it down on the armoured back of Count Bertrich, roaring the word "ANVIL!"

The armour splintered like crushed ice, and Count Bertrich fell prone on his face and lay there. There was instant cry of "Treason! Treason!" and shouts of "No man may draw arms in the Emperor's presence."

"My Lord Emperor," cried the Count of Burg Arras, "I crave pardon if I have done amiss. A man does not forget the tricks of his old calling when he takes on new honours. Your Majesty has said that I am a Count. This man, having heard your Majesty's word, proclaims me blacksmith, and so gave the lie to his Emperor. For this I struck him, and would again, even though he stood before the throne in a palace, or the altar in a cathedral. If that be treason, take from me your honours, and let me back to my forge, where this same hammer will mend the armour it has broken, or beat him out a new back-piece."

"You have broken no tenet of the feudal law," said the Emperor. "You have broken nothing, I trust, but the Count's armour, for, as I see, he is arousing himself, doubtless no bones are broken as well. The feudal law does not regard a blacksmith's hammer as a weapon. And as for treason, Count of Burg Arras, may my throne always be surrounded by such treason as yours."

And for centuries after, the descendants of the blacksmith were Counts of Burg Arras, and held the castle of that name, whose ruins to-day attest the excellence of the Archbishop's building.

COUNT KONRAD'S COURTSHIP

It was nearly midnight when Count Konrad von Hochstaden reached his castle on the Rhine, with a score of very tired and hungry men behind him. The warder at the gate of Schloss Hochstaden, after some cautious parley with the newcomers, joyously threw apart the two great iron-studded oaken leaves of the portal when he was convinced that it was indeed his young master who had arrived after some tumultuous years at the crusades, and Count Konrad with his followers rode clattering under the stone arch, into the ample courtyard. It is recorded that, in the great hall of the castle, the Count and his twenty bronzed and scarred knights ate such a meal as had never before been seen to disappear in Hochstaden, and that after drinking with great cheer to the downfall of the Saracene and the triumph of the true cross, they all lay on the floor of the Rittersaal and slept the remainder of the night, the whole of next day, and did not awaken until the dawn of the second morning. They had had years of hard fighting in the east, and on the way home they had been compelled to work their passage through the domains of turbulent nobles by good stout broadsword play, the only argument their opposers could understand, and thus they had come through to the Rhine without contributing aught to their opponents except fierce blows, which were not commodities as marketable as yellow gold, yet with this sole exchange did the twenty-one win their way from Palestine to the Palatinate, and thus were they so long on the road that those in Schloss Hochstaden had given up all expectation of their coming.

Count Konrad found that his father, whose serious illness was the cause of his return, had been dead for months past, and the young man wandered about the castle which, during the past few years, he had beheld only in dreams by night and in the desert mirages by day, saddened because of his loss. He would return to the Holy Land, he said to himself, and let the castle be looked after by its custodian until the war with the heathen was ended.

The young Count walked back and forth on the stone paved terrace which commanded from its height such a splendid view of the winding river, but he paid small attention to the landscape, striding along with his hands clasped behind him; his head bent, deep in thought. He was awakened from his reverie by the coming of the ancient custodian of the castle, who shuffled up to him and saluted him with reverential respect, for the Count was now the last of his race; a fighting line, whose members rarely came to die peaceably in their beds as Konrad's father had done.

The Count, looking up, swept his eye around the horizon and then to his astonishment saw the red battle flag flying grimly from the high northern tower of Castle Bernstein perched on the summit of the next hill to the south. In the valley were the white tents of an encampment, and fluttering over it was a flag whose device, at that distance, the Count could not discern.

"Why is the battle flag flying on Bernstein, Gottlieb, and what means those tents in the valley?" asked Konrad.

The old man looked in the direction of the encampment, as if the sight were new to him, but Konrad speedily saw that the opposite was the case. The tents had been there so long that they now seemed a permanent part of the scenery.

"The Archbishop of Cologne, my Lord, is engaged in the besiegement of Schloss Bernstein, and seems like to have a long job of it. He has been there for nearly a year now."

"Then the stout Baron is making a brave defence; good luck to him!"

"Alas, my Lord, I am grieved to state that the Baron went to his rest on the first day of the assault. He foolishly sallied out at the head of his men and fell hotly on the Archbishop's troops, who were surrounding the castle. There was some matter in dispute between the Baron and the Archbishop, and to aid the settlement thereof, his mighty Lordship of Cologne sent a thousand armed men up the river, and it is said that all he wished was to have parley with Baron Bernstein, and to overawe him in the discussion, but the Baron came out at the head of his men and fell upon the Cologne troops so mightily that he nearly put the whole battalion to flight, but the officers rallied their

414

panic-stricken host, seeing how few were opposed to them, and the order was given that the Baron should be taken prisoner, but the old man would not have it so, and fought so sturdily with his long sword, that he nearly entrenched himself with a wall of dead. At last the old man was cut down and died gloriously, with scarcely a square inch unwounded on his whole body. The officers of the Archbishop then tried to carry the castle by assault, but the Lady of Bernstein closed and barred the gate, ran, up the battle flag on the northern tower and bid defiance to the Archbishop and all his men."

"The Lady of Bernstein? I thought the Baron was a widower. Whom, then, did he again marry?"

"'Twas not his wife, but his daughter."

"His daughter? Not Brunhilda? She's but a child of ten."

"She was when you went away, my Lord, but now she is a woman of eighteen, with all the beauty of her mother and all the bravery of her father."

"Burning Cross of the East, Gottlieb! Do you mean to say that for a year a prince of the Church has been warring with a girl, and her brother, knowing nothing of this cowardly assault, fighting the battles for his faith on the sands of the desert? Let the bugle sound! Call up my men and arouse those who are still sleeping."

"My Lord, my Lord, I beg of you to have caution in this matter."

"Caution? God's patience! Has caution rotted the honour out of the bones of all Rhine men, that this outrage should pass unmolested before their eyes! The father murdered; the daughter beleaguered; while those who call themselves men sleep sound in their safe castles! Out of my way, old man! Throw open the gates!"

But the ancient custodian stood firmly before his over-lord, whose red angry face seemed like that of the sun rising so ruddily behind him.

"My Lord, if you insist on engaging in this enterprise it must be gone about sanely. You need the old head as well as the young arm. You have a score of well-seasoned warriors, and we can gather into the castle another hundred. But the Archbishop has a thousand men around Bernstein. Your score would but meet the fate of the old Baron and would not better the case of those within the castle. The Archbishop has not assaulted Bernstein since the Baron's death, but has drawn a tight line around it and so has cut off all supplies, daily summoning the maiden to surrender. What they now need in Bernstein is not iron, but food. Through long waiting they keep slack watch about the castle, and it is possible that, with care taken at midnight, you might reprovision Bernstein so that she could hold out until her brother comes, whom it is said she has summoned from the Holy Land."

"Thou art wise, old Gottlieb," said the Count slowly, pausing in his wrath as the difficulties of the situation were thus placed in array before him; "wise and cautious, as all men seem to be who now keep ward on the Rhine. What said my father regarding this contest?"

"My Lord, your honoured father was in his bed stricken with the long illness that came to be his undoing at the last, and we never let him know that the Baron was dead or the siege in progress."

"Again wise and cautious, Gottlieb, for had he known it, he would have risen from his deathbed, taken down his two-handed sword from the wall, and struck his last blow in defence of the right against tyranny."

"Indeed, my Lord, under danger of your censure, I venture to say that you do not yet know the cause of the quarrel into which you design to precipitate yourself. It may not be tyranny on the part of the overlord, but disobedience on the part of the vassal, which causes the environment of Bernstein. And the Archbishop is a prince of our holy Church."

"I leave those nice distinctions to philosophers like thee, Gottlieb. It is enough for me to know that a thousand men are trying to starve one woman, and as for being a prince of the Church, I shall give his devout Lordship a taste of religion hot from its birthplace, and show him how we uphold the cause in the East, for in this matter the Archbishop grasps not the cross but the sword, and by the sword shall he be met. And now go, Gottlieb, set ablaze the fires on all our ovens and put the bakers at work. Call in your hundred men as speedily as possible, and bid each man bring with him a sack of wheat.

416

Spend the day at the baking and fill the cellars with grain and wine. It will be reason enough, if any make inquiry, to say that the young Lord has returned and intends to hold feasts in his castle. Send hither my Captain to me."

Old Gottlieb hobbled away, and there presently came upon the terrace a stalwart, grizzled man, somewhat past middle age, whose brown face showed more seams of scars than remnants of beauty. He saluted his chief and stood erect in silence.

The Count waved his hand toward the broad valley and said grimly:

"There sits the Archbishop of Cologne, besieging the Castle of Bernstein."

The Captain bowed low and crossed himself.

"God prosper his Lordship," he said piously.

"You may think that scarcely the phrase to use, Captain, when I tell you that you will lead an assault on his Lordship to-night."

"Then God prosper us, my Lord," replied the Captain cheerfully, for he was ever a man who delighted more in fighting than in inquiring keenly into the cause thereof.

"You may see from here that a ridge runs round from this castle, bending back from the river, which it again approaches, touching thus Schloss Bernstein. There is a path along the summit of the ridge which I have often trodden as a boy, so I shall be your guide. It is scarce likely that this path is guarded, but if it is we will have to throw its keepers over the precipice; those that we do not slay outright, when we come upon them."

"Excellent, my Lord, most excellent," replied the Captain, gleefully rubbing his huge hands one over the other.

"But it is not entirely to fight that we go. You are to act as convoy to those who carry bread to Castle Bernstein. We shall leave here at the darkest hour after midnight and you must return before daybreak so that the Archbishop cannot estimate our numbers. Then get out all the old armour there is in the castle and masquerade the peasants in it. Arrange them along the battlements so that they will appear as numerous as possible while I stay in Castle Bernstein and make terms with the Archbishop, for it seems he out-mans us, so we must resort, in some measure, to strategy. On the night assault let each man yell as if he were ten and lay about him mightily. Are the knaves astir yet?"

"Most of them, my Lord, and drinking steadily the better to endure the dryness of the desert when we go eastward again."

"Well, see to it that they do not drink so much as to interfere with clean sword-play against to-night's business."

"Indeed, my Lord, I have a doubt if there is Rhine wine enough in the castle's vaults to do that, and the men yell better when they have a few gallons within them."

At the appointed hour Count Konrad and his company went silently forth, escorting a score more who carried sacks of the newly baked bread on their backs, or leathern receptacles filled with wine, as well as a stout cask of the same seductive fluid. Near the Schloss Bernstein the rescuing party came upon the Archbishop's outpost, who raised the alarm before the good sword of the Captain cut through the cry. There were bugle calls throughout the camp and the sound of men hurrying to their weapons, but all the noise of preparation among the besiegers was as nothing to the demoniac din sent up by the Crusaders, who rushed to the onslaught with a zest sharpened by their previous rest and inactivity. The wild barbaric nature of their yells, such as never before were heard on the borders of the placid Rhine, struck consternation into the opposition camp, because some of the Archbishop's troops had fought against the heathen in the East, and they now recognised the clamour which had before, on many an occasion, routed them, and they thought that the Saracenes had turned the tables and invaded Germany; indeed from the deafening clamour it seemed likely that all Asia was let loose upon them. The alarm spread quickly to Castle Bernstein itself, and torches began to glimmer on its battlements. With a roar the Crusaders rushed up to the foot of the wall, as a wave dashes against a rock, sweeping the frightened bread-carriers with them. By the light of the torches Konrad saw standing on

418

the wall a fair young girl clad in chain armour whose sparkling links glistened like countless diamonds in the rays of the burning pitch. She leaned on the cross-bar of her father's sword and, with wide-open, eager eyes peered into the darkness beyond, questioning the gloom for reason of the terrifying tumult. When Konrad strode within the radius of the torches, the girl drew back slightly and cried:

"So the Archbishop has at last summoned courage to attack, after all this patient waiting."

"My Lady," shouted the Count, "these are my forces and not the Archbishop's. I am Konrad, Count of Hochstaden."

"The more shame, then, that you, who have fought bravely with men, should now turn your weapons against a woman, and she your neighbour and the sister of your friend."

"Indeed, Lady Brunhilda, you misjudge me. I am come to your rescue and not to your disadvantage.. The Archbishop's men were put to some inconvenience by our unexpected arrival, and to gather from the sounds far down the valley they have not ceased running yet. We come with bread, and use the sword but as a spit to deliver it."

"Your words are welcome were I but sure of their truth," said the lady with deep distrust in her tone, for she had had experience of the Archbishop's craft on many occasions, and the untimely hour of the succour led her to fear a ruse. "I open my gates neither to friend nor to foe in the darkness," she added.

"Tis a rule that may well be commended to others of your bewitching sex," replied the Count, "but we ask not the opening of the gates, although you might warn those within your courtyard to beware what comes upon them presently."

So saying, he gave the word, and each two of his servitors seized a sack of bread by the ends and, heaving it, flung it over the wall. Some of the sacks fell short, but the second effort sent them into the courtyard, where many of them burst, scattering the round loaves along the cobble-stoned pavement, to be eagerly pounced upon by the starving servitors and such men-at-arms as had escaped from the encounter with the Archbishop's troops when the Baron was slain. The cries of joy that rang up from within the castle delighted the ear of the Count and softened the suspicion of the lady on the wall.

"Now," cried Konrad to his Captain, "back to Schloss Hochstaden before the dawn approaches too closely, and let there be no mistake in the Archbishop's camp that you are on the way."

They all departed in a series of earsplitting, heart-appalling whoops that shattered the still night air and made a vocal pandemonium of that portion of the fair Rhine valley. The colour left the cheeks of the Lady of Bernstein as she listened in palpable terror to the fiendish outcry which seemed to scream for blood and that instantly, looking down she saw the Knight of Hochstaden still there at the foot of her wall gazing up at her.

"My Lord," she said with concern, "if you stay thus behind your noisy troop you will certainly be captured when it comes day."

"My Lady of Bernstein, I am already a captive, and all the Archbishop's men could not hold me more in thrall did they surround me at this moment."

"I do not understand you, sir," said Brunhilda coldly, drawing herself up with a dignity that well became her, "your language seems to partake of an exaggeration that doubtless you have learned in the tropical East, and which we have small patience with on the more temperate banks of the Rhine."

"The language that I use, fair Brunhilda, knows neither east nor west; north nor south, but is common to every land, and if it be a stranger to the Rhine, the Saints be witness 'tis full time 'twere introduced here, and I hold myself as competent to be its spokesman, as those screeching scoundrels of mine hold themselves the equal in battle to all the archbishops who ever wore the robes of that high office."

"My Lord," cried Brunhilda, a note of serious warning in her voice, "my gates are closed and they remain so. I hold myself your debtor for unasked aid, and would fain see you in a place of safety."

"My reverenced Lady, that friendly wish shall presently be gratified," and saying this, the Count unwound from his waist a thin rope woven of horse-hair, having a long loop at the end of it. This he whirled round his head and with an art learned in the scaling of eastern walls flung the loop so that it surrounded one of the machicolations of the bastion, and, with his feet travelling against the stone work, he walked up the wall by aid of this cord and was over the parapet before any could hinder his ascent. The Maid of the Schloss, her brows drawn down in anger, stood with sword ready to strike, but whether it was the unwieldiness of the clumsy weapon, or whether it was the great celerity with which the young man put his nimbleness to the test, or whether it was that she recognised him as perhaps her one friend on earth, who can tell; be that as it may, she did not strike in time, and a moment, later the Count dropped on one knee and before she knew it raised one of her hands to his bending lips.

"Lovely Warder of Bernstein," cried Count Konrad, with a tremor of emotion in his voice that thrilled the girl in spite of herself, "I lay my devotion and my life at your feet, to use them as you will."

"My Lord," she said quaveringly, with tears nearer the surface than she would have cared to admit, "I like not this scaling of the walls; my permission unasked."

"God's truth, my Lady, and you are not the first to so object, but the others were men, and I may say, without boasting, that I bent not the knee to them when I reached their level, but I have been told that custom will enable a maid to look more forgivingly on such escapades if her feeling is friendly toward the invader, and I am bold enough to hope that the friendship with which your brother has ever regarded me in the distant wars, may be extended to my unworthy self by his sister at home."

Count Konrad rose to his feet and the girl gazed at him in silence, seeing how bronzed and manly he looked in his light well-polished eastern armour, which had not the cumbrous massiveness of western mail, but, while amply protecting the body, bestowed upon it lithe freedom for quick action; and unconsciously she compared him, not to his disadvantage, with the cravens on the Rhine, who, while sympathising with her, dared not raise weapon on

421

her behalf against so powerful an over-lord as the warlike Archbishop. The scarlet cross of the Crusader on his broad breast seemed to her swimming eyes to blaze with lambent flame in the yellow torchlight. She dared not trust her voice to answer him, fearing its faintness might disown the courage with which she had held her castle for so long, and he, seeing that she struggled to hold control of herself, standing there like a superb Goddess of the Rhine, pretended to notice nothing and spoke jauntily with a wave of his hand: "My villains have brought to the foot of the walls a cask of our best wine which we dared not adventure to cast into the courtyard with that freedom which forwarded the loaves; there is also a packet of dainties more suited to your Ladyship's consideration than the coarse bread from our ovens. Give command, I beg of you, that the gates be opened and that your men bring the wine and food to safety within the courtyard, and bestow on me the privilege of guarding the open gate while this is being done."

Then gently, with insistent deference, the young man took from her the sword of her father which she yielded to him with visible reluctance, but nevertheless yielded, standing there disarmed before him. Together in silence they went down the stone steps that led from the battlements to the courtyard, followed by the torch-bearers, whom the lightening east threatened soon to render unnecessary. A cheer went up, the first heard for many days within those walls, and the feasters, flinging their caps in the air, cried "Hochstaden! Hochstaden!" The Count turned to his fair companion and said, with a smile:

"The garrison is with me, my Lady."

She smiled also, and sighed, but made no other reply, keeping her eyes steadfast on the stone steps beneath her. Once descended, she gave the order in a low voice, and quickly the gates were thrown wide, creaking grumblingly on their hinges, long unused. Konrad stood before the opening with the sword of Bernstein in his hands, swinging it this way and that to get the hang of it, and looking on it with the admiration which a warrior ever feels for a well hung, trusty blade, while the men-at-arms nodded to one another and said: "There stands a man who knows the use of a weapon. I would that he had the crafty Archbishop before him to practise on."

When the barrel was trundled in, the Lady of Bernstein had it broached at once, and with her own hand served to each of her men a flagon of the golden wine. Each took his portion, bowing low to the lady, then doffing cap, drank first to the Emperor, and after with an enthusiasm absent from the Imperial toast, to the young war lord whom the night had flung thus unexpectedly among them. When the last man had refreshed himself, the Count stepped forward and begged a flagon full that he might drink in such good company, and it seemed that Brunhilda had anticipated such a request, for she turned to one of her women and held out her hand, receiving a huge silver goblet marvellously engraved that had belonged to her forefathers, and plenishing it, she gave it to the Count, who, holding it aloft, cried, "The Lady of Bernstein," whereupon there arose such a shout that the troubled Archbishop heard it in his distant tent.

"And yet further of your hospitality must I crave," said Konrad, "for the morning air is keen, and gives me an appetite for food of which I am deeply ashamed, but which nevertheless clamours for an early breakfast."

The lady, after giving instruction to the maids who waited upon her, led the way into the castle, where Konrad following, they arrived in the long Rittersaal, at the end of which, facing the brightening east, was placed a huge window of stained glass, whose great breadth was gradually lightening as if an unseen painter with magic brush was tinting the glass with transparent colour, from the lofty timbered ceiling to the smoothly polished floor. At the end of the table, with her back to the window, Brunhilda sat, while the Count took a place near her, by the side, turning so that he faced her, the ever-increasing radiance illumining his scintillating armour. The girl ate sparingly, saying little and glancing often at her guest. He fell to like the good trencherman he was, and talked unceasingly of the wars in the East, and the brave deeds done there, and as he talked the girl forgot all else, rested her elbows on the table and her chin in her hands, regarding him intently, for he spoke not of himself but of her brother, and of how, when grievously pressed, he had borne himself so nobly that more than once, seemingly certain defeat was changed into glorious victory. Now and then when Konrad gazed upon Brunhilda, his eloquent tongue faltered for a moment and he lost the thread of his narrative, for all trace of the warrior maid had departed, and there, outlined against the glowing window of dazzling colours, she seemed indeed a saint with her halo of golden hair, a fit companion to the angels that the marvellous skill of the artificer had placed in that gorgeous collection of pictured panes, lead-lined and cut in various shapes, answering the needs of their gifted designer, as a paint-brush follows the will of the artist. From where the young man sat, the girl against the window seemed a member of that radiant company, and thus he paused stricken speechless by her beauty.

She spoke at last, the smile on her lips saddened by the down turning of their corners, her voice the voice of one hovering uncertain between laughter and tears.

"And you," she said, "you seem to have had no part in all this stirring recital. It was my brother and my brother and my brother, and to hear you one would think you were all the while hunting peacefully in your Rhine forests. Yet still I do believe the Count of Hochstaden gave the heathen to know he was somewhat further to the east of Germany."

"Oh, of me," stammered the Count. "Yes, I was there, it is true, and sometimes—well, I have a fool of a captain, headstrong and reckless, who swept me now and then into a melee, before I could bring cool investigation to bear upon his mad projects, and once in the fray of course I had to plead with my sword to protect my head, otherwise my bones would now be on the desert sands, so I selfishly lay about me and did what I could to get once more out of the turmoil."

The rising sun now struck living colour into the great window of stained glass, splashing the floor and the further wall with crimson and blue and gold. Count Konrad sprang to his feet. "The day is here," he cried, standing in the glory of it, while the girl rose more slowly. "Let us have in your bugler and see if he has forgotten the battle call of the Bernsteins. Often have I heard it in the desert. 'Give us the battle call,' young Heinrich would cry and then to its music all his followers would shout 'Bernstein! Bernstein!' until it seemed the far-off horizon must have heard."

The trumpeter came, and being now well fed, blew valiantly, giving to the echoing roof the war cry of the generations of fighting men it had sheltered.

"That is it," cried the Count, "and it has a double significance. A challenge on the field, and a summons to parley when heard from the walls. We shall now learn whether or no the Archbishop has forgotten it, and I crave your permission to act as spokesman with his Lordship."

"That I most gratefully grant," said the Lady of the Castle.

Once more on the battlements, the Lord of Hochstaden commanded the trumpeter to sound the call The martial music rang out in the still morning air and was echoed mockingly by the hills on the other side of the river. After that, all was deep silence.

"Once again," said Konrad.

For a second time the battle blast filled the valley, and for a second time returned faintly back from the hills. Then from near the great tent of the Archbishop, by the margin of the stream, came the answering call, accepting the demand for a parley.

When at last the Archbishop, mounted on a black charger, came slowly up the winding path which led to the castle, attended by only two of his officers, he found the Count of Hochstaden awaiting him on the battlements above the gate. The latter's hopes arose when he saw that Cologne himself had come, and had not entrusted the business to an envoy, and it was also encouraging to note that he came so poorly attended, for when a man has made up his mind to succumb he wishes as few witnesses as possible, while if he intends further hostilities, he comes in all the pomp of his station.

"With whom am I to hold converse?" began the Archbishop, "I am here at the behest of the Bernstein call to parley, but I see none, of that name on the wall to greet me."

"Heinrich, Baron Bernstein, is now on his way to his castle from the Holy Land, and were he here it were useless for me to summon a parley, for he would answer you with the sword and not with the tongue when he learned his father was dead at your hand."

"That is no reply to my question. With whom do I hold converse?"

"I am Konrad, Count of Hochstaden, and your Lordship's vassal."

"I am glad to learn of your humility and pleased to know that I need not call your vassalage to your memory, but I fear that in the darkness you have less regard for either than you now pretend in the light of day."

"In truth, my Lord, you grievously mistake me, for in the darkness I stood your friend. I assure you I had less than a thousand rascals at my back last night, and yet nothing would appease them but that they must fling themselves upon your whole force, had I not held them in check. I told them you probably outnumbered us ten to one, but they held that one man who had gone through an eastern campaign was worth ten honest burghers from Cologne, which indeed I verily believe, and for the fact that you were not swept into the Rhine early this morning you have me and my peaceful nature to thank, my Lord. Perhaps you heard the rogues discussing the matter with me before dawn, and going angrily home when I so ordered them."

"A man had need to be dead and exceedingly deep in his grave not to have heard them," growled the Archbishop.

"And there they stand at this moment, my Lord, doubtless grumbling among themselves that I am so long giving the signal they expect, which will permit them to finish this morning's work. The men I can generally control, but my captains are a set of impious cut-throats who would sooner sack an Archbishop's palace than listen to the niceties of the feudal law which protects over-lords from such pleasantries."

The Archbishop turned on his horse and gazed on the huge bulk of Schloss Hochstaden, and there a wonderful sight met his eye. The walls bristled with armed men, the sun glistening on their polished breastplates like the shimmer of summer lightning. The Archbishop turned toward the gate again, as though the sight he beheld brought small comfort to him.

"What is your desire?" he said with less of truculence in his tone than there had been at the beginning.

"I hold it a scandal," said the Count gravely, "that a prince of the Church

426

should assault Christian walls while their owner is absent in the East venturing his life in the uplifting of the true faith. You can now retreat without loss of prestige; six hours hence that may be impossible. I ask you then to give your assurance to the Lady of Bernstein, pledging your knightly word that she will be no longer threatened by you, and I ask you to withdraw your forces immediately to Cologne where it is likely they will find something to do if Baron Heinrich, as I strongly suspect, marches directly on that city."

"I shall follow the advice of my humble vassal, for the strength of a prince is in the sage counsel of his war lords. Will you escort the lady to the battlements?"

Then did Count Konrad von Hochstaden see that his cause was won, and descending he came up again, leading the Lady Brunhilda by the hand.

"I have to acquaint you, madame," said the Archbishop, "that the siege is ended, and I give you my assurance that you will not again be beleaguered by my forces."

The Lady of Bernstein bowed, but made no answer. She blushed deeply that the Count still held her hand, but she did not withdraw it.

"And now, my Lord Archbishop, that this long-held contention is amicably adjusted," began Von Hochstaden, "I crave that you bestow on us two your gracious blessing, potentate of the Church, for this lady is to be my wife."

"What!" cried Brunhilda in sudden anger, snatching her hand from his, "do you think you can carry me by storm as you did my castle, without even asking my consent?"

"Lady of my heart," said Konrad tenderly, "I did ask your consent. My eyes questioned in the Rittersaal and yours gave kindly answer. Is there then no language but that which is spoken? I offer you here before the world my open hand; is it to remain empty?"

He stood before her with outstretched palm, and she gazed steadfastly at him, breathing quickly. At length a smile dissolved the sternness of her charming lips, she glanced at his extended hand and said:

"'Twere a pity so firm and generous a hand should remain tenantless," and with that she placed her palm in his.

The Archbishop smiled grimly at this lovers' by-play, then solemnly, with upraised hands, invoked God's blessing upon them.

THE LONG LADDER

Every fortress has one traitor within its walls; the Schloss Eltz had two. In this, curiously enough, lay its salvation; for as some Eastern poisons when mixed neutralise each other and form combined a harmless fluid, so did the two traitors unwittingly react, the one upon the other, to the lasting glory of Schloss Eltz, which has never been captured to this day.

It would be difficult to picture the amazement of Heinrich von Richenbach when he sat mute upon his horse at the brow of the wooded heights and, for the first time, beheld the imposing pile which had been erected by the Count von Eltz. It is startling enough to come suddenly upon a castle where no castle should be; but to find across one's path an erection that could hardly have been the product of other agency than the lamp of Aladdin was stupefying, and Heinrich drew the sunburned back of his hand across his eyes, fearing that they were playing him a trick; then seeing the wondrous vision still before him, he hastily crossed himself, an action performed somewhat clumsily through lack of practice, so that he might ward off enchantment, if, as seemed likely, that mountain of pinnacles was the work of the devil, and not placed there, stone on stone, by the hand of man. But in spite of crossing and the clearing of his eyes, Eltz Castle remained firmly seated on its stool of rock, and, when his first astonishment had somewhat abated, Von Richenbach, who was a most practical man, began to realise that here, purely by a piece of unbelievable good luck, the very secret he had been sent to unravel had been stumbled upon, the solving of which he had given up in despair, returning empty-handed to his grim master, the redoubtable Archbishop Baldwin of Treves.

It was now almost two months since the Archbishop had sent him on the mission to the Rhine from which he was returning as wise as he went, well knowing that a void budget would procure him scant welcome from his imperious ruler. Here, at least, was important matter for the warlike Elector's stern consideration—an apparently impregnable fortress secretly built in the very centre of the Archbishop's domain; and knowing that the Count von Eltz claimed at least partial jurisdiction over this district, more especially that portion known as the Eltz-thal, in the middle of which this mysterious citadel had been erected. Heinrich rightly surmised that its construction had been the work of this ancient enemy of the Archbishop.

Two months before, or nearly so, Heinrich von Richenbach had been summoned into the presence of the Lion of Treves at his palace in that venerable city. When Baldwin had dismissed all within the room save only Von Richenbach, the august prelate said:

"It is my pleasure that you take horse at once and proceed to my city of Mayence on the Rhine, where I am governor. You will inspect the garrison there and report to me."

Heinrich bowed, but said nothing.

"You will then go down the Rhine to Elfield, where my new castle is built, and I shall be pleased to have an opinion regarding it."

The Archbishop paused, and again his vassal bowed and remained silent.

"It is my wish that you go without escort, attracting as little attention as possible, and perhaps it may be advisable to return by the northern side of the Moselle, but some distance back from the river, as there are barons on the banks who might inquire your business, and regret their curiosity when they found they questioned a messenger of mine. We should strive, during our brief sojourn on this inquisitive earth, to put our fellow creatures to as little discomfort as possible."

Von Richenbach saw that he was being sent on a secret and possibly dangerous mission, and he had been long enough in the service of the crafty Archbishop to know that the reasons ostensibly given for his journey were probably not those which were the cause of it, so he contented himself with inclining his head for the third time and holding his peace. The Archbishop regarded him keenly for a few moments, a derisive smile parting his firm lips; then said, as if his words were an afterthought:

"Our faithful vassal, the Count von Eltz, is, if I mistake not, a neighbor of ours at Elfield?"

The sentence took, through its inflection, the nature of a query, and for the first time Heinrich von Richenbach ventured reply.

"He is, my Lord."

The Archbishop raised his eyes to the vaulted ceiling, and seemed for a time lost in thought, saying, at last, apparently in soliloquy, rather than by direct address:

"Count von Eltz has been suspiciously quiet of late for a man so impetuous by nature. It might be profitable to know what interests him during this unwonted seclusion. It behooves us to acquaint ourselves with the motives that actuate a neighbour, so that, opportunity arising, we may aid him with counsel or encouragement. If, therefore, it should so chance that, in the intervals of your inspection of governorship or castle, aught regarding the present occupation of the noble count comes to your ears, the information thus received may perhaps remain in your memory until you return to Treves."

The Archbishop withdrew his eyes from the ceiling, the lids lowering over them, and flashed a keen, rapier-like glance at the man who stood before him.

Heinrich von Richenbach made low obeisance and replied:

"Whatever else fades from my memory, my Lord, news of Count von Eltz shall remain there."

"See that you carry nothing upon you, save your commission as inspector, which my secretary will presently give to you. If you are captured it will be enough to proclaim yourself my emissary and exhibit your commission in proof of the peaceful nature of your embassy. And now to horse and away."

Thus Von Richenbach, well mounted, with his commission legibly engrossed in clerkly hand on parchment, departed on the Roman road for Mayence, but neither there nor at Elfield could he learn more of Count von Eltz than was already known at Treves, which was to the effect that this nobleman, repenting him, it was said, of his stubborn opposition to the

Archbishop, had betaken himself to the Crusades in expiation of his wrong in shouldering arms against one who was both his temporal and spiritual over-lord; and this rumour coming to the ears of Baldwin, had the immediate effect of causing that prince of the Church to despatch Von Richenbach with the purpose of learning accurately what his old enemy was actually about; for Baldwin, being an astute man, placed little faith in sudden conversion.

When Heinrich von Richenbach returned to Treves he was immediately ushered into the presence of his master.

"You have been long away," said the Archbishop, a frown on his brow. "I trust the tidings you bring offer some slight compensation for the delay." Then was Heinrich indeed glad that fate, rather than his own perspicacity, had led his horse to the heights above Schloss Eltz.

"The tidings I bring, my Lord, are so astounding that I could not return to Treves without verifying them. This led me far afield, for my information was of the scantiest; but I am now enabled to vouch for the truth of my well-nigh incredible intelligence."

"Have the good deeds of the Count then translated him bodily to heaven, as was the case with Elijah? Unloose your packet, man, and waste not so much time in the vaunting of your wares."

"The Count von Eltz, my Lord, has built a castle that is part palace, part fortress, and in its latter office well-nigh impregnable."

"Yes? And where?"

"In the Eltz-thal, my Lord, a league and a quarter from the Moselle."

"Impossible!" cried Baldwin, bringing his clenched fist down on the table before him. "Impossible! You have been misled, Von Richenbach."

"Indeed, my Lord, I had every reason to believe so until I viewed the structure with my own eyes."

"This, then, is the fruit of Von Eltz's contrition! To build a castle without permission within my jurisdiction, and defy me in my own domain. By the

Coat, he shall repent his temerity and wish himself twice over a captive of the Saracen ere I have done with him. I will despatch at once an army to the Eltz-thal, and there shall not be left one stone upon another when it returns."

"My Lord, I beseech you not to move with haste in this matter. If twenty thousand men marched up to the Eltz-thal they could not take the castle. No such schloss was ever built before, and none to equal it will ever be built again, unless, as I suspect to be the case in this instance, the devil lends his aid."

"Oh, I doubt not that Satan built it, but he took the form and name of Count von Eltz while doing so," replied the Archbishop, his natural anger at this bold defiance of his power giving way to his habitual caution, which, united with his resources and intrepidity, had much to do with his success. "You hold the castle, then, to be unassailable. Is its garrison so powerful, or its position so strong?"

"The strength of its garrison, my Lord, is in its weakness; I doubt if there are a score of men in the castle, but that is all the better, as there are fewer mouths to feed in case of siege, and the Count has some four years' supplies in his vaults. The schloss is situated on a lofty, unscalable rock that stands in the centre of a valley, as if it were a fortress itself. Then the walls of the building are of unbelievable height, with none of the round or square towers which castles usually possess, but having in plenty conical turrets, steep roofs, and the like, which give it the appearance of a fairy palace in a wide, enchanted amphitheatre of green wooded hills, making the Schloss Eltz, all in all, a most miraculous sight, such as a man may not behold in many years' travel."

"In truth, Von Richenbach," said the Archbishop, with a twinkle in his eye, "we should have made you one of our scrivening monks rather than a warrior, so marvellously do you describe the entrancing handiwork of our beloved vassal, the Count von Eltz. Perhaps you think it pity to destroy so fascinating a creation."

"Not so, my Lord. I have examined the castle well, and I think were I entrusted with the commission I could reduce it."

"Ah, now we have modesty indeed! You can take the stronghold where

I should fail."

"I did not say that you would fail, my Lord. I said that twenty thousand men marching up the valley would fail, unless they were content to sit around the castle for four years or more."

"Answered like a courtier, Heinrich. What, then, is your method of attack?"

"On the height to the east, which is the nearest elevation to the castle, a strong fortress might be built, that would in a measure command the Schloss Eltz, although I fear the distance would be too great for any catapult to fling stones within its courtyard. Still, we might thus have complete power over the entrance to the schloss, and no more provender could be taken in."

"You mean, then, to wear Von Eltz out? That would be as slow a method as besiegement."

"To besiege would require an army, my Lord, and would have this disadvantage, that, besides withdrawing from other use so many of your men, rumour would spread abroad that the Count held you in check. The building of a fortress on the height would merely be doing what the Count has already done, and it could be well garrisoned by twoscore men at the most, vigilant night and day to take advantage of any movement of fancied security to force way into the castle. There need be no formal declaration of hostilities, but a fortress built in all amicableness, to which the Count could hardly object, as you would be but following his own example."

"I understand. We build a house near his for neighbourliness. There is indeed much in your plan that commends itself to me, but I confess a liking for the underlying part of a scheme. Remains there anything else which you have not unfolded to me?"

"Placing in command of the new fortress a stout warrior who was at the same time a subtle man——"

"In other words, thyself, Heinrich—well, what then?"

"There is every chance that such a general may learn much of the castle from one or other of its inmates. It might be possible that, through neglect or inadvertence, the drawbridge would be left down some night and the portcullis raised. In other words, the castle, impervious to direct assault, may fall by strategy."

"Excellent, excellent, my worthy warrior! I should dearly love to have captain of mine pay such an informal visit to his estimable Countship. We shall build the fortress you suggest, and call it Baldwineltz. You shall be its commander, and I now bestow upon you Schloss Eltz, the only proviso being that you are to enter into possession of it by whatever means you choose to use."

Thus the square, long castle of Baldwineltz came to be builded, and thus Heinrich von Richenbach, brave, ingenious, and unscrupulous, was installed captain of it, with twoscore men to keep him company, together with a plentiful supply of gold to bribe whomsoever he thought worth suborning.

Time went on without much to show for its passing, and Heinrich began to grow impatient, for his attempt at corrupting the garrison showed that negotiations were not without their dangers. Stout Baumstein, captain of the gate, was the man whom Heinrich most desired to purchase, for Baumstein could lessen the discipline at the portal of Schloss Eltz without attracting undue attention. But he was an irascible German, whose strong right arm was readier than his tongue; and when Heinrich's emissary got speech with him, under a flag of truce, whispering that much gold might be had for a casual raising of the portcullis and lowering of the drawbridge, Baumstein at first could not understand his purport, for he was somewhat thick in the skull; but when the meaning of the message at last broke in upon him, he wasted no time in talk, but, raising his ever-ready battle-axe, clove the Envoy to the midriff. The Count von Eltz himself, coming on the scene at this moment, was amazed at the deed, and sternly demanded of his gate-captain why he had violated the terms of a parley. Baumstein's slowness of speech came near to being the undoing of him, for at first he merely said that such creatures as the messenger should not be allowed to live and that an honest soldier was insulted by holding converse with him; whereupon the Count, having nice notions, picked up in polite countries, regarding the sacredness of a flag of truce, was about to hang Baumstein, scant though the garrison was, and even then it was but by chance that the true state of affairs became known to the Count. He was on the point of sending back the body of the Envoy to Von Richenbach with suitable apology for his destruction and offer of recompense, stating that the assailant would be seen hanging outside the gate, when Baumstein said that while he had no objection to being hanged if it so pleased the Count, he begged to suggest that the gold which the Envoy brought with him to bribe the garrison should be taken from the body before it was returned, and divided equally among the guard at the gate. As Baumstein said this, he was taking off his helmet and unbuckling his corselet, thus freeing his neck for the greater convenience of the castle hangman. When the Count learned that the stout stroke of the battle-axe was caused by the proffer of a bribe for the betraying of the castle, he, to the amazement of all present, begged the pardon of Baumstein; for such a thing was never before known under the feudal law that a noble should apologise to a common man, and Baumstein himself muttered that he wot not what the world was coming to if a mighty Lord might not hang an underling if it so pleased him, cause or no cause.

The Count commanded the body to be searched, and finding thereon some five bags of gold, distributed the coin among his men, as a good commander should, sending back the body to Von Richenbach, with a most polite message to the effect that as the Archbishop evidently intended the money to be given to the garrison, the Count had endeavoured to carry out his Lordship's wishes, as was the duty of an obedient vassal. But Heinrich, instead of being pleased with the courtesy of the message, broke into violent oaths, and spread abroad in the land the false saying that Count von Eltz had violated a flag of truce.

But there was one man in the castle who did not enjoy a share of the gold, because he was not a warrior, but a servant of the Countess. This was a Spaniard named Rego, marvellously skilled in the concocting of various dishes of pastry and other niceties such as high-born ladies have a fondness for. Rego was disliked by the Count, and, in fact, by all the stout Germans who formed the garrison, not only because it is the fashion for men of one country justly to abhor those of another, foreigners being in all lands regarded as benighted creatures whom we marvel that the Lord allows to live when he might so easily have peopled the whole world with men like unto ourselves; but, aside from this, Rego had a cat-like tread, and a furtive eye that never met another honestly as an eye should. The count, however, endured the presence of this Spaniard, because the Countess admired his skill in confections, then unknown in Germany, and thus Rego remained under her orders.

The Spaniard's eye glittered when he saw the yellow lustre of the gold, and his heart was bitter that he did not have a share of it. He soon learned where it came from, and rightly surmised that there was more in the same treasury, ready to be bestowed for similar service to that which the unready Baumstein had so emphatically rejected; so Rego, watching his opportunity, stole away secretly to Von Richenbach and offered his aid in the capture of the castle, should suitable compensation be tendered him. Heinrich questioned him closely regarding the interior arrangements of the castle, and asked him if he could find any means of letting down the drawbridge and raising the portcullis in the night. This, Rego said quite truly, was impossible, as the guard at the gate, vigilant enough before, had become much more so since the attempted bribery of the Captain. There was, however, one way by which the castle might be entered, and that entailed a most perilous adventure. There was a platform between two of the lofty, steep roofs, so elevated that it gave a view over all the valley. On this platform a sentinel was stationed night and day, whose duty was that of outlook, like a man on the cross-trees of a ship. From this platform a stair, narrow at the top, but widening as it descended to the lower stories, gave access to the whole castle. If, then, a besieger constructed a ladder of enormous length, it might be placed at night on the narrow ledge of rock far below this platform, standing almost perpendicular, and by this means man after man would be enabled to reach the roof of the castle, and, under the guidance of Rego, gain admittance to the lower rooms unsuspected.

"But the sentinel?" objected Von Richenbach.

"The sentinel I will myself slay. I will steal up behind him in the night when you make your assault, and running my knife into his neck, fling him over the castle wall; then I shall be ready to guide you down into the courtyard."

Von Richenbach, remembering the sheer precipice of rock at the foot of the castle walls and the dizzy height of the castle roof above the rock, could scarcely forbear a shudder at the thought of climbing so high on a shaky ladder, even if such a ladder could be made, of which he had some doubts. The scheme did not seem so feasible as the Spaniard appeared to imagine.

"Could you not let down a rope ladder from the platform when you had slain the sentinel, and thus allow us to climb by that?"

"It would be impossible for me to construct and conceal a contrivance strong enough to carry more than one man at a time, even if I had the materials," said the wily Spaniard, whose thoughtfulness and ingenuity Heinrich could not but admire, while despising him as an oily foreigner. "If you made the rope ladder there would be no method of getting it into Schloss Eltz; besides, it would need to be double the length of a wooden ladder, for you can place your ladder at the foot of the ledge, then climb to the top of the rock, and, standing there, pull the ladder up, letting the higher end scrape against the castle wall until the lower end stands firm on the ledge of rock. Your whole troop could then climb, one following another, so that there would be no delay."

Thus it was arranged, and then began and was completed the construction of the longest and most wonderful ladder ever made in Germany or anywhere else, so far as history records. It was composed of numerous small ladders, spliced and hooped with iron bands by the castle armourer. At a second visit, which Rego paid to Baldwineltz when the ladder was completed, all arrangements were made and the necessary signals agreed upon.

It was the pious custom of those in the fortress of Baldwineltz to ring the great bell on Saints' days and other festivals that called for special observance, because Von Richenbach conducted war on the strictest principles, as a man knowing his duty both spiritual and temporal. It was agreed that on the night of the assault, when it was necessary that Rego should assassinate the sentinel, the great bell of the fortress should be rung, whereupon the Spaniard was to hie himself up the stair and send the watchman into another sphere of duty by means of his dagger. The bell-ringing seems a perfectly justifiable device, and one that will be approved by all conspirators, for the sounding of the bell, plainly heard in Schloss Eltz, would cause no alarm, as it was wont to sound at uncertain intervals, night and day, and was known to give tongue only during moments allotted by the Church to devout thoughts. But the good monk Ambrose, in setting down on parchment the chronicles of this time, gives it as his opinion that no prosperity could have been expected in thus suddenly changing the functions of the bell from sacred duty to the furtherance of a secular object. Still, Ambrose was known to be a sympathiser with the house of Eltz, and, aside from this, a monk in his cell cannot be expected to take the same view of military necessity that would commend itself to a warrior on a bastion; therefore, much as we may admire Ambrose as an historian, we are not compelled to accept his opinions on military ethics.

On the important night, which was of great darkness, made the more intense by the black environment of densely-wooded hills which surrounded Schloss Eltz, the swarthy Spaniard became almost pale with anxiety as he listened for the solemn peal that was to be his signal. At last it tolled forth, and he, with knife to hand in his girdle, crept softly along the narrow halls to his fatal task. The interior of Schloss Eltz is full of intricate passages, unexpected turnings, here a few steps up, there a few steps down, for all the world like a maze, in which even one knowing the castle might well go astray. At one of the turnings Rego came suddenly upon the Countess, who screamed at sight of him, and then recognising him said, half laughing, half crying, being a nervous woman:

"Ah, Rego, thank heaven it is you! I am so distraught with the doleful ringing of that bell that I am frightened at the sound of my own footsteps. Why rings it so, Rego?"

"'Tis some Church festival, my Lady, which they, fighting for the Archbishop, are more familiar with than I," answered the trembling Spaniard, as frightened as the lady herself at the unexpected meeting. But the Countess was a most religious woman, well skilled in the observances of her Church, and she replied:

"No, Rego. There is no cause for its dolorous music, and to-night there seems to me something ominous and menacing in its tone, as if disaster impended."

"It may be the birthday of the Archbishop, my Lady, or of the Pope himself."

"Our Holy Father was born in May, and the Archbishop in November. Ah, I would that this horrid strife were done with! But our safety lies in Heaven, and if our duty be accomplished here on earth, we should have naught to fear; yet I tremble as if great danger lay before me. Come, Rego, to the chapel, and light the candles at the altar."

The Countess passed him, and for one fateful moment Rego's hand hovered over his dagger, thinking to strike the lady dead at his feet; but the risk was too great, for there might at any time pass along the corridor one of the servants, who would instantly raise the alarm and bring disaster upon him. He dare not disobey. So grinding his teeth in impotent rage and fear, he followed his mistress to the chapel, and, as quickly as he could, lit one candle after another, until the usual number burned before the sacred image. The Countess was upon her knees as he tried to steal softly from the room. "Nay, Rego," she said, raising her bended head, "light them all to-night. Hearken! That raven bell has ceased even as you lighted the last candle."

The Countess, as has been said was a devout lady, and there stood an unusual number of candles before the altar, several of which burned constantly, but only on notable occasions were all the candles lighted. As Rego hesitated, not knowing what to do in this crisis, the lady repeated: "Light all the candles to-night, Rego."

"You said yourself, my Lady," murmured the agonised man, cold sweat breaking out on his forehead, "that this was not a Saint's day."

"Nevertheless, Rego," persisted the Countess, surprised that even a favourite servant should thus attempt to thwart her will, "I ask you to light each candle. Do so at once."

She bowed her head as one who had spoken the final word, and again her fate trembled in the balance; but Rego heard the footsteps of the Count entering the gallery above him, that ran across the end of the chapel, and he at once resumed the lighting of the candles, making less speed in his eagerness than if he had gone about his task with more care.

The monk Ambrose draws a moral from this episode, which is sufficiently obvious when after-events have confirmed it, but which we need not here pause to consider, when an episode of the most thrilling nature is going forward on the lofty platform on the roof of Eltz Castle.

The sentinel paced back and forward within his narrow limit, listening to the depressing and monotonous tolling of the bell and cursing it, for the platform was a lonely place and the night of inky darkness. At last the bell ceased, and he stood resting on his long pike, enjoying the stillness, and peering into the blackness surrounding him, when suddenly he became aware of a grating, rasping sound below, as if some one were attempting to climb the precipitous beetling cliff of castle wall and slipping against the stones. His heart stood still with fear, for he knew it could be nothing human. An instant later something appeared over the parapet that could be seen only because it was blacker than the distant dark sky against which it was outlined. It rose and rose until the sentinel saw it was the top of a ladder, which was even more amazing than if the fiend himself had scrambled over the stone coping, for we know the devil can go anywhere, while a ladder cannot. But the soldier was a common-sense man, and, dark as was the night, he knew that, tall as such a ladder must be, there seemed a likelihood that human power was pushing it upward. He touched it with his hands and convinced himself that there was nothing supernatural about it. The ladder rose inch by inch, slowly, for it must have been no easy task for even twoscore men to raise it thus with ropes or other devices, especially when the bottom of it neared the top of the ledge. The soldier knew he should at once give the alarm: but he was the second traitor in the stronghold, corrupted by the sight of the glittering gold he had shared, and only prevented from selling himself because the rigours of military rule did not give him opportunity of going to Baldwineltz as the less exacting civilian duties had allowed the Spaniard to do and thus market his ware. So the sentry made no outcry, but silently prepared a method by which he could negotiate with advantage to himself when the first head appeared above the parapet. He fixed the point of his lance against a round of the ladder, and when the leading warrior, who was none other than Heinrich von Richenbach, himself came slowly and cautiously to the top of the wall, the sentinel, exerting all his strength, pushed the lance outward, and the top of the ladder with it, until it stood nearly perpendicular some two yards back from the wall.

"In God's name, what are you about? Is that you, Rego?"

The soldier replied, calmly:

"Order your men not to move, and do not move yourself, until I have some converse with you. Have no fear if you are prepared to accept my terms; otherwise you will have ample time to say your prayers before you reach the ground, for the distance is great."

Von Richenbach, who now leaned over the top round, suspended thus between heaven and earth, grasped the lance with both hands, so that the ladder might not be thrust beyond the perpendicular. In quivering voice he passed down the word that no man was to shift foot or hand until he had made bargain with the sentinel who held them in such extreme peril.

"What terms do you propose to me, soldier?" he asked, breathlessly.

"I will conduct you down to the courtyard, and when you have surprised and taken the castle you will grant me safe conduct and give me five bags of gold equal in weight to those offered to our captain."

"All that will I do and double the treasure. Faithfully and truly do I promise it."

"You pledge me your knightly word, and swear also by the holy coat of Treves?"

"I pledge and swear. And pray you be careful; incline the ladder yet a little more toward the wall."

"I trust to your honour," said the traitor, for traitors love to prate

442

of honour, "and will now admit you to the castle; but until we are in the courtyard there must be silence."

"Incline the ladder gently, for it is so weighted that if it come suddenly against the wall, it may break in the middle."

At this supreme moment, as the sentinel was preparing to bring them cautiously to the wall, when all was deep silence, there crept swiftly and noiselessly through the trap-door the belated Spaniard. His catlike eyes beheld the shadowy form of the sentinel bending apparently over the parapet, but they showed him nothing beyond. With the speed and precipitation of a springing panther, the Spaniard leaped forward and drove his dagger deep into the neck of his comrade, who, with a gurgling cry, plunged headlong forward, and down the precipice, thrusting his lance as he fell. The Spaniard's dagger went with the doomed sentinel, sticking fast in his throat, and its presence there passed a fatal noose around the neck of Rego later, for they wrongly thought the false sentinel had saved the castle and that the Spaniard had murdered a faithful watchman.

Rego leaned panting over the stone coping, listening for the thud of the body. Then was he frozen with horror when the still night air was split with the most appalling shriek of combined human voice in an agony of fear that ever tortured the ear of man. The shriek ended in a terrorising crash far below, and silence again filled the valley.

"GENTLEMEN: THE KING!"

The room was large, but with a low ceiling, and at one end of the lengthy, broad apartment stood a gigantic fireplace, in which was heaped a pile of blazing logs, whose light, rather than that of several lanterns hanging from nails along the timbered walls, illuminated the faces of the twenty men who sat within. Heavy timbers, blackened with age and smoke, formed the ceiling. The long, low, diamond-paned window in the middle of the wall opposite the door, had been shuttered as completely as possible, but less care than usual was taken to prevent the light from penetrating into the darkness beyond, for the night was a stormy and tempestuous one, the rain lashing wildly against the hunting châlet, which, in its time, had seen many a merry hunting party gathered under its ample roof.

Every now and then a blast of wind shook the wooden edifice from garret to foundation, causing a puff of smoke to come down the chimney, and the white ashes to scatter in little whirlwinds over the hearth. On the opposite side from the shuttered window was the door, heavily barred. A long, oaken table occupied the centre of the room, and round this in groups, seated and standing, were a score of men, all with swords at their sides; bearing, many of them, that air of careless hauteur which is supposed to be a characteristic of noble birth.

Flagons were scattered upon the table, and a barrel of wine stood in a corner of the room farthest from the fireplace, but it was evident that this was no ordinary drinking party, and that the assemblage was brought about by some high purport, of a nature so serious that it stamped anxiety on every brow. No servants were present, and each man who wished a fresh flagon of wine had to take his measure to the barrel in the corner and fill for himself.

The hunting châlet stood in a wilderness, near the confines of the kingdom of Alluria, twelve leagues from the capital, and was the property of Count Staumn, whose tall, gaunt form stood erect at the head of the table as he silently listened to the discussion which every moment was becoming more and more heated, the principal speaking parts being taken by the obstinate, rough-spoken Baron Brunfels, on the one hand, and the crafty, fox-like ex-Chancellor Steinmetz on the other.

"I tell you," thundered Baron Brunfels, bringing his fist down on the table, "I will not have the King killed. Such a proposal goes beyond what was intended when we banded ourselves together. The King is a fool, so let him escape like a fool. I am a conspirator, but not an assassin."

"It is justice rather than assassination," said the ex-Chancellor suavely, as if his tones were oil and the Baron's boisterous talk were troubled waters.

"Justice!" cried the Baron, with great contempt. "You have learned that cant word in the Cabinet of the King himself, before he thrust you out. He eternally prates of justice, yet, much as I loathe him, I have no wish to compass his death, either directly or through gabbling of justice."

"Will you permit me to point out the reason that induces me to believe his continued exemption, and State policy, will not run together?" replied the advocate of the King's death. "If Rudolph escape, he will take up his abode in a neighbouring territory, and there will inevitably follow plots and counter-plots for his restoration—thus Alluria will be kept in a state of constant turmoil. There will doubtless grow up within the kingdom itself a party sworn to his restoration. We shall thus be involved in difficulties at home and abroad, and all for what? Merely to save the life of a man who is an enemy to each of us. We place thousands of lives in jeopardy, render our own positions insecure, bring continual disquiet upon the State, when all might be avoided by the slitting of one throat, even though that throat belong to the King."

It was evident that the lawyer's persuasive tone brought many to his side, and the conspirators seemed about evenly divided upon the question of life or death to the King. The Baron was about to break out again with some strenuousness in favour of his own view of the matter, when Count Staumn made a proposition that was eagerly accepted by all save Brunfels himself.

"Argument," said Count Staumn, "is ever the enemy of good comradeship. Let us settle the point at once and finally, with the dice-box. Baron Brunfels, you are too seasoned a gambler to object to such a mode of terminating a discussion. Steinmetz, the law, of which you are so distinguished a representative, is often compared to a lottery, so you cannot look with disfavour upon a method that is conclusive, and as reasonably fair as the average decision of a judge. Let us throw, therefore, for the life of the King. I, as chairman of this meeting, will be umpire. Single throws, and the highest number wins. Baron Brunfels, you will act for the King, and, if you win, may bestow upon the monarch his life. Chancellor Steinmetz stands for the State. If he wins, then is the King's life forfeit. Gentlemen, are you agreed?"

"Agreed, agreed," cried the conspirators, with practically unanimous voice.

Baron Brunfels grumbled somewhat, but when the dice-horn was brought, and he heard the rattle of the bones within the leathern cylinder, the light of a gambler's love shone in his eyes, and he made no further protest.

The ex-Chancellor took the dice-box in his hand, and was about to shake, when there came suddenly upon them three stout raps against the door, given apparently with the hilt of a sword. Many not already standing, started to their feet, and nearly all looked one upon another with deep dismay in their glances. The full company of conspirators was present; exactly a score of men knew of the rendezvous, and now the twenty-first man outside was beating the oaken panels. The knocking was repeated, but now accompanied by the words:

"Open, I beg of you."

Count Staumn left the table and, stealthily as a cat, approached the door.

"Who is there?" he asked.

"A wayfarer, weary and wet, who seeks shelter from the storm."

"My house is already filled," spoke up the Count. "I have no room for another."

"Open the door peacefully," cried the outlander, "and do not put me to the necessity of forcing it."

There was a ring of decision in the voice which sent quick pallor to more than one cheek. Ex-Chancellor Steinmetz rose to his feet with chattering teeth, and terror in his eyes; he seemed to recognise the tones of the invisible speaker. Count Staumn looked over his shoulder at the assemblage with an expression that plainly said: "What am I to do?"

"In the fiend's name," hissed Baron Brunfels, taking the precaution, however, to speak scarce above his breath, "if you are so frightened when it comes to a knock at the door, what will it be when the real knocks are upon you. Open, Count, and let the insistent stranger in. Whether he leave the place alive or no, there are twenty men here to answer."

The Count undid the fastenings and threw back the door. There entered a tall man completely enveloped in a dark cloak that was dripping wet. Drawn over his eyes was a hunter's hat of felt, with a drooping bedraggled feather on it.

The door was immediately closed and barred behind him, and the stranger, pausing a moment when confronted by so many inquiring eyes, flung off his cloak, throwing it over the back of a chair; then he removed his hat with a sweep, sending the raindrops flying. The intriguants gazed at him, speechless, with varying emotions. They saw before them His Majesty, Rudolph, King of Alluria.

If the King had any suspicion of his danger, he gave no token of it. On his smooth, lofty forehead there was no trace of frown, and no sign of fear. His was a manly figure, rather over, than under, six feet in height; not slim and gaunt, like Count Staumn, nor yet stout to excess, like Baron Brunfels. The finger of Time had touched with frost the hair at his temples, and there were threads of white in his pointed beard, but his sweeping moustache was still as black as the night from which he came.

His frank, clear, honest eyes swept the company, resting momentarily on each, then he said in a firm voice, without the suspicion of a tremor in it:

"Gentlemen, I give you good evening, and although the hospitality of Count Staumn has needed spurring, I lay that not up against him, because I am well aware his apparent reluctance arose through the unexpectedness of my visit; and, if the Count will act as cup-bearer, we will drown all remembrance of a barred door in a flagon of wine, for, to tell truth, gentlemen, I have ridden hard in order to have the pleasure of drinking with you."

As the King spoke these ominous words, he cast a glance of piercing intensity upon the company, and more than one quailed under it. He strode to the fireplace, spurs jingling as he went, and stood with his back to the fire, spreading out his hands to the blaze. Count Staumn left the bolted door, took an empty flagon from the shelf, filled it at the barrel in the corner, and, with a low bow, presented the brimming measure to the King.

Rudolph held aloft his beaker of Burgundy, and, as he did so, spoke in a loud voice that rang to the beams of the ceiling:

"Gentlemen, I give you a suitable toast. May none here gathered encounter a more pitiless storm than that which is raging without!"

With this he drank off the wine, and, inclining his head slightly to the Count, returned the flagon. No one, save the King, had spoken since he entered. Every word he had uttered seemed charged with double meaning and brought to the suspicious minds of his hearers visions of a trysting place surrounded by troops, and the King standing there, playing with them, as a tiger plays with its victims. His easy confidence appalled them.

When first he came in, several who were seated remained so, but one by one they rose to their feet, with the exception of Baron Brunfels, although he, when the King gave the toast, also stood. It was clear enough their glances of fear were not directed towards the King, but towards Baron Brunfels. Several pairs of eyes beseeched him in silent supplication, but the Baron met none of these glances, for his gaze was fixed upon the King.

Every man present knew the Baron to be reckless of consequences; frankly outspoken, thoroughly a man of the sword, and a despiser of diplomacy. They feared that at any moment he might blurt out the purport of the meeting, and more than one was thankful for the crafty ex-Chancellor's planning, who throughout had insisted there should be no documentary evidence of their designs, either in their houses or on their persons. Some startling rumour must have reached the King's ear to bring him thus unexpectedly upon them.

The anxiety of all was that some one should persuade the King they were merely a storm-besieged hunting party. They trembled in anticipation of Brunfels' open candor, and dreaded the revealing of the real cause of their conference. There was now no chance to warn the Baron; a man who spoke his mind; who never looked an inch beyond his nose, even though his head should roll off in consequence, and if a man does not value his own head, how can he be expected to care for the heads of his neighbours?

"I ask you to be seated," said the King, with a wave of the hand.

Now, what should that stubborn fool of a Baron do but remain standing, when all but Rudolph and himself had seated themselves, thus drawing His Majesty's attention directly towards him, and making a colloquy between them well-nigh inevitable. Those next the ex-Chancellor were nudging him, in God's name, to stand also, and open whatever discussion there must ensue between themselves and His Majesty, so that it might be smoothly carried on, but the Chancellor was ashen grey with fear, and his hand trembled on the table.

"My Lord of Brunfels," said the King, a smile hovering about his lips, "I see that I have interrupted you at your old pleasure of dicing; while requesting you to continue your game as though I had not joined you, may I venture to hope the stakes you play for are not high?"

Every one held his breath, awaiting with deepest concern the reply of the frowning Baron, and when it came growling forth, there was little in it to ease their disquiet.

"Your Majesty," said Baron Brunfels, "the stakes are the highest that a gambler may play for."

"You tempt me, Baron, to guess that the hazard is a man's soul, but I see that your adversary is my worthy ex-Chancellor, and as I should hesitate to impute to him the character of the devil, I am led, therefore, to the conclusion that you play for a human life. Whose life is in the cast, my Lord of Brunfels?"

Before the Baron could reply, ex-Chancellor Steinmetz arose, with some indecision, to his feet. He began in a trembling voice:

"I beg your gracious permission to explain the reason of our gathering—"

"Herr Steinmetz," cried the King sternly, "when I desire your interference I shall call for it; and remember this, Herr Steinmetz; the man who begins a game must play it to the end, even though he finds luck running against him."

The ex-Chancellor sat down again, and drew his hand across his damp forehead.

"Your Majesty," spoke up the Baron, a ring of defiance in his voice, "I speak not for my comrades, but for myself. I begin no game that I fear to finish. We were about dice in order to discover whether Your Majesty should live or die."

A simultaneous moan seemed to rise from the assembled traitors. The smile returned to the King's lips.

"Baron," he said, "I have ever chided myself for loving you, for you were always a bad example to weak and impressionable natures. Even when your overbearing, obstinate intolerance compelled me to dismiss you from the command of my army, I could not but admire your sturdy honesty. Had I been able to graft your love of truth upon some of my councillors, what a valuable group of advisers might I have gathered round me. But we have had enough of comedy and now tragedy sets in. Those who are traitors to their ruler must not be surprised if a double traitor is one of their number. Why am I here? Why do two hundred mounted and armed men surround this doomed châlet? Miserable wretches, what have you to say that judgment be not instantly passed upon you?"

"I have this to say," roared Baron Brunfels, drawing his sword, "that whatever may befall this assemblage, you, at least, shall not live to boast of it."

450

The King stood unmoved as Baron Brunfels was about to rush upon him, but Count Staumn and others threw themselves between the Baron and his victim, seeing in the King's words some intimation of mercy to be held out to them, could but actual assault upon his person be prevented.

"My Lord of Brunfels," said the King, calmly, "sheath your sword. Your ancestors have often drawn it, but always for, and never against the occupant of the Throne. Now, gentlemen, hear my decision, and abide faithfully by it. Seat yourselves at the table, ten on each side, the dice-box between you. You shall not be disappointed, but shall play out the game of life and death. Each dices with his opposite. He who throws the higher number escapes. He who throws the lower places his weapons on the empty chair, and stands against yonder wall to be executed for the traitor that he is. Thus half of your company shall live, and the other half seek death with such courage as may be granted them. Do you agree, or shall I give the signal?"

With unanimous voice they agreed, all excepting Baron Brunfels, who spoke not.

"Come, Baron, you and my devoted ex-Chancellor were about to play when I came in. Begin the game."

"Very well," replied the Baron nonchalantly. "Steinmetz, the dice-box is near your hand: throw."

Some one placed the cubes in the leathern cup and handed it to the ex-Chancellor, whose shivering fingers relieved him of the necessity of shaking the box. The dice rolled out on the table; a three, a four, and a one. Those nearest reported the total.

"Eight!" cried the King. "Now, Baron."

Baron Brunfels carelessly threw the dice into their receptacle, and a moment after the spotted bones clattered on the table.

"Three sixes!" cried the Baron. "Lord, if I only had such luck when I played for money!"

The ex-Chancellor's eyes were starting from his head, wild with fear.

"We have three throws," he screamed.

"Not so," said the King.

"I swear I understood that we were to have three chances," shrieked Steinmetz, springing from his chair. "But it is all illegal, and not to be borne. I will not have my life diced away to please either King or commons."

He drew his sword and placed himself in an attitude of defence.

"Seize him; disarm him, and bind him," commanded the King. "There are enough gentlemen in this company to see that the rules of the game are adhered to."

Steinmetz, struggling and pleading for mercy, was speedily overpowered and bound; then his captors placed him against the wall, and resumed their seats at the table. The next man to be doomed was Count Staumn. The Count arose from his chair, bowed first to the King and then to the assembled company; drew forth his sword, broke it over his knee, and walked to the wall of the condemned.

The remainder of the fearful contest was carried on in silence, but with great celerity, and before a quarter of an hour was past, ten men had their backs to the wall, while the remaining ten were seated at the table, some on one side, and some on the other.

The men ranged against the wall were downcast, for however bravely a soldier may meet death in hostile encounter, it is a different matter to face it bound and helpless at the hands of an executioner.

A shade of sadness seemed to overspread the countenance of the King, who still occupied the position he had taken at the first, with his back towards the fire.

Baron Brunfels shifted uneasily in his seat, and glanced now and then with compassion at his sentenced comrades. He was first to break the silence.

"Your Majesty," he said, "I am always loath to see a coward die. The whimpering of your former Chancellor annoys me; therefore, will I gladly

452

take his place, and give to him the life and liberty you perhaps design for me, if, in exchange, I have the privilege of speaking my mind regarding you and your precious Kingship."

"Unbind the valiant Steinmetz," said the King. "Speak your mind freely, Baron Brunfels."

The Baron rose, drew sword from scabbard, and placed it on the table.

"Your Majesty, backed by brute force," he began, "has condemned to death ten of your subjects. You have branded us as traitors, and such we are, and so find no fault with your sentence; merely recognising that you represent, for the time being, the upper hand. You have reminded me that my ancestors fought for yours, and that they never turned their swords against their sovereign. Why, then, have our blades been pointed towards your breast? Because, King Rudolph, you are yourself a traitor. You belong to the ruling class and have turned your back upon your order. You, a King, have made yourself a brother to the demagogue at the street corner; yearning for the cheap applause of the serf. You have shorn nobility of its privileges, and for what?"

"And for what?" echoed the King with rising voice. "For this; that the ploughman on the plain may reap what he has sown; that the shepherd on the hillside may enjoy the increase which comes to his flock; that taxation may be light; that my nobles shall deal honestly with the people, and not use their position for thievery and depredation; that those whom the State honours by appointing to positions of trust shall content themselves with the recompense lawfully given, and refrain from peculation; that peace and security shall rest on the land; and that bloodthirsty swashbucklers shall not go up and down inciting the people to carnage and rapine under the name of patriotism. This is the task I set myself when I came to the Throne. What fault have you to find with the programme, my Lord Baron?"

"The simple fault that it is the programme of a fool," replied the Baron calmly. "In following it you have gained the resentment of your nobles, and have not even received the thanks of those pitiable hinds, the ploughman in the valley or the shepherd on the hills. You have impoverished us so that the clowns may have a few more coins with which to muddle in drink their already stupid brains. You are hated in cot and castle alike. You would not stand in your place for a moment, were not an army behind you. Being a fool, you think the common people love honesty, whereas, they only curse that they have not a share in the thieving."

"The people," said the King soberly, "have been misled. Their ear has been abused by calumny and falsehood. Had it been possible for me personally to explain to them the good that must ultimately accrue to a land where honesty rules, I am confident I would have had their undivided support, even though my nobles deserted me."

"Not so, Your Majesty; they would listen to you and cheer you, but when the next orator came among them, promising to divide the moon, and give a share to each, they would gather round his banner and hoot you from the kingdom. What care they for rectitude of government? They see no farther than the shining florin that glitters on their palm. When your nobles were rich, they came to their castles among the people, and scattered their gold with a lavish hand. Little recked the peasants how it was got, so long as they shared it. 'There,' they said, 'the coin comes to us that we have not worked for.'

"But now, with castles deserted, and retainers dismissed, the people have to sweat to wring from traders the reluctant silver, and they cry: 'Thus it was not in times of old, and this King is the cause of it,' and so they spit upon your name, and shrug their shoulders, when your honesty is mentioned. And now, Rudolph of Alluria, I have done, and I go the more jauntily to my death that I have had fair speech with you before the end."

The King looked at the company, his eyes veiled with moisture. "I thought," he said slowly, "until to-night, that I had possessed some qualities at least of a ruler of men. I came here alone among you, and although there are brave men in this assembly, yet I had the ordering of events as I chose to order them, notwithstanding that odds stood a score to one against me. I still venture to think that whatever failures have attended my eight years' rule in Alluria arose from faults of my own, and not through imperfections in the plan, or want of appreciation in the people.

"I have now to inform you that if it is disastrous for a King to act without the co-operation of his nobles, it is equally disastrous for them to plot against their leader. I beg to acquaint you with the fact that the insurrection so carefully prepared has broken out prematurely. My capital is in possession of the factions, who are industriously cutting each other's throats to settle which one of two smooth-tongued rascals shall be their President. While you were dicing to settle the fate of an already deposed King, and I was sentencing you to a mythical death, we were all alike being involved in common ruin.

"I have seen to-night more property in flames than all my savings during the last eight years would pay for. I have no horsemen at my back, and have stumbled here blindly, a much bedraggled fugitive, having lost my way in every sense of the phrase. And so I beg of the hospitality of Count Staumn another flagon of wine, and either a place of shelter for my patient horse, who has been left too long in the storm without, or else direction towards the frontier, whereupon my horse and I will set out to find it."

"Not towards the frontier!" cried Baron Brunfels, grasping again his sword and holding it aloft, "but towards the capital. We will surround you, and hew for you a way through that fickle mob back to the throne of your ancestors."

Each man sprang to his weapon and brandished it above his head, while a ringing cheer echoed to the timbered ceiling.

"The King! The King!" they cried.

Rudolph smiled and shook his head.

"Not so," he said. "I leave a thankless throne with a joy I find it impossible to express. As I sat on horseback, half-way up the hill above the burning city, and heard the clash of arms, I was filled with amazement to think that men would actually fight for the position of ruler of the people. Whether the insurrection has brought freedom to themselves or not, the future alone can tell, but it has at least brought freedom to me. I now belong to myself. No man may question either my motives or my acts. Gentlemen, drink with me to the new President of Alluria, whoever he may be."

But the King drank alone, none other raising flagon to lip. Then Baron Brunfels cried aloud:

"Gentlemen: the King!"

And never in the history of Alluria was a toast so heartily honoured.

THE HOUR-GLASS

Bertram Eastford had intended to pass the shop of his old friend, the curiosity dealer, into whose pockets so much of his money had gone for trinkets gathered from all quarters of the globe. He knew it was weakness on his part, to select that street when he might have taken another, but he thought it would do no harm to treat himself to one glance at the seductive window of the old curiosity shop, where the dealer was in the habit of displaying his latest acquisitions. The window was never quite the same, and it had a continued fascination for Bertram Eastford; but this time, he said to himself resolutely, he would not enter, having, as he assured himself, the strength of mind to forego this temptation. However, he reckoned without his window, for in it there was an old object newly displayed which caught his attention as effectually as a half-driven nail arrests the hem of a cloak. On the central shelf of the window stood an hour-glass, its framework of some wood as black as ebony. He stood gazing at it for a moment, then turned to the door and went inside, greeting the ancient shopman, whom he knew so well.

"I want to look at the hour-glass you have in the window," he said.

"Ah, yes," replied the curiosity dealer; "the cheap watch has driven the hour-glass out of the commercial market, and we rarely pick up a thing like that nowadays." He took the hour-glass from the shelf in the window, reversed it, and placed it on a table. The ruddy sand began to pour through into the lower receptacle in a thin, constant stream, as if it were blood that had been dried and powdered. Eastford watched the ever-increasing heap at the bottom, rising conically, changing its shape every moment, as little avalanches of the sand fell away from its heightening sides.

"There is no need for you to extol its antiquity," said Eastford, with a smile. "I knew the moment I looked at it that such glasses are rare, and you are not going to find me a cheapening customer."

"So far from over-praising it," protested the shopman, "I was about to call your attention to a defect. It is useless as a measurer of time."

"It doesn't record the exact hour, then?" asked Eastford.

"Well, I suppose the truth is, they were not very particular in the old days, and time was not money, as it is now. It measures the hour with great accuracy," the curio dealer went on—"that is, if you watch it; but, strangely enough, after it has run for half an hour, or thereabouts, it stops, because of some defect in the neck of the glass, or in the pulverising of the sand, and will not go again until the glass is shaken."

The hour-glass at that moment verified what the old man said. The tiny stream of sand suddenly ceased, but resumed its flow the moment its owner jarred the frame, and continued pouring without further interruption.

"That is very singular," said Eastford. "How do you account for it?"

"I imagine it is caused by some inequality in the grains of sand; probably a few atoms larger than the others come together at the neck, and so stop the percolation. It always does this, and, of course, I cannot remedy the matter because the glass is hermetically sealed."

"Well, I don't want it as a timekeeper, so we will not allow that defect to interfere with the sale. How much do you ask for it?"

The dealer named his price, and Eastford paid the amount.

"I shall send it to you this afternoon."

"Thank you," said the customer, taking his leave.

That night in his room Bertram Eastford wrote busily until a late hour. When his work was concluded, he pushed away his manuscript with a sigh of that deep contentment which comes to a man who has not wasted his day. He replenished the open fire, drew his most comfortable arm-chair in front of it, took the green shade from his lamp, thus filling the luxurious apartment with a light that was reflected from armour and from ancient weapons standing in corners and hung along the walls. He lifted the paper-covered package, cut the string that bound it, and placed the ancient hour-glass on his table, watching the thin stream of sand which his action had set running. The constant, unceasing, steady downfall seemed to hypnotise him. Its descent was as silent as the footsteps of time itself. Suddenly it stopped, as it had done in the shop, and its abrupt ceasing jarred on his tingling nerves like an unexpected break in the stillness. He could almost imagine an unseen hand clasping the thin cylinder of the glass and throttling it. He shook the bygone time-measurer and breathed again more steadily when the sand resumed its motion. Presently he took the glass from the table and examined it with some attention.

He thought at first its frame was ebony, but further inspection convinced him it was oak, blackened with age. On one round end was carved rudely two hearts overlapping, and twined about them a pair of serpents.

"Now, I wonder what that's for?" murmured Eastford to himself. "An attempt at a coat of arms, perhaps."

There was no clue to the meaning of the hieroglyphics, and Eastford, with the glass balanced on his knee, watched the sand still running, the crimson thread sparkling in the lamplight. He fancied he saw distorted reflections of faces in the convex glass, although his reason told him they were but caricatures of his own. The great bell in the tower near by, with slow solemnity, tolled twelve. He counted its measured strokes one by one, and then was startled by a decisive knock at his door. One section of his brain considered this visit untimely, another looked on it as perfectly usual, and while the two were arguing the matter out, he heard his own voice cry: "Come in."

The door opened, and the discussion between the government and the opposition in his mind ceased to consider the untimeliness of the visit, for here, in the visitor himself, stood another problem. He was a young man in military costume, his uniform being that of an officer. Eastford remembered seeing something like it on the stage, and knowing little of military affairs, thought perhaps the costume of the visitor before him indicated an officer in the Napoleonic war.

"Good evening!" said the incomer. "May I introduce myself? I am

Lieutenant Sentore, of the regular army."

"You are very welcome," returned his host. "Will you be seated?"

"Thank you, no. I have but a few moments to stay. I have come for my hour-glass, if you will be good enough to let me have it."

"Your hour-glass?" ejaculated Eastford, in surprise. "I think you labour under a misapprehension. The glass belongs to me; I bought it to-day at the old curiosity shop in Finchmore Street."

"Rightful possession of the glass would appear to rest with you, technically; but taking you to be a gentleman, I venture to believe that a mere statement of my priority of claim will appeal to you, even though it might have no effect on the minds of a jury of our countrymen."

"You mean to say that the glass has been stolen from you and has been sold?"

"It has been sold undoubtedly over and over again, but never stolen, so far as I have been able to trace its history."

"If, then, the glass has been honestly purchased by its different owners, I fail to see how you can possibly establish any claim to it."

"I have already admitted that my claim is moral rather than legal," continued the visitor. "It is a long story; have I your permission to tell it?"

"I shall be delighted to listen," replied Eastford, "but before doing so I beg to renew my invitation, and ask you to occupy this easy-chair before the fire."

The officer bowed in silence, crossed the room behind Eastford, and sat down in the arm-chair, placing his sword across his knees. The stranger spread his hands before the fire, and seemed to enjoy the comforting warmth. He remained for a few moments buried in deep reflection, quite ignoring the presence of his host, who, glancing upon the hour-glass in dispute upon his knees, seeing that the sands had all run out silently reversed it and set them flowing again. This action caught the corner of the stranger's eye, and brought him to a realisation of why he was there. Drawing a heavy sigh, he began his story.

"In the year 1706 I held the post of lieutenant in that part of the British Army commanded by General Trelawny, the supreme command, of course, being in the hands of the great Marlborough."

Eastford listened to this announcement with a feeling that there was something wrong about the statement. The man sitting there was calmly talking of a time one hundred and ninety-two years past, and yet he himself could not be a day more than twenty-five years old. Somewhere entangled in this were the elements of absurdity. Eastford found himself unable to unravel them, but the more he thought of the matter, the more reasonable it began to appear, and so, hoping his visitor had not noted the look of surprise on his face, he said, quietly, casting his mind back over the history of England, and remembering what he had learned at school:—

"That was during the war of the Spanish Succession?"

"Yes: the war had then been in progress four years, and many brilliant victories had been won, the greatest of which was probably the Battle of Blenheim."

"Quite so," murmured Eastford.

"It was the English," Casper cried,

"That put the French to rout;

"But what they killed each other for,

"I never could make out."

The officer looked up in astonishment.

"I never heard anything like that said about the war. The reason for it was perfectly plain. We had to fight or acknowledge France to be the dictator of Europe. Still, politics have nothing to do with my story. General Trelawny and his forces were in Brabant, and were under orders to join the Duke of Marlborough's army. We were to go through the country as

461

speedily as possible, for a great battle was expected. Trelawny's instructions were to capture certain towns and cities that lay in our way, to dismantle the fortresses, and to parole their garrisons. We could not encumber ourselves with prisoners, and so marched the garrisons out, paroled them, destroyed their arms, and bade them disperse. But, great as was our hurry, strict orders had been given to leave no strongholds in our rear untaken.

"Everything went well until we came to the town of Elsengore, which we captured without the loss of a man. The capture of the town, however, was of little avail, for in the centre of it stood a strong citadel, which we tried to take by assault, but could not. General Trelawny, a very irascible, hotheaded man, but, on the whole, a just and capable officer, impatient at this unexpected delay, offered the garrison almost any terms they desired to evacuate the castle. But, having had warning of our coming, they had provisioned the place, were well supplied with ammunition, and their commander refused to make terms with General Trelawny.

"'If you want the place,' said the Frenchman, 'come and take it.'

"General Trelawny, angered at this contemptuous treatment, flung his men again and again at the citadel, but without making the slightest impression on it.

"We were in no wise prepared for a long siege, nor had we expected stubborn resistance. Marching quickly, as was our custom heretofore, we possessed no heavy artillery, and so were at a disadvantage when attacking a fortress as strong as that of Elsengore. Meanwhile, General Trelawny sent mounted messengers by different roads to his chief giving an account of what had happened, explaining his delay in joining the main army, and asking for definite instructions. He expected that one or two, at least, of the mounted messengers sent away would reach his chief and be enabled to return. And that is exactly what happened, for one day a dusty horseman came to General Trelawny's headquarters with a brief note from Marlborough. The Commander-in-Chief said:—

"'I think the Frenchman's advice is good. We want the place; therefore, take it.'

462

"But he sent no heavy artillery to aid us in this task, for he could not spare his big guns, expecting, as he did, an important battle. General Trelawny having his work thus cut out for him, settled down to accomplish it as best he might. He quartered officers and men in various parts of the town, the more thoroughly to keep watch on the citizens, of whose good intentions, if the siege were prolonged, we were by no means sure.

"It fell to my lot to be lodged in the house of Burgomaster Seidelmier, of whose conduct I have no reason to complain, for he treated me well. I was given two rooms, one a large, low apartment on the first floor, and communicating directly with the outside, by means of a hall and a separate stairway. The room was lighted by a long, many-paned window, leaded and filled with diamond-shaped glass. Beyond this large drawing-room was my bedroom. I must say that I enjoyed my stay in Burgomaster Seidelmier's house none the less because he had an only daughter, a most charming girl. Our acquaintance ripened into deep friendship, and afterwards into——but that has nothing to do with what I have to tell you. My story is of war, and not of love. Gretlich Seidelmier presented me with the hour-glass you have in your hand, and on it I carved the joined hearts entwined with our similar initials."

"So they are initials, are they?" said Eastford, glancing down at what he had mistaken for twining serpents.

"Yes," said the officer; "I was more accustomed to a sword than to an etching tool, and the letters are but rudely drawn. One evening, after dark, Gretlich and I were whispering together in the hall, when we heard the heavy tread of the general coming up the stair. The girl fled precipitately, and I, holding open the door, waited the approach of my chief. He entered and curtly asked me to close the door.

"'Lieutenant,' he said, 'it is my intention to capture the citadel to-night. Get together twenty-five of your men, and have them ready under the shadow of this house, but give no one a hint of what you intend to do with them. In one hour's time leave this place with your men as quietly as possible, and make an attack on the western entrance of the citadel. Your attack is to be but a feint and to draw off their forces to that point. Still, if any of your men succeed in gaining entrance to the fort they shall not lack reward and promotion. Have you a watch?'

"'Not one that will go, general; but I have an hourglass here.'

"'Very well, set it running. Collect your men, and exactly at the hour lead them to the west front; it is but five minutes' quick march from here. An hour and five minutes from this moment I expect you to begin the attack, and the instant you are before the western gate make as much noise as your twenty-five men are capable of, so as to lead the enemy to believe that the attack is a serious one.'

"Saying this, the general turned and made his way, heavy-footed, through the hall and down the stairway.

"I set the hour-glass running, and went at once to call my men, stationing them where I had been ordered to place them. I returned to have a word with Gretlich before I departed on what I knew was a dangerous mission. Glancing at the hour-glass, I saw that not more than a quarter of the sand had run down during my absence. I remained in the doorway, where I could keep an eye on the hour-glass, while the girl stood leaning her arm against the angle of the dark passageway, supporting her fair cheek on her open palm; and, standing thus in the darkness, she talked to me in whispers. We talked and talked, engaged in that sweet, endless conversation that murmurs in subdued tone round the world, being duplicated that moment at who knows how many places. Absorbed as I was in listening, at last there crept into my consciousness the fact that the sand in the upper bulb was not diminishing as fast as it should. This knowledge was fully in my mind for some time before I realised its fearful significance. Suddenly the dim knowledge took on actuality. I sprang from the door-lintel, saying:—

"'Good heavens, the sand in the hour-glass has stopped running!'

"I remained there motionless, all action struck from my rigid limbs, gazing at the hour-glass on the table.

"Gretlich, peering in at the doorway, looking at the hour-glass and not at me, having no suspicion of the ruin involved in the stoppage of that miniature sandstorm, said, presently:—

"'Oh, yes, I forgot to tell you it does that now and then, and so you must shake the glass.'

"She bent forward as if to do this when the leaden windows shuddered, and the house itself trembled with the sharp crash of our light cannon, followed almost immediately by the deeper detonation of the heavier guns from the citadel. The red sand in the glass began to fall again, and its liberation seemed to unfetter my paralysed limbs. Bareheaded as I was, I rushed like one frantic along the passage and down the stairs. The air was resonant with the quick-following reports of the cannon, and the long, narrow street was fitfully lit up as if by sudden flashes of summer lightning. My men were still standing where I had placed them. Giving a sharp word of command, I marched them down the street and out into the square, where I met General Trelawny coming back from his futile assault. Like myself, he was bareheaded. His military countenance was begrimed with powder-smoke, but he spoke to me with no trace of anger in his voice.

"'Lieutenant Sentore,' he said, 'disperse your men.'

"I gave the word to disband my men, and then stood at attention before him.

"'Lieutenant Sentore,' he said, in the same level voice, 'return to your quarters and consider yourself under arrest. Await my coming there.'

"I turned and obeyed his orders. It seemed incredible that the sand should still be running in the hour-glass, for ages appeared to have passed over my head since last I was in that room. I paced up and down, awaiting the coming of my chief, feeling neither fear nor regret, but rather dumb despair. In a few minutes his heavy tread was on the stair, followed by the measured tramp of a file of men. He came into the room, and with him were a sergeant and four soldiers, fully armed. The general was trembling with rage, but held strong control over himself, as was his habit on serious occasions.

"'Lieutenant Sentore,' he said, 'why were you not at your post?'"

"'The running sand in the hour-glass' (I hardly recognised my own voice on hearing it) 'stopped when but half exhausted. I did not notice its interruption until it was too late.'

"The general glanced grimly at the hour-glass. The last sands were falling through to the lower bulb. I saw that he did not believe my explanation.

"'It seems now to be in perfect working order,' he said, at last.

"He strode up to it and reversed it, watching the sand pour for a few moments, then he spoke abruptly:—

"'Lieutenant Sentore, your sword.'

"I handed my weapon to him without a word. Turning to the sergeant, he said: 'Lieutenant Sentore is sentenced to death. He has an hour for whatever preparations he cares to make. Allow him to dispose of that hour as he chooses, so long as he remains within this room and holds converse with no one whatever. When the last sands of this hour-glass are run, Lieutenant Sentore will stand at the other end of this room and meet the death merited by traitors, laggards, or cowards. Do you understand your duty, sergeant?'

"'Yes, general.'

"General Trelawny abruptly left the room, and we heard his heavy steps echoing throughout the silent house, and later, more faintly on the cobble-stones of the street. When they had died away a deep stillness set in, I standing alone at one end of the room, my eyes fixed on the hour-glass, and the sergeant with his four men, like statues at the other, also gazing at the same sinister object. The sergeant was the first to break the silence.

"'Lieutenant,' he said, 'do you wish to write anything——?'

"He stopped short, being an unready man, rarely venturing far beyond 'Yes' and 'No.'

"'I should like to communicate with one in this household,' I said, 'but the general has forbidden it, so all I ask is that you shall have my body conveyed from this room as speedily as possible after the execution.'

"'Very good, lieutenant,' answered the sergeant.

"After that, for a long time no word was spoken. I watched my life run redly through the wasp waist of the transparent glass, then suddenly the sand ceased to flow, half in the upper bulb, half in the lower.

"'It has stopped,' said the sergeant; 'I must shake the glass.'

"'Stand where you are!' I commanded, sharply. 'Your orders do not run to that.'

"The habit of obedience rooted the sergeant to the spot.

"'Send one of your men to General Trelawny,' I said, as if I had still the right to be obeyed. 'Tell him what has happened, and ask for instructions. Let your man tread lightly as he leaves the room.'

"The sergeant did not hesitate a moment, but gave the order I required of him. The soldier nearest the door tip-toed out of the house. As we all stood there the silence seeming the deeper because of the stopping of the sand, we heard the hour toll in the nearest steeple. The sergeant was visibly perturbed, and finally he said:—

"'Lieutenant, I must obey the general's orders. An hour has passed since he left here, for that clock struck as he was going down the stair. Soldiers, make ready. Present.'

"The men, like impassive machines levelled their muskets at my breast. I held up my hand.

"'Sergeant,' I said as calmly as I could, 'you are now about to exceed your instructions. Give another command at your peril. The exact words of the general were, 'When the last sands of this hour-glass are run.' I call your attention to the fact that the conditions are not fulfilled. Half of the sand remains in the upper bulb.'

"The sergeant scratched his head in perplexity, but he had no desire to kill me, and was only actuated by a soldier's wish to adhere strictly to the letter of his instructions, be the victim friend or foe. After a few moments he muttered, 'It is true,' then gave a command that put his men into their former position.

"Probably more than half an hour passed, during which time no man moved; the sergeant and his three remaining soldiers seemed afraid to breathe; then we heard the step of the general himself on the stair. I feared that this would give the needed impetus to the sand in the glass, but, when Trelawny entered, the status quo remained. The general stood looking at the suspended sand, without speaking.

"'That is what happened before, general, and that is why I was not at my place. I have committed the crime of neglect, and have thus deservedly earned my death; but I shall die the happier if my general believes I am neither a traitor nor a coward.'

"The general, still without a word, advanced to the table, slightly shook the hour-glass, and the sand began to pour again. Then he picked the glass up in his hand, examining it minutely, as if it were some strange kind of toy, turning it over and over. He glanced up at me and said, quite in his usual tone, as if nothing in particular had come between us:—

"'Remarkable thing that, Sentore, isn't it?'

"'Very,' I answered, grimly.

"He put the glass down.

"'Sergeant, take your men to quarters. Lieutenant Sentore, I return to you your sword; you can perhaps make better use of it alive than dead; I am not a man to be disobeyed, reason or no reason. Remember that, and now go to bed.'

"He left me without further word, and buckling on my sword, I proceeded straightway to disobey again.

"I had a great liking for General Trelawny. Knowing how he fumed and raged at being thus held helpless by an apparently impregnable fortress in the unimportant town of Elsengore, I had myself studied the citadel from all points, and had come to the conclusion that it might be successfully attempted, not by the great gates that opened on the square of the town, nor by the inferior west gates, but by scaling the seemingly unclimbable cliffs at the north side. The wall at the top of this precipice was low, and owing to the height of the beetling cliff, was inefficiently watched by one lone sentinel, who paced the battlements from corner tower to corner tower. I had made my plans, intending to ask the general's permission to risk this venture, but now I resolved to try it without his knowledge or consent, and thus retrieve, if I could, my failure of the foregoing part of the night.

"Taking with me a long, thin rope which I had in my room, anticipating such a trial for it, I roused five of my picked men, and silently we made our way to the foot of the northern cliff. Here, with the rope around my waist, I worked my way diagonally up along a cleft in the rock, which, like others parallel to it, marked the face of the precipice. A slip would be fatal. The loosening of a stone would give warning to the sentinel, whose slow steps I heard on the wall above me, but at last I reached a narrow ledge without accident, and standing up in the darkness, my chin was level with the top of the wall on which the sentry paced. The shelf between the bottom of the wall and the top of the cliff was perhaps three feet in width, and gave ample room for a man careful of his footing. Aided by the rope, the others, less expert climbers than myself, made their way to my side one by one, and the six of us stood on the ledge under the low wall. We were all in our stockinged feet, some of the men, in fact, not even having stockings on. As the sentinel passed, we crouching in the darkness under the wall, the most agile of our party sprang up behind him. The soldier had taken off his jacket, and tip-toeing behind the sentinel, he threw the garment over his head, tightening it with a twist that almost strangled the man. Then seizing his gun so that it would not clatter on the stones, held him thus helpless while we five climbed up beside him. Feeling under the jacket, I put my right hand firmly on the sentinel's throat, and nearly choking the breath out of him, said:—

"'Your life depends on your actions now. Will you utter a sound if I let go your throat?'

"The man shook his head vehemently, and I released my clutch.

"'Now,' I said to him, 'where is the powder stored? Answer in a whisper, and speak truly.'

"'The bulk of the powder,' he answered, 'is in the vault below the citadel.'

"'Where is the rest of it?' I whispered.

"'In the lower room of the round tower by the gate.'

"'Nonsense,' I said: 'they would never store it in a place so liable to attack.'

"'There was nowhere else to put it,' replied the sentinel, 'unless they left it in the open courtyard, which would be quite as unsafe.'

"'Is the door to the lower room in the tower bolted?'

"'There is no door,' replied the sentry, 'but a low archway. This archway has not been closed, because no cannon-balls ever come from the northern side.'

"'How much powder is there in this room?'

"'I do not know; nine or ten barrels, I think.'

"It was evident to me that the fellow, in his fear, spoke the truth. Now, the question was, how to get down from the wall into the courtyard and across that to the archway at the southern side? Cautioning the sentinel again, that if he made the slightest attempt to escape or give the alarm, instant death would be meted to him, I told him to guide us to the archway, which he did, down the stone steps that led from the northern wall into the courtyard. They seemed to keep loose watch inside, the only sentinels in the place being those on the upper walls. But the man we had captured not appearing at his corner in time, his comrade on the western side became alarmed, spoke to him, and obtaining no answer, shouted for him, then discharged his gun. Instantly the place was in an uproar. Lights flashed, and from different guard-rooms soldiers poured out. I saw across the courtyard the archway the sentinel had spoken of, and calling my men made a dash for it. The besieged garrison, not expecting an enemy within, had been rushing up the stone steps at each side to the outer wall to man the cannon they had so recently quitted, and it was some minutes before a knowledge of the real state of things came to them. These few minutes were all we needed, but I saw there was no chance for a slow match, while if we fired the mine we probably would die under the tottering tower.

"By the time we reached the archway and discovered the powder barrels, the besieged, finding everything silent outside, came to a realisation of the true condition of affairs. We faced them with bayonets fixed, while Sept, the man who had captured the sentinel, took the hatchet he had brought with him at his girdle, flung over one of the barrels on its side, knocked in the head of it, allowing the dull black powder to pour on the cobblestones. Then filling his hat with the explosive, he came out towards us, leaving a thick trail behind him. By this time we were sorely beset, and one of our men had gone down under the fire of the enemy, who shot wildly, being baffled by the darkness, otherwise all of us had been slaughtered. I seized a musket from a comrade and shouted to the rest:—

"'Save yourselves', and to the garrison, in French, I gave the same warning; then I fired the musket into the train of powder, and the next instant found myself half stunned and bleeding at the farther end of the courtyard. The roar of the explosion and the crash of the falling tower were deafening. All Elsengore was groused by the earthquake shock, I called to my men when I could find my voice, and Sept answered from one side, and two more from another. Together we tottered across the débris-strewn courtyard. Some woodwork inside the citadel had taken fire and was burning fiercely, and this lit up the ruins and made visible the great gap in the wall at the fallen gate. Into the square below we saw the whole town pouring, soldiers and civilians alike coming from the narrow streets into the open quadrangle. I made my way, leaning on Sept, over the broken gate and down the causeway into the square, and there, foremost of all, met my general, with a cloak thrown round him, to make up for his want of coat.

"'There, general,' I gasped, 'there is your citadel, and through this gap can we march to meet Marlborough.'

"'Pray, sir, who the deuce are you?' cried the general, for my face was like that of a blackamoor.

"'I am the lieutenant who has once more disobeyed your orders, general, in the hope of retrieving a former mistake.'

"'Sentore!' he cried, rapping out an oath. 'I shall have you court-martialled, sir.'

"'I think, general,' I said, 'that I am court-martialled already,' for I thought then that the hand of death was upon me, which shows the effect of imagination, for my wounds were not serious, yet I sank down unconscious at the general's feet. He raised me in his arms as if I had been his own son, and thus carried me to my rooms. Seven years later, when the war ended, I got leave of absence and came back to Elsengore for Gretlich Seidelmier and the hour-glass."

As the lieutenant ceased speaking, Eastford thought he heard again the explosion under the tower, and started to his feet in nervous alarm, then looked at the lieutenant and laughed, while he said:—

"Lieutenant, I was startled by that noise just now, and imagined for the moment that I was in Brabant. You have made good your claim to the hour-glass, and you are welcome to it."

But as Eastford spoke, he turned his eyes towards the chair in which the lieutenant had been seated, and found it vacant. Gazing round the room, in half somnolent dismay, he saw that he was indeed alone. At his feet was the shattered hour-glass, which had fallen from his knee, its blood-red sand mingling with the colours on the carpet. Eastford said, with an air of surprise:—

"By Jove!"

THE WARRIOR MAID OF SAN CARLOS

The young naval officer came into this world with two eyes and two arms; he left it with but one of each—nevertheless the remaining eye was ever quick to see, and the remaining arm ever strong to seize. Even his blind eye became useful on one historic occasion. But the loss of eye or arm was as nothing to the continual loss of his heart, which often led him far afield in the finding of it. Vanquished when he met the women; invincible when he met the men; in truth, a most human hero, and so we all love Jack—the we, in this instant, as the old joke has it, embracing the women.

In the year 1780 Britain ordered Colonel Polson to invade Nicaragua. The task imposed on the gallant Colonel was not an onerous one, for the Nicaraguans never cared to secure for themselves the military reputation of Sparta. In fact, some years after this, a single American, Walker, with a few Californian rifles under his command, conquered the whole nation and made himself President of it, and perhaps would have been Dictator of Nicaragua to-day if his own country had not laid him by the heels. It is no violation of history to state that the entire British fleet was not engaged in subduing Nicaragua, and that Colonel Polson felt himself amply provided for the necessities of the crisis by sailing into the harbour of San Juan del Norte with one small ship. There were numerous fortifications at the mouth of the river, and in about an hour after landing, the Colonel was in possession of them all.

The flight of time, brief as it was, could not be compared in celerity with the flight of the Nicaraguans, who betook themselves to the backwoods with an impetuosity seldom seen outside of a race-course. There was no loss of life so far as the British were concerned, and the only casualties resulting to the Nicaraguans were colds caught through the overheating of themselves in their feverish desire to explore immediately the interior of their beloved country. "He who bolts and runs away will live to bolt another day," was the motto of the Nicaraguans. So far, so good, or so bad, as the case may be.

The victorious Colonel now got together a flotilla of some half a score of boats, and the flotilla was placed under the command of the young naval officer, the hero of this story. The expedition proceeded cautiously up the river San Juan, which runs for eighty miles, or thereabouts, from Lake Nicaragua to the salt water. The voyage was a sort of marine picnic. Luxurious vegetation on either side, and no opposition to speak of, even from the current of the river; for Lake Nicaragua itself is but a hundred and twenty feet above the sea level, and a hundred and twenty feet gives little rapidity to a river eighty miles long.

As the flotilla approached the entrance to the lake caution increased, for it was not known how strong Fort San Carlos might prove. This fort, perhaps the only one in the country strongly built, stood at once on the shore of the lake and bank of the stream. There was one chance in a thousand that the speedy retreat of the Nicaraguans had been merely a device to lure the British into the centre of the country, where the little expedition of two hundred sailors and marines might be annihilated. In these circumstances Colonel Poison thought it well, before coming in sight of the fort, to draw up his boats along the northern bank of the San Juan River, sending out scouts to bring in necessary information regarding the stronghold.

The young naval officer all through his life was noted for his energetic and reckless courage, so it was not to be wondered at that the age of twenty-two found him impatient with the delay, loth to lie inactive in his boat until the scouts returned; so he resolved upon an action that would have justly brought a court-martial upon his head had a knowledge of it come to his superior officer. He plunged alone into the tropical thicket, armed only with two pistols and a cutlass, determined to force his way through the rank vegetation along the bank of the river, and reconnoitre Fort San Carlos for himself. If he had given any thought to the matter, which it is more than likely he did not, he must have known that he ran every risk of capture and death, for the native of South America, then as now, has rarely shown any hesitation about shooting prisoners of war. Our young friend, therefore, had slight chance for his life if cut off from his comrades, and, in the circumstances, even a civilised nation would have been perfectly within its right in executing him as a spy.

After leaving the lake the river San Juan bends south, and then north again. The scouts had taken the direct route to the fort across the land, but the young officer's theory was that, if the Nicaraguans meant to fight, they would place an ambush in the dense jungle along the river, and from this place of concealment harass the flotilla before it got within gunshot of the fort. This ambuscade could easily fall back upon the fort if directly attacked and defeated. This, the young man argued was what he himself would have done had he been in command of the Nicaraguan forces, so it naturally occurred to him to discover whether the same idea had suggested itself to the commandant at San Carlos.

Expecting every moment to come upon this ambuscade, the boy proceeded, pistol in hand, with the utmost care, crouching under the luxuriant tropical foliage, tunnelling his way, as one might say, along the dark alleys of vegetation, roofed in by the broad leaves overhead. Through cross-alleys he caught glimpses now and then of the broad river, of which he was desirous to keep within touch. Stealthily crossing one of these riverward alleys the young fellow came upon his ambuscade, and was struck motionless with amazement at the form it took. Silhouetted against the shining water beyond was a young girl. She knelt at the very verge of the low, crumbling cliff above the water; her left hand, outspread, was on the ground, her right rested against the rough trunk of a palm-tree, and counter-balanced the weight of her body, which leaned far forward over the brink. Her face was turned sideways towards him, and her lustrous eyes peered intently down the river at the British flotilla stranded along the river's bank. So intent was her gaze, so confident was she that she was alone, that the leopard-like approach of her enemy gave her no hint of attack. Her perfect profile being towards him, he saw her cherry-red lips move silently as if she were counting the boats and impressing their number upon her memory.

A woman in appearance, she was at this date but sixteen years old, and the breathless young man who stood like a statue regarding her thought he had never seen a vision of such entrancing beauty, and, as I have before intimated, he was a judge of feminine loveliness. Pulling himself together, and drawing a deep but silent breath, he went forward with soft tread, and the next instant there was a grip of steel on the wrist of the young girl that rested on the earth. With a cry of dismay she sprang to her feet and confronted her assailant, nearly toppling over the brink as she did so; but he grasped her firmly, and drew her a step or two up the arcade. As he held her left wrist there was in the air the flash of a stiletto, and the naval officer's distinguished career would have ended on that spot had he not been a little quicker than his fair opponent. His disengaged hand gripped the descending wrist and held her powerless.

"Ruffian!" she hissed, in Spanish.

The young man had a workable knowledge of the language, and he thanked his stars now that it was so. He smiled at her futile struggles to free herself, then said:—

"When they gave me my commission, I had no hope that I should meet so charming an enemy. Drop the knife, señorita, and I will release your hand."

The girl did not comply at first. She tried to wrench herself free, pulling this way and that with more strength than might have been expected from one so slight. But finding herself helpless in those rigid bonds, she slowly relaxed the fingers of her right hand, and let the dagger drop point downward into the loose soil, where it stood and quivered.

"Now let me go," she said, panting. "You promised."

The young man relinquished his hold, and the girl, with the quick movement of a humming-bird, dived into the foliage, and would have disappeared, had he not with equal celerity intercepted her, again imprisoning her wrist.

"You liar!" she cried, her magnificent eyes ablaze with anger. "Faithless minion of a faithless race, you promised to let me go."

"And I kept my promise," said the young man, still with a smile. "I said I would release your hand, and I did so; but as for yourself, that is a different matter. You see, señorita, to speak plainly, you are a spy. I have caught you almost within our lines, counting our boats, and, perhaps, our men. There is war between our countries, and I arrest you as a spy."

"A brave country, yours," she cried, "to war upon women!"

"Well," said the young man, with a laugh, "what are we to do? The men won't stay and fight us."

She gave him a dark, indignant glance at this, which but heightened her swarthy beauty.

"And what are you," she said, "but a spy?"

"Not yet," he replied. "If you had found me peering at the fort, then, perhaps, I should be compelled to plead guilty. But as it is, you are the only spy here at present, señorita. Do you know what the fate of a spy is?"

The girl stood there for a few moments, her face downcast, the living gyves still encircling her wrists. When she looked up it was with a smile so radiant that the young man gasped for breath, and his heart beat faster than ever it had done in warfare.

"But you will not give me up?" she murmured, softly.

"Then would I be in truth a faithless minion," cried the young man, fervently; "not, indeed, to my country, but to your fascinating sex, which I never adored so much as now."

"You mean that you would be faithless to your country, but not to me?"

"Well," said the young man, with some natural hesitation, "I shouldn't care to have to choose between my allegiance to one or the other. England can survive without warring upon women, as you have said; so I hope that if we talk the matter amicably over, we may find that my duty need not clash with my inclination."

"I am afraid that is impossible," she answered, quickly. "I hate your country."

"But not the individual members of it, I hope."

"I know nothing of its individual members, nor do I wish to, as you shall soon see, if you will but let go my wrist."

"Ah, señorita," exclaimed the young man, "you are using an argument now that will make me hold you forever."

"In that case," said the girl, "I shall change my argument, and give instead a promise. If you release me I shall not endeavour to escape—I may even be so bold as to expect your escort to the fort, where, if I understand you aright, you were but just now going."

"I accept your promise, and shall be delighted if you will accept my escort. Meanwhile, in the interest of our better acquaintance, can I persuade you to sit down, and allow me to cast myself at your feet?"

The girl, with a clear, mellow laugh, sat down, and the young man reclined in the position he had indicated, gazing up at her with intense admiration in his eyes.

"If this be war," he said to himself, "long may I remain a soldier." Infatuated as he certainly was, his natural alertness could not but notice that her glance wandered to the stiletto, the perpendicular shining blade of which looked like the crest of a glittering, dangerous serpent, whose body was hidden in the leaves. She had seated herself as close to the weapon as possible, and now, on one pretext or another, edged nearer and nearer to it. At last the young man laughed aloud, and, sweeping his foot round, knocked down the weapon, then indolently stretching out his arm, he took it.

"Señorita," he said, examining its keen edge, "will you give me this dagger as a memento of our meeting?"

"It is unlucky," she murmured, "to make presents of stilettos."

"I think," said the young man, glancing up at her with a smile on his lips, "it will be more lucky for me if I place it here in my belt than if I allow it to reach the possession of another."

"Do you intend to steal it, señor?"

"Oh, no. If you refuse to let me have it, I will give it back to you when our interview ends; but I should be glad to possess it, if you allow me to keep it."

478

"It is unlucky, as I have said; to make a present of it, but I will exchange. If you will give me one of your loaded pistols, you may have the stiletto."

"A fair exchange," he laughed, but he made no motion to fulfil his part to the barter. "May I have the happiness of knowing your name, señorita?" he asked.

"I am called Donna Rafaela Mora," answered the girl, simply. "I am daughter of the Commandant of Fort San Carlos. I am no Nicaraguan, but a Spaniard And, señor, what is your name?"

"Horatio Nelson, an humble captain in His Majesty's naval forces, to be heard from later, I hope, unless Donna Rafaela cuts short my thread of life with her stiletto."

"And does a captain in His Majesty's forces condescend to play the part of a spy?" asked the girl, proudly.

"He is delighted to do so when it brings him the acquaintance of another spy so charming as Donna Rafaela. My spying, and I imagine yours also, is but amateurish, and will probably be of little value to our respective forces. Our real spies are now gathered round your fort, and will bring to us all the information we need. Thus, I can recline at your feet, Donna Rafaela, with an easy conscience, well aware that my failure as a spy will in no way retard our expedition."

"How many men do you command, Señor Captain?" asked the girl, with ill-concealed eagerness.

"Oh, sometimes twenty-five, sometimes fifty, or a hundred or two hundred, or more, as the case may be," answered the young man, carelessly.

"But how many are there in your expedition now?"

"Didn't you count them, Donna? To answer truly, I must not, to answer falsely, I will not, Donna."

"Why?" asked the girl, impetuously. "There is no such secrecy about our forces; we do not care who knows the number in our garrison."

"No? Then how many are there, Donna?"

"Three hundred and forty," answered the girl.

"Men, or young ladies like yourself, Donna? Be careful how you answer, for if the latter, I warn you that nothing will keep the British out of Fort San Carlos. We shall be with you, even if we have to go as prisoners. In saying this, I feel that I am speaking for our entire company."

The girl tossed her head scornfully.

"There are three hundred and forty men," she said, "as you shall find to your cost, if you dare attack the fort."

"In that case," replied Nelson, "you are nearly two to one, and I venture to think that we have not come up the river for nothing."

"What braggarts you English are!"

"Is it bragging to welcome a stirring fight? Are you well provided with cannon?"

"You will learn that for yourself when you come within sight of the fort. Have you any more questions to ask, Señor Sailor?"

"Yes; one. The number in the fort, which you give, corresponds with what I have already heard. I have heard also that you were well supplied with cannon, but I have been told that you have no cannonballs in Fort San Carlos."

"That is not true; we have plenty.

"Incredible as it may seem, I was told that the cannon-balls were made of clay. When I said you had none, I meant that you had none of iron."

"That also is quite true," answered the girl. "Do you mean to say that you are going to shoot baked clay at us? It will be like heaving bricks," and the young man threw back his head and laughed.

"Oh, you may laugh," cried the girl, "but I doubt if you will be so merry when you come to attack the fort. The clay cannon-balls were made under the superintendence of my father, and they are filled with links of chain, spikes, and other scraps of iron."

"By Jove!" cried young Nelson, "that's an original idea. I wonder how it will work?"

"You will have every opportunity of finding out, if you are foolish enough to attack the fort."

"You advise us then to retreat?"

"I most certainly do."

"And why, Donna, if you hate our country, are you so anxious that we shall not be cut to pieces by your scrap-iron?"

The girl shrugged her pretty shoulders.

"It doesn't matter in the least to me what you do," she said, rising to her feet. "Am I your prisoner, Señor Nelson?"

"No," cried the young man, also springing up; "I am yours, and have been ever since you looked at me."

Again the girl shrugged her shoulders. She seemed to be in no humour for light compliments, and betrayed an eagerness to be gone.

"I have your permission, then, to depart? Do you intend to keep your word?"

"If you will keep yours, Donna."

"I gave you no promise, except that I would not run away, and I have not done so. I now ask your permission to depart."

"You said that I might accompany you to the fort."

"Oh, if you have the courage, yes," replied the girl, carelessly.

They walked on together through the dense alleys of vegetation, and finally came to an opening which showed them a sandy plain, and across it the strong white stone walls of the fort, facing the wide river, and behind it the blue background of Lake Nicaragua.

Not a human form was visible either on the walls or on the plain. Fort San Carlos, in spite of the fact that it bristled with cannon, seemed like an abandoned castle. The two stood silent for a moment at the margin of the jungle, the young officer running his eye rapidly over the landscape, always bringing back his gaze to the seemingly deserted stronghold.

"Your three hundred and forty men keep themselves well hidden," he said at last.

"Yes," replied the girl, nonchalantly, "they fear that if they show themselves you may hesitate to attack a fortress that is impregnable."

"Well, you may disabuse their minds of that error when you return."

"Are you going to keep my stiletto?" asked the girl, suddenly changing the subject.

"Yes, with your permission."

"Then keep your word, and give me your pistol in return."

"Did I actually promise it?"

"You promised, Señor."

"Then in that case, the pistol is yours."

"Please hand it to me."

Her eagerness to obtain the weapon was but partially hidden, and the young man laughed as he weighed the fire-arm in his hand, holding it by the muzzle.

"It is too heavy for a slim girl like you to handle," he said, at last. "It can hardly be called a lady's toy."

"You intend, then, to break your word," said the girl, with quick intuition, guessing with unerring instinct his vulnerable point.

"Oh, no," he cried, "but I am going to send the pistol half-way home for you," and with that, holding it still by the barrel, he flung it far out on the sandy plain, where it fell, raising a little cloud of dust. The girl was about to speed to the fort, when, for the third time, the young man grasped her wrist. She looked at him with indignant surprise.

"Pardon me," he said, "but in case you should wish to fire the weapon, you must have some priming. Let me pour a quantity of this gunpowder into your hand."

"Thank you," she said, veiling her eyes, to hide their hatred.

He raised the tiny hand to his lips, without opposition, and then into her satin palm, from his powderhorn, he poured a little heap of the black grains.

"Good-bye, señor," she said, hurrying away. She went directly to where the pistol had fallen, stooped and picked it up. He saw her pour the powder from her hand on its broad, unshapely pan. She knelt on the sand, studied the clumsy implement, resting her elbow on her knee. The young man stood there motionless, bareheaded, his cap in his hand. There was a flash and a loud report; and the bullet cut the foliage behind him, a little nearer than he expected. He bowed low to her, and she, rising with an angry gesture, flung the weapon from her.

"Donna Rafaela," he shouted, "thank you for firing the pistol. Its report brings no one to the walls of San Carlos. Your fortress is deserted, Donna. Tomorrow may I have the pleasure of showing you how to shoot?"

The girl made no answer, but turning, ran as fast as she could towards the fort.

The young man walked toward the fort, picked up his despised weapon, thrust it in his belt, and went back to the camp. The scouts were returning, and reported that, as far as they could learn, the three hundred and forty Nicaraguans had, in a body, abandoned Fort San Carlos.

"It is some trick," said the Colonel. "We must approach the fortress cautiously, as if the three hundred and forty were there."

The flotilla neared the fort in a long line. Each boat was filled with men, and in each prow was levelled a small cannon—a man with a lighted match beside it—ready to fire the moment word was given. Nelson himself stood up in his boat, and watched the silent fort. Suddenly the silence was broken by a crash of thunder, and Nelson's boat (and the one nearest to it) was wrecked, many of the men being killed, and himself severely wounded.

"Back, back!" cried the commander. "Row out of range, for your lives!" The second cannon spoke, and the whole line of boats was thrown into inextricable confusion. Cannon after cannon rang out, and of the two hundred men who sailed up the river San Juan only ten reached the ship alive.

The Commandant of the fort lay ill in his bed, unable to move, but his brave daughter fired the cannon that destroyed the flotilla. Here Nelson lost his eye, and so on a celebrated occasion was unable to see the signals that called upon him to retreat. Thus victory ultimately rose out of disaster.

The King of Spain decorated Donna Rafaela Mora, made her a colonel, and gave her a pension for life. So recently as 1857, her grandson, General Martinez, was appointed President of Nicaragua solely because he was a descendant of the girl who defeated Horatio Nelson.

THE AMBASSADOR'S PIGEONS

Haziddin, the ambassador, stood at the door of his tent and gazed down upon the famous city of Baalbek, seeing it now for the first time. The night before, he had encamped on the heights to the south of Baalbek, and had sent forward to that city, messengers to the Prince, carrying greetings and acquainting him with the fact that an embassy from the Governor of Damascus awaited permission to enter the gates. The sun had not yet risen, but the splendour in the East, lighting the sky with wondrous colourings of gold and crimson and green, announced the speedy coming of that god which many of the inhabitants of Baalbek still worshipped. The temples and palaces of the city took their tints from the flaming sky, and Haziddin, the ambassador, thought he had never seen anything so beautiful, notwithstanding the eulogy Mahomet himself had pronounced upon his own metropolis of Damascus.

The great city lay in silence, but the moment the rim of the sun appeared above the horizon the silence was broken by a faint sound of chanting from that ornate temple, seemingly of carven ivory, which had bestowed upon the city its Greek name of Heliopolis. The Temple of the Sun towered overall other buildings in the place, and, as if the day-god claimed his own, the rising sun shot his first rays upon this edifice, striking from it instantly all colour, leaving its rows of pillars a dazzling white as if they were fashioned from the pure snows of distant Lebanon. The sun seemed a mainspring of activity, as well as an object of adoration, for before it had been many minutes above the horizon the ambassador saw emerging from the newly opened gate the mounted convoy that was to act as his escort into the city; so, turning, he gave a quick command which speedily levelled the tents, and brought his retinue; into line to receive their hosts.

The officer, sent by the Prince of Baalbek to welcome the ambassador and conduct him into the city, greeted the visitor with that deferential ceremony so beloved of the Eastern people, and together they journeyed down the hill to the gates, the followers of the one mingling fraternally with the followers of the other. As if the deities of the wonderful temples they were approaching wished to show the futility of man's foresight, a thoughtless remark made by one of the least in the ambassador's retinue to one of the least who followed the Baalbek general, wrought ruin to one empire, and saved another from disaster.

A mule-driver from Baalbek said to one of his lowly a profession from Damascus that the animals of the northern city seemed of superior breed to those of the southern. Then the Damascus man, his civic pride disturbed by the slighting remark, replied haughtily that if the mules of Baalbek had endured such hardships as those of Damascus, journeying for a month without rest through a rugged mountain country, they would perhaps look in no better condition than those the speaker then drove.

"Our mules were as sleek as yours a month ago, when we left Damascus."

As Baalbek is but thirty-one miles north of Damascus, the muleteer of the former place marvelled that so long a time had been spent on the journey, and he asked his fellow why they had wandered among the mountains. The other could but answer that so it was, and he knew no reason for it, and with this the man of Baalbek had to content himself. And so the tale went from mouth to ear of the Baalbek men until it reached the general himself. He thought little of it for the moment, but, turning to the ambassador, said, having nothing else to say:

"How long has it taken you from Damascus to Baalbek?"

Then the ambassador answered:

"We have done the journey in three days; it might have taken us but two, or perhaps it could have been accomplished in one, but there being no necessity for speed we travelled leisurely."

Then the general, remaining silent, said to himself:

"Which has lied, rumour or the ambassador?"

He cast his eyes over the animals the ambassador had brought with him, and saw that they indeed showed signs of fatigue, and perhaps of irregular and improper food.

Prince Ismael himself received Haziddin, ambassador of Omar, Governor of Damascus, at the gates of Baalbek, and the pomp and splendour of that reception was worthy of him who gave it, but the general found opportunity to whisper in the ear of the Prince:

"The ambassador says he was but three days coming, while a follower of his told a follower of mine that they have been a month on the road, wandering among the mountains."

Suspicion is ever latent in the Eastern mind, and the Prince was quick to see a possible meaning for this sojourn among the mountains. It might well be that the party were seeking a route at once easy and unknown by which warriors from Damascus might fall upon Baalbek; yet, if this were the case, why did not the explorers return directly to Damascus rather than venture within the walls of Baalbek? It seemed to Prince Ismael that this would have been the more crafty method to pursue, for, as it was, unless messengers had returned to Damascus to report the result of their mountain excursion, he had the whole party practically prisoners within the walls of his city, and he could easily waylay any envoy sent by the ambassador to his chief in Damascus. The Prince, however, showed nothing in his manner of what was passing through his mind, but at the last moment he changed the programme he had laid out for the reception of the ambassador. Preparation had been made for a great public breakfast, for Haziddin was famed throughout the East, not only as a diplomatist, but also as physician and a man of science. The Prince now gave orders that his officers were to entertain the retinue of the ambassador at the public breakfast, while he bestowed upon the ambassador the exceptional honour of asking him to his private table, thus giving Haziddin of Damascus no opportunity to confer with his followers after they had entered the gates of Baalbek.

It was impossible for Haziddin to demur, so he could but bow low and accept the hospitality which might at that moment be most unwelcome, as indeed it was. The Prince's manner was so genial and friendly that, the physician, Haziddin, soon saw he had an easy man to deal with, and he suspected no sinister motive beneath the cordiality of the Prince.

The red wine of Lebanon is strong, and his Highness, Ismael, pressed it upon his guest, urging that his three days' journey had been fatiguing. The ambassador had asked that his own servant might wait upon him, but the Prince would not hear of it, and said that none should serve him who were not themselves among the first nobles in Baalbek.

"You represent Omar, Governor of Damascus, son of King Ayoub, and as such I receive you on terms of equality with myself."

The ambassador, at first nonplussed with a lavishness that was most unusual, gradually overcame his diffidence, became warm with the wine, and so failed to notice that the Prince himself remained cool, and drank sparingly. At last the head of Haziddin sank on his breast, and he reclined at full length on the couch he occupied, falling into a drunken stupor, for indeed he was deeply fatigued, and had spent the night before sleepless. As his cloak fell away from him it left exposed a small wicker cage attached to his girdle containing four pigeons closely huddled, for the cage was barely large enough to hold them, and here the Prince saw the ambassador's swift messengers to Damascus. Let loose from the walls of Baalbek, and flying direct, the tidings would, in a few hours, be in the hands of the Governor of Damascus. Haziddin then was spy as well as ambassador. The Prince also possessed carrier pigeons, and used them as a means of communication between his armies at Tripoli and at Antioch, so he was not ignorant of their consequence. The fact that the ambassador himself carried this small cage under his cloak attached to his girdle showed the great importance that was attached to these winged messengers, otherwise Haziddin would have entrusted them to one of his subordinates.

"Bring me," whispered the Prince to his general, "four of my own pigeons. Do not disturb the thongs attached to the girdle when you open the cage, but take the ambassador's pigeons out and substitute four of my own. Keep these pigeons of Damascus separate from ours; we may yet have use for them in communicating with the Governor."

The general, quick to see the scheme which was in the Prince's mind, brought four Baalbek pigeons, identical with the others in size and colour. He brought with him also a cage into which the Damascus pigeons were put, and thus the transfer was made without the knowledge of the slumbering ambassador. His cloak was arranged about him so that it concealed the cage attached to the girdle, then the ambassador's own servants were sent for, and he was confided to their care.

When Haziddin awoke he found himself in a sumptuous room of the palace. He had but a hazy remembrance of the latter part of the meal with the Prince, and his first thought went with a thrill of fear towards the cage under his cloak; finding, however, that this was intact, he was much relieved in his mind, and could but hope that in his cups he had not babbled anything of his mission which might arouse suspicion in the mind of the Prince. His first meeting with the ruler of Baalbek after the breakfast they had had together, set all doubts finally at rest, because the Prince received him with a friendship which was unmistakable. The physician apologised for being overcome by the potency of the wine, and pleaded that he had hitherto been unused to liquor of such strength. The Prince waved away all reference to the subject, saying that he himself had succumbed on the same occasion, and had but slight recollection of what had passed between them.

Ismael assigned to the ambassador one of the palaces near the Pantheon, and Haziddin found himself free to come and go as he pleased without espionage or restriction. He speedily learned that one of the armies of Baalbek was at the north, near Antioch, the other to the west at Tripoli, leaving the great city practically unprotected, and this unprecedented state of affairs jumped so coincident with the designs of his master, that he hastened to communicate the intelligence. He wrote:

"If Baalbek is immediately attacked, it cannot be protected. Half of the army is on the shore of the Mediterranean, near Tripoli, the other half is north, at Antioch. The Prince has no suspicion. If you conceal the main body of your army behind the hills to the south of Baalbek, and come on yourself with a small: retinue, sending notice to the Prince of your arrival, he will likely himself come out to the gates to meet you, and having secured his person, while I, with my followers, hold the open gates, you can march into Baalbek unmolested. Once with a force inside the walls of Baalbek, the city is as nearly as possible impregnable, and holding the Prince prisoner, you may make with him your own terms. The city is indescribably rich, and probably never before in the history of the world has there been opportunity of accumulating so much treasure with so little risk."

This writing Haziddin attached to the leg of a pigeon, and throwing the bird aloft from the walls, it promptly disappeared over the housetops, and a few moments later was in the hands of its master, the Prince of Baalbek, who read the treacherous message with amazement. Then, imitating the ambassador's writing, he penned a note, saying that this was not the time to invade Baalbek, but as there were rumours that the armies were about to leave the city, one going to the north and the other to the west, the ambassador would send by another pigeon news of the proper moment to strike.

This communication the Prince attached to the leg of one of the Damascus pigeons, and throwing it into the air, saw with satisfaction that the bird flew straight across the hills towards the south.

Ismael that night sent messengers mounted on swift Arabian horses to Tripoli and to Antioch recalling his armies, directing his generals to avoid Baalbek and to join forces in the mountains to the south of that city and out of sight of it. This done, the Prince attended in state a banquet tendered to him by the ambassador from Damascus, where he charmed all present by his genial urbanity, speaking touchingly on the blessings of peace, and drinking to a thorough understanding between the two great cities of the East, Damascus and Baalbek, sentiments which, were cordially reciprocated by the ambassador.

Next morning the second pigeon came to the palace of the Prince.

"Ismael is still unsuspicious," the document ran. "He will fall an easy prey if action be prompt. In case of a failure to surprise, it would be well to impress upon your generals the necessity of surrounding the city instantly so that messengers cannot be sent to the two armies. It will then be advisable to cut off the water-supply by diverting the course of the small river which flows into Baalbek. The walls of the city are incredibly strong, and a few men can defend them successfully against a host, once the gates are shut. Thirst, however, will soon compel them, to surrender. Strike quickly, and Baalbek is yours."

The Prince sent a note of another tenor to Damascus, and the calm days passed serenely on, the ambassador watching anxiously from his house-top, his eyes turned to the south, while the Prince watched as anxiously from the roof of his palace, his gaze turning now westward now northward.

The third night after the second message had been sent, the ambassador paced the long level promenade of his roof, ever questioning the south. A full moon shone down on the silent city, and in that clear air the plain outside the walls and the nearer hills were as distinctly visible as if it were daylight. There was no sign of an approaching army. Baalbek lay like a city of the dead, the splendid architecture of its countless temples gleaming ghostlike, cold, white and unreal in the pure refulgence of the moon. Occasionally the ambassador paused in his walk and leaned on the parapet. He had become vaguely uneasy, wondering why Damascus delayed, and there crept over him that sensation of dumb fear which comes to a man in the middle of the night and leaves him with the breaking of day. He realised keenly the extreme peril of his own position—imprisoned and at the mercy of his enemy should his treachery be discovered. And now as he leaned over the parapet in the breathless stillness, his alert ear missed an accustomed murmur of the night. Baalbek was lulled to sleep by the ever-present tinkle of running water, the most delicious sound that can soothe an Eastern ear, accustomed as it is to the echoless silence of the arid rainless desert.

The little river which entered Baalbek first flowed past the palace of the Prince, then to the homes of the nobles and the priests, meandering through every street and lane until it came to the baths left by the Romans, whence it flowed through the poorer quarters, and at last disappeared under the outer wall. It might be termed a liquid guide to Baalbek, for the stranger, leaving the palace and following its current, would be led past every temple and residence in the city. It was the limpid thread of life running through the veins of the town, and without it Baalbek could not have existed. As the ambassador leaned over the parapet wondering whether it was his imagination which made this night seem more still than all that had gone before since he came to the city, he suddenly became aware that what he missed was the purling trickle of the water. Peering over the wall of his house, and gazing downward on the moonlit street, he saw no reflecting glitter of the current, and realised, with a leap of the heart, that the stream had run dry.

The ambassador was quick to understand the meaning of this sudden drying of the stream. Notwithstanding his vigilance, the soldiers of Damascus had stolen upon the city unperceived by him, and had already diverted the water-course. Instantly his thoughts turned toward his own escape. In the morning the fact of the invasion would be revealed, and his life would lie at the mercy of an exasperated ruler. To flee from Baalbek in the night he knew to be no easy task; all the gates were closed, and not one of them would be opened before daybreak, except through the intervention of the Prince himself. To spring from even the lowest part of the wall would mean instant death. In this extremity the natural ingenuity of the man came to his rescue. That which gave him warning would also provide an avenue of safety.

The stream, conveyed to the city by a lofty aqueduct, penetrated the thick walls through a tunnel cut in the solid stone, just large enough to receive its volume. The tunnel being thus left dry, a man could crawl on his hands and knees through it, and once outside, walk upright on the top of the viaduct, along the empty bed of the river, until he reached the spot where the water had been diverted, and there find his comrades. Wasting not a thought on the jeopardy in which he left his own followers, thus helplessly imprisoned in Baalbek, but bent only on his own safety, he left his house silently, and hurried, deep in the shadow, along the obscure side of the street. He knew he must avoid the guards of the palace, and that done, his path to the invading army was clear. But before he reached the palace of the Prince there remained for him another stupefying surprise.

Coming to a broad thoroughfare leading to the square in which stood the Temple of Life, he was amazed to see at his feet, flowing rapidly, the full tide of the stream, shattering into dancing discs of light the reflection of the full moon on its surface, gurgling swiftly towards the square. The fugitive stood motionless and panic-stricken at the margin of this transparent flood.

He knew that his retreat had been cut off. What had happened? Perhaps the strong current had swept away the impediment placed against it by the invaders, and thus had resumed its course into the city. Perhaps—but there was little use in surmising, and the ambassador, recovering in a measure his self-possession, resolved to see whether or not it would lead him to his own palace.

Crossing the wide thoroughfare into the shadow beyond, he followed it towards the square, keeping his eye on the stream that rippled in the moonlight. The rivulet flowed directly across the square to the Temple of Life; there, sweeping a semicircle half round the huge building, it resumed its straight course. The ambassador hesitated before crossing the moonlit square, but a moment's reflection showed him that no suspicion could possibly attach to his movements in this direction, for the Temple of Life was the only sacred edifice in the city for ever open.

The Temple of Life consisted of a huge dome, which was supported by a double circle of pillars, and beneath this dome had been erected a gigantic marble statue, representing the God of Life, who stood motionless with outstretched arms, as if invoking a blessing upon the city. A circular opening at the top of the dome allowed the rays of the moon to penetrate and illuminate the head of the statue. Against the white polished surface of the broad marble slab, which lay at the foot of the statue, the ambassador saw the dark forms of several prostrate figures, and knew that each was there to beg of the sightless statue, life for some friend, lying at that moment somewhere on a bed of illness. For this reason the Temple of Life was always open, and supplicants prostrated themselves within it at any hour of the night or day. Remembering this, and knowing that it was the resort of high and low alike, for Death respects not rank, Haziddin, with gathering confidence, entered the moonlit square. At the edge of the great circular temple he paused, meeting there his third surprise. He saw that the stream was not deflected round the lower rim of the edifice, but that a stone had been swung at right angles with the lower step, cutting off the flow of the stream to the left, and allowing its waters to pour underneath the temple. Listening, the ambassador heard the low muffled roar of pouring water, and instantly his quick mind jumped at an accurate conclusion. Underneath the Temple was a gigantic tank for the storage of water, and it was being filled during the night. Did the authorities of Baalbek expect a siege, and were they thus preparing for it? Or was the filling of the tank an ordinary function performed periodically to keep the water sweet? The ambassador would have given much for an accurate answer to these questions, but he knew not whom to ask.

Entering the Temple he prostrated himself on the marble slab, and remained there for a few moments, hoping that, if his presence had been observed, this action would provide excuse for his nocturnal wanderings. Rising, he crossed again the broad square, and hurried up the street by which he had entered it. This street led to the northern gate, whose dark arch he saw at the end of it, and just as he was about to turn down a lane which led to his palace, he found himself confronted with a fourth problem. One leaf of the ponderous gate swung inward, and through the opening he caught a glimpse of the moonlit country beyond. Knowing that the gates were never opened at night, except through the direct order of the Prince, he paused for a moment, and then saw a man on horseback enter, fling himself hurriedly from his steed, leaving it in care of those in charge of the gates, and disappear down the street that led directly to the Prince's palace. In a most perturbed state of mind the ambassador sought his own house, and there wrote his final despatch to Damascus. He told of his discovery of the water-tank, and said that his former advice regarding the diverting of the stream was no longer of practical value. He said he would investigate further the reservoir under the Temple of Life, and discover, if possible, how the water was discharged. If he succeeded in his quest he would endeavour, in case of a long siege, to set free Baalbek's store of water; but he reiterated his belief that it was better to attempt the capture of the city by surprise and fierce assault. The message that actually went to Damascus, carried by the third pigeon, was again different in tenor.

"Come at once," it said. "Baalbek is unprotected, and the Prince has gone on a hunting expedition. March through the Pass of El-Zaid, which is unprotected, because it is the longer route. The armies of Baalbek are at Tripoli and at Antioch, and the city is without even a garrison. The southern gate will be open awaiting your coming."

Days passed, and the ambassador paced the roof of his house, looking in vain towards the south. The streamed flowed as usual through the city. Anxiety at the lack of all tidings from Damascus began to plough furrows in his brow. He looked careworn and haggard. To the kindly inquiries of the Prince regarding his health, he replied that there was nothing amiss.

One evening, an urgent message came from the palace requesting his attendance there. The Prince met him with concern on his brow.

"Have you had word from your master, Omar, Governor of Damascus, since you parted with him?" asked Ismael.

"I have had no tidings," replied the ambassador.

"A messenger has just come in from Damascus, who says that Omar is in deadly peril. I thought you should know this speedily, and so I sent for you."

"Of what nature is this peril?" asked the ambassador, turning pale.

"The messenger said something of his falling a prisoner, sorely wounded, in the hands of his enemies."

"Of his enemies," echoed the ambassador. "He has many. Which one has been victorious?"

"I have had no particulars and perhaps the news may not be true," answered the Prince, soothingly.

"May I question your messenger?"

"Assuredly. He has gone to the Temple of Life, to pray for some of his own kin, who are in danger. Let us go there together and find him."

But the messenger had already left the Temple before the arrival of his master, and the two found the great place entirely empty. Standing near the edge of the slab before the mammoth statue, the Prince said:

"Stand upon that slab facing the statue, and it will tell you more faithfully than any messenger whether your master shall live or die, and when."

495

"I am a Moslem," answered Haziddin, "and pray to none but Allah."

"In Baalbek," said the Prince, carelessly, "all religions are tolerated. Here we have temples for the worship of the Roman and the Greek gods and mosques for the Moslems. Here Christian, or Jew, Sun-worshipper or Pagan implore their several gods unmolested, and thus is Baalbek prosperous. I confess a liking for this Temple of Life, and come here often. I should, however, warn you that it is the general belief of those who frequent this place that he who steps upon the marble slab facing the god courts disaster, unless his heart is as free, from treachery and guile as this stone beneath him is free from flaw. Perhaps you have heard the rumour, and therefore hesitate."

"I have not heard it heretofore, but having heard it, do not hesitate." Saying which, the ambassador stepped upon the stone. Instantly, the marble turned under him, and falling, he clutched its polished surface in vain, dropping helplessly into the reservoir beneath. The air under his cloak bore him up and kept him from sinking. The reservoir into which he had fallen proved to be as large as the Temple itself, circular in form, as was the edifice above it. Steps rose from the water in unbroken rings around it, but even if he could have reached the edge of the huge tank in which he found himself, ascent by the steps was impossible, for upon the first three burned vigorously some chemical substance, which luridly illuminated the surface of this subterranean lake. He was surrounded immediately by water, and beyond that by rising rings of flame, and he rightly surmised that this substance was Greek fire, for where it dripped into the water it still burned, floating on the surface. A moment later the Prince appeared on the upper steps, outside the flaming circumference.

"Ambassador," he cried, "I told you that if you stepped on the marble slab, you would be informed truly of the fate of your master. I now announce to you that he dies to-night, being a prisoner in my hands. His army was annihilated in the Pass of El-Zaid, while he was on his way to capture this city through your treachery. In your last communication to him you said that you would investigate our water storage, and learn how it was discharged. This secret I shall proceed to put you in possession of, but before doing so, I beg to tell you that Damascus has fallen and is in my possession. The reservoir, you will observe, is emptied by pulling this lever, which releases a trap-door at the centre of the bottom of the tank."

The Prince, with both hands on the lever, exerted his strength and depressed it. Instantly the ambassador felt the result. First, a small whirlpool became indented in the placid surface of the water, exactly in the centre of the disc: enlarging its influence, it grew and grew until it reached the outer edges of the reservoir, bringing lines of fire round with it. The ambassador found himself floating with increased rapidity, dizzily round and round. He cried out in a voice that rang against the stone ceiling:

"An ambassador's life is sacred, Prince of Baalbek. It is contrary to the law of nations to do me injury, much less to encompass my death."

"An ambassador is sacred," replied the Prince, "but not a spy. Aside from that, it is the duty of an ambassador to precede his master, and that you are about to do. Tell him, when you meet him, the secret of the reservoir of Baalbek."

This reservoir, now a whirling maelstrom, hurled its shrieking victim into its vortex, and then drowned shriek and man together.

About Author

Robert Barr (16 September 1849 – 21 October 1912) was a Scottish-Canadian short story writer and novelist.

Early years in Canada

Robert Barr was born in Barony, Lanark, Scotland to Robert Barr and Jane Watson. In 1854, he emigrated with his parents to Upper Canada at the age of four years old. His family settled on a farm near the village of Muirkirk. Barr assisted his father with his job as a carpenter, and developed a sound work ethic. Robert Barr then worked as a steel smelter for a number of years before he was educated at Toronto Normal School in 1873 to train as a teacher.

After graduating Toronto Normal School, Barr became a teacher, and eventually headmaster/principal of the Central School of Windsor, Ontario in 1874. While Barr worked as head master of the Central School of Windsor, Ontario, he began to contribute short stories—often based on personal experiences, and recorded his work. On August 1876, when he was 27, Robert Barr married Ontario-born Eva Bennett, who was 21. According to the 1891 England Census, the couple appears to have had three children, Laura, William, and Andrew.

In 1876, Barr quit his teaching position to become a staff member of publication, and later on became the news editor for the Detroit Free Press. Barr wrote for this newspaper under the pseudonym, "Luke Sharp." The idea for this pseudonym was inspired during his morning commute to work when Barr saw a sign that read "Luke Sharp, Undertaker." In 1881, Barr left Canada to return to England in order to start a new weekly version of "The Detroit Free Press Magazine."

London years

In 1881 Barr decided to "vamoose the ranch", as he called the process of immigration in search of literary fame outside of Canada, and relocated to London to continue to write/establish the weekly English edition of the Detroit Free Press. During the 1890s, he broadened his literary works, and started writing novels from the popular crime genre. In 1892 he founded the magazine The Idler, choosing Jerome K. Jerome as his collaborator (wanting, as Jerome said, "a popular name"). He retired from its co-editorship in 1895.

In London of the 1890s Barr became a more prolific author—publishing a book a year—and was familiar with many of the best-selling authors of his day, including :Arnold Bennett, Horatio Gilbert Parker, Joseph Conrad, Bret Harte, Rudyard Kipling, H. Rider Haggard, H. G. Wells, and George Robert Gissing. Barr was well-spoken, well-cultured due to travel, and considered a "socializer."

Because most of Barr's literary output was of the crime genre, his works were highly in vogue. As Sherlock Holmes stories were becoming well-known, Barr wrote and published in the Idler the first Holmes parody, "The Adventures of "Sherlaw Kombs" (1892), a spoof that was continued a decade later in another Barr story, "The Adventure of the Second Swag" (1904). Despite those jibes at the growing Holmes phenomenon, Barr remained on very good terms with its creator Arthur Conan Doyle. In Memories and Adventures, a serial memoir published 1923–24, Doyle described him as "a volcanic Anglo—or rather Scot-American, with a violent manner, a wealth of strong adjectives, and one of the kindest natures underneath it all".

In 1904, Robert Barr completed an unfinished novel for Methuen & Co. by the recently deceased American author Stephen Crane entitled The O'Ruddy, a romance.Despite his reservations at taking on the project, Barr reluctantly finished the last eight chapters due to his longstanding friendship with Crane and his common-law wife, Cora, the war correspondent and bordello owner.

Death

The 1911 census places Robert Barr, "a writer of fiction," at Hillhead, Woldingham, Surrey, a small village southeast of London, living with his wife, Eva, their son William, and two female servants. At this home, the author died from heart disease on 21 October 1912.

500

Writing Style

Barr's volumes of short stories were often written with an ironic twist in the story with a witty, appealing narrator telling the story. Barr's other works also include numerous fiction and non-fiction contributions to periodicals. A few of his mystery stories and stories of the supernatural were put in anthologies, and a few novels have been republished. His writings have also attracted scholarly attention. His narrative personae also featured moral and editorial interpolations within their tales. Barr's achievements were recognized by an honorary degree from the University of Michigan in 1900.

His protagonists were journalists, princes, detectives, deserving commercial and social climbers, financiers, the new woman of bright wit and aggressive accomplishment, and lords. Often, his characters were stereotypical and romanticized.

Barr wrote fiction in an episode-like format. He developed this style when working as an editor for the newspaper Detroit Press. Barr developed his skill with the anecdote and vignette; often only the central character serves to link the nearly self-contained chapters of the novels. (Source: Wikipedia)

NOTABLE WORKS

In a Steamer Chair and Other Stories (Thirteen short stories by one of the most famous writers in his day -1892)

"The Face And The Mask" (1894) consists of twenty-four delightful short stories.

In the Midst of Alarms (1894, 1900, 1912), a story of the attempted Fenian invasion of Canada in 1866.

From Whose Bourne (1896) Novel in which the main character, William Brenton, searches for truth to set his wife free.

One Day's Courtship (1896)

Revenge! (Collection of 20 short stories, Alfred Hitchcock-like style, thriller with a surprise ending)

The Strong Arm

A Woman Intervenes (1896), a story of love, finance, and American journalism.

Tekla: A Romance of Love and War (1898)

Jennie Baxter, Journalist (1899)

The Unchanging East (1900)

The Victors (1901)

A Prince of Good Fellows (1902)

Over The Border: A Romance (1903)

The O'Ruddy, A Romance, with Stephen Crane (1903)

A Chicago Princess (1904)

The Speculations of John Steele (1905)

The Tempestuous Petticoat (1905–12)

A Rock in the Baltic (1906)

The Triumphs of Eugène Valmont (1906)

The Measure of the Rule (1907)

Stranleigh's Millions (1909)

The Sword Maker (Medieval action/adventure novel, genre: Historical Fiction-1910)

The Palace of Logs (1912)

"The Ambassadors Pigeons" (1899)

"And the Rigor of the Game" (1892)

"Converted" (1896)

"Count Conrad's Courtship" (1896)

"The Count's Apology" (1896)

"A Deal on Change " (1896)

"The Exposure of Lord Stanford" (1896)

"Gentlemen: The King!"

"The Hour-Glass" (1899)

"An invitation" (1892)

" A Ladies Man"

"The Long Ladder" (1899)

"Mrs. Tremain" (1892)

" Transformation" (1896)

"The Understudy" (1896)

" The Vengeance of the Dead" (1896)

"The Bromley Gibbert's Story" (1896)

" Out of Thun" (1896)

"The Shadow of Greenback" (1896)

"Flight of the Red Dog" (fiction)

"Lord Stranleigh Abroad" (1913)

"One Day's Courtship and the Herald's of Fame" (1896)

"Cardillac"

"Dr. Barr's Tales"

"The Triumphs of Eugene Valmont"

CPSIA information can be obtained
at www.ICGtesting.com
Printed in the USA
LVHW030502140720
660560LV00012B/535

9 789390 208456